EMP LOS ANGELES

Frank LaFlamme

This book is a work of fiction. Names, characters, places, and incidents are either products of the author's imagination or, if real, used fictitiously. Any material resemblance to actual events or persons, living or dead, is coincidental.

ISBN: 1500980153
ISBN 13: 9781500980153
Library of Congress Control Number: 2014916118
CreateSpace Independent Publishing Platform
North Charleston, South Carolina

FOREWORD

While I sincerely hope those who read this novel are entertained by the story, I must admit that when I first began this project my primary intention was to provide a "cautionary tale" for any and all Americans concerned about the perils facing our nation. Although the specific contents of this book are fictional, and the severity depicted represents only a worst case scenario, I think the underlying concept is a valid one.

It is my hope that many who read this will reconsider what constitutes a diverse insurance portfolio. In today's world, perhaps auto, homeowners, and life insurance are no longer sufficient.

--Frank LaFlamme

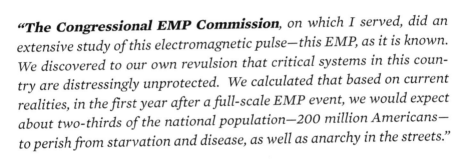

*"**The Congressional EMP Commission**, on which I served, did an extensive study of this electromagnetic pulse—this EMP, as it is known. We discovered to our own revulsion that critical systems in this country are distressingly unprotected. We calculated that based on current realities, in the first year after a full-scale EMP event, we would expect about two-thirds of the national population—200 million Americans—to perish from starvation and disease, as well as anarchy in the streets."*

----Dr. Peter Vincent Pry, Executive Director, Task Force on National and Homeland Security. Taken from the foreword in the non-fiction book titled *A NATION FORSAKEN; EMP: The Escalating Threat of an American Catastrophe* by F. Michael Maloof.

For my wife Dee, whose persistent encouragement, love, and support made this book possible. Even if you were the only person to ever enjoy this story, it would have been worth all the hours spent writing it for that reason alone.

TABLE OF CONTENTS

THOUSAND OAKS, CA

Rob Flynn couldn't believe he was going to have to really hustle to avoid being late for the 6:00 AM briefing and roll call for the Nadeau Sheriff's Station day shift. Not only had he set his alarm for four AM, he had actually jumped out of bed immediately upon hearing the obnoxious buzzing of the dreaded device. He hadn't even used the snooze button for the extra five minutes. A quick glance at his Swiss Army watch revealed that it was now 4:45.

How the hell have I wasted forty five minutes already, he asked himself.

It was a week day, and the drive from his suburban Thousand Oaks home to the Los Angeles Sheriff's Department Nadeau Station, located in the unincorporated area of Watts, normally required more than a full hour of driving even at this early hour. Rob realized he would have to push his luck with his freeway speed in order to arrive at his locker, get suited up for his patrol shift, and grab a seat in the briefing room by 6 AM.

Sergeant David Marino would run the briefing roll call. At almost six foot five, and about 280 pounds, the well preserved fifty one year old former SWAT deputy and college football lineman could still be plenty intimidating in a physical way if need be. But his physical stature and capability wasn't the crux of what made his reputation, which was both well respected and formidable. His exploits and unassailable police experience were well known throughout the huge sheriff's department and within other police agencies in L.A. County. The few on the department who had crossed him during his career had suffered derision from supervisors and the rank and file alike. As a result, regardless of rank, not many wanted to get on the wrong side of big Dave Marino.

It was no secret the sergeant had a problem with his deputies showing up late for briefings, and with this in mind, Rob told himself for at least the third time this morning, he would have to push his driving speed a little more than usual when he got on the freeway. Actually, he would have to push it a lot harder. Hell yeah; when it came down to it, it was better to be stopped and scolded by a California Highway Patrol traffic cop than to have a sergeant as respected as Dave Marino make you feel like he was disappointed in you—even if it were only communicated with his facial expression.

As Rob finished his last gulp of coffee and headed for the front door, he quietly opened his son's bedroom door to see if his four year old, Charlie Wyatt, was still asleep. Seeing he was in fact still sleeping, Rob considered waking him to say good bye but realized he was being selfish. He closed the door to his son's room and called out to his wife Stephanie, "Bye honey. Love you!"

A couple of days prior, Daylight Savings Time had arrived, requiring the "spring forward" changing of the clocks. As a result, it seemed as though it were even earlier than his watch indicated. He heard the early stirrings indicating that Stephanie had gotten out of bed, but he had not actually seen her yet this morning. She hadn't responded to his good bye but he could hear her talking in an affectionate voice to their two female Australian Shepherds. He and Stephanie had been married for almost fifteen years, and the current pair of Aussies was the second for them. That was the biggest downside to bringing pets into the family: their short lifespans meant having to deal with more emotional loss than most cared to deal with.

Rob and Stephanie had their first and only child, Charlie Wyatt Flynn, after eleven years of marriage. She had been thirty four at the time. Stephanie's nurturing tendency, which had won Rob over two months into their courtship, showed in the attention she gave their dogs during the years before their son was born. But when Charlie Wyatt came along the dogs became a secondary focus of her affection.

A slight smile appeared on Rob's face as he allowed himself to enjoy these memories.

Rob had acknowledged to himself many years ago that he possessed a stronger tendency than most to let his mind wander. He didn't regard this tendency as being necessarily good or bad--unless it happened at inopportune times--it was just a part of his personality.

Finally getting ready to leave the house, he instinctively felt for his "essentials" as he walked toward the door: cell phone, Smith & Wesson model M&P 9mm pistol, an extra loaded magazine, and his wallet. He had just exited the front door when he realized he had left his *bug-out* pack inside the living room, a precaution taken due to an increasing number of window smash vehicle break ins. He had spent far too much time and money putting together his bug-out pack to risk having some car burglar rip it off.

He could remember when "bug-out pack" was a new term that required explanation to the uninformed. Now the term used to describe an emergency 72 hour "essentials" bag was part of many Americans' lexicons. Ever since Rob had been assigned to the Nadeau Sheriff Station's terrorism liaison officer (TLO) position following the September 11th attacks, he made sure to keep a bug-out pack in his truck for more reasons than just the possibility of earthquakes.

Thinking about the recent car burglaries in his own neighborhood and his bug-out pack, Rob considered how he would react if he or Stephanie should ever become victims. It was not going to be a perfunctory "police report for the insurance company" if they broke into any of the Flynn family's cars. He would devote all of his spare time for as long as it took to find the responsible parties. And God help anyone who ever hurt, or even threatened, Stephanie or Charlie Wyatt.

Rob was a decent and fair man, but forgiveness for serious transgressions was not part of his psychological makeup.

He quickly spun around on the ball of his foot and picked up his pace as he bee-lined it back to the front door of the house. After letting himself in and announcing that he had forgotten his pack, Rob spotted the tan colored *So Tech* pack and hoisted the thirty pound sack over his shoulder. He briefly relished the psychological comfort provided by the pack and its contents.

At just over six feet tall, and slightly north of a solid 200 pounds, Rob found the pack's load easy to handle. He felt a little bit of pride as he considered how he had managed to keep himself reasonably fit for a forty one year old American male surrounded by culinary temptations and all manner of things encouraging a sedentary lifestyle in twenty first century America.

He didn't possess the physique of a body builder or professional athlete, but Rob was built solid and knew how to use his body to good effect when necessary. He used the sheriff's station gym to maintain his strength but preferred to get his cardio exercise by strapping a small pack on his back and hiking at a semi wilderness location not far from his home.

He opened the driver side door of his four wheel drive Chevy pick-up truck and tossed his bug-out pack onto the passenger seat. Rob experienced a brief and inexplicable sensation as he watched his pack come to rest on the seat. A premonition? Unable to place or categorize the feeling, he dismissed it as merely one of those myriad instances where the human brain creates a sensation, however brief or faint, that even modern science couldn't explain. Terms like "intuition", "sixth sense", or "gut feeling" all attempted to label it, however inadequately.

Dismissing the unidentifiable feeling as unimportant, Rob fired up his truck, put it into gear, and pulled away from the curb. He gave his residential block a quick but practiced scan in an attempt to check if anything was out of the ordinary. Not noticing anything giving cause for concern, he flipped his visor down and allowed the half used can of *Skoal* chewing tobacco to slide down the visor and fall into his hand. Unlike some of his fellow patrol deputies, he was not a constant user of the smokeless tobacco, but he allowed himself to enjoy its flavor and attendant "buzz" several times a week.

He grabbed an empty Dr. Pepper can from the console's cup holder while simultaneously removing his *Zero Tolerance* tactical folding knife from his jeans pocket. He flipped open the four inch blade with his left hand and used its tip to cut the top of the Dr. Pepper can into a large hole so that he could use it as a spittoon for his *Skoal* while driving into work. As he closed his knife, he automatically glanced at the four inch scar resembling a pink worm that decorated the back of his left hand. It was a healed wound acquired while handling a family disturbance between a pissed off construction worker and his fed-up wife.

At the time Rob had tried to stop the angry woman from arming herself with the sharp eight inch kitchen knife but had failed to do so until *after* she had sliced the back of his left hand. The deputy had thrown his hand up to prevent the knife from reaching his face, the consequences of which would surely have been more devastating than the scar he now wore on his hand.

Enjoying the small nicotine rush from the *Skoal* as he entered the south-bound 101 freeway, Rob mused over how the use of chewing tobacco, or snuff, had become such a widespread habit for patrol cops in Southern California despite its usage being criticized by most holding management ranks within law enforcement agencies.

While Rob had never experienced so much as a supervisory disdainful look for using smokeless tobacco, this was only because he rarely if ever used the stuff indoors. But he had seen it with his co-workers plenty of times. Rob had always found these managers' outspoken criticisms to be somewhere between laughable and irritating. Every time he witnessed such rebukes he had the same thought.

We've got more shootings and murders around here than fucking Baghdad and you're worried about guys using chewing tobacco? Really?

Police work, especially in high crime areas, was still a testosterone filled world. Habits, like using smokeless tobacco, were often undertaken by the guys and even some of the "A" personality gals as a means of wearing their "I fear nothing and am always up for a confrontation" attitudes on their sleeves. Rob laughed aloud in his truck as he thought about how many considered it to be settled psychological science that those who went out of their way to display their "forward" personalities were people who really doubted their own capabilities. He was convinced this was just psycho-babble. He had known more men than he could count who had proved this theory to be nothing more than academic bullshit.

Add it to the long list of bullshit espoused by academic experts, he mused.

The truth was that Rob's world contained lots of guys that flaunted their proclivity for action. The strong silent type may have also been represented in the alpha world of high activity police work, but there was no shortage of loud extraverts, putting it all on display whenever and however possible, for anyone who cared to notice. It was largely an environment where alpha males competed for rank, even if informally, among other alpha males.

The ranking personnel overseeing hiring practices could try as hard as they wanted to screen this aspect out of the dynamic, but in the end this kind of work drafted heavily from the pool of society's alpha males (and to a lesser degree alpha females) who were willing to confront others in adversarial circumstances and environments--circumstances and environments that the vast majority of the public were willing to pay someone else to deal with. Why shovel shit yourself when you can just pay someone else to do it?

Rob was anxious to get to work today as he had just finished doing a three day suspension without pay that stemmed from a field contact with a local politician. The administrative investigation's findings had concluded Rob had been "discourteous to the public" during his contact with the obnoxious politician during a traffic violation stop. Traffic enforcement was a rare part of Rob's approach to police work. In a typical year the number of tickets he issued could be counted on one hand. But on the day in question, the community organizer turned politician had been driving a new model BMW in a manner that bordered on reckless driving. Rob felt he had no choice but to pull the driver over.

The driver had been hostile at the outset of the contact. Rob had no sooner requested the man's driver's license and car registration than the irate politician had identified himself by elected position title, adding that he could cause Rob a lot of trouble if he wanted to. In typical form, Rob had failed to keep his contempt in check, telling the self-important wind bag he wasn't as big a deal as he thought he was. Rob had seasoned his response with a couple of profanities as well as mentioning something about who would be performing the "water boy" services for the other if somehow the two of them were to find themselves stranded on a deserted island together.

The politician hadn't been impressed with the patrol cop's wit, or his insight, in the least, a fact he made known to Rob's watch commander five minutes following the traffic stop. Rob had used the three day suspension to spend time with Stephanie and Charlie Wyatt. You never wasted your suspension days on self-pity or remorse. You made damn sure to have fun or do something otherwise enjoyable.

Rob turned on the radio in his truck. Most of the patrol cops in Rob's approximate age group either listened to classic rock, country, or "head banger" music. A few preferred jazz or old Motown. Of course some of the younger guys favored the *hip-hop* stuff. Rob liked both classic rock and country music. In fact he enjoyed them a lot. But at the very top of Rob's list of audio entertainment was talk radio. So he found the AM station that hosted one of his favorite talk radio personalities, a local talent, and waited to hear what the topic of the morning would be.

This morning the host was interviewing a scientist of some sort about the probability of Southern California suffering a major magnitude earthquake in the near future. The scientist, obviously very knowledgeable about the subject matter, offered her opinion in the flat monotone and overly scientific manner that served as a stereotype for those in her profession.

The radio host, clearly attempting to elicit some semblance of audible passion from his guest speaker, followed up by asking the geologist what she thought the impact on Southern California's infrastructure would be following such an event. Rob answered aloud for the scientist before she could get the words out to her radio host in the studio.

"All of L.A. would be in deep shit; that's what!"

No longer having the patience to listen to the insipid scientist who was today's guest speaker, Rob decided to find some music to listen to for the remainder of his drive. He switched the radio to an FM classic rock station in time to hear the 1970's Ted Nugent classic: *STRANGLEHOLD*.

Rob was instantly reminded of September 11th, 2001. He remembered, with absolute detail, how he had heard this song while driving on route to the station from home on his day off after having been awakened by a phone call informing him of unfolding events, and then watching the second plane fly into the World Trade Center tower on live television that morning. For Rob, music had always contained a certain ability to create, or enhance, his mood, and the cut by Ted Nugent called *Stranglehold* was what he categorized as "battle music".

It turned out there had been no additional attacks on the west coast, but at the time, the American law enforcement community as a whole was anticipating the worst. Cops across the nation packed their gear, told their family members they loved them, and went to work not knowing what was to be expected.

Rob dismissed the memory and focused on his driving. Responding to the hard driving Ted Nugent tune, Rob pushed his speed to over 80 miles per hour after transitioning onto the south-bound 405 freeway from the 101. He was now changing lanes frequently to get around those driving at more normal speeds. Traffic was still light by L.A. standards, but there were definitely plenty of vehicles on the freeway. He eased off the accelerator a bit as the song came to an end, reducing his speed to between seventy and seventy five MPH. He enjoyed listening to an old Credence Clearwater song followed by a Lynyrd Skynyrd classic before he transitioned again onto the east-bound Century Freeway toward South Central Los Angeles.

Suddenly, and without explanation, not long after passing through the city of Inglewood and into South Central L.A., Rob felt his truck lose power at the same time he saw most of the lights go black all around him as far as he could see. When he put more weight into the gas pedal there was no response whatsoever. He also experienced a loss in the truck's power steering.

Shit; now I'm going to be seriously late, Rob thought in frustration as he struggled to steer his truck without benefit of power steering.

His truck was rapidly losing speed, and Rob realized his first priority was to get the truck over to the shoulder and to get it stopped. It would also be nice to avoid getting struck by one of the now growing number of cars on the freeway. It was only seconds later that he noticed all of the other cars on the freeway were also decelerating quickly.

Uh-oh; this isn't good, he said to himself.

Many of the drivers were jockeying their non-running, yet still rolling, vehicles in an attempt to get to the freeway shoulder. Others were making no such effort, instead allowing their cars to slow and then stop in the traffic lanes. Rob noted that the city lights were blacked out.

The only illumination on the freeway was provided by car lights, yet most of them seemed to have lost this function too.

Weird. Some headlights are still working, Rob noted.

The reality of the current situation struck him like a punch to the gut. For the second time this morning, Rob spoke out loud despite there being no one to hear him.

"Holy shit. I can't believe it actually happened!" Rob was pretty sure what he was looking at was an electromagnetic pulse event.

The phenomenon of electromagnetic pulse (aka: EMP) was something he had learned about during a department sponsored terrorism seminar a little over a year ago. Although an EMP could result from natural causes (referred to as "solar flares"), the course addressed the "weaponized" version. The type caused by a nuclear device detonated at high altitude.

A high altitude detonation, unlike a similar blast at ground level, produced a pulse of much larger amplitude, due to interactions with the earth's magnetic field. In layman's terms, the pulse caused by such a detonation would fry anything that used electronics of any type. The instructor had indicated he feared the right EMP event had the potential to crush much of the nation's infrastructure for quite a long time.

He had stressed that an EMP event could impact virtually every unprotected device reliant upon electronics, circuit boards, and in many cases, other electrical motors. The power grid, all vehicles (including aircraft) that used electronics in their function, train systems, hospitals, retail stores, and wholesale distributors were all vulnerable to EMP. Fuel supply sources, hospitals, and emergency response (police, fire, and medical) would likely be unavailable or at least severely hampered.

Most modern emergency electrical power generators would be ruined as well. Of course cell phones and satellite phones would be toast. The presenter mentioned that vehicles manufactured prior to the early 1970's would likely be unaffected due to the lack of electronics used in the vehicle designs.

"For many intents and purposes we would immediately be thrown back into the 19th century without a minute's warning," the instructor had told the class.

After he said this, an unusual thing happened. All classroom sub-volume discussions, cell phone texting, and note taking came to an immediate and conspicuous halt. The course attendees looked up at the instructor.

Rob could still hear the man's derisive tone as he addressed the class.

"The good news is that there are ways to protect vulnerable electronic mechanisms against EMP. But the bad news is that very few local governments, private industry companies, or utility companies, have done anything to 'harden' their sensitive equipment."

The class had responded audibly with a collective groan.

"And it gets even better," the presenter had said, "the politicians seem to be willfully choosing to ignore the problem even though it has been brought to their attention many a time."

Totally irresponsible assholes, Rob had said under his breath when he had heard this.

Later that week, after raising the issue with his superiors at the sheriff's station, Rob's surprise was transformed into disappointment and irritation. Nobody seemed to care.

Rob had not broached the subject with Sergeant Marino after returning from the terrorism course. But Marino had attended the same course a month later, and eventually he and Rob had discussed the information presented in the class. The sergeant had shared Rob's concerns. Marino had stopped short of criticizing his superiors, but it was clear enough to Rob that he was aware of the problem that an apathetic sheriff's department presented when it came to this issue. If nobody cared enough to even acknowledge the preparation problem, it damn sure wasn't going to get fixed. So things continued as usual.

Rob brought his mind back to the current situation on the freeway. Unable to come up with another explanation for what was happening, he felt a sinking realization that one of the worst scenarios discussed in the entire terrorism seminar--an EMP event--was possibly a reality now. And he was thinking that he couldn't be in a worse place than the gang infested neighborhoods of South Los Angeles.

2

SOUTH CENTRAL LOS ANGELES

The violent jarring came out of nowhere and without warning. It was the unmistakable crunching sound of one automobile striking another that provided the first indication he had been hit. But it wasn't the sound that occupied Rob's brain right now; it was the excruciating pain that radiated down his neck as the back of his head struck the head rest, rebounded forward, and then hit the headrest again.

Although he tried to maintain control of his slowly moving truck's steering wheel, the pain he was experiencing rendered him incapable of doing so. Unable to control the truck's path of travel, he struck the metal guardrail with enough impact to activate the truck's air bags, and then came to a stop.

The first thing he did after realizing he was in pain yet still conscious, was to wait for the driver side airbag to deflate. The second thing he did was spit out the "dip" of *Skoal* from his mouth onto the floor of his truck. He wanted it out of his mouth immediately, and couldn't care less if there was a small mess to clean up later. He was pretty sure that his truck wasn't going to be in his possession much longer anyway. He slowly moved his head and instantly experienced neck spasms.

Shit. This is all I need right now.

Luckily, he was able to move his neck, gradually and marginally, from side to side and back and forth despite the spasms. He checked the basic function of his entire body, looking and feeling for additional injuries, as he sat in the driver's seat. He did so slowly, trying his best not to overlook anything. He knew from experience that the adrenaline in one's body after something like this could do a pretty good job of masking injury.

Other than his neck, he seemed to be free of any significant injury. He silently thanked God for this despite the fact that it seemed so much else had gone terribly wrong in a very short period of time.

Rob always kept the passenger side seat belt locked when he had his bug-out pack there in order to avoid the truck's seatbelt alarm from being activated. As a result, it had activated the passenger side airbag as well as the bag on the driver's side.

For some reason, the passenger airbag had failed to deflate, and now it prevented him from reaching his pack. He opened his folding knife and used the blade to cut away the airbag. He winced with pain as he reached for his pack and then gingerly stepped out of his damaged truck.

The vehicle that had crashed into the back of his truck was a 1970 Cadillac Eldorado Fleetwood. The Cadillac's engine was still running, despite the fact it was leaking fluid from under the engine compartment at a fast rate. The motor continued running for almost twenty seconds before it quit. Looking at the big old damaged luxury sedan, Rob was convinced an EMP was responsible for what he was seeing all around him.

He recalled the terrorism instructor had said older cars would not be affected by EMP. Looking at the older Cadillac with its engine still running seemed to support this. He regretted that he was not mechanically inclined as he watched the Cadillac leaking fluid from its motor compartment.

While Rob thought this over, the driver's door of the Cadillac opened, and a black man, appearing to be at least seventy years old, climbed out. He was dressed in jeans and a plain cotton work shirt. Daylight was beginning to make its appearance over the south L.A. landscape, and Rob was aware of how different his surroundings appeared without the normal intrusion of the vehicles and all things electrical.

Like most patrol cops, Rob made it a habit to watch the hands of most people he contacted. He saw the man's thick hands. A working man's hands, tough and strong.

Rob asked him if he was injured.

"No, I don't think so, but that was crazy man! What in hell's goin' on anyway? Earthquake or somethin'? Looks like all the power went out."

Rob started to shake his head, instantly stopping as he was painfully reminded of his injury.

"Naw. I think this is something a lot worse than an earthquake. A whole helluva lot worse."

Both of the men heard the faint sound of the distant explosion, although this was only possible because there was no traffic on the freeway to cover the sound. Shortly afterward the men saw smoke rising from the presumed source of the sound. Rob determined the blast was considerably west and slightly north of where they stood, but it was difficult to estimate how far away the explosion was from where they were. He estimated it to be several miles away, maybe even ten or more.

Whatever had caused the explosion, it was big, and it was serious. And then an odd thing happened, or more accurately, did *not* happen. They saw no emergency vehicles responding to the scene of the explosion. Nor did they hear any sirens. The freeway scene was eerily quiet and still. Rob was consumed by a sinking feeling as he began to realize just how terrible this event was going to be.

He was trying to remember what had been said during his terrorism training about EMP and commercial aircraft. Rob realized that they were less than ten miles from the Los Angeles International Airport. He now feared that the explosion may have been the result of a large jet losing power and crashing into one of the heavily populated residential areas below the flight path for the LAX Airport.

No sooner had these thoughts gone through his mind than Rob observed something so frighteningly bizarre that his mind had difficulty accepting it as reality. While surveying the sky around him, he saw an airliner several miles to the east. It was precipitously losing altitude, its nose plummeting toward the ground.

The plane's image was quite small due the distance, but there was no mistaking what it was. Moments later, he saw the plane disappear from view. Then, not long after that, he saw a small but definite dark column of smoke rising from that location. While Rob could not estimate in what part of the city the plane had gone down, he had no doubt what he had just witnessed.

Rob was convinced they were looking at the aftermath of two airliners that had undergone electronics systems failures as a result of an electromagnetic pulse. He tried to conjure up any explanation for the crazy events of the morning other than EMP. Nothing else explained it all. He avoided thinking about the massive number of deaths and injuries at the airline crash sites. He told himself it was imperative he be able to avoid letting his emotions guide his actions.

Rob was almost positive that the older man hadn't seen the second airliner going down, and he didn't think there was any point in telling him. For that matter, Rob wasn't at all sure the older man had realized the first explosion had been caused by a downed plane. But he obviously knew something serious had just happened.

Thinking he had possibly detected a bit of hesitancy on the part of the senior man next to him, Rob removed the wallet that housed his badge and Sheriff's Department identification card from his rear pocket. He showed it to him, and offered what he hoped would be a comforting gesture.

"Sir, I just want to put you at ease if I can. I'm a deputy sheriff. I'm just letting you know this because I don't want you to think I'm going to hurt you or take advantage of you in any way."

Rob thought he saw the slightest indication of tension reduction in the man's expression as he nodded to acknowledge the information.

This guy is old school, he thought. *He still views us as the good guys. That's a nice change.*

Gesturing toward the front of the Cadillac, he asked the man, "Do you know much about fixing cars?"

He was hoping the damaged engine could be repaired well enough to allow the car to run for a while. It would mean transportation for them at least. Rob was pretty certain the Cadillac had escaped any damage from the EMP, but that didn't help the damage caused by the collision with his truck.

The older man chuckled and said, "Hell, I hope so young man. I was an auto mechanic for almost forty five years."

Rob showed him a rare smile and shrugged his shoulders as if to apologize for missing the obvious, even though there was no way he could've been expected to know this.

"Hey young fellah, I'm sorry I hit your truck and all. I guess I didn't know you was stopping so all-of-a-sudden. Why *did* you stop like that? All those cars stopped for no reason."

Before Rob could answer, the man asked him if he wanted to make a police report about the accident.

Rob let out a half-hearted laugh and added that if he was right about what had just happened, the whole state, and maybe even much of the country, was going to be shut down hard for quite a while.

"A police report is the last thing to be worrying about at this point," said Rob.

"Hell, I'm bettin' most police services aren't even going to be available for quite a while," he added.

"And that is something we need to start thinking about starting right now," Rob stated matter-of-factly as he slowly looked around at his surroundings, turning his whole torso so as to minimize using his sore neck muscles.

The retired mechanic just looked at Rob with an expression that suggested he was trying to figure out whether the younger off-duty deputy sheriff was kidding him, knew something that the older man didn't, or was perhaps just crazy.

Slowly and carefully massaging his sore neck, Rob read the expression on his face and began to provide the incredulous man with an abbreviated explanation of EMP and why he believed this was what had taken place. In a voice infused with more than a little sarcasm, Rob commented that they both could probably predict how this scenario was likely to play out before long. They both knew that with so many normal day-to-day goods and services being unavailable, trouble wasn't far behind.

Still holding the thought, Rob asked him if he had been living around here during the riots of 1992. The older man nodded his head and then directed his attention at the pavement as he spoke.

"Yeah I was here when all those evil mother..." He stopped mid-sentence before completing the profanity he felt like uttering to describe the savage predators that had been active in his neighborhood at the time. The man stopped speaking and simply shook his head from side to side as he recalled the three days of violence and destruction that had besieged certain regions of Los Angeles in April of 1992 prior to order having been restored.

Rob knew that almost a hundred deaths, and easily ten times as many serious injuries, had been attributed to that shit storm. And these were neighborhoods that were surrounding the spot where they now stood.

Time to get moving, thought Rob.

"Well, I don't think there's going to be any police or firemen showing up for quite a while," Rob said with a stern face.

The man looked at Rob with a puzzled expression and responded, "Yeah you said that. Why you think that anyway?"

He ignored the question for the moment.

"Pardon my manners. I'm Rob."

"My name's Gerald Brown," replied the man as he extended his hand.

Rob shook his hand, noting the firmness in his grasp. Gerald asked him again about the lack of emergency response.

He took a minute to provide Gerald with more detail about electromagnetic pulse and how virtually none of the first responders in the greater L.A. area were prepared for such an event.

"Being an auto mechanic I figure you know all about the new cars having all the electronics in 'em now. Well, all the emergency vehicles have those same systems. They don't have any cars that are protected from EMP effects. Don't ask me how come; they just don't is all. Trust me on this," Rob grumbled.

He recalled how he had tried unsuccessfully to get his superiors to attempt to prepare the station, its equipment, or its personnel for serious terrorist incidents. The most he had been able to accomplish was to get the station's captain to allow the installation of a thousand gallon water tank in the building's parking lot. The tank was to be paid for with money collected from the station deputies. And they were still waiting for the new tank to be installed. Before this could happen, an ancient corroded steel water tank planted in the corner of the parking lot had to be removed. And who the hell knew how long that would take. It was, after all, the county.

"You probably know this since you're a mechanic, but the reason your Caddy was still running is because it was built before the engines had all the electronics."

He nodded his head in understanding.

"I hate all that computer stuff the new cars have. Some of 'em got so much of it that I can't even work on 'em."

The topic being discussed apparently prompted Gerald to consider their present situation.

"Lemme get a look under the hood and see how bad the Caddy is."

He slowly walked to the front end of his car. After a bit of difficulty with opening the crumpled hood, he eventually popped it up so that he could examine the engine area. He shook his head in disappointment.

"This baby ain't gonna be working for a while. No way man. Damn."

"Okay Gerald. Let me think about this for a minute here."

Rob set his bug-out pack on the ground and opened the main compartment. He found his first aid "blow-out" kit, and withdrew four 200 milligram ibuprofen tablets. He swallowed all four of them dry, two at a time. All he could do now was hope that by taking the ibuprofen so soon after the injury, the pills' anti-inflammatory properties would kick in before the inflammation itself.

It was obvious that any hope of traveling in a vehicle was out of the question. He also realized time was of the essence. As if reading the younger man's mind, Gerald asked, "Where you gonna be headed to?"

"I'm not really sure right this second. I'm gonna have to think about that for a minute I guess," he responded as he surveyed the scene on the Century Freeway around them.

Most of the drivers were staying inside of their cars. Some of these were on the freeway's shoulder while many remained in the freeway lanes. But they were all stopped. No doubt about that. A few of the occupants were milling about trying to use their cell phones. This was all to no avail of course. Rob saw one man take his cell phone and violently throw it across the freeway in frustration as he let loose with a long string of profanities.

Good problem solving skills you got there buddy, Rob said to himself.

He asked Gerald if he lived anywhere near their present location. Gerald indicated that he lived in Inglewood, located only a few miles from where they were standing. The city of Inglewood was one of the many incorporated cities that were independent of Los Angeles proper. Yet it could be difficult to know when a person had left one city and entered another.

The majority of Inglewood's population was comprised of persons of color, mostly Hispanic and African-American. It included some areas where the residents possessed considerable wealth, quite a few middle class neighborhoods, and plenty of poorer sections that housed hard-core gang populations amidst regular residents.

Rob suggested they walk together until it was time for Gerald to get off the freeway and head for his home via surface streets.

"We might as well both get the advantage of bein' with each other in case any trouble finds us, right?" Rob asked.

"Yeah, that makes sense to me okay."

Rob asked him if there was anything he wanted to get from his car to carry with him. He added that there was a good chance neither of them would see their vehicles, or any of their vehicles' contents, ever again once they left on foot.

"I'd take another look to be sure" Rob advised. Following his own advice, he walked to the bed of his truck and lifted the truck bed cover to examine what lay beneath it.

After giving considerable thought to his plan of action, Rob had decided he would find a way to return home, no matter how long it would take him. Despite the heavy pull of his sense of duty as a cop and the specific obligation he felt to make his way to the Nadeau Station to help in whatever capacity he could, Rob had already made the decision to make the journey to his home. Or had he?

Rob knew the real struggle would lie with his efforts to forgive himself for abandoning his buddies. Buddies who would be forced to deal with whatever ugly shit would soon be happening at the Nadeau Station in the coming hours and days. Similar to wartime military friendships, the personal bonds forged under the circumstances of high action law enforcement carried with them a much heavier sense of loyalty than co-workers in normal professions Making a deliberate decision to abandon these friends, regardless of the justification, was a big deal--a hell of a big deal.

But his home was where his wife and little boy would be worried and scared. To leave them to fend for themselves with what was possibly going to be heading their way was simply out of the question for Rob. There was no way in hell that was going to happen.

He estimated the distance to his Thousand Oaks home was close to 50 miles. He let his mind go to a bad place as he pictured Stephanie and Charlie Wyatt being left alone to deal with the chaos of a post-EMP setting. He reminded himself about what the terrorism instructor had said about the awful impact an EMP would have on the nation. The only question in Rob's mind was how long it would take to start happening, and how quickly things would deteriorate from there.

Rob knew without a doubt that his most important duty was to get home to his family, and he made a commitment right then and there to do whatever it took to make that happen.

He scanned the contents in his truck bed: a full length round-nosed shovel, a full sized axe, a six-by-eight foot plastic tarp, several lengths of half inch diameter rope, a few aluminum high strength oval shaped aluminum "D" shaped clips called *Carabiners* that were used for attaching ropes or miscellaneous other functions. There was a small tool box, two full one gallon plastic water jugs, and a sleeping bag. Rob thought intently about which items, if any, were worth taking with him on this fifty mile hike he was about to embark upon.

He immediately rejected the idea of taking the shovel or the axe. Both were too heavy and awkward to carry for any distance. Besides, his pack contained a large knife that could handle most of the functions an axe would be needed for. It was a *Kabar Cutlass* model compact machete. A proven wilderness tool.

Its slightly thicker than typical machete blade and ten inch length cutting edge made it almost as effective as a hatchet for chopping, and in Rob's opinion the big knife was actually better than a hatchet for splitting small logs into kindling when using the "batoning" method. Another advantage of the big knife was that, unlike a hatchet or standard machete, the tip of the blade came to a point, which allowed it to be used to pierce things if required.

He had included a half dozen ten foot lengths of military 550 cord (aka: *Paracord*) in his pack as well. About the same size as the cord used for clothes lines, its namesake suggested that it had a load bearing strength of up to 550 pounds. He couldn't think of any likely scenario he would encounter where he would need a full-sized rope rather than the much smaller diameter *Paracord*, so he left the heavier rope in the truck bed. He did take one of the high strength aluminum alloy *Carabiners* and attached it to one of the "D" rings on his pack's shoulder strap. Rob then opened the tool box in his truck bed and sifted through the miscellaneous item located within.

Why am I even bothering with this stuff? I'm just wasting time now. I already have what I need in my pack.

But he couldn't help himself.

He decided to make a deal with himself to continue looking through the items in his truck that might be worth taking with him, but to do so quickly.

Gotta haul ass so we can hurry up and start walking.

He realized there was really no need to look through his tool box for items worth taking with him since he had already spent a lot of time selecting those items he felt were most essential when he put his pack together in the first place. Besides, he had the invaluable Leatherman multi-tool in his pack. The modern version of an old school *Swiss Army Knife,* the multi-tool was the closest thing to a tool box in a package not much bigger than a pack of chewing gum that a guy could have.

He dumped the tool box contents and scanned the items, trying to consider whether there was likely to be a need for any of them. Finally, he opted to take only two items from all of the contents he had dumped from the tool box.

Rob removed the hacksaw blade from its relatively large steel frame and placed the thin and insignificantly weighted blade into his front pocket. He retrieved a roll of duct tape from the truck and set it on his tailgate.

He used both hands to massage his sore neck. Trying to ignore the pain, he grabbed the roll of duct tape and wound approximately four feet of tape around each of the pack shoulder straps, effectively using the straps as the cores, or spools, for the tape. He separated the tape pieces from the roll with his knife, and then folded approximately a quarter inch of the tape ends over on themselves to facilitate removing sections of tape in a hurry later on if needed. Rob knew full well how valuable duct tape could be for a whole host of uses.

Looking at the jugs of water, Rob grabbed one and began to slowly and carefully drink from it, ever mindful of his sore neck. He noticed the pain had begun to subside. Looking at his watch he saw that twenty minutes had gone by since he had taken the ibuprofen tablets. Enough time for the medicine to have begun its work.

Setting the water jug he had been drinking from back in the truck, he called out to Gerald. "Better drink as much of this stuff as you can. Who knows how long till you get home where you can have a decent drink of water."

"Okay. Yeah, you're right about that."

Rob blurted out, "Hey; hold on a sec; I got an idea," as he once again produced his folding knife, flicked the blade open, and took one of the pieces of rope from his truck bed.

He cut a piece of rope several feet in length and tied both ends around the handle of the full water jug that was still in the truck bed. Rob handed the jug, now complete with an improvised carrying strap, to Gerald.

"Here, put this over your shoulder so you can carry this thing. And you can keep it by the way."

Rob stopped and faced Gerald.

"That reminds me. Be careful about the water you drink from now on. If the power grid and utilities are down everywhere--and they either are already or they soon will be--I wouldn't trust the water to be safe from germs or whatever. All the damn treatment centers and everything else are totally reliant on electronics based systems to make the water safe to drink, not to mention getting the water to everyone's house. "

Rob stopped for a second to gather his thoughts.

"Here's what you need to do. After getting it out of the faucet or garden hose, boil the water first before drinking it or even brushing your teeth or washing your face with it. Boiling the water for thirty seconds or so will kill the germs. No sense taking any chances".

Gerald nodded in acknowledgment, his expression showing that he liked the situation he was faced with less and less.

Rob asked Gerald if he was ready to head out. He answered as he took another look at his Cadillac, and once again shook his head back and forth. "Might as well I guess. Man, this is some crazy shit; crazy shit."

Rob replied, "Yeah, and it's gonna get a lot crazier if I'm right about this." Rob hoisted his pack over his shoulder and onto his back feeling a sharp spasm of pain as a reminder of his injury despite the relief he was starting to get from the ibuprofen.

Rob had a 27 ounce stainless steel water bottle and a flexible plastic *Platypus* water bag that held two quarts, in his pack. Both containers were full of water. He grabbed the partially empty plastic water jug from the truck bed with his left hand as he started walking. He left the two smaller water containers in his pack for later. He planned to carry the half empty jug with him, taking small drinks along the route until he had drained it completely.

Rob told himself he would tie the empty plastic jug to his pack in case he came across a water source during his journey. He lifted the jug, carefully tilted his head back no more than necessary in light of his injury, and drew heavily from it, fully aware but not caring that he was making loud gulping sounds as a slight stream of water dripped down the front of his chin and down over his shirt.

He drank past the point of feeling full. He drank until he felt he would burst, having consumed at least a quart of the stuff in the last few minutes. He suddenly remembered he had left his can of *Skoal* over the truck's visor. He walked back and flipped down the visor, catching the small three quarters full can and putting it into a pocket on his pack.

Rob called out to Gerald, now a good twenty feet in front of him as he began hiking down the side of the freeway, "I'm sorry but I gotta do just one more thing before we start off. It'll only take a minute."

The older man stopped, then turned and looked at Rob the way a father would look at his pre-adolescent son when his patience was being tried. Rob ignored the expression and shrugged out of his pack, letting it hit the pavement with a thud. He ignored the spasm that accompanied the action as he withdrew the sheathed machete from his pack.

He examined the big knife and its custom *Kydex* sheath. Affixed to the sheath was a small pouch containing a *Bic* butane cigarette lighter, a safety pin, single-edged razor blade, a couple of storm proof matches, and two cotton balls smeared with *Vaseline* petroleum jelly.

Rob had learned about the cotton balls with *Vaseline* being used as emergency fire starting tinder from an old woodsman in a bar years earlier. The petroleum in the *Vaseline* was extremely flammable and would start fire with only a spark if needed. Being able to make a fire, whether during wilderness activities or a "shit hit the fan" disaster like the one he now faced, was important. So the cotton balls had also earned a place in his bug-out pack.

He made one last trip to his truck bed to retrieve the duct tape roll. He used the tape to attach the *Kabar* machete to the front of his pack's left shoulder strap, handle pointing downward. After having made close to a half dozen wrapping rotations with the tape he tested the strength of the attachment with a few short tugs.

This thing is snug, he told himself.

He took an extra few seconds to open the small pouch attached to the opposite pack strap and ensure that the small *Steiner* monocular was still there. Admittedly not as effective as a set of good binoculars, the little monocular was far better than the naked eye for seeing at distances, and it took up very little space and weighed next to nothing. Satisfied that everything was secure in its position, Rob donned his pack, called out to Gerald, and began walking west-bound on the freeway shoulder.

Gerald watched him do all of the above as he thought to himself, *This guy has thought about this before today.*

"Okay, I'm good to go now," Rob announced as he adjusted the pack and cinched down the shoulder straps. This time Gerald waited for Rob to get next to him before he began his stride, both of them walking in silence. Not more than five minutes after having begun the hike, Rob removed his *boonie* hat from where it had been loosely tethered to the side of his pack and threw it over his head. He wanted to avoid sun burn if at all possible.

As both men walked at a decent pace Rob watched the activity of those on the freeway around them. More of the people were outside of their cars now than the last time he had observed them. He knew that as time passed, more and more of those on the freeway would become aware of the fact there wasn't going to be any help on the way for quite a while. They were going to start coming to the unpleasant realization that they were on their own.

3

UNINCORPORATED SOUTHEAST

LOS ANGELES

The geographical area patrolled by the Nadeau Sheriff's Station deputies included some of the nation's most violent neighborhoods, mainly due to the heavy gang populations that existed here. The fact that such a large area of "inner city" land had somehow never been incorporated into the city proper of Los Angeles was one of those odd phenomena that probably had some historical reason behind it, but it was a safe bet none of the deputies assigned here had any idea why it was so. Like the residents of the area themselves, they only knew the unincorporated areas were patrolled by the L.A. Sheriff's Department and the incorporated areas were patrolled by the LAPD.

Over the decades a relatively large number of sheriff's deputies and LAPD officers had been killed in the line of duty while working in this region. And, unlike the national average of law enforcement deaths, these numbers were not attributed to vehicle accidents. They were the result of cops being *murdered* in the line of duty. There were a lot of seriously dangerous people residing in, or passing through, the Nadeau Station patrol jurisdiction.

In the 1990's, before the Islamic jihadists had converted our mostly peacetime military into a battle hardened one, military surgeons spent lots of time at the Watts Trauma Center, located close to the border of the LAPD and LASD patrol jurisdictions. The reason for this was simple. The trauma center provided exposure to injuries similar to those encountered on battlefields. Specifically, gunshot wounds. And lots of them.

Every deputy assigned to Nadeau Station knew all of this, and these patrol cops wore it as an informal badge of honor. All LASD patrol cops received equal pay, but the work required and the risk they were subjected to was anything but equal.

In short, anyone who wanted to work at this station was advised to buckle his or her chin strap and hold on tight. The ride could get bumpy indeed.

By any definition, Sergeant Dave Marino was a pillar of the Nadeau Station. It was a title he had earned starting many years prior to the day the EMP happened.

In the 1980's, before every patrol deputy carried a two-way radio on his person, then *Deputy* Marino and his partner had arrested a pair of extremely dangerous killers that made national headlines. The pair of serial robbers had murdered a family of four in their home at the culmination of an hour long home invasion robbery. No witnesses meant less chance of being caught, and less chance of being convicted if you were caught. And innocent human life meant nothing to the pair.

Adding to this newsworthy event was the fact the arrest itself was a violent one. Marino had fought with one of the ex-convicts—an unusually muscular 250 pound bruiser—for almost two full minutes before finally ending it with a carotid choke hold. Marino's partner had held the second murderer at gunpoint during the entire fight.

As it turned out, both men associated with the arrest were provided with a very rarely administered ticket to California's death row, and Dave Marino would become something akin to a legend on the Sheriff's Department. Although he rarely mentioned the incident, to this day it was recounted to virtually every new trainee that was assigned to the Nadeau Station as a rookie.

Marino's performance while assigned to LASD SWAT--one of the nation's top tier special weapons teams--only added to his reputation. As a SWAT cop he had been involved in several shooting incidents as well as additional scenarios that showcased his capabilities and commitment to the position. He had definitely earned his promotion to sergeant. And as a patrol sergeant he was the supervisor you wanted to run field operations when you found yourself in the middle of a fecal blizzard.

***

Sergeant Marino was enjoying his second large cup of black coffee in the Nadeau Station watch sergeant's office when the EMP happened. All of the electrical power for the station went out as if God himself had simply snapped his fingers and killed all the juice. While a power outage in this area was rare in itself, it was not unheard of. What was unheard of was the failure of the building's emergency generator to kick in and supply back-up power to the station.

This ain't good, he thought.

4

THOUSAND OAKS, CA

Rob's wife, Stephanie, had just finished feeding Charlie Wyatt and was preparing to feed their two dogs when the EMP event happened. She always made it a point to have her own breakfast last. This was part of her giving nature, already formed in her childhood, and an aspect of her personality that shortened the time it took for Rob to fall in love with her during their courtship.

Stephanie had spent close to twenty years working in both the public and private sectors. She had been a medical office manager for several doctors as well as serving as a valued assistant for two large hospital CEO's. In these positions she had been an effective trouble shooter and problem solver, always highly respected by her employers for her above average capabilities.

After Charlie Wyatt was born she and Rob had decided it would be better to do with less than to have their son raised in large part by strangers. So Stephanie changed jobs. She resigned from the medical office manager position and took a promotion as a full-time mother and household manager. She still wasn't sure which position was more demanding, but she damn well knew which was more rewarding. She never regretted her decision, and neither did Rob.

In contrast with how Rob had experienced the EMP on the freeway, at the Flynn residence that morning the EMP occurred in a wholly unspectacular manner. Stephanie had started to make her morning coffee when the coffee machine, along with everything else in the house reliant upon the power grid, simply ceased to work.

There was no loud noise, no intense burst of bright light, and no felt shock wave; everything just stopped working was all.

She spent the first hour after the EMP without much fanfare or any serious concern. She dismissed it as being nothing more than a typical power outage, which had occurred a handful of times during the past ten years. She assumed power would be turned back on within a few hours at the most.

Determined not to allow a power outage to deprive her of her morning coffee, Stephanie recalled how she had made coffee for herself and Rob on their most recent camping trip. She walked into the attached garage and retrieved an old fashioned coffee pot from a duffle bag kept on a shelf that stored their camping gear. The appearance of the coffee pot reminded Stephanie of campfire scenes in old western movies with its blue speckled enamel exterior.

Stephanie fished out a medium-sized wire mesh basket strainer from the cupboard and rested it over the coffee pot's opening. She went to the coffee maker that had quit on her moments earlier and removed the paper coffee filter that still contained the unused coffee grounds. She placed the filter and its contents inside of the strainer so that when she poured hot water over it the coffee would drip into the coffee pot below it. All that was left for her to do at this point was to heat some water in another pot for this purpose.

After a failed attempt at trying to turn on the stove using the normal procedure, it occurred to her that without power she would have to light the stove's burner manually with a flame. She rummaged through a drawer filled with miscellaneous items ranging from masking tape to rubber-bands, eventually locating a disposable plastic cigarette lighter. Applying the lighter's flame to the stove burner, the stove came to life.

She placed a small cooking pot full of water over the flame. Just before the water came to a boil, she poured the steaming liquid over the filter containing the coffee as it rested in the strainer over the coffee pot. She savored the unique and comforting aroma of fresh coffee brewing as the hot water made its way through the coffee grounds and filter before collecting in the pot below. She repeated the process until she had used all of the water and had filled the old fashioned coffee pot half full of freshly brewed coffee.

In less than five minutes Stephanie was enjoying a good cup of coffee. Charlie Wyatt was sitting at the table, watching with great interest, while his mom engaged in this new endeavor. Not for the first time, she made a mental note of thanks for having received the good fortune of giving birth to a child who possessed such a happy personality. It had not escaped her notice how so many other kids Charlie Wyatt's age were not so easily contented, and she counted her blessings.

While savoring her coffee Stephanie decided to make a phone call to her friend. She realized the house landline was dead, which didn't really surprise her. When she tried to use her cell phone she discovered that it didn't work either. In fact, she soon realized that her cell phone couldn't even be turned on at all. This did surprise her.

Thinking that the phone's battery was dead, she went to charge it. Then she realized that the house had no electrical power, so the wall charger would be pointless. She grabbed Charlie Wyatt and went out to the driveway where her Honda Pilot SUV was parked so she could use her car charger.

After sitting her son in the front passenger seat she climbed in behind the wheel. She was well aware it was best to start the car's engine if she planned to use the cigarette lighter outlet to charge her cell phone to avoid draining the car's battery. But when she tried to do so nothing happened.

She repeated the action twice more before she accepted the fact that the car wasn't going to start. Charlie Wyatt was bouncing up and down and looking all around, obviously intent upon maximizing the unusual treat of sitting in the "grown up" seat next to his mom. He was trying to communicate with his mom to the best of his ability, but Stephanie was becoming increasingly concerned with the growing number of equipment failures she was experiencing.

The capable mom dropped her cell phone onto her lap and smacked the SUV's steering wheel with the palm of her hand, stopping herself just in time before uttering a profanity with Charlie Wyatt sitting right next to her.

She told herself, *Okay Steph; think. What's the problem here, and how can you fix it?*

While sitting there in her car trying to mentally connect the dots and make sense out of all of the morning's power loss events and equipment failures, she suddenly experienced a moment of near panic.

The recollection surged through her with a jolt of adrenaline as she suddenly remembered something Rob had told her a while back. The thought scared her to the point where she jumped out of the parked car and ran around to the passenger side. She flung open the door and pulled Charlie Wyatt from his seat and out of the car as quickly as she could.

Her actions were so uncharacteristically abrupt and forceful that her normally happy-go-lucky little boy became visibly shaken as he looked at his mother trying to figure out what had suddenly made her so upset. She implored him, "Come on Charlie Wyatt; we need to go inside now" as she quickly walked back into the house with her son in tow. He complied without saying a word, knowing somehow that this was not a time to question his mother.

Stephanie wracked her brain as she tried to bring her memory into sharper focus. Over a year prior, Rob had returned from a two day terrorism course whereupon she had pressed him for details about the class. At first Rob had merely shrugged off her questions, but eventually he explained about the threats of biological and chemical terrorism. He had also talked about nuclear weapons being used for purposes of terrorism. But it was what he had shared with her about a phenomenon called "EMP" that she was now trying to recall.

Rob had gone into detail in his explanation, describing how a large geographical area of the country could suffer a loss of its infrastructure following an EMP event. His explanation included a list of electronic components--found in everything from cell phones to cars—that would likely be destroyed.

"Now I know where the saying 'ignorance is bliss' comes from," Stephanie had retorted at the time as she shook her head.

Thinking everything over on the morning of the EMP incident, Stephanie began connecting the dots. She knew in the deepest recesses of her gut that the only thing that could explain the loss of the electric grid, her cell phone not working, and her car's engine and battery being inoperable, was the strange phenomenon that Rob had told her about after returning from that terrorism course. She also knew that she was going to have to deal with whatever was coming her way by herself.

Laden with the heavy weight of tremendous responsibility, Stephanie began to replay, as best she could, some of the previous conversations she had had with Rob about disaster planning. Six months ago Rob had sat her down and attempted to establish protocols for handling miscellaneous disasters that could impact their family. She had somewhat reluctantly agreed to go along with the idea, but she had never truly bought into it. Rob being a cop and all, it was his usual practice to worry about things whether it warranted serious concern or not.

After the one-sided discussion, Rob had begun to assemble a few items to be stored at their house that could be used to make their lives a more comfortable under disaster conditions. He described it as being nothing more than an insurance policy. Not having a lot of extra money with which to purchase these things, Rob had made affordable purchases every couple of weeks.

He started off by setting up an emergency food supply, much of which Stephanie had taken care of by adding larger numbers of canned goods to their pantry. Rob also bought a few long term storage food items of the freeze dried variety. It hadn't taken much more a month to acquire thirty days of emergency disaster food for the three of them and the two dogs.

The following month Rob had sought to establish a thirty day reserve of water for the family. Estimating that ten gallons of water per day would be the minimal amount required to sustain his family during a disaster that shut off the public water supply, Rob had purchased a half dozen fifty five gallon plastic drums and then filled them with tap water in the event they should ever need water during a disaster scenario. He stored four of the barrels in the garage and two outside of the house, just in case a major earthquake should ever cause the house's walls to collapse, making access to the barrels a problem.

A basic camping stove that used readily available propane canisters for fuel, and a couple of good quality flashlights with attendant extra batteries, completed the second month's shopping objective for the family's disaster preparation items. Rob had also purchased a couple of inexpensive old fashioned oil lamps and a five gallon can of high grade kerosene a few weeks later on a whim. Spotting the items while waiting in line to pay for some sprinkler parts at his local hardware store, he had thought that they might be put to good use during a prolonged power outage.

He admitted to himself that the oil lamps weren't bought so much for practical reasons as they were for the "cool factor". He had long ago discovered that he found comfort in the soothing effect of an open flame, whether it be a candle light, a campfire, or anything in between.

Rob also knew that the comfort he gleaned from fire was very common, if not universal, with other persons. This was one of the reasons that wilderness survival experts emphasized the value of making a fire when lost.

Although he had never been lost in the wilderness, throughout many years of outdoor activities Rob had taken great pleasure in the simple observation of a small fire, letting his normally busy mind drift off to a slow and peaceful ebb as he watched the flames. In fact, he had been so content in watching his campfires in this manner during his extensive outdoor experiences that he referred to the practice as "mountain man TV".

Three large standard plastic garbage cans were the final addition to the disaster preparation supplies at the Flynn residence. These were stacked empty inside of each other and then suspended with rope from the garage rafters where they were completely out of the way of everyday activities.

The concept here was to have available water storage contain-ers that could be retrieved and used to acquire any water remaining in the city water lines immediately following a disaster that would cause a cessation in water availability after time. Rob's thinking was that even if the water retrieved from compromised public water lines were contaminated with bacteria or other pathogens, boiling the liq-uid, over a camp stove if need be, provided an easy solution. Having the water in the first place was the important thing.

Looking around the kitchen, Stephanie found herself becoming increasingly concerned about Rob, and then she started to worry even more about how she and Charlie Wyatt would be able to contend with this disaster without Rob being here with them.

She fought to hold back her tears, but she soon lost the battle as small pools ran down her cheeks. She hugged her son tightly, silently hoping and praying that she could handle the looming challenge. Charlie Wyatt, rarely seen with anything but a smile on his face, somehow grasped the fact that his mother was close to despair and he began to cry also. Immediately aware of how she had transferred her emotions to her young son, Stephanie forced herself back from the dark place she had started to enter and committed herself to get to work with what needed to be done.

She wrapped one arm around Charlie Wyatt's little waist tightly and brushed his hair with the fingers of her other hand, soothing the growing anxiety for both of them in the process. He wasn't smiling again as of yet, but he no longer wore his expression of concern and worry. He definitely seemed to be doing better than he had been a few minutes ago.

The Australian Shepherds, one of whom licked Charlie Wyatt on the back of his head while trotting over to Stephanie, both sat down in front of her. The dogs wagged their tails, demonstrating their hap-piness, as always, just to be in the company of their human masters. "Lady", the older of the two, turned her head inquisitively, looking directly at Stephanie. The other dog, "Bella", rolled over on her back exposing her canine belly; no doubt a not so subtle request to be scratched or petted. The female Aussie seemed to be conveying the message that just because an EMP event had occurred didn't mean that a dog couldn't still enjoy the basic comforts of life. Stephanie actually laughed aloud.

The memory came to her without her even trying to pull it up. She recalled how Rob had created a detailed list of the things Stephanie should do in his absence during a major disaster such as a major earthquake. He placed this detailed list, complete with instructions for using equipment and the storage locations of the items, in two separate locations of their house. She agreed to memorize where the lists were located. This way she didn't have to be bothered with remembering the details—only where the lists were kept.

The couple acknowledged it wasn't the best approach—the idea of waiting to try out gear for the first time when there was an emergency unfolding was inviting trouble. But it was in essence a compromise.

For their meals, Stephanie and Charlie Wyatt began using the food in the refrigerator first since she knew it would be the earliest to spoil. He ate his food without complaint. She was thankful her son was not a picky eater. When she took Charlie Wyatt to brush his teeth before going to bed, she saw that the water volume and pressure was only about half of what it normally was. Too tired to even think about what to do about the water issue, she walked him to his room she put him to bed just after dark.

He asked her where his dad was, and Stephanie hesitated before answering. She told Charlie Wyatt that his father would be home late tonight because he was at work trying to help people. The little guy was asleep almost as soon as his head hit the pillow. She kissed him goodnight and left the door to his room open so that she could easily hear him if he cried out in the night.

She used her *Surefire* LED flashlight to brush her teeth and prepare for bed. She even thought about using the flashlight to read the novel she had started a few days prior before deciding she had better save her batteries. She climbed into bed exhausted. As she lay there in her bed she told herself that she would take another look at everything in the morning. With any luck, in the morning things might be back to normal. But In her heart she knew that they wouldn't be.

Charlie Wyatt woke her in the middle of the night asking if he could sleep in her bed with her. She broke the normal rule and allowed him in, realizing what he had endured throughout the day and wanting to comfort him. He may have only been four years old, but he sensed that things were anything but normal.

The next day Stephanie located one of the "disaster procedure" lists from the garage and began to look it over. She immediately regretted not treating the idea with interest when Rob had wanted to show her how to use the various items.

Oh well; that's just how things go in life. Can't rewind the clock of time at this point, she thought.

Following the recommendations on the list, she removed the empty plastic garbage cans suspended from the rafters and stood them just outside their back door. She used the garden hose to fill the containers, noting that the water was flowing at only a fraction of its normal volume. Eventually she filled the three trash cans. By the time she had accomplished this, the water coming out of the hose was barely a trickle. She doubted whether there would be any water flowing at all the next day. She tried to heat some water on the kitchen stove but the gas flame sputtered and died less than a minute after she lit the burner.

There goes the natural gas supply, she thought.

Stephanie set up the propane camp stove in the kitchen, remembering to open a window a few inches behind it for ventilation as her husband's directions indicated. His directions had indicated that despite the manufacturer issuing a "Do not use indoors" warning, it was generally safe to use the camp stoves indoors, provided a few precautions were followed.

Cracking a window a few inches near the stove was one, and not burning the stove for more than a half hour to forty five minutes at a time was another. She also set up two of the kerosene lamps that Rob had stored. She made sure she knew how to light the lamps, fill the reservoirs with kerosene, and adjust the wick height. It was fairly easy for her to figure out in the daylight, but she was definitely glad she had not waited until dark to attempt to familiarize herself with their operation.

The directions stated that the main gas supply valve should be shut off if there was any concern about a broken gas line being involved. The concern was based on the risk of even a small amount of escaping natural gas being ignited by a spark or open flame, thereby causing an explosion.

Stephanie had given the decision no more than a couple of seconds thought when she was startled by a loud and insistent pounding at her front door. Both dogs erupted into a chain of continuous, loud, and energetic barking. Whoever was at the door wanted the attention of the occupants, and he/she wanted it immediately. She told Charlie Wyatt to stay where he was in the garage before she stepped through the doorway and re-entered the house.

As she began walking toward the front door, where the banging persisted and grew louder, Stephanie was reminded of the uncomfortable fact that she had no way to contact outside help, whether it was the police, a neighbor, or anyone else. The only exception to this was if she were able to make contact on foot. She was also aware that she had no immediate means of protecting herself or her son.

Stephanie was irritated with herself for having failed to arm herself earlier with the revolver secured in the small lock box in their bedroom. Rob had encouraged her to embrace the concept of keeping a secured yet reasonably accessible gun in the house so that she could at least have the option of arming herself should she ever choose to. She had initially refused to even consider the idea at all, but had eventually changed her mind after thinking it over for a month or two. The worried mom had forgotten about having the revolver available to her until now.

Having the presence of mind to at least look out the living room window to see who was at the front door before opening it blindly, Stephanie saw her neighbor Rosalyn standing there, banging away with her fists. The attractive forty-one year-old brunette was wearing jeans and a loose fitting tan cotton blouse. She was uncharacteristically disheveled. And she was barefoot.

5

SOUTH-CENTRAL LOS ANGELES

As the two men walked along the freeway shoulder about eight feet apart from each other, Rob asked Gerald, "So, do you live in a house or an apartment, or what?"

"We live in a house. Nothing real big or fancy--just a nice simple house."

Rob continued with his questions. "You got a family Gerald? Wife or kids; grandkids?"

After picking up on the slightest suggestion of irritation, Rob quickly added, "I'm sorry if I sound like I'm getting into your business. Only reason I'm asking is so I can figure out the best way for you to get ready for what might be coming down the road regarding this situation, that's all. I guess I shouldn't assume that everyone wants my suggestions anyway. Bad habit I have I guess," he said somewhat sheepishly.

Gerald seemed to be considering Rob's comments, and after a few seconds had gone by, he nodded his head indicating he was okay with the younger man's intrusion into his private life.

"Just me and the wife, and my lazy-ass son. He's forty one damn years old and don't do nothin' but watch that damn TV all day drinkin'!".

Rob smiled to acknowledge Gerald's complaint. He considered the information the older man had given him and thought about it for a while as they walked along the freeway shoulder. After a minute or more had passed he decided to offer a little advice.

Trying to make brief eye contact with Gerald as they continued walking, he said, "I guess it's hard to give advice without seeing your place, but I'll say this much. Have a talk with your family and try to get them to understand what this thing means. They're gonna have to be ready to start living completely different from how they are now."

Gerald didn't respond, and Rob couldn't get a good read on what the man was thinking.

As they continued walking in a westerly direction along the freeway shoulder, they noticed that increasingly more people were milling about in the freeway lanes and shoulder area. They saw an attractive woman in her mid-forties, dressed in a professional business skirt and blouse, standing beside her car, a new model Lexus, looking as though it had recently been washed and detailed.

She was sipping water from her plastic water bottle. Tall, slender, and attractive, the African-American woman had the looks and posture that suggested life had been very good to her and that she was accustomed to success in all areas of her life. The woman almost appeared to be waiting for a ride that was soon to be taking her away from all of this unnecessary inconvenience. Her attention was drawn to a young woman who had exited an older model Toyota Camry, stopped twenty yards away, and was now walking toward her. Rob ignored the professional woman and now focused on the younger of the two.

The approaching woman was no more than twenty years old. She was overweight, but carried her weight in a manner suggesting there was physical power beneath her body fat. She had short cropped hair, and numerous earrings and a nose ring. She had a large word or name tattooed on the right side of her neck in bold cursive writing, but Rob couldn't make out what it said. The tattoo was done with ink dark and thick enough to be clearly visible despite the almost ebony skin tone of the young woman's neck. She carried herself as though she were used to intimidating people.

As the tough looking younger woman reached the corporate looking lady standing next to her Lexus, she thrust out her hand and said, "Gimme that. I thirsty." The older woman physically reacted, indicating the shock she felt at the abrupt request. It was actually more of a demand than a request of course.

Apparently not satisfied with the speed in which the refined woman was responding, the coarse young woman yelled at her.

"I said gimme that water bitch. Better give it up right now befoe I slap yo ritch ass!"

The slender woman, now quite obviously frightened by the unexpected, and possibly dangerous encounter, handed her water bottle to the female bully without delay. The bully snatched it from her hand, turned around, and walked back to her Toyota with what was now her very own water bottle. The victim, obviously completely out of her element and suddenly realizing she had no capability to control what happened in her present environment, began looking around at her surroundings, possibly for the first time since the EMP event had happened.

A young tough looking black man in his early twenties now sat on the hood of the Toyota and laughed in a loud and obnoxious manner pumping his fist up and down and slapping his hands together a few times as he did so. The young man shouted out at the professional woman who had now locked herself inside of her Lexus, "That's right bitch. We take what the fuck we want from you, stupid bitch!"

Several persons that were within hearing distance looked at the young man sitting on the car making all of the noise. Almost every one of them took in the scene and decided to get into their cars and lock the doors.

The man sitting on the Toyota wore his hair in braids and had a sparse goatee. He was slender but muscular, possessing a body type that, when covered with clothing, belied the musculature that lay hidden beneath. However, the man was wearing a white tank top t-shirt (commonly referred to as a "slingshot" in this area) that revealed the developed muscles bunching beneath his tattooed arms. There was no mistaking the hardness of the man.

Rob looked him over quickly. He made him as a Crip gang member for a number of reasons, including the fact his shoes had blue shoe laces and he had a large tattoo of a cartoon figure leaning against a street sign and wearing an old school gangster fedora hat. Looking at the tattoo, Rob couldn't make out the name on the street sign at this distance, but he had no doubt that the name tattooed inside the sign would reveal which specific gang "set" the thug was affiliated with.

The *Crip* sitting on the Toyota had apparently been seated inside of the car earlier and had managed to get out and seat himself on the hood without Rob's notice at some point during the encounter between the two women. Rob was a little unhappy with himself for not having noticed this earlier. He took his partially filled water jug and used the *Carabiner* to clip the jug through the handle to attach it to his pack. He realized that he wanted it out of his way, or at least out of his hand, should he have to use his hands in a sudden fight with this guy. Thinking it over a moment, he changed his mind and held the container in his hand so that he could drop it at a split second's notice.

Rob tried to avoid direct eye contact with the Crip gangbanger for now, but at the same time wanted to make sure he didn't get attacked by surprise, so he kept an eye on the gangster using his peripheral vision as he continued walking.

"Try not to let them see you looking at them," he said to Gerald in a voice not much louder than a whisper. Rob knew that he (and to a lesser extent Gerald with his water jug) were likely to draw attention due to the backpack he was wearing. He figured as time went on, and the harsh realization sunk in that there was not going to be any help arriving, his pack would become increasingly attractive to predators and opportunistic reprobates roaming about. But there was no real way to hide the pack.

He made it a point to touch his 9mm pistol through his un-tucked shirt tail with his right elbow while rubbing his hands together as if trying to rid them of dirt. It was done in an attempt to conceal what he was really doing. He wanted to confirm *exactly* where his pistol was positioned on his belt so he could draw and present the weapon without any delay whatsoever. It was the kind of thing that could determine the winner and loser if things turned ugly

The *Crip* looked at Gerald quickly, and then at Rob. The thug's eyes moved from Rob's face, then to his pack, and lastly, to the machete knife affixed to the pack's shoulder strap covering the left side of Rob's chest. He had given a lot of thought about where to keep the large knife while hiking home and concluded its present position was best. He hoped having the compact machete visible and in a position allowing immediate access would make a potential opponent focus his attention on the knife. The knife was the obvious threat.

Most potential predators would be deterred by this alone. A big knife being quickly accessible to a man of Rob's physical stature was no joke to those in the know. Those that wouldn't be deterred by this would still likely focus on the knife instinctively as a means of sizing up Rob's capability of hurting them during an attack or robbery.

Of course Rob had a much more effective weapon (his Smith & Wesson 9mm) holstered and concealed on his belt in his right center front waist band—the best place to carry a handgun when wearing civilian clothes since it allowed the pistol to be instantly located, drawn, brought on target. He flashed back to an off duty security detail he had worked a couple years prior. During the "meet and greet" introduction to the guys he would be working with, Rob met a recently retired U.S. Navy special ops man. Seemed like a good guy. Probably was a good guy—maybe even a great guy.

However, Rob couldn't help but notice the former military operator, at the time wearing normal civilian clothes, carried his pistol tucked into his rear waistband area of his belt. It was situated almost in the center of his lower back. It was not a good location to carry a pistol in a tactical sense, but it looked cool—just like in the movies. Right then and there Rob told himself never to assume a guy was squared away based on his official pedigree alone.

Returning his attention to the fact the *Crip* was taking in the big knife taped to his pack's shoulder strap, Rob formed a quick game plan. He didn't think the *Crip* was going to jump him, but one never knew for sure. He wouldn't hesitate to shoot him while he was looking at his knife if the situation came to that.

He couldn't tell whether the man sitting on the Toyota had any kind of weapon on his person, or in the car for that matter, but at least he wasn't presenting one at this point. He told Gerald to keep his eyes on the woman, no matter what happened. He added that he needed

Gerald to tell him right away if she was doing anything that could be dangerous to them, like going into the car to retrieve a weapon.

Rob lowered his voice slightly and told Gerald, "It doesn't matter that she's a woman. If she picks up a weapon or comes at either of us, you hit her like she was a man that you need to put down fast. You get me on this Gerald?"

It was the first time since their contact that Gerald had heard Rob use this tone of voice. Despite being slightly taken aback by the menace it contained, he responded with not much more than a stage whisper, "Oh yeah. I got you on that alright. Don't you worry."

Rob realized that Gerald was way past his physical prime, but he also knew that every professional mechanic he had ever known had forearm and grip strength far greater than the average guy. He only hoped Gerald still possessed enough of that strength, not to mention the will to fight, to be effective if things went bad.

Rob knew one thing for damn sure: he wasn't going to be playing "Mr. Nice Guy" if things started going south with this situation. This *Crip* and his girlfriend, or whatever she was to him, were going to get the surprise of their lives if they failed to size Rob up correctly.

6

UNINCORPORATED SOUTHEAST

LOS ANGELES

At **Nadeau Station**, just after the electromagnetic pulse took place, the situation was anything but business as usual. Being no different than virtually all of the civilian cars on the road at the time, the station's patrol cars all came to a sudden halt immediately following the monster pulse. The reaction by the deputies who happened to be inside their squad cars at the time was to follow standard protocol. They tried to communicate their car problems to station personnel so that they could receive some sort of assistance.

Of course these attempts were all unsuccessful on the morning of the EMP. The L.A. Sheriff's Department radio system had been rendered inoperable instantly after the giant pulse. The computers mounted inside of the patrol cars were similarly disabled, as were all telephone landlines.

When the deputies realized that even their personal cell phones weren't working, they felt frustrated and puzzled. Some of the patrol cops began the walk to Nadeau Station while others remained in their halted vehicles for a while, believing that their communications capability, and subsequent help, would soon return in one form or another. Eventually all of the deputies working at the time of the EMP ended up walking back to the station.

Sergeant Marino was instantly aware of both the power outage and the fact the backup generator had failed. The sun had risen a while earlier, but the cinderblock building's virtual absence of windows meant there was only minimal natural lighting that made its way inside. The small battery powered emergency lights mounted throughout the hallways helped somewhat.

Marino, who had attended the same terrorism course that Rob Flynn had, suspected the power outage was the result of an EMP. And the suspicion grew stronger with almost every passing minute.

He walked out of the station and into the parking lot where the patrol vehicles were parked. Like all sworn personnel, he had been issued a vehicle ignition key that fit every patrol car at the station. The sergeant tried every car in the lot to see if he could find one that would start. Nothing. He tried the radios in several of the cars as well. No luck there.

Damnit!

He returned to the station, running a myriad of scenarios and possible courses of action through his head. He found the deputy assigned to the front desk and pulled him aside. Looking at Marino's face, the deputy became concerned. Not much affected the battle hardened sergeant, but now he appeared a bit shaken.

The deputy, a fifteen year veteran named Lee Harris, had worked through the night and was due to be replaced within the hour by the day shift deputy assigned to the front desk. Harris was not a cop that sought desk duty; in fact he avoided it whenever possible. He loved working in the field, demonstrating a seemingly limitless reservoir of enthusiasm for being in the mix of any type of excitement related to police work.

He had been temporarily assigned to station duty pending the conclusion of an internal investigation for his use of force during an incident over a month ago. A gangbanger driving a stolen car had crashed the ill-gotten vehicle into a parked car and had then taken Harris on a foot chase over hill and dale before finally being caught by the short muscular deputy.

Harris absolutely hated to run. But the difference between Harris and lots of other cops who hated to run was that he *would* run after fleeing bad guys, he just *hated* to do it. When he caught up to the felon, he wasn't in a good mood.

He would most likely be cleared of any wrongdoing when the investigation was over, particularly since several witnesses had supported his version of the event. However, it was common knowledge that the department higher-ups were stalling the results for the purpose of sending a message to Harris and others.

Harris was a unique kind of patrol cop to be sure. At five foot eight inches tall, and a solidly built two hundred pounds, he was physically impressive, but not exactly rare for an LASD patrol cop working in the ghetto. His face reminded many viewers of a wholesome mid-western farm boy despite his never having set foot on such a place in his life. A glimpse of his uncovered arms suggested a life lived that was a far cry from farm life. Harris had acquired bi-lateral tattoos on his arms, the designs of a type that were commonly found on career combat military men or "motorcycle enthusiasts" throughout the world.

He had earned a colorful reputation over the years—not all of it positive to be sure. He liked to push the envelope. During his career Harris had been involved in several fatal shootings, including an incident while off duty after being confronted by two armed robbers as he walked out of a restaurant.

Standing in the dimly lit post EMP Station, Sergeant Marino informed Harris that while he hoped he was wrong, the power outage was possibly going to be a protracted ordeal.

"I think we could have a whole bunch of collateral damage on this one Lee. And I'm talkin' about some pretty serious stuff—and long lasting too."

He gave Harris a tutorial on EMP and what it might mean for them at the station. Marino could see him processing the information, and actually thought he saw a small glimmer of excitement register behind Harris's eyes. It was a glimmer that those who had worked him often enough had come to recognize. It was the glimmer of an anticipation of excitement.

Harris had no family, other than a wife who had long ago accepted that Lee Harris would always subordinate their marriage to his first love--the Los Angeles County Sheriff's Department. Unlike every other deputy around him, he looked forward to the excitement the catastrophic event called "electromagnetic pulse" potentially offered. He was, first and foremost, a man who lived for new adventure of any kind. He pursued life like it was an adrenaline producing carnival ride that should be sought after with great zeal whenever possible. For Harris, the draw was as powerful and controlling as a drug addiction.

Marino asked Harris to turn off as many of the battery powered emergency hallway lights as possible until nighttime in order to preserve battery life.

"We only want the bare minimum we gotta have so we can see to walk through the building."

"Yeah; makes sense. I'll handle it boss."

Marino encountered two patrol deputies in the station parking lot who were standing next to their inoperable patrol car. The vehicle was stopped in the middle of the parking lot, approximately midway between the security gate and the gas pumps, its hood opened up to afford Deputy Mark Gattuso--a view of the engine. Cindy Anderson, his patrol partner, looked like she was irritated by the whole situation.

Gattuso stepped away from the car's engine compartment and approached his supervisor. He shrugged his shoulders. Anderson merely looked at Marino as if hoping he would provide some sort of solution to the problem where her partner had failed.

"Let me guess--your car just quit on you without warning, right? It was probably working fine until right before it stalled out wasn't it?"

Anderson responded with a strange expression on her face.

"Well, yeah actually. That's exactly what happened. How did you know?"

Marino just looked at the ground for a few seconds. Then, shaking his size eight head, he simply said, "We're in some serious trouble here."

If the legendary sergeant had had any way of knowing how prophetic his words were, at that moment he would have packed up and started walking home--or anywhere--right then and there. And he would have encouraged as many of the other deputies around him as possible to do the same.

7

SOUTH CENTRAL LOS ANGELES

Giving a slight but measured nod as he did so, Rob now made it a point to look directly at the *Crip* sitting on the car, making full and deliberate eye contact. He did so without uttering a word, just giving the nod. It was his intention that the head nod would convey a couple of messages: a somewhat respectful greeting, and a clear message that Rob knew the *Crip* was sizing him up. But most importantly, Rob knew the simple head nod along with eye contact and strong body language contained a subliminal message indicating he was ready to receive any challenge or attack the young thug might be willing to attempt.

The *Crip* gave a slight nod of his own as he addressed Rob.

"Serious pack you be carryin' there dawg."

Rob hated the popular street term "dawg" that every urban street punk, and even the suburban wannabes, seemed to use when addressing one another these days. He responded to the comment with an obviously forced and tight-lipped smile.

"Oh yeah. This pack is my whole life, dawg."

The way Rob used the hated term contained a slight trace of contempt for the word, and if the hood was paying attention, he would pick up on this fact. Rob didn't care.

He held eye contact with the *Crip* and hoped he had successfully sent the message that he would fight to the death to retain his pack. The *Crip* only offered a crocodile smile by way of response and remained seated on the Toyota's hood.

Good decision, shithead, Rob said to himself.

The mentality of two legged predators was something Rob had become very familiar with during his tenure as a street cop, and the *Crip* proved to be no exception. Unless the scenario included some unusual element of desperation, or a high level of intoxication of some sort was in play, the typical predator wanted no part of a confrontation where he/she wasn't confident of having a clear advantage over the victim. While there were exceptions to this, they were definitely not the norm.

The thug must've figured that trying to take Rob's pack was too risky under the circumstances at that time. He was absolutely right too.

Rob picked up his pace and began working his way to the other side of the freeway where west-bound traffic had also come to a halt following the EMP. Using his peripheral vision, Rob kept an eye on the *Crip* as he crossed the freeway just in case he changed his mind and wanted to make a try for his pack. As it turned out it was an unnecessary precaution. Gerald kept pace with Rob and asked him what he would've done if the thug had tried to take their stuff from them.

"I'm not sure Gerald. But I know for damn sure I wasn't going to give them any of our stuff no matter what." replied Rob.

Gerald responded with a subtle laugh, "Yeah. I figure that punk knew you wasn't gonna be playing games with him too."

Rob realized that during the confrontation his neck had been nowhere near as painful as it had been earlier, but now the pain had begun to return. It was probably just the adrenaline pumping through his system at that moment that had temporarily reduced the pain.

Trying to make some use of the time spent walking together, Rob suggested to Gerald as soon as he made it to his house he should start fortifying his home in a manner that would make it more difficult for hoodlums in the area to be able to force their way into the residence. He recommended that Gerald fortify the front door and figure a different means of going in and out of the house.

"I know this probably sounds pretty crazy, but there ain't gonna be any police or anyone else to keep things right for a while Gerald.

It's gonna be up to you and your family to keep each other safe until things get back to normal. And that might take a pretty long time. So I'm just sayin'..." Rob let the tail end of his sentence hang there unfinished as he looked Gerald in the eye. Gerald held Rob's eye contact for a moment and then just nodded his head saying "I hear what you sayin'."

The two men walked side by side for another two or three miles with very little conversation taking place between them. Gerald took a long pull of water from the jug he was carrying, and Rob followed suit, leaving only a small amount left in his jug. Gerald was tired and Rob was in pain. Gerald began surveying the neighborhoods located below where they walked along the freeway shoulder. They were now in the city of Inglewood and out of South L.A., but the demographics were very similar. More specifically, the city of Inglewood was primarily populated by black and Hispanic residents.

Rob felt the pain in his neck growing even more severe than he had remembered it being when they had first started walking. He had developed a severe headache now as well, and was beginning to have doubts about whether continuing on for much farther was a good idea. He thought about Stephanie and Charlie Wyatt. Rob figured she would be irritated at first by the electrical power being off, not to mention the fact that both her cell phone service and landline were probably unavailable.

Rob figured Stephanie would become even more irritated when she discovered her car wouldn't start. He also knew that at some point her irritation would be replaced by fear. He felt sorry for her having to endure this without him being there. Despite her being a strong woman who viewed herself as not needing much help to get things done, he knew she would be frightened after she took a good hard look at the circumstances surrounding Charlie Wyatt and her. At this point he only hoped his wife would be able to find and use the things he had stocked their home with to make living conditions more comfortable during a prolonged disaster.

Rob considered taking some more ibuprofen, but realized it had only been a few hours since his original dose. He had to make his supply last. It was too soon for another dose. Having emptied and discarded his water jug earlier, he removed his stainless steel water bottle and drank heavily from it. It held just under a quart, which didn't seem like much now that he was sweating under the L.A. springtime sun. At least he still had his half gallon of water in his flexible *Platypus* container buried inside his pack.

Gerald told Rob that they were close to his home and that he was going to be breaking off to head into his neighborhood shortly. The off-duty deputy was uncomfortable in more ways than one as he prepared to present his friend with his request. But he just plain didn't want to press on any farther today with his neck in a state of spasm.

"Hey Gerald, I have a favor to ask, and don't feel like you have to say yes. I'm really heading into some serious pain here with my neck. Is there any way I could go to your place with you and just stay there until morning... until I feel better?"

Rob added that he had his own food (energy bars in his pack) and that he would be fine with sleeping on a couch, chair, or even on the floor. Gerald gave the request some thought. Watching the older man hesitate with his answer led Rob to withdraw the request and apologize to Gerald for imposing on him. Gerald shook his head back and forth and said, "Naw. That ain't the problem."

"So what's the problem then?" asked Rob.

Gerald looked at Rob and said, "The problem is how much we should tell my wife. I'm gonna tell my son everything cause he need to know how serious this shit is, but I'm not sure what to tell my wife."

Rob responded, "Yeah. Sounds like a legitimate question to be asking yourself."

Rob's thoughts returned yet again to Stephanie being alone to deal with whatever happened at their house in Thousand Oaks. He was brought back to the present situation by Gerald telling him that he could stay at his place until he felt better.

Gerald indicated they should get off the freeway and head into the neighborhood of his home located just to the north of their present location. It was early afternoon and the men had not seen a single motorized vehicle, or aircraft for that matter, since the EMP had occurred. They saw groups of people hanging out on front porches and even in the streets here and there, but overall things didn't appear to be that much different than normal.

The men passed by a small group of African-American tough-looking men in their late teens and early twenties. All of them held forty ounce bottles of *Colt 45* malt liquor and were talking loudly. The conversation was laced with vulgar profanities and raucous laughter. Lots of references about "hoes", "niggas", and "straps".

Noticing the change in Rob's apprehension level, Gerald attempted to assure his new friend.

"These guys ain't gonna bother us none. I see 'em all the time around here. We just need to keep on walkin' through is all.

Rob relaxed slightly, but kept his senses dialed up anyway. He still felt uneasy but put his trust in Gerald's inside knowledge and familiarity with the men in the group.

Although they were aware of a big power outage, none of those in the group was yet aware of the absolute lack of police response under the current circumstances. However, they did know that--for whatever reason--there were no police cars patrolling the neighborhood. This was an obvious deviation from normal conditions. They had experienced this on rare occasions in the past—always explained by some major incident demanding virtually all available police resources elsewhere—but even under those conditions, emergency police response was available, just slow to arrive. These guys were under the impression that this was the current situation. It was enough to embolden them. Plenty of time to caper and split to some relative sanctuary or another before the cops showed up.

One of the group, a guy with a shaved head, ginger-colored complexion and striking green eyes, looked toward Rob and stopped his participation in the conversation. He hit the muscle shirt wearing ringleader standing next to him on the side of his biceps with the back of his hand. The blow was hard enough to move his torso several inches despite his being a solid two hundred pounds of hardened muscle. Upon getting the larger man's attention, he nodded toward Rob and Gerald.

The head man in the *slingshot* undershirt wore his hair in braids. There was really nothing that made the guy stand out in Rob's mind. Nothing remarkable about his face. A dark ink tattoo on the side of his neck as well as on the insides of both forearms—nothing atypical there. Complexion too dark for Rob to make out the tattoo designs. Big guy, but not unusually so. The alarm bells started sounding inside Rob's head. Loudly.

Shit. Why did I take Gerald's word about what I need or don't need to worry about? I knew better than that....damn rookie mistake.

The leader stepped up and faced Rob, leaving less than five feet between the two of them.

"Hey, whatcha doin' here in our hood white boy?"

Through his peripheral vision Rob saw the newfound concern manifest itself on Gerald's face.

I'm a dumb-ass for sure, thought Rob. *Now I doubt I can get to any of my weapons in time if I get jumped. And I'm all bound up with my pack on my back too. What the fuck was I thinking?!*

Rob said nothing by way of response. He made eye contact with muscle shirt and held it. He angled his body to the guy a little bit without being obvious--he hoped. He wanted to have a slightly better position to defend against an attack, and he could only hope this asshole didn't pick up on what he had done.

He'll likely jump me if he picks up on me shifting my body position. Hell, there's a good chance I'm going to get jumped anyway. I guess I'll know soon enough.

Gerald's voice caused *slingshot* shirt to break eye contact with Rob in order to look at the older man.

"We just passin' through is all. He ain't no problem," Gerald said in a placating but nervous tone as he indicated Rob with a jerk of his thumb.

Another in the group added his opinion on the matter, his voice slow and calm compared to the others who had spoken up to this point.

"I knows that ol' nigga. He alright. He used to be fixin' my momma's car back in the day. That ol' bucket she used to be havin'. Yeah, he alright."

Muscle shirt didn't seem to be convinced about who was "alright" and who wasn't quite yet. Besides, as the alpha of the group, he was going to be the one to decide that. He eyed Rob's pack.

"What da fuck you got in da bag white boy?"

Rob decided to answer this time. "Just some camping stuff. Nothin' worth anything."

He noticed muscle shirt's eyes as they shifted for a second--no doubt taking in the small machete taped to the pack strap--and then returned to Rob's face.

"Take that shit off Dawg. Lemme take a look."

Shit...here we go.

Rob knew the robbery was now in progress. But the thug didn't know that Rob knew it yet. Changing tactics, Rob now made it a point to avoid eye contact with muscle shirt as he put what he hoped was a soft expression on his face. The wheels of his brain were turning fast now. To be more precise, they were flat out hauling ass as he put together his impromptu plan.

Feigning a lack of concern—or at least a lack of panic—he shrugged his shoulders as he began to loosen the pack's straps.

"Like I said, there really isn't anything in here you want," Rob said in an affected pleading voice. When preparing to engage in battle, try to appear weak to your enemy. Let him be over confident.

This asshole just made a big mistake that he's going to pay for. He should've never let me put my hands all over my pack while he's standing this close to me. Now school is going to be in session for this motherfucker. And today's lesson is a tough one.

Rob tried to make out, as best he could, whether any of the young toughs in the bunch were armed. All of them had shirts tucked into oversized pants with belts cinched up tight. No sign of guns--hopefully no one had a loaded *strap* tucked into the rear of his waist band where he couldn't see it. He decided not to use his pistol to address the problem. Just a judgment call really.

With his pack still on his back, Rob worked his left and right hand fingers to loosen both straps. He allowed the first strap to lazily slide off his shoulder and then dipped his opposite shoulder--the one with the machete taped to it--in the normal manner of shedding a pack.

Without telegraphing his intention, he exploded into the action he had been mentally rehearsing during the past ten seconds. As his pack slid down over his left arm he used this hand to grab the pack's carry handle to hold the sack suspended for a split second. During this split second he reached across his chest with his right hand to grab the handle of the sheathed machete. He flicked open the sheath's retention strap, and yanked the blade free with the spine--or dull side of the blade--facing away from him.

Without stalling in his movement, Rob thrust the pack at muscle shirt's face as he stepped back from him. He gripped the machete's handle with both hands and raised it over his shoulder with incredible speed. He brought the spine of the blade down with all the force he could deliver. It struck his left collarbone, shattering the clavicle. The thug cried out and started to slump under the terrible pain.

Still maintaining a double-handed grip, Rob swung the side of the machete blade at the man's head, the wide part of the blade's impact making a smacking sound that announced to anyone within earshot the violence contained in the blow. *Slingshot* shirt hit the pavement hard and stayed there with a shattered collar bone and serious concussion, unable to focus on anything other than basic life-sustaining breathing.

Rob raised the machete over his shoulder in preparation for meting out additional blows should any of the rest of the group decide to come to their fellow hoodlum's defense. But each of them either raised his hands in a position of surrender or quickly stepped back from Rob, creating as much distance as possible, and doing so as quickly as they could.

Without taking his eyes from the retreating tough guys, he called out to Gerald.

"Let's get the hell outta here—right now Gerald."

His friend needed no prompting. After taking one last look at the guy lying on the ground in a stupefied and agonizing state, his mouth and breathing pattern reminding him of a dying fish on dry land, he headed out at a fast clip with Rob trailing behind him. Rob glanced back over his shoulder every few seconds until they had created enough distance between the hoods and themselves to feel safe for the time being.

After he was comfortable in his belief they weren't being followed, Gerald shook his head from side to side a few times and said to Rob, "Damn man; you're one serious customer; I'll give you that for sure." He chuckled in a manner that Rob wasn't sure what to make of.

"Course, now I gotta problem whenever I see any a those punks again."

"Yeah well, I hate to say it but I think it's gonna be a long while before you go anywhere without worrying about danger anyway. What happened just now won't make any difference."

Gerald looked at him, mulling over what he had said, and not for the first time today.

Rob considered the situation. He admitted to himself that because he had seriously injured the thug attempting to rob him of his pack, he had created a heightened risk of retaliation against Gerald. Should he decide to separate from Gerald now, this risk would become far greater—especially during that time between now and when the older man arrived at his home. Although he felt no guilt about what he had done to the thug trying to rob him of his pack, his conscience prompted him to stay with Gerald until they reached the comparative safety of his home. Not only that, but wearing his pack had now become a source of considerable neck pain. He thought hard about his options.

If he continued on his way home now while suffering borderline debilitating pain he would be putting himself in jeopardy when it came to being able to defend himself or otherwise deal with problems he might encounter. Emotionally he wanted to press on and get home, but intellectually he realized he was only hurting his chances. He had to rest.

It's not going to cause that much of a delay, he thought.

They arrived at Gerald's residential block twenty minutes later. The street contained mostly single story modest houses with neatly kept yards indicative of a neighborhood where the majority of residents took pride in their homes. Gerald's house was a simple neat single story home with a well maintained front lawn, detached garage, and a small cement patio located in the rear. The entire lot was enclosed with a chain link fence about four feet high.

Rob considered that even though the fence wasn't high enough to physically prevent most people from jumping over it, there was another benefit. If Gerald were to lock the front gate, it would create a situation where anyone wanting access to the property would have to scale the fence. This pretty much eliminated the "Awe shucks, I didn't mean any harm" excuse...which in turn meant any member of Gerald's household wouldn't have to hesitate to confront a trespasser with a serious "high security" greeting. It could often be the little things that made the difference.

Of course this whole concept meant nothing if Gerald, or his family, didn't want to go along with the idea. He hoped they would grasp the seriousness of the situation.

Well, all I can do is try, he figured.

Gerald entered the yard of the Brown residence and made his way to the front door holding his house key in his hand. Before inserting his key in the door lock, Gerald announced himself. He did this loudly, and he did it twice. It was only then that he knocked forcefully on the door, repeating his earlier announcements. Rob wondered if the family kept guns in the house. Maybe he didn't want his wife or son to shoot him thinking it was an intruder coming through the door. Then again, perhaps he was just being courteous, not wanting to startle anyone inside.

A large fortyish man with a mahogany complexion opened the door. Despite Gerald's earlier description of a man who didn't take life seriously, preferring instead to watch TV and drink all day, the man Rob was looking at seemed to be both sober and serious. In fact, by the look of him at the moment, he was all business. The man was easily over six feet tall and close to 230 pounds. He didn't have the type of physique indicative of regular visits to a gym or the by-product of physically demanding work conditions, but rather that of a man who had simply inherited a large and powerful body. He had a neatly trimmed beard and a shaved bald head.

Rob, standing several feet behind Gerald, was now holding his pack rather than wearing it--to lessen his pain. He noticed the man in the doorway had a medium sized revolver tucked into the front of his waistband. The large man said, "Hey Pops, who is this?" as he gestured toward Rob with his head. Gerald explained how they had met and had then decided to travel together for practical reasons.

Gerald introduced his son Kevin to Rob. The two shook hands and sized each other up. Kevin addressed his father and asked, "Where's your Caddy at?" Gerald motioned for Kevin and Rob to step off the porch and into the front yard in an effort to avoid being overheard by his wife. He wanted to shield her from the harsh realities of what lay ahead. Looking all around for a brief second before starting, Gerald informed his son that Rob was a deputy sheriff and that they had helped each other in order to get here.

While the sullen looking and skeptical man didn't seem to be very impressed by any of this, he at least listened.

Rob explained in a couple of sentences how he had come to be informed about what an electromagnetic pulse attack was, promising to provide more details later. First he wanted to let Kevin know what the results of the EMP attack were likely to be for the local area, the state, and possibly even the entire nation. Kevin looked at Rob as if he wasn't sure whether to believe him or make him leave.

"Yeah, we don't have anything working here now. Not even cell phones," Kevin said.

Rob looked at Kevin and gave him a slight smile and head nod. He apologized in advance for possibly coming across as disrespect-ful of the Brown family and their home. His smile evaporated as he added that he had advice to give them that could be important in the near future. Kevin looked as though he wasn't about to have any of it. And Rob respected the man for his position. He was being protective of his family after all. But the AWOL cop wasn't ready to give up.

"Hey, I can give you some advice on what you should be thinking about doing here, but if you don't want to hear it, just tell me." Rob shrugged his shoulders, which radiated pain across his neck.

"I can show you a few moves, and if it gets to the point where you don't want my help anymore and it's time for me to leave, just let me know and I'll respect that." Rob made eye contact with Gerald first, and then with Kevin in an effort to communicate his sincerity. "I'll be leaving in the morning anyway," he added as an afterthought.

The father and son exchanged looks but said nothing.

Finally, Kevin responded in what was close to a baritone voice.

"Okay. We'll let you know."

Rob liked this guy despite his being such a hard-ass.

"Okay then. Let me explain about what I'm pretty sure has happened."

Even though Gerald had already heard much of it, Rob started at the beginning. He explained briefly about what could cause EMP and why he was certain electromagnetic pulse was responsible for the current situation. He spent more time on what the consequences were likely to be.

Just in case Kevin wasn't getting the full message, Rob said point blank, "This means there aren't likely to be any 9-1-1, no cell phones, no TV, and no cops or fire department to respond to help--or even to patrol neighborhoods for that matter. None of their cars are working most likely. This is some serious shit I'm talking about here."

Kevin just looked at Rob with an expression that revealed his concern. Actually, that was putting it mildly; Kevin looked like he had just seen a ghost. Gerald looked back and forth a few times between his son and Rob, but made no remark.

Gerald invited Rob into the house and called out to his wife, Eunice. She wore a conservative dress which almost seemed to be from a different decade. She had the appearance of a woman who would not wear jeans or other casual clothing unless performing a specific task that required it, such as gardening. She looked to be about the same age as her husband, and carried herself with a posture that made Rob wonder if she had been a school teacher.

After introductions were made, Rob apologized for the intrusion. Then he cast aside his reservation and asked if he could bother them for any medication for his neck pain. Eunice responded, "Well it so happens that I am a retired nurse. I think we might have some medications that will help you. But first please tell me what happened and explain the pain you're feeling."

The woman sounded like she was inquiring of a patient in a medical clinic. He described his injury and the pain.

After being invited into the home, Rob asked Eunice if the kitchen stove used natural gas. She nodded but made no verbal response, as if awaiting the rest of Rob's question. He asked her if gas was still being supplied to the stove burners. As she answered that she wasn't sure, Rob followed Gerald into the kitchen. "Let's check it out," he said.

Rob asked for a cigarette lighter or matches. Gerald fished a lighter from his shirt pocket and handed it to him. After opening the stove's valve Rob applied the lighter's flame to the burner and lit it. It burned for twenty seconds before it died. The stove had obviously used up the small amount of gas contained within the line. The natural gas supply probably incorporated electronics somewhere in the delivery system. And that system had no doubt been damaged by the EMP.

So much for having any natural gas, Rob thought.

He asked if he could check the faucet water. Eunice nodded and pointed at the kitchen sink. He turned it on for a few seconds, observing that water still flowed, and then shut it off. When he turned around he saw Eunice was no longer in the kitchen. When she returned moments later she was holding two pills in her hand.

"One of these is a muscle relaxer and the other is a prescription strength *Motrin.*"

Rob accepted the pills and threw them into his mouth, swallowing them dry. She went to a hallway closet and returned with a blanket and pillow.

"You can sleep on the couch," Eunice said as she handed the items to Rob.

She asked him if he was hungry. Rob thanked her for the offer but insisted that he would eat his own food. He was reminded of something that needed to be addressed immediately. He asked Eunice if they had any plastic liners used for garbage cans or waste baskets.

"Yes we do. Why do you ask?"

"I think you should fill 'em with water as soon as possible."

Rob summoned Kevin and Gerald while she went to retrieve the plastic bags. He advised the Browns the water supply was in jeopardy because virtually all of the municipal water systems were dependent upon electronics to deliver the substance. He stressed that all four of them should get busy filling any receptacles they could find that were capable of holding water, including bathtubs and sinks. He even recommended taking a couple of large garbage cans, emptying them of their contents, and filling them too.

Gerald and Eunice both looked at him with confused expressions.

"You won't want to use the water right from the garbage cans, but you can always filter it through a t-shirt and then boil it somehow. You wanna get all the water you can right now while it's still available from the tap. It could run dry any time."

Rob grabbed several of the garbage can liners and placed one bag inside of another to double them up for added strength. He then went to find a hose bib outside of the house. He sought out the hose bib at the lowest location on the property he could find in order to take full advantage of gravity. This hose bib would be the last one to run out of water.

Rob used every one of the twenty four bags remaining in the box to improvise a dozen water containers. He spent the next half hour or more filling each of these bags with several gallons of water, placing them on the back porch where he hoped they would remain out of public view.

Satisfied that the family had filled every conceivable container in the house capable of holding water, Rob sat on the sofa in the living room and picked up his pack. He excused himself for a few minutes. He carried his pack to the back porch and removed his lightweight hiking boots. He peeled off his sweat soaked socks and placed them into a plastic shopping bag he had placed in his pack for this purpose.

Since the house's water system was still providing water--although at significantly reduced water pressure now--he used a garden hose to wash off his feet. He removed his toothbrush from his pack and brushed his teeth using water but no toothpaste. Finally, he took a small terrycloth rag from his pack, soaked it in water, and performed a quick hygiene drill to relieve some of the day's sweat and grime. No telling when he would have access to water again, other than what he absolutely needed to stay hydrated.

After airing out his feet for several minutes, Rob took a small plastic bag of foot powder from his pack and applied it sparingly to his feet. This was something he had learned during his Marine Corps days. Taking care of your feet was not merely a comfort issue; it was paramount in importance if one expected to avoid problems that could easily turn serious. He removed a clean pair of socks from the pack and put them on, re-entering the house with his pack when he had finished.

Rob removed a *Millenium* brand 400 calorie energy bar from his pack. He noticed that Kevin was positioned where he could keep an eye on what was going on in front of the house, while Eunice was busy taking inventory of the kitchen cupboards. Not seeing Gerald anywhere, he asked Eunice where he had gone.

Before she could even answer, Gerald walked in from the home's side door carrying a large steel teapot. It appeared to be full, judging by the way it was being carried.

"I remember what you said about boiling the water before drinking it, so I boiled it on the grill," Gerald quipped.

Rob realized he was probably referring to a barbeque powered by a refillable twenty pound propane tank. He asked him how much fuel was left in the barbeque tank.

"I dunno, but I got two more in the garage that're full." Gerald showed Rob a rare full-fledged smile that held more than a little self-satisfaction.

Gerald told Rob that the man at the big box hardware store had told him that propane could be stored indefinitely, unlike other fuels which had a definite shelf life. Gerald said he had thought it over at the time. He had figured it would only be more expensive when he had to buy it later, so he had decided to purchase two extra tanks of the propane then and there. He was now especially proud of his smart decision.

Reiterating his security concerns for the near future, Rob offered to give the Browns some ideas about setting up a security protocol for their home. Gerald answered for the family.

"Yeah. I think we should listen to what the man has to say."

Rob noticed that Kevin had a dour look on his face.

"Okay then. I'll offer the best help I can. I'll look around at everything here first thing tomorrow before I get back on the road. But for tonight someone should be up no matter what time it is."

He decided to elaborate.

"This means sleeping in shifts. And a second family member should sleep with most of their clothes on so that they can jump into action fast to help out whoever is on security duty."

None of the Brown family responded to Rob's comments. Kevin looked as though he wanted a reason to object, but couldn't come up with anything suitable.

Rob indicated that tonight he would sleep in his clothes. Kevin said he would take the watch throughout the night, patting the revolver in his waistband for emphasis.

"Is that a .38?" asked Rob, pointing his chin in the direction of Kevin's revolver.

"Yeah; why?"

"Good. Do you have any other guns in the house besides that one?"

Gerald spoke up to answer Rob's question. "No; that's it. It's the family gun I guess. I bought it back after the 92 riots. After the police didn't do shit to help us," he added. Realizing that he might have offended Rob with this comment about the police, he quickly added,

"No offense Rob." Rob ignored the comment other than to shrug his shoulders.

He had not been part of law enforcement back then, but he had heard plenty of stories about LAPD's anemic police response at the riot's epicenter. He had even heard that the LASD sheriff of the nine thousand man department at the time had made contact with the LAPD chief, or assistant chief, and had given him an ultimatum.

According to the story, the sheriff had uttered words to the effect of, "Either the LAPD starts protecting these people, or I'll send in my deputies to handle the problem, even if it is in LAPD's jurisdiction. It's still in Los Angeles County after all."

Rob had no way of knowing if this story was an accurate account, an outright fabrication, or exaggeration rooted in fact. But it certainly served to fuel the ongoing rivalry between the state's two largest full service law enforcement agencies. It reminded him of the rivalry between the Army and the Marine Corps. Two good outfits that seemed to live for the opportunity to give each other shit whenever possible.

Rob asked Gerald if he had any flashlights in the house.

"Yeah, we got a couple flashlights. I hope the batteries still work," he replied.

Gerald disappeared for a few minutes and returned with two large sturdy metal *Maglite* flashlights.

"They both still work," he said as he handed one of the flashlights to his son and put the other in his back pocket. They weren't exactly state of the art flashlights for tactical use, as they used the older technology incandescent bulbs rather than the state of the art LED bulbs. But they were certainly better than nothing.

Rob indicated his approval with a "thumbs up" gesture and then excused himself as he walked to the couch and set up his temporary sleeping quarters. He sought out Eunice, who was still in the kitchen taking inventory. He mentioned to her it might be a good idea to take inventory of any first aid, medicines, and other medical supplies, as well as food supplies.

She replied, "Yes. I've already thought of that." Rob smiled with a touch of embarrassment as he remembered the woman was a nurse by profession.

He made himself as comfortable as he could as he prepared himself to sleep in a sitting position rather than lying flat. Although the men of the house had declined his offer to take a shift at staying up to perform watch duty at the house--possibly because Kevin didn't trust him enough to do so--he remained fully clothed, except for his boots, as he lay on the couch in the Brown's living room. The pain in his neck was an incessant source of discomfort, and he slept little throughout the night.

As Rob slept fitfully, two unusual events happened without his knowledge only a few blocks from where he rested.

8

THOUSAND OAKS, CA

Stephanie opened the door as fast as she was able. Rosalyn was in a panic and speaking so rapidly that Stephanie could only understand part of what she was saying. She understood that Rosalyn's husband needed help because he had injured himself, but not much more. Her barefoot neighbor and friend, now shedding tears as she spoke, was speaking in a voice that was close to becoming an unintelligible chain of sobs.

Stephanie turned around, ran to her son, and took his hand. With Charlie Wyatt in tow, she ran back to the open front door and forcefully rotated Rosalyn around so that she was facing away from the house. She gave her a gentle push.

"Let's go!"

Rosalyn ran next door her driveway, pushed her way through a closed but unlocked wooden gate, and continued into the back yard. Her husband, Rick, was lying on the ground next to numerous pieces of firewood. A small pool of blood had gathered next to his leg. Stephanie could see that Rick was probably in shock, as his slightly olive complexion was now pasty white. He was still awake and marginally lucid, but Stephanie guessed this might not be the case for long.

She saw a large axe lying on the ground next to the pool of blood, its blade covered with blood as well. Stephanie knelt next to his leg and located the tear in Rick's jeans where the blood was oozing out. The wound was located just below his left knee on the inside of his leg. She tried to talk to him, but he only responded by groaning unintelligibly.

Think Stephanie, think. What's the first thing that needs to be done here, she silently asked herself.

She glanced at Charlie Wyatt, who appeared to be getting ready to cry.

"Charlie Wyatt, it's okay. Mommy needs to help this man."

She frantically waved an arm to get Rosalyn's attention, and then told her to take charge of Charlie Wyatt while she worked on her husband's injury.

"Don't let him watch what I'm doing if you can help it," she implored.

Rosalyn looked like she was close to passing out herself but, to her credit, she followed Stephanie's directive and took the four-year-old by the hand, turning him so that he was no longer looking at the man with the heavily bleeding leg.

Stephanie and Rob had enjoyed the occasional company of their two childless neighbors, Rosalyn and Rick, for more than eight years. Rick, a successful contractor, enjoyed the outdoors, as did Rob. Rosalyn hadn't been much of a fan of that type of activity, preferring instead to spend their money on designer furniture, expensive clothes, manicures, costly hairstylists, and similar expenditures.

Stephanie remembered how she and Rob had laughed until their stomachs ached when Rick had come home with a small backpack to be used on a hike in the local mountains. Before Rick had gone shopping for a pack, Rob had taken the time to recommend a couple of them that were affordable while still being good practical designs.

Unfortunately, Rick had taken his wife Rosalyn with him to pick out the pack. At her insistence, he had discarded Rob's suggestions and bought a designer pack. It was in vogue with jet setters, but really impractical for outdoor activities. However, it did have a clothing designer label. Upon seeing the silly looking pack Rick had selected, Rob had given him no quarter on his ridiculous selection.

Rob teased him for quite a while afterward. He had even suggested to his thoroughly embarrassed friend that he should cover it with a plastic garbage bag to hide it from view of other hikers on the trail. Later on during the hike he had recommended Rick consider doing a photo shoot for a magazine with the designer pack. Rick had never lived it down.

Rosalyn's idiosyncrasies notwithstanding, Stephanie enjoyed her company, even if preferably only in small doses. The two of them certainly had a good relationship as neighbors. The couples attended barbeques at each other's homes several times a year, always saying they should get together more often. Yet, for whatever reason, they had never gotten past the infrequent nature of their get-togethers.

Rosalyn was an unusually attractive woman who made it a priority to display her good looks whenever possible. She enjoyed her ability to turn the heads--or at least the eyes--of most men in social settings. On several occasions Stephanie had observed her neighbor use this subtle influence to her advantage. Little things like getting a better price or other small favors.

Some of Rosalyn's good looks were the result of above average genetics, while some were credited to a couple of good cosmetic surgeons. Stephanie had no doubt that Rosalyn's large symmetrical breasts were surgical implants, but that was her business alone. Rosalyn's shapely firm legs were a feature she worked on at the local gym with regularity, and expensive makeup applied over a genetically good bone structure was how she presented herself to the public every day. Looks were important to the woman, and she made it a priority to maintain them, as well as accentuating them with expensive clothing at almost every opportunity.

Stephanie quickly examined Rick's leg wound as she tried to use the man's jeans and the palm of her hand to apply direct pressure to slow down the blood loss. She overheard Rosalyn trying to distract Charlie Wyatt. Something about chickens. Rosalyn must have remembered Stephanie sharing with her that her son was intrigued with the funny birds. She appreciated the effort on her friend's part to keep the four-year-old preoccupied, as she was convinced there was too much blood here for a little boy to be viewing.

Charlie Wyatt, apparently not sufficiently distracted despite Rosalyn's efforts, began to cry. Stephanie, still working to slow down the blood loss, coaxed him to stop crying. She tried to convince him that everything would be alright, but her efforts were only marginally successful. He was still sobbing, although more quietly now. She had to ignore her motherly instincts to comfort her son. She would soothe him later. Right now she had to address Rick's leg wound before he bled to death.

She yelled at Rosalyn, "Go into the house and get me a towel of some kind. Dish towel, bathroom towel, anything! And bring me a knife to cut with too. Hurry up! Leave Charlie Wyatt here!"

Half a minute later, Rosalyn came running back with a small dish towel and handed it to Stephanie. She then thrust a steak knife at her, blade first. Fearing that the frantic woman might accidentally cut her with the protruding knife blade, Stephanie told her to drop it on the ground to ensure this wouldn't happen. Rosalyn seemed confused for a second by the request.

Stephanie raised her voice and ordered her friend, "Rosalyn, just drop it." Eventually realizing that it was more important to comply with Stephanie and her demand than to understand the reason for the request, Rosalyn simply dropped the knife, letting it fall on the grass without making a sound.

The housewife and mother picked up the steak knife and went to work cutting the jeans away from the leg wound of the man lying on the ground before her. After getting the wound exposed, she saw that it was a nasty one, easily four inches in length--and deep. The blood flow continued seemingly unabated regardless of her efforts. Stephanie folded the towel over a couple of times and applied it against the gash, hoping to at least stem the blood loss. She leaned in hard against the towel, applying as much pressure as she could in an attempt to get some kind of result. Within a few seconds the blood began to seep through the towel at a volume indicating something else had to be done if she wanted to prevent him from bleeding out. And it had to be done soon.

"Rosalyn, go get me a blanket and a pillow. Now!"

To her credit, Rosalyn was no longer frantic. She was now focused and listening to Stephanie's every word. She turned and ran into the house.

She had given Rosalyn the request mostly for the purpose of giving her something constructive to do. However, Stephanie also wanted to use the pillow to elevate Rick's legs and cover him with a blanket to help with the shock. Nothing wrong with killing two birds with one stone she figured. She now came to the realization that if she didn't stop the wound's bleeding, there was a good chance Rick would die. She glanced at Charlie Wyatt, who was now staring, wide eyed, as he watched his mother work on the wounded man.

A decade earlier Stephanie had spent three years employed as a medical office manager at a major Los Angeles hospital. She had been fascinated with the work performed by the doctors assigned to the emergency room and had been granted permission to observe these physicians in practice on many occasions in the hospital's trauma center.

She now recalled a conversation she had overheard between two physicians in the ER years ago about the use of tourniquets to stop bleeding. One doctor was bemoaning the use of tourniquets, claiming they often caused severe damage to the affected limb due to *necrosis*. In regular speak, this meant all of the tissue located between the tourniquet location and the end of that limb was subject to "dying" without the life sustaining blood being circulated there.

The second physician had vehemently disagreed with his colleague, arguing for the importance of using tourniquets to stop otherwise uncontrollable blood loss. She could still remember his emphatic declaration: "When direct pressure or other methods aren't working, tourniquets save lives."

Redoubling her efforts to stem the wound's blood flow, Stephanie removed the belt from his jeans and wrapped it around his injured leg a few inches above his knee. She pulled the belt as tightly as she was able and then tied it in a knot. Clearly, the belt was not tight enough to constrict the blood flow, so Stephanie desperately looked around at her surroundings for some object that she could use to make the belt tighter.

Rosalyn returned with a blanket and a pillow that appeared to have been removed from a sofa or stuffed chair. She yelled at Rosalyn so that she would be heard above the sound of her crying son.

"Go find me a stick, or screwdriver, or anything like that you can get! I need something to shove under the belt here!"

Rosalyn turned and sped toward the house. She returned seconds later with a medium sized screwdriver. Stephanie took the tool from her and inserted the six inch blade under the belt and began to rotate it clockwise, effectively taking up the slack in the belt. After a couple more rotations she saw that the blood had stopped seeping through the towel bandage. She tried to remember what she had overheard a decade earlier while listening to the two doctors discussing the use of tourniquets.

It came to her with abrupt clarity. First, the tourniquet should only be tight enough to cut off the blood seepage from the wound. Better yet, it should only be tight enough to allow a slight trickle of blood. This theory held that the trickle could be effectively managed using only direct pressure at that point. This was a safer approach because it lessened the likelihood of necrosis occurring since there was still a little bit of blood being allowed to flow to the region. The only negative aspect of this approach was the fact that it required having someone remain with the victim to apply this direct pressure if the victim wasn't capable of doing so himself.

The second thing she remembered was the importance of loosening the tourniquet every twenty to thirty minutes, depending on how wide the band was and how tightly it was applied. Letting the blood flow periodically like this would better the odds for saving the limb. If you were only trying to save a life, and the limb wasn't important, then it was best to cinch the tourniquet up tight and leave it that way.

She backed the screwdriver counterclockwise in a loosening direction about a quarter rotation and watched for any blood seepage through the improvised wound dressing. After watching for half a minute without seeing any seepage, she rotated the screwdriver backward another quarter rotation to further loosen the constriction, even if only slightly. She finally observed a small amount of blood making its way through the bandage. She decided this was pretty close to what she was after.

Stephanie directed Rosalyn to hold the screwdriver while using her other hand to press on the improvised bandage. Stephanie placed the pillow under Rick's lower legs, elevating them several inches off the ground. She then covered him with the blanket as best she could while still leaving the wound accessible to Rosalyn. Glancing at her watch, which thankfully still worked, Stephanie made a note of the time for future reference as to when the tourniquet would need adjusting.

The mom now playing medic looked at Rosalyn as she held the screwdriver blade in place inside the tourniquet. She tried to focus on what needed to be done next.

"See if you can find some strong tape like duct tape or anything like that. We need to tape this screwdriver down to his leg so it won't move. I'll hold it while you go look."

Rosalyn returned a few minutes later with a roll of the invaluable grey colored multi-purpose tape. Stephanie tore a piece about a foot long from the roll and used it to secure the position of the screwdriver.

"Okay; you saw how I did this, so just do it pretty much the same way I did after you change the bandage out later."

Rosalyn acknowledged the information and exhaled a deep breath. Stephanie stood up.

"Alright; I'll be back in a minute. I'm gonna take Charlie Wyatt and go get some help. Hang tight, okay."

She had managed to get some blood on her hand while working on Rick's wound. Ignoring the sticky feeling created by the substance between her palm and her son's, she walked quickly to the house across the street. The house was occupied by a retired couple who had lived there for twenty plus years.

She began pounding on the front door with her free hand, not wanting to release Charlie Wyatt and risk his transferring the blood to his face or clothes. Stephanie wished she could remember the couple's last name. She seemed to recall the woman was a lawyer, but could not remember either of their names.

Within seconds, a short fit woman in her late sixties opened the door. Stephanie didn't waste time asking the woman if any of her phones were working; she knew the answer. Speaking rapidly, Stephanie explained what had happened across the street and requested the woman's immediate help. The retired woman's husband appeared in the doorway and asked what was going on, looking at Stephanie and Charlie Wyatt with an expression of apprehension and puzzlement.

Oh great, thought Stephanie. *This guy is now going to ask a hundred questions before he allows his wife to help me.*

The woman gave her husband a disdainful look and turned to put her shoes on. She would make her own decision, and she had already done so.

Another idea occurred to Stephanie.

I'm going to get both of them to help me. And right now!

"I need both of you to come with me right now. It's an emergency. Let's go. Both of you. Let's go; come on!"

The senior couple followed her at a fast walk to where Rosalyn was attending to her husband. She was no longer applying direct pressure to his wound. Rick had not moved from the spot where he lay minutes earlier, and he still appeared to be in shock. Stephanie took a closer look at the wound and was relieved to see the blood on the bandage appeared to be drying, indicating the bleeding had been arrested.

She tried to talk to Rick but he was only minimally responsive, his voice not much more than a whisper. He wasn't going to be able to get into the house without being carried. Stephanie told Rosalyn she needed to look in their garage for something that could be used as a stretcher. She asked the woman from across the street to stay with Rosalyn and Rick while she beckoned the woman's husband to accompany Charlie Wyatt and her to the garage.

Clearly aware that Stephanie was effectively running the show, the husband complied without comment. After explaining in as few words as possible what she was looking for and why, the two of them spent several minutes canvassing the garage for a suitable object that could be improvised as a stretcher. No luck. Charlie Wyatt, who was trying his best to keep up with his mother's seemingly unending endeavors, was still crying.

Stephanie realized how tough this situation must have been on such a young boy, and she questioned herself briefly as to whether she should have even become involved in this medical debacle involving her neighbors. For now, there was no alternative. But she would have time to think about the whole situation more later on after they had returned to their own home.

Suddenly a thought came to her. She considered removing one of the interior doors of the house so that it could be used as a stretcher, but opted against doing so because she feared it might take too long to find the simple tools needed to separate the two piece hinges in order to free up the door.

Stephanie was truly afraid that Rick might succumb to his leg wound if he wasn't stabilized somehow. She beckoned her male neighbor and went directly into the dining room. She quickly identified the dining table, an adjustable type with removable leafs allowing for changing its overall size.

Several candles had been placed in an aluminum pie tin that rested on the table. They were obviously being used to provide some light under the circumstances. She pulled a eighteen by sixty inch table leaf free and handed one end to the man beside her.

They brought the finished wood plank outside and placed it directly next to Rick. As the four of them prepared to move Rick onto the table leaf, Stephanie warned them to be careful not to disturb his wound any more than was absolutely necessary. After some straining and frustration they managed to slide the injured man onto the makeshift stretcher. The board was too narrow to be a truly suitable stretcher, but it would work for the task at hand. The four neighbors carried the wounded man into the living room. After considerable effort on everyone's part, he was placed on the large sofa and the leaf pulled out from under him.

Stephanie loosened the tourniquet for about twenty seconds and then cinched it back to where it had been seconds earlier. Just prior to her returning the tourniquet to its original position, she observed the blood had started seeping through the towel bandage again. She couldn't remember how long she was supposed to have the tourniquet loosened, but she knew it was better than not loosening it at all--at least if saving the leg was still a priority.

Unsolicited by anyone, Rosalyn started explaining how Rick had sustained his injury. Since they had no electricity to power their electric stove top, Rick had decided to use their charcoal barbeque in lieu of the stove. And given the fact they had no charcoal briquettes for the device, Rick thought he would simply split some of their firewood into thinner pieces, and then use it to build a fire in the barbeque. Performing the task with the axe too quickly--at the price of caution--had resulted in his sustaining a serious injury.to his leg.

Rosalyn was once again trying to maintain her composure, and she seemed to be losing the struggle. Stephanie tried to soothe her neighbor as best she could, but her mind was already thinking about what she needed to do at her own house. Yet despite her preoccupation with getting home, Stephanie did harbor some serious concerns about the threat of infection with Rick's wound.

Leaving Rosalyn with the best directions she could about how to look after Rick and his wound, she told her that she was sorry she couldn't stay with her, but she had to get home to address several of her own problems. After thanking them for their help, Stephanie left the senior neighbors standing in the living room and began walking out of the house.

She looked over her shoulder, promising Rosalyn she would be back to check on her before nightfall. She stopped to use a garden hose to wash off her hands as well as her son's. The hose only produced a small trickle, but it was enough to clean off the blood that had found its way onto both of their hands.

Charlie Wyatt was not doing well at this point, whining and complaining a bit more than usual, the stress of the recent events being a lot for any boy his age to handle. Stephanie gave him a hug and ran her fingers through his hair, telling him that things were going to be okay. She then used their camp stove to make him macaroni and cheese. It did the trick--at least for the time being.

The exhausted mom did what mothers have been doing since the beginning of time. She pushed past her own fatigue and despair to provide for her child. Stephanie took his shoes off and put him down for a nap, hoping that she could get some necessary things done while he slept. Having fallen asleep unintentionally, she awoke some time later next to Charlie Wyatt, who was still soundly asleep. She got up quietly so as not to disturb her sleeping son. She hardly knew where to begin.

9

UNINCORPORATED SOUTHEAST
LOS ANGELES

Standing next to the dead squad car assigned to Deputies Mark Gattuso and Cindy Anderson in the station parking lot, Marino tried to think about what needed to be done. Actually, he only tried to come up with a plan for the next fifteen minutes. He had no doubt that after fifteen minute had gone by another fifteen minute plan would be necessary.

Shit is happening fast around here, he told himself.

Gattuso, being somewhat of an amateur auto mechanic, addressed the sergeant while wearing a look of confusion.

He nodded his head toward the patrol car to indicate the source of his perplexity.

"Sarge, I can't figure out what the hell's wrong with this thing. At first I was thinkin' it might be the alternator, but then..."

An impatient Marino held up his hand before Gattuso could finish.

"Stop. The problem's got nothing to do with normal car mechanics stuff. Let me explain this." He glanced at both of the deputies just long enough to make sure he had their attention before beginning his explanation. He then described the phenomenon of electromagnetic pulse and why he believed this was what they were now dealing with.

Both deputies just looked at him with expressions of confusion and disbelief. If this information had been coming from just about any other sergeant, it might well have been dismissed as crazy talk.

He thought back to the terrorism class presenter and his comments about EMP. The instructor had told the students not only could an EMP event shut down the power grids of the affected area(s), but also the other utilities that required electronics of any type to function. This held true for most emergency power generators as well as newer cars.

But what stood out for the sergeant more than anything else were the instructor's comments about how an EMP could be much larger than merely regional. It could easily impact a large portion of the entire country, making any effective efforts at recovery a very slow and problematic proposition. His worry deepened.

Marino explained further.

"The country's worst disasters have only been regional. So these places could always expect lots of outside help from other parts of the state or even the country. If this EMP thing is what we're talkin' about here, we could have a way bigger problem—like most of the country being in the same boat."

He ordered the shift partners to check every squad car in the lot to see if any could be started. A few minutes later the deputies reported to him with the disappointing results. He was now convinced that EMP had caused the power grid crash.

He told the two deputies that he had a request, adding that it was going to be an unusual one.

"I wouldn't ask you to do it if I didn't think it was important though, so just hear me out on this."

He asked them to walk to the liquor store located two blocks from the station and tell the owner, Phil Goldstein, that the power grid might be down for a very long time.

"Tell him to make plans accordingly."

Goldstein was a World War Two veteran and had owned and operated the little liquor store for decades. Most of the Nadeau Station deputies considered Phil a friend and looked in after him with regularity.

"Don't go into any detail about what EMP is all about, just tell him I said this is what I think we might be looking at...you know, a really long power outage and equipment failure scenario."

Both cops nodded in response, each of them still trying to process the unusual information that had been dumped on them during the past hour.

"Listen up now. Here's the other thing. This thing could be something that's worse than anything we've ever dealt with in our lifetimes. I need you both to ask Phil to load up boxes with as many foods and non-alcoholic drinks as he can manage. I'm talking everything and anything: from beef jerky to *Twinkies*. Also, we need all the water that he has in the store. We'll have to figure a way to carry it over here. Tell him I think this situation is going to get really bad, and his store may not even survive this thing."

The deputies exchanged looks and then stared at their sergeant with uncomprehending expressions.

"Make sure Phil knows the county will compensate him at full retail price for everything we take. And scratch out an itemized receipt for him also, but get this done as fast as possible."

A quarter minute after the two patrol cops had headed toward the liquor store, Marino called out to the pair and asked them to wait. This time he walked over to them before he began talking.

"Get as much chewing tobacco as you can--brands don't matter--along with all the food and water. I know some of the deputies will appreciate it later. Don't let Phil give you any booze even if he insists. We don't need to have anyone getting liquored up around here. I got a feeling we aren't going to have any *off duty* time till this whole thing is over."

A frown creased the sergeant's brow as he entertained another idea.

"Ya know what," he said, "Tell Phil he should consider coming to the station until this thing gets back to normal. There's no way he should try to walk home--I think he lives over in West LA. That's way too far. And Phil can tell anyone who asks that I said it was okay." He held up his index finger and said, "Hold on just a second. I think I got something you can use to carry all this stuff," and then turned and walked into the station

He returned moments later pulling a four-wheeled hand cart behind him. The cart was normally used by the station janitor to transport his miscellaneous supplies around the building. Gattuso looked at his partner and said, "This situation is getting weirder by the minute," and then let loose with his signature chuckle.

Showing no reaction to the patrolman's attempt at humor, Marino told the deputies to take the cart with them to the liquor store and use it to carry as many supplies as possible back with them. They both looked somewhat put off by the request.

"Hey, I know this might seem kinda weird," Marino said, "but when you see all the cars out there stopped in the streets it won't seem so dumb--trust me."

Gattuso chuckled again.

"Yeah, whatever Sarge." Anderson just shrugged her shoulders as if to suggest it was all just part of the job for her. Marino made one last comment as the deputies walked away with Gattuso towing the cart, the pair looking like a couple of overgrown grade school kids pulling a wagon.

"You two watch your butts real good out there. I think you'll be back here before everyone figures out there might not be food and other stuff available for a long time, but you never know. Remember you got no backup at all. Be careful, and get back here as soon as you can."

"Okay Dad," Gattuso answered with a big smile that fell just short of developing into a laugh.

"And by the way, if the power comes back on in a little while you know your rep will be ruined forever Sarge." Gattuso continued to laugh good naturedly after making the wisecrack.

"Yeah, well, somebody has to look out for the mentally challenged. And I seriously doubt the good will fairy is going to visit our parking lot and magically fix all of our cars any time soon," the sergeant said with a smile.

Marino liked the stocky deputy, and they both laughed together now. It was a welcomed respite from the problems they faced, even if only brief.

Gattuso was in his mid-30's, five foot nine (if he stood perfectly straight), and had a ready smile that broke into laughter without much stimulus needed. Short and stocky by nature, his borderline fanatical weight lifting regimen only added to this appearance. On a good day he could bench press over four hundred pounds, making him the strongest, or second strongest, deputy at the station, depending on whether he or Harris were having a better day. Many of his peers attributed this feat to the fact that he, like Harris, had short arms and therefore didn't have to move the weight very far off of his barrel chest. But four hundred pounds was a hell of a lot of weight, short arms or not.

Due to his Sicilian ancestry, Gattuso often passed for being Hispanic, a fact that served as a constant irritation for him while working in the field at Nadeau Station. The irritation was due to the fact he was often approached by local residents within the substantial Latino population who would begin speaking to him in rapid fire Spanish. They just assumed he was Hispanic and fluent in Spanish. Like the majority of non-Hispanic deputies assigned to this area, he spoke only limited Spanish, but at times had difficulty convincing Latino residents of this.

Still standing in the station parking lot, a thought came to Marino. He wanted to take inventory of the bicycles that had been seized and booked into the large evidence room at the station. He was hoping that they could be used as a means of transportation in this new environment of non-working automobiles.

As he registered this, he suddenly realized he had overlooked something when he had sent the two deputies out on the liquor store detail. Batteries for the lights.

Inside his office, the sergeant found a note pad and began scribbling down miscellaneous notes. As a seasoned sheriff's supervisor, Marino had no problem with handing out orders and directives. And he had never asked any of his charges to do anything he hadn't either done himself, or was willing to do himself. He asked Harris to lock up the station doors, something that had never been done since the station had been officially opened. He also asked him to bring out any usable bicycles from the evidence room and park them outside of the station's back door. The latter request caused Harris to look at the sergeant with a quizzical expression.

"Okay Boss, I gotta ask on this one. What's the plan with the bikes?"

Marino answered with a shrug, "Well, I dunno, but I'm thinking we might want to use them to do some patroling. I'm not sure right now. Whatcha think?"

Harris cocked his head to the side and paused for a second before answering.

"I guess that might work. I don't know though. Might be a problem. Not a bad idea to have 'em ready in case we want to use 'em anyway. I'll go see what I can find."

With that, Harris turned and walked off to carry out the task, his excitement about the adventure he anticipated seeping out in his body language and facial expressions. He returned with a bicycle--a single speed cruiser--a few minutes later. Using the kickstand, he parked it in front of the sergeant's office. Within the next ten minutes he located two more bicycles suitable for riding.

Later on, while walking one of the bicycles to the rear of the station, the sergeant heard a string of rapid fire gun shots. He estimated about ten rounds fired. It was difficult to determine where gun shots were coming from most of the time, but he thought it sounded like they were within a couple of blocks of the station.

Within seconds of the first volley, Marino heard another burst of rounds. He estimated this volley to be at least twice as long as the first. He thought of the two deputies on route to the liquor store and hoped the shots he had heard were unrelated.

Marino had tried to order back all of the early morning watch patrol deputies who were scheduled to end their shifts at 6 AM. Most of these claimed emergency hardships that had to be addressed at their homes. They insisted they needed to get home, even if it required doing so on foot.

While Marino told them that he understood and wouldn't formally force the issue, he let them know their decisions could potentially be interpreted as violations of department policy, maybe even ending in employment termination. To a person, the deputies heading for their homes each made it clear they would take the risk. They were going to get home to their families or die trying.

Marino briefly reflected on the fact he had never married or had any children. As far as competing loyalties were concerned, he, unlike most LASD cops, had no conflicting sense of duty to sort out. The closest thing to family he had was the department.

It may be a dysfunctional family a lot of the time, but it's the only family I have.

He was now questioning whether it had been a good idea to explain the whole EMP thing to the patrol deputies. By explaining the severity of the situation, he now thought he may have created the very motivation for so many to leave for home. There was nothing he could do about it anyway.

One deputy had a bicycle fortuitously mounted on his small SUV bike rack in preparation for a ride later in the day at a destination far from South Central L.A. After realizing the grid would likely be down for quite some time, and that the travelling conditions were probably going to get worse as time went on, he got on his bike, put his small backpack on, and headed for home.

The sergeant noted that only four of the scheduled twelve *day-watch* deputies had arrived at the station for their 6AM shifts. It was now 7:20, so it was possible some of them would still arrive later in the day. He tried to do the math in his head and wasn't encouraged by what he concluded. If the EMP event had occurred at between 5:30 and 5:45 AM, then most likely any patrol deputies on route to the 6AM briefing would have been within a five to ten mile distance of the station at that time.

Marino was a realist if nothing else. He fully accepted the possibility that some of the deputies on route to their day-shift would opt to head home to their loved ones rather than come into work. It would be a tough call for most to make. The sergeant recalled how this very topic had been raised and discussed at a law enforcement supervisors' course a while back. The class was divided as to whether individual peace officers had an obligation, legal or ethical, to come into work during a major disaster that impacted the area's entire infrastructure.

Ten o'clock came and went without a single additional patrol cop having shown up at the station. By 11 AM, Marino had accepted the fact there weren't going to be any more deputies coming to work.

Marino hadn't spoken to the station captain since the EMP had taken place, having been too busy to go to the other side of the building where her office was located. He briefly wondered why she hadn't made an effort to contact him. Maybe she was working on some sort of plan.

A half hour to forty five minutes later Deputies Gattuso and Anderson returned with their cart piled high with boxes containing miscellaneous items from the liquor store. They unloaded the boxes in front of the sergeant's office, awaiting further instructions. Marino asked them to stand by for a minute, and the patrol partners looked at each other with an expression of *now what?*

A half dozen shots rang out, probably within a few blocks of where they stood. They all held still. When there were no more shots they continued with what they were doing.

Marino summoned the remaining patrol deputies from the positions or duties he had assigned them to earlier that morning. He ordered all of the officers, save those transporting the goods from the liquor store, to remain within the station or its parking lot until further notice. He prepared to address the patrol cops now before him. Once again he sucked in a deep breath and then exhaled before beginning.

"I'm not gonna sugar coat this situation guys. I think we could be screwed on this one. I got no communication at all with the outside world--not department headquarters, not other stations, no television, radio, or anything else. It's lookin' pretty damn ugly right now for sure."

He saw all eyes were on him.

"Hey, by the way," Marino digressed as he looked briefly in the direction of Gattuso and Anderson, "what's the scoop with Phil at the liquor store? Is he heading over here to the station or what?"

Anderson responded before her partner could form his answer.

"We told him what you said and he looked at us like we were from Mars. When he finally seemed to figure out what we were telling him he said he would head over here after he took care of some stuff at his store."

The sergeant looked at Anderson and considered what she had said.

"I don't like this at all. A lot of bad things could happen while he's walking over here."

He shifted his gaze to the others.

"I want everyone to organize into two deputy teams and run relays over to the liquor store with that hand cart. Let's get all the stuff we can out of there as soon as we can. And the next team over there needs to get Phil's ass over here ASAP."

Marino told the deputies they needed to organize a security perimeter detail that used all deputies present.

"You guys can set it up yourself. I'm sure you'll get it done right. If I have a problem with it I'll speak up—but I doubt I will."

The LASD—at least at the high activity stations—had a culture that deviated somewhat from most police agencies in Los Angeles County. Generally speaking, the patrol deputies were allowed to handle a lot of their own field incidents. The result was a rank-and-file patrol cop who could typically step up and run a major incident with little help from a supervisor. Marino was confident his charges could set up an adequate defensive plan.

The sergeant decided to add a couple of points.

"You're gonna have to figure out sleeping shifts. And I'll take a shift along with everyone else by the way." The middle aged former SWAT cop tapped the stock of his tactical shotgun that hung suspended over his shoulder for emphasis. A few of the deputies exchanged looks and slight smiles as if to acknowledge they had no doubt the older sergeant could still take care of business if circumstances required it.

Noticing that Gattuso was wearing an uncharacteristically serious expression, Marino asked him if he was okay.

"I'm not complaining exactly Sarge...well maybe I am actually. I mean, shit, what's really going on here? How come we haven't got any relief or even any information at all?"

Marino said to himself, *Oh shit; here we go. I have no idea what to tell these guys. They deserve a straight answer, and they're looking to me to get that answer, but I just don't know what to tell them. Oh well, here goes.*

"I don't know how long it's gonna take to get any reinforcements here. Hell, I'm not sure if sheriff headquarters has any way to talk to the rest of the country or what. For that matter, I don't know how much of the country's been hit as bad as we have. I'm just like you guys. I don't have a clue how this is all gonna shake out for us. I don't know anyone who's ever been in this kind of situation before. I'll say this much though: I'm not counting on getting any help from anyone for quite a while."

Realizing that three of the cops in front of him hadn't heard his explanation about EMP and its consequences, Marino gave them the short version.

One of the deputies, Mike Mori, a twenty something year-old Japanese American with a pair of Oakley sunglasses wrapped around the rear of his head for temporary storage, began asking questions.

"What about the military? Don't they have vehicles built to resist the EMP effects? They gotta have 'em, right? Maybe they'll start sending some help to us, although they'll probably take forever to get it done...knowing how slow the feds work."

Marino replied, "I dunno. Yeah, they may have vehicles that are hardened against EMP, but depending how big the area is that's been affected by this, they might have a problem getting out help to where it's needed. It's possible they aren't gonna have enough vehicles to send to all of the areas that are in deep shit, so I don't know."

"Well what about older cars? You said that EMP destroys the electronics, but the older cars that don't use that stuff should still run, right?"

He slowly nodded his head, the realization coming over him slowly. Phil Goldstein, the owner of the nearby liquor store, used an old early 1970's model full sized Chevy station wagon to commute to and from his store every day. It was possible he had used the old car and driven it home. The deputies he had sent to the store had recently reported that Phil was no longer there, but they hadn't mentioned whether or not his station wagon was parked behind the building in its usual location.

He would have to address the issue later—if he could.

Again, he considered the situation at the station.

We have to keep all of our resources here at the station. I can't have anybody leaving this building or property from now on unless we get some goddamn relief. If the higher ups want to chew my ass later for my decision then so be it, but I have to take care of my people.

The tired cops, several of them having worked the midnight shift the previous night, responded to their sergeant's earlier request and began discussing among themselves how they were going to set up station security. Holding out his big hand in a halting motion, Marino addressed the collection of deputies with one last directive before they all headed off.

"Everyone hang on here for a minute."

He walked into the station armory and noted there were eight Remington Tactical 870 model shotguns in the station armory.

Marino walked past the shotgun racks and directly to the large safe that rested against the far wall. He knew the container housed half a dozen AR-15 rifles, as well as numerous twenty-round magazines and two thousand round cases of ammunition for the rifles. The four foot high safe was approximately three feet wide and three feet deep with one inch thick walls.

Marino fished the small piece of paper from his wallet that held the safe's combination and looked at it. He tapped out the combination on the safe's electronic keypad. Nothing happened. He tried it again. Nothing.

Shit. The EMP fried the electronics of the damn safe door. Damn it!

The sergeant used his meaty fist to tap the side of the massively thick safe in appreciation of the heavy duty construction as he contemplated a way to force entry into the device. There was simply no way to get into it with the limited tools they had available to them. He tried entering the combination once more, but again failed to gain entry. The electronics had been destroyed.

As the sergeant walked out of the armory, he told the deputies he wanted each and every one of them to carry one of the standard patrol issue tactical shotguns at all times until further notice. He reminded them they should remove all shotguns still in the patrol car racks before taking any from the armory.

"I just thought of somethin'. Someone should check all of the lockers and the detective desks. See what you can find. That includes ammo for the shotguns or handguns. Hell, if yer lucky, you might even find a candy bar in one of their desks."

Marino laughed as he said this, but the truth of the matter was that every little bit would help.

Another thought struck the sergeant. An old rusted steel water tank was located in the far back corner of the parking lot. It was mostly hidden and few even noticed it was there. He had no idea if there was any water inside the tank, but he definitely planned to find out.

The station hallway was filled with the unmistakable sounds of pump action shotguns being operated to confirm the weapons' actions were in working order. After all of the deputies had armed themselves with shotguns, Marino re-entered the armory and removed a shotgun for himself.

Upon entering the rear parking lot of the station Marino saw Gattuso and another deputy jogging into the parking lot driveway. Apparently they had been outside the defensive perimeter.

"What's goin' on out there guys," Marino asked.

Gattuso answered, "The whole area looks like a fuckin' bomb went off Sarge. I mean all the stores are trashed big time. And we got all kinds of assholes out there running amuck now. They looked right at us and didn't even care that we were there. This shit looks like some third world country now."

Well, so much for having any bicycle patrols. There's no way I'm going to let any of my deputies ride around this war zone on a damn bicycle now.

10

INGLEWOOD, CA

On the first night after the electromagnetic pulse had shut down most of the nation, a local Inglewood troublemaker and sometimes hoodlum, known to everyone in his neighborhood except his mother as "Big J", participated in an event that was really not so unusual for him: he got high on malt liquor and methamphetamine.

As far as Big J was concerned, the first unusual event to take place on this night was that he deviated from his normal routine. Rather than staying home or inside of one of his friends' residences to enjoy his high, Big J got out of hand and began punching parked car windows, shattering the glass of over a dozen cars while sustaining only superficial injuries to his hands. Then, aware that the police were seriously delayed in their response, he started throwing rocks the size of baseballs through several of the occupied houses in the residential area where he lived.

Obviously not satisfied with his vandalistic bender, Big J removed a forty pound cement water main cover and hoisted it over his head while walking down the middle of the street yelling profanities. He threw the big cement block through the windshield of a parked compact van with the name of a local church stenciled on the doors. Big J, laughing maniacally and yelling profanities the whole time, removed the cement block from where it had come to rest inside the van's front passenger area. He used the chunk of concrete to repeat similar acts for another half hour, leaving numerous smashed windshields in his wake. The destructive rampage lasted for over ninety minutes.

The second unusual event of the evening was that nothing happened to stop him. The police weren't slow to respond--they simply never responded at all. Big J eventually passed out on the sidewalk at about four AM, bringing his wing-ding to a halt.

Several local gangbangers watched Big J's uninterrupted rampage, and they found it entertaining. But the fact there was no police response was what they really found interesting.

***

As the day's first light arrived, Rob sat on the Brown family's living room sofa and tried to figure out what he needed to do first. He had attempted to sleep on the couch the previous night, but had only met with partial success. His neck was so sore that when he tried to put on his pack the pain was excruciating. As if all of this weren't bad enough, he was dealing with a nasty headache to boot. If he hadn't known better he would have thought he had spent the night drinking.

Rubbing his neck, he forced himself to think about his current situation. He wanted to get started on route to Thousand Oaks. Eunice, who, as always, was the earliest riser of the Brown family, happened to observe Rob as he unsuccessfully attempted to get his pack onto his back. As she watched him wince in pain, she told him in a very direct tone of voice, "You can't go anywhere until your neck feels a little better. Especially if you want to wear that pack you have there. We've got to get those neck muscles to calm down and reduce the spasm effect."

It was a simple truth Rob had to acknowledge whether he wanted to or not. He was going to have to wait until his neck spasms had diminished before he could begin his trek home. Thinking over his predicament some more, he realized he wasn't likely to find a better opportunity to heal up than his present environment, so he counted his blessings and swallowed his pride. Along with a few more pills provided by Eunice.

Eunice offered him breakfast. He declined at first, but this time she wouldn't accept his refusal. Despite his initial reluctance to accept the offer, his physical needs won out over his desire to leave the family with as much of their food supply as possible. He thanked her and agreed to have a cup of hot tea and some bread, butter, and honey. He watched Eunice try to light the gas stove with a match. Still no luck.

Looks like they're stuck using the propane powered barbeque, he reckoned.

Rob spent the rest of the next twenty four hours trying to manage the pain in his neck as best he could. He slept off and on, only getting up from the couch when he had to go outside to relieve himself. He promised to help the family create some sort of a latrine as soon as his neck felt a little bit better.

At one point, while convalescing on the sofa, Rob overheard Gerald and his son arguing in another part of the house. The argument was over Rob. Kevin was not happy with the fact that Rob was still staying in their home. Gerald, on the other hand, was insistent that they owed their new house guest a place to stay and some food and drink for at least a few days.

The argument culminated with Gerald saying, "Just how the hell you think that man's neck got hurt anyway? His neck got hurt cause I ran my damn car into him, that's how. And you don't think I owe him shit? C'mon now!"

Kevin's rejoinder was brief but insistent. "Well two days is all he's gettin' then. After that he needs to be movin' on. And that's the straight up truth."

On the third day following the EMP Rob woke after he had actually slept for most of the night. His neck pain was still there but it was definitely on the mend. He was relieved to find that he could hoist his pack and slide his arms into the straps without feeling the severe pain he had a couple of days prior. It was still uncomfortable, but he felt that he could manage the discomfort.

He asked Gerald and Kevin if they had building supplies and carpentry tools of any kind that did not require power. Gerald said he had hammers, nails, and hand saws. He offered to show him what they had in the garage. Kevin was a bit reluctant, but agreed to go along with this. As they walked from the house to the detached garage, they heard about a half dozen gun shots. It was difficult to identify where they were coming from, but it sounded like the shots had originated within close proximity of the Brown residence. A few seconds later, an additional four rounds were heard, followed by a half dozen after that. These shots sounded like they were fired from an even closer location.

All three men entered the garage. Rob looked around and pointed out several sheets of plywood that were resting on saw horses and functioning as table tops. He also indicated a couple of one by six boards about eight feet in length. Rob suggested that they use the lumber to board up the front windows first. Any remaining lumber could be used to cover as many additional windows as possible. Rob asked if they had any wire mesh or chicken wire anywhere on the property. Both Browns shook their heads in the negative.

Rob said, "Well if you find any chicken wire or anything like that, think about nailing it over any windows that are still uncovered. You also might want to cut a couple of holes about this big in the boards covering the windows." Rob positioned his two thumbs and index fingers in a square to indicate the size he was suggesting.

All three men were startled by the sound of several gunshots being fired in quick succession. They seemed to have originated fairly close to their present location too. Rob pulled his Smith & Wesson 9mm from its holster and took a two handed combat grip as he went toward the garage door and looked around the neighborhood outside of the Brown's yard.

Two men in their early twenties, one Hispanic and one black, ran past the Brown residence on the sidewalk. The Hispanic man held a small semi auto pistol extended in his hand as he chased after the other man, yelling profanities and racial slurs as he did so. The fleeing man was running in a zig-zag pattern, no doubt in an attempt to keep from being shot. None of the three men in the garage showed any desire to intervene in the event taking place in front of the house. Rob opined, "Right now it's all about taking care of your own family and nothing else."

Kevin, still not willing to fully open up to this stranger in their midst, showed no reaction to Rob's comment, while Gerald shook his head slowly from side to side. He wasn't disagreeing with what Rob had said, but was merely showing his disdain for the way things had begun to deteriorate in his immediate world. Of course no sirens were heard, as there was no emergency response.

Rob retrieved a shovel and offered to make a latrine in the yard, insisting it would be better than nothing under the circumstances. Gerald gave him the go ahead and followed him to the far end of the back yard. Rob dug a trench about five feet long and eighteen inches deep that he thought would serve the purpose. He was thankful for the fact that the soil was soft and required only a modest effort to remove with the shovel. When he had completed the trench he asked Gerald for a piece of rope. When the older man returned with the rope, Rob took one end and tied it around a nearby tree while taking the other end and fashioned a six inch diameter loop in it.

"This will make it easier to support yourself when you're squatting over the trench to do your business. I'll show you how this works."

Gerald watched Rob hold onto the loop and lean back against the rope while squatting on his haunches over the trench to demonstrate his concept. He nodded his head in understanding and approval.

After returning to the living room and sliding his shoulders into his pack, all the while forcing himself to mask the feeling that was now somewhere between pain and discomfort, Rob thanked the Brown family and indicated he wanted to get going to start his journey home. Rob watched Eunice pour a dozen ibuprofen tablets from a huge white plastic bottle of *Advil* into a small plastic bag.

She handed him the bag and its contents, and said, "These are only 200 milligrams each. You need to keep that inflammation in your neck under control. Try to get some food in your stomach when you take these if you can." Rob nodded his understanding and stuffed the pills into his shirt pocket. He considered the fact that Eunice was a trained nurse and concluded she probably had a decent assortment of first aid supplies and medications in the house. He felt good about that.

Before leaving the house, Rob checked his weapon, slightly pulling the slide to the rear to confirm a round was loaded in the chamber. He tapped the bottom of the pistol's magazine to ensure that it was seated properly. He then tossed his now worthless cell phone into the bottom of his pack (although he questioned why) and took a quick inventory of the pack's contents.

He made sure his folding knife was in his front pocket, confirmed that his extra pistol magazine was in place on his belt, and then slid into his pack as he said his good byes, and then headed out the door, scanning his surroundings as he did so.

11

THOUSAND OAKS, CA

With only a few hours of fading daylight left, Stephanie went back to her neighbors' house to take another look at Rick's leg wound. With Charlie Wyatt standing at her side her, she knocked on the front door. Rosalyn answered the door a minute later, waving them in without comment. Her smile appeared to be forced, and failed to hide the signs that she had been doing a lot of crying over the last few hours.

"How's he doing?"

"I'm not sure. I'm really scared right now." Rosalyn released a couple of tears and sniffled loudly. A slight trace of mucous trickled down from her nostril before she used her forearm to wipe it away.

Stephanie couldn't help but think how a few days ago Rosalyn would have been embarrassed or even horrified to have knowingly been observed performing such a crass act.

Funny how tragic events can erase all of that trivial nonsense, she thought. *Not funny like watching a comedy funny; but funny like when a large truck unexpectedly "T-bones" you in an intersection. Yeah; that kind of funny.*

Stephanie asked Rosalyn if they had a camping stove or any other means of heating water.

"No; that was what Rick was trying to do when he cut his leg. You know, cut firewood to make a fire for all that kinda stuff." Stephanie realized she had already known this and now felt foolish for asking the question.

"How about a first aid kit?" Stephanie asked.

"We don't have one."

"Okay; we'll figure something out."

Stephanie followed her neighbor into the house as she considered the situation.

"How about just bringing me a pan of water and a bottle of bleach. You do have bleach don't you," Stephanie said with a touch of irritation.

She regretted making the sarcastic comment to her emotionally taxed friend as soon as the words left her mouth. But she was frustrated over how her neighbors were so completely unprepared to deal with the situation. She knew Rob had tried many times, all to no avail, to persuade them to buy a couple of things that would make their lives a lot better should any number of types of disasters occur. Then she caught herself, realizing that she had resisted her own husband's urgings for them to do this or that to better prepare their own family for emergencies.

Stephanie was aware using bleach treated water for wound cleaning was somewhat controversial. Since bleach was known to destroy small amounts of healthy tissue at the wound site and the weakened tissue was often more susceptible to infection, some argued against its use altogether. Others claimed the germ killing features of the chemical and its subsequent ability to stave off infection trumped the potential issue of minor tissue damage.

She decided to use the bleach treated water.

She removed one of Rick's socks and examined his foot for color. It looked like the foot was getting enough circulation to be okay, but she was less than confident in her ability to know for certain. She also observed that there appeared to be some debris caught in the wound. Stephanie knew it was important to try to remove as much of the foreign debris from an open wound as possible to minimize the likelihood of infection. The question was how best to accomplish the task.

She asked Rosalyn to bring a new toothbrush as well as the other items she had requested.

"Uh, I don't think we have a new one. Can we use his toothbrush?"

"Yeah, that's fine. We'll just have to soak it in the bleach water for a few minutes first to sterilize it, that's all."

Rosalyn disappeared for a few minutes before returning with a pot of water, bleach, and Rick's toothbrush. Stephanie prepared a bleach water solution in a large drinking glass and dropped the head of the toothbrush into the liquid.

"We need to let this soak for about ten minutes before we use it to clean his wound," she said. Looking at the two quart cooking pot Rosalyn had brought her, Stephanie said, "Actually, I think we can just use the glass. We won't need this pot."

The women began to talk about the situation they faced. Stephanie shared the little bit she had gleaned from Rob's explanation of electromagnetic pulse with Rosalyn.

"I can't remember exactly what Rob said this thing was called, but I remember he told me about some kind of situation caused by either the sun or by the explosion of a nuclear bomb really high in the atmosphere," she said.

"He said when this happened not only would the power go off, but the cell phones and most of the cars would quit working too. I thought it sounded too weird to be real when he told me...sorta like something in a science-fiction movie."

Rosalyn and Rick merely looked at their neighbor with similar expressions of confusion as they listened to Stephanie share this information with them.

"Anyway," Stephanie continued, "The reason I mention this is because neither my cell phone or my car work. Have you tried to see if your car works?"

Rick inhaled and then slowly expelled a large volume of air as he examined his wound, shaking his head in answer to Stephanie's question.

Rosalyn replied for both of them. "Neither of our cars will start, and neither of our cell phones are working either."

Rosalyn asked several questions--most of which Stephanie had no answers for--about what this all meant. She inquired about how long it was likely to take before the electrical grid returned and whether the cars would be returned to working order after the power grid was repaired.

Stephanie was only marginally successful in her attempt to stifle her laughter in response to Rosalyn's question. She looked over at Charlie Wyatt, who for some reason known only to him had decided to remove his shoes and "adjust" their laces. She hoped it would appear as though it was her son's actions, not her friend's ridiculous question, that had struck her as being so funny.

"The cars are all going to have to be fixed by a mechanic one at a time just like any other car repair," Stephanie replied. "I remember Rob said this thing would destroy some of the parts in most of the cars' engines, so bringing the power back on won't repair the cars. Same with our phones and anything else that was ruined."

Rick was mostly quiet, letting his wife and Stephanie do all of the talking. He was clearly using all of his personal strength and reserves to try to manage his pain and discomfort.

After the toothbrush had soaked for close to ten minutes and there weren't any more questions to be asked or opinions to be shared, Stephanie requested that Rosalyn watch how she cleaned the wound so that she could do it later by herself. She added that unless the wound started bleeding through the bandage again, she should leave the tourniquet loose.

"You can probably take it off altogether, really," Stephanie said. "I would keep it handy though, just in case it starts bleeding again."

After mixing a half teaspoon of bleach with approximately a pint of water, Stephanie dropped the toothbrush into the water. She then removed the tourniquet. She failed to notice any blood oozing through the bandage--a good sign to be sure. She took the risk of removing the towel being used as a bandage so she could work on cleaning the wound. There was a little bit of bleeding, but nothing to cause her alarm.

Despite the fact that it had to be uncomfortable when she pulled it away from the wound, Rick made no sounds of protest. He seemed to be flirting with the edge of blacking out.

Probably in shock, she thought.

Stephanie reiterated to Rosalyn the need to keep his legs elevated and to make sure he was warm. She opted not to mention her concerns about the possibility of having to deal with shock.

Stephanie, relieved the wound was bleeding only slightly, used the toothbrush and bleach water solution to clean out the large gash as best she could. Despite it being a bad indicator as far as Rick's condition was concerned, she was thankful that he didn't offer much resistance to her efforts as she performed the crude wound cleaning procedure.

When she had finished cleaning the open wound, leaving no visible debris in the four inch gash, Stephanie placed the dirty bandage in the water filled pot and handed it to Rosalyn.

"You need to clean this bandage as best you can in the bleach water. Get another clean dry towel, or whatever you want to use, to make more bandages. I'd cut a large towel into several smaller bandages--about six inches square-- if it were me. Fold the bandages in half when you put 'em on. Just make sure the bandage is dry, and as clean as you can get it as far as germs are concerned."

Rosalyn gave a slight nod to acknowledge her friend.

"Since you might not have a decent way to boil water, I would use a bleach water solution to clean them, like I said. You saw how I did that, right," Stephanie asked.

Rosalyn indicated she understood, looking at Stephanie with large eyes the whole time.

Stephanie squinted and slightly wrinkled her nose as she looked again at Rick's wound.

"Yeah, I really don't think you need to use the tourniquet anymore Rosalyn. He isn't bleeding enough to have to do that. But I would definitely keep it nearby in case that changes."

She saw that Rosalyn was beginning to appear overwhelmed with everything that had gone on, and was still going on. Stephanie approached her and hugged her tightly.

"It's going to be okay." She then turned and headed for the front door, calling for Charlie Wyatt to join her.

"Oh yeah, one more thing," Stephanie said as she stopped mid-stride, "Don't give him any aspirin or ibuprofen. You don't want it to bleed any easier than it is right now."

Rosalyn nodded her head, obviously digesting this latest information. She had the look of a woman who was near the limit of her ability to endure. A woman who was merely waiting for that last proverbial straw to be delivered at any moment.

Stephanie, sensing the level of despair her neighbor was suffering, stepped forward and threw one arm around Rosalyn while holding her son's hand tightly with the other. She gave her a one-armed but substantial hug. She held the embrace as she consoled her friend.

"You have to hang in there Rosalyn. You can get through this. I'll be back in the morning to see how things are going, okay?"

Rosalyn's only answer was a slight head movement that fell short of a nod and a loud sniffle. She wiped her tears with the back of her free hand.

Stephanie broke away from the hug and gave Rosalyn a nurturing smile before turning away and stepping out the door. She walked back to her home with her son in tow, feeling a mixture of relief and apprehension as she prepared to focus on their own situation for the evening.

12

UNINCORPORATED SOUTHEAST LOS ANGELES

Shortly after noon on the day of the EMP event, Nadeau Station's patrol area of South L.A. was approaching the realm of chaos, but it was not really violent--at least not on a wholesale level--yet.

It has been said that those living in the greater Los Angeles area have seen it all: earthquakes, riots, fires, and mudslides. But the EMP event promised to eclipse all of these in terms of its devastation and disruption of normal life. The difference was twofold. First, the nature of the EMP had rendered the entire infrastructure that was typically used to coordinate responses to disasters unworkable. Second, the EMP had rendered the problem much larger than merely a regional one, thereby making help from outside of the affected area unavailable. Every area had been affected this time. Exactly how long this was to be the case was anybody's guess. It was of a size and scope that the nation had never experienced until now.

In the areas normally patrolled by Nadeau Station deputies, cars were abandoned in the middle of the streets, left where they had come to a halt after they had given up the mechanical ghost. The sudden and unexpected cessation of virtually all vehicle functions was arguably a good thing since there were now no working traffic control lights, a condition that would have resulted in more than a few traffic collisions had the vehicles still been driven on the streets under these circumstances.

People could be seen walking about on the sidewalks and streets, many displaying the mannerisms associated with the irritation that went along with unforeseen major inconvenience. And this was before any of them were even aware of the magnitude of what had happened. Of course some were calmly and purposefully walking with a specific destination in mind, whether it be a residence or work location. Others were meandering about with some expectation that they would be rescued. Of course for others, help simply wasn't coming fast enough, so they demonstrated their frustration by yelling profanities, throwing cell phones, kicking immovable cars, and blaming everyone under the sun for their present circumstances.

Many of the affected parties thought it strange that there were no emergency vehicles responding to the massive disorder. This soon became another object on which to focus their anger. It was the cops' fault. Where were they? By early afternoon on day one--largely due to the conspicuous absence of law enforcement--the stores in Nadeau Station's jurisdiction were being looted.

It began with the younger teenage aspiring thugs entering the stores in large numbers, many of whom took advantage of the store keepers' inability to monitor or prevent theft. Young delinquents, suddenly aware of their virtual anonymity and the lack of any controlling influence, ran amuck. They grabbed anything they could in the way of store items, concealed them by whatever means was available, and then fled from the places of business with their stolen loot.

The situation went from bad to worse. Within an hour of the initial larcenous activity, the simple stealing devolved into a scene where thefts were being performed in full view of frantic but helpless storekeepers. Teenagers filled their hands and arms, loaded up their book bags--or anything else available--with whatever items they could get ahold of inside the stores. All while the store owners retreated, fearing for their personal safety.

It wasn't long before these thefts were accompanied by the destruction of the stores themselves. And then it was no longer only the teenagers that were taking part in the madness; other residents in the adjacent neighborhoods had joined in the activities as well.

Those that couldn't get access to the stores focused their attention on the ubiquitous cars left unattended in the streets. Vehicle contents perceived to have any value whatsoever were taken from the cars, while other valueless contents were strewn about the roads and sidewalks for the mere sake of being destructive.

Others, either frustrated by their inability to find anything to steal, or simply to satisfy some nihilistic urge, began destroying abandoned cars. Interior and exterior mirrors were ripped from their mounting brackets, side windows and windshields were smashed, and vehicle exteriors were kicked and dented until the vandals grew tired.

Several of the larger vandals broke car doors completely free of their host vehicles after slamming them repeatedly against the hinge stops. In these cases the car doors were left in the street while the violent and vandalistic teenagers moved on to find more vehicles on which to practice their newfound hobby. There was no law enforcement infrastructure in place to prevent the lawlessness, and this absence accelerated the mayhem like hot wind on a brushfire. Anarchy was now the rule of the day.

By mid-afternoon the real thugs had been awake for a few hours. Many had watched with interest the events as they unfolded in their neighborhoods and adjacent areas. Very few of the local hard core criminals were involved in the chaotic wholesale level stealing and vandalism taking place, but they were paying attention.

The complete absence of LASD patrol deputies, or any law enforcement response for that matter, was certainly not lost on them. The gangbangers had noticed, and they were going to take advantage of this latest situation. By nightfall the real violence would be in full swing.

One of the Los Angeles area's oldest Hispanic street gangs had its roots in the Nadeau Station's jurisdiction. Over the previous half century, the gang called "L Street" had gone to war with most of the nearby rival street gangs, both black and Latino, for one reason or another. It had no shortage of members capable of performing the savagery that led to respect inside this ultra-violent subculture.

After darkness had arrived on the first day of the EMP event, five of the L Street gang's most influential members had a meeting for the purpose of coming up with ways to exploit the situation at hand. The five gangbanger shot callers decided a rival gang member, who was suspected of shooting up an "L Street" house a week ago, would be killed before dawn.

There were two equally important reasons for this decision. The first was simply for revenge. Not a big deal in these parts. The second reason for the hit was to see what kind of law enforcement response, if any, would follow the shooting.

The usual notifications were made within the L Street gang infrastructure. One shot caller ordered a low ranking gangster to retrieve two *library guns* for the night's planned murder. One weapon was a .357 magnum revolver, the other a .40 caliber pistol. The guns were hidden in a semi-public location where they could be withdrawn on an "as needed" basis for hits of this nature.

The handguns were retrieved and delivered to the gang leader making the request. Soon afterward two trusted female L Street gang affiliates were sent out to perform reconnaissance for the shooters assigned to tonight's hit. The main shooter and his "back-up" were given their respective weapons and briefed on the plan of attack.

Within the hour, the girls reported back that the intended target was hanging out on the front porch of a house in the neighborhood where he lived. The two gangsters assigned the hit were sent on their way.

The primary shooter, a small shaved head Latino twenty year old with the street name of "Chaos", was heavily tattooed even by gang standards. Along with the plethora of tattoos covering his hands, arms, chest, and back, he had the two inch high numbers "187" tattooed across his forehead, the numbers indicating the California Penal Code section defining the crime of murder. Subtlety wasn't his strong suit, but he didn't give a shit.

The .357 revolver was his weapon for tonight's event. The advantage of the revolver for doing the hit lay with the fact it did not expend the empty fired cartridge cases onto the ground where law enforcement could recover them as evidence. All the expended cartridge casings remained in the revolver's closed cylinder after they had been fired.

The second gangster's responsibility was to provide security for the primary should things not go as planned and the two found themselves under fire by either superior numbers of rival gangbangers or any other unforeseen problem that warranted a serious defense.

His weapon was the high capacity .40 caliber pistol. It had more firepower than the revolver in case things went unexpectedly bad for the assassin.

"Chaos" wore a black hooded sweatshirt that was pulled tight around his face. A "hoodie" was an effective means of making identification more difficult by witnesses. And a "hoodie", unlike a ski mask or nylon stocking, was a normal piece of clothing commonly worn in L.A. The tactics used by the bad guys evolved, just like they did with the police.

Gripping the .357 magnum revolver in both of his hands in preparation for the hit, "Chaos" began to pump himself up mentally for what was about to happen. The truth of the matter was that he loved the thrill, or the "juice" that went along with doing a murder for the gang. His back-up, another Hispanic man in his early twenties, was also wearing a dark hooded sweatshirt in a similar manner. He carried a Beretta .40 caliber semi-automatic pistol and a fully loaded extra magazine in his front pocket.

The L Street hit went off without a hitch for the most part. Using small flashlights to illuminate their route as little as possible, the shooter and his backup partner walked from the rear of the house, along the side of the house to the front, and then went right up to the intended target as he sat on the porch. The porch's occupants, all gangbangers or affiliates, had placed a steel fifty gallon barrel on top of some bricks laid on the porch and then made a fire inside of the steel drum.

The female, a nineteen year old light skinned black woman with a pretty face and a slender yet curvaceous figure, was sitting on the lap of the intended victim of this evening's shooting. She wore a tight skirt that was so short that it was doubtful whether it would even conceal her black skimpy panties when she walked. But at this moment, she wasn't walking at all. She was sitting astride the soon to be targeted gangster's lap.

Sitting in this position, the young woman's bikini panties, as well as much of the often pursued natural treasure that lay beneath the lacy undergarment, was on display for all of those seated on the fire illuminated porch to view. She slid up and down against the thug's thigh beneath her, creating a slow lascivious motion that kept timing with an unknown rhythm.

The intended victim, along with two other young men and the sensual young vixen, all immediately recognized what was about to take place when the Hispanic gangbangers abruptly appeared, guns gripped in their outstretched fists. The gang member with the revolver yelled, "This is for L Street!" as he swung the revolver's barrel around toward the people on the porch.

The shooter wasn't concerned in the least about which of the persons in front of him were actually responsible for last week's shooting of one of their own. To him, at this point it was only about shooting as many of them as possible before he ran out of rounds. And that's exactly what he did.

Taken completely by surprise, and terrified that they were about to be shot, the victim and his friends all instinctively held their hands up, palms out, in front of their faces as if this would prevent the bullets from fatally harming them. It was a futile gesture of course, a point that was cruelly driven home as the first two bullets passed through the victim's outstretched palm before punching holes in his liver and heart.

As the gangster-turned-victim slid to the porch and lay there dying, the shooter fired the revolver's remaining four rounds into the first victim's friends. One of these rounds missed its target altogether. It passed through the front wall of the house before coming to rest in the living room's inoperable television. The last three all found human flesh—one striking a twenty year old gangster in the thigh, and two hitting the pretty girl in her abdomen and upper arm.

The L Street gangbanger serving as back-up never fired a shot, remembering that he was to save his ammo in case he had to protect the primary shooter and himself. It was a level of discipline that was rare in the circles he travelled.

The first victim and the girl died on the porch then and there, while the third victim would succumb to his leg wound several days later due to a massive and untreated infection. Both of the L Street gangsters ran back to the alley, jumped a fence that deposited them into a residential back yard, and then made their way out onto the sidewalk bordering the front yard of the residence. They walked from there to the pre-arranged meeting location with the gang's shot callers. Now it was time to watch.

The deputies didn't respond to the murder location within the first hour following the shooting. Nor had they responded by the time dawn had arrived the next morning. By that point, it was accurately concluded, there was not going to be any response unless the power came back on and working cars were available.

What the "L Street" gangsters did see was a lot of destruction that had been suffered by the commercial buildings in their neighborhoods. Although none would openly admit it to their peers, they were surprised at the level of destruction that had taken place. It looked like something they would watch on a rented "B" movie while sitting around getting high on their drug of choice.

The absence of any law enforcement or other first responders had served as an accelerant for the violence and other lawlessness in the area. Something the gangsters could not actually see, but would not have been surprised to hear, was the fact the nation's deadly violence level had skyrocketed within the last twelve hours. It had surpassed anything seen in the United States since the Civil War, and there was no indication things were going to improve any time soon.

13

INGLEWOOD, CA

Upon leaving the Brown's home, Rob didn't like what he saw taking place in the neighborhood as he walked through it. He observed several groups of young toughs loitering in different locations, including front porches, parking lots, and around parked cars in the street. He saw one hard looking youngster, an average sized guy in his late teens to early twenties, with a red ball cap turned backwards, holding a woman of similar age by her hair as he yelled at her in the middle of the residential street.

The street seasoned looking young man swung her around by her braids, fully exploiting the complete physical control he had over her. Yanking on her braids, he pulled her face up to his, no more than a couple of inches separating the two. He yelled vulgar insults at her, and then slapped her hard across the face. The woman screamed and then sobbed, prompting a repeated performance of the same sequence of events at the hands of her tormentor. Several in the crowd laughed raucously as they watched the performance. The girl's growing terror was evident in her eyes. She knew she was in for a long day and night--or worse.

Rob didn't like what he was seeing, but this wasn't the part that bothered him the most. What really disturbed him was the lack of any police response. He was pretty sure this would mean things were not only going to end badly for the girl who was at the mercy of the man who was abusing her, it was also going to embolden all of the other criminals in the area. It wouldn't take long for word to get out that the cops weren't patrolling or responding under the present circumstances, and he knew this would spell serious trouble.

He recalled how following instances where deputies had been shot in the line of duty, typically there would be a huge law enforcement presence in the area of occurrence for days, sometimes longer, depending on the circumstances surrounding the shooting. During these periods none of the gangsters and other thugs could be found at their usual haunts. In fact, they typically couldn't be found at all while the extra police presence continued. It was as if they were all either hiding inside their residences all hours of the day and night or had simply left the area entirely.

Rob also understood the flip side of this coin. Whenever police presence was scarce, the thugs became more active. What Rob didn't yet realize was that word of the seriously diminished, or even nonexistent, police presence had already begun to make the rounds in the neighborhood he was walking through.

He had travelled no more than a quarter mile from the Brown residence when he saw five gangbangers, all with red bandanas covering their faces, approach a house not half a block from where he was walking. The red bandanas told Rob they were members of the *Bloods* gang, but nothing more. Nor did he give a damn. He knew all he needed to know based on what he had just seen.

Four of the gangsters were holding guns. Three had handguns while one held a shortened single shot shotgun. He recognized the design of the shotgun as a break action, and it was clearly too short to be legal—not that this even mattered under the circumstances. Despite the fact the little shotgun held only one round, Rob was well aware of the devastation a single shotgun round could accomplish at close range.

Much like a hand grenade in rough concept, a short barreled shotgun firing buckshot delivered numerous small to medium sized projectiles in its payload, in contrast with a single more powerful projectile such as that of a rifle cartridge. The devastation of a buckshot round was not just academic for Rob. He had been provided more than a couple first hand and close-up views of the damage these rounds could produce during his tenure as a patrol officer.

The gangsters never noticed Rob across the street from them. He stopped and positioned himself behind a tree located adjacent to the sidewalk, hoping to continue to remain concealed from their view. The tree wasn't big enough to hide him entirely, but he hoped it would at least break up the outline of his body. For the second time that morning Rob pulled his pistol from its holster and held it in his hands in preparation for combat.

Watching the gang members standing on the porch of the house, he could hear them yelling but could not make out their words. The largest gangbanger of the group (the only one who was not holding a gun) kicked at the door. It held fast. He kicked the thick door a second and then a third time before it finally gave way and allowed all five thugs entry into the home. They left the front door wide open behind them as they went in.

Rob left the partial concealment of the tree and approached the house. As he crouched behind a small hedge forming a border between the yard of the house in question and a neighbor's yard, he strained to listen to what was happening inside. He could hear at least two female voices screaming and a male voice. The man sounded like he was desperate and pleading. Rob heard two gunshots, soon followed by three more in rapid succession. They all sounded like handgun rounds to Rob. The hysterical screaming of the women was ratcheted up even further following the gunshots. The sounds unnerved him. He could no longer hear a male voice.

He wanted badly to enter the home and help the victims still inside, but he was conflicted once again by competing pulls of duty and obligation. He told himself to stay focused on his main objective: getting home to look after Stephanie and Charlie Wyatt. Anything lessening the odds of accomplishing his objective had to be disregarded. It had to be this way or he wouldn't make it. He was no longer a law enforcement officer charged with protecting the citizenry. He was a husband who had to protect his own family now--because nobody else was going to do that.

Yet Rob still wanted to try to see what was going on inside the house. He snuck up to one of the windows at the side of the house that afforded a view of the small dining area and living room. He saw a woman in her late 30's, tall with short cropped hair, high cheekbones and smooth chocolate colored skin, wearing designer jeans and a sleeveless blouse. Next to the woman stood a girl in her mid-teens that looked so much like the older woman that Rob concluded it had to be her daughter. The mother dropped down to the floor, sobbing uncontrollably, as she bent over a man who lay on the living room carpet in a pool of blood.

The man was dressed in a business suit, and Rob briefly wondered where he thought he was going to be going dressed in a suit under the current post EMP circumstances. Maybe he had no idea as to the magnitude of what was in store. No matter; it was now quite clear that the business suit would never be worn again by the man on the floor or anyone else. To Rob, he appeared to be dead. In any case, even if the man were still alive, there would be no emergency help coming to give him assistance. He was almost certainly going to die if he hadn't already.

The teenage girl was sobbing loudly and moaning as she stared at the man on the floor presumed to be her father. One of the gangbangers attempted to hit the mother on the side of her head with the barrel of his handgun, but the woman managed to raise her hand defensively in time to mitigate some of the intended impact. Nonetheless, the result was not much better for the poor woman. The blow broke her ring finger and yet still contained enough force to create a three inch laceration to her head, knocking her into a semi-prone position on the ground as blood spurted from the fresh head wound. She somehow remained awake despite suffering a concussion.

The poor woman vomited onto the floor, a reaction to serious trauma Rob had seen many times. Screaming in response to what she had just witnessed, the daughter rushed the savage bandana clad gangster responsible for pistol whipping her mother. She desperately swung her impotent fists at the man as she collided with him.

He easily grabbed one of her wrists with his non-gun hand while he shoved the revolver into his waistband, allowing him the use of both of his hands. Then he grabbed her other wrist, effectively preventing her from hitting him. It was a cruel little move in and of itself—the prevention of her ability to hit him only making her feel even more helpless and doomed.

"Bitch; I gonna teach you not to be hittin no *Blood*! You gonna pay for that shit now bitch!"

Retaining his firm grip on her wrists, he kicked the girl's feet out from under her and shoved her, face first, to the ground. Hard. The blow rattled her and brought her to the brink of passing out, but she remained aware of what was happening. As she lay face down on the living room floor, not five feet from her dead father and barely conscious mother, the psychopathic hood struck her in the back of her head with his right fist a half dozen times. His cohort with the shotgun yelled at him from across the room.

"Don't kill that bitch. We need to find the damn money Dawg!"

Not sure if the traumatized girl was still awake or even alive, her tormenter yanked her head up by grabbing a fistful of her hair. Through broken sobs she begged with the savage thug, imploring him not to hurt her any more. But he paid no attention to her requests.

The girl had now made the transition from grief and shock over what these predators had done to her parents. Now she was only focused on that most basic of human conditions: simple survival. Somewhere within the deepest recesses of her brain she wanted to live through this ordeal. Her mother, watching what was happening in the living room as she lay immobile on the floor, moaned with a combination of physical and mental agony.

At this point Rob wasn't exactly sure why he had made the decision to inch up to the window to investigate what was happening inside the house. He suspected he mostly wanted to make sure it was "only" a robbery, so that he might be able to excuse himself for not taking action. Unfortunately, fate was not to be so kind to him.

Rob was now watching a worst case scenario unfold before his very eyes. And he couldn't do anything about it without making the odds of his returning home a hell of a lot smaller than they were if he did nothing. He now seriously regretted his decision to make sure nothing too bad was happening inside the house.

What the hell made me think I would get any indication of good news by looking through this window?

As Rob agonized over whether or not he should take action at this point, one of the gangsters in the living room indicated to his fellow thugs that he didn't care about the money; he just wanted to use the two women for sexual purposes.

"We can get the damn money after we done with these bitches, Dawg. I'm gettin me some right now!"

As the young rapist began to visit his sexual debauchery upon the mother, he laughed and told her that her daughter was going to be next. He performed miscellaneous sexual acts upon the mother in full view of her daughter as well as the other gangsters.

Apparently encouraged and emboldened by the savagery of the first rapist, a second gang member unzipped his pants and prepared to sexually assault the daughter while the mother was still enduring the brutal sexual assault from the first. Rob had to turn his head away. He considered himself to be a hardened man, having seen more than his share of man's inhumanity to his fellow man (and woman), but he could not take watching this scene from a hellish nightmare any longer.

Rob seethed with a hot burning hatred that exceeded anything he had ever experienced. He came so close to entering that house and shooting as many of the gangsters as he could, that he actually wasn't sure whether he might risk his life—and by extension his family's life--to do so. It took him the better part of a minute to power down his emotions and refocus on his objective.

So he walked away with gun in hand, taking quick and repeated glances over his shoulder as he created distance between himself and the scene of horrors he had just witnessed. Rob could not recall having ever felt so ashamed and powerless. But he pushed on, all the while trying to figure out the best way to get home.

14

THOUSAND OAKS, CA

The next morning Stephanie made it a point to walk over to her neighbors' house to check on Rick's injury status before she made breakfast or fed the dogs. Rosalyn answered the front door, her face telling the tale about how the recent stress had affected her. She looked as though she had been crying quite a bit over the past several hours, and it was obvious sleep had evaded her as well.

Stephanie asked how they both were doing, but Rosalyn responded with no more than a shrug.

This woman is in way over her head. I have to try to help her, but I'm not sure how much I can.

She walked past Rosalyn with Charlie Wyatt once again in tow. She headed directly into the living room to take a look at Rick. Charlie Wyatt began to protest in a whiny voice. She gave him a stern look and told him to sit down and wait for her. He had brought a book with him that she hoped would suffice to keep him occupied.

Rick mentioned to Stephanie that he hadn't slept very well due to his leg throbbing throughout the night. She winced mildly in response. She made a mental note to check her own first aid supplies to see if they included any pain killers even though she wasn't sure if she wanted to share them with her injured neighbor.

"Well at least I can see you got the bleeding to stop. No more tourniquet anyway," Stephanie said.

Rick replied, "Yeah, we took it off a few hours ago."

Stephanie asked Rosalyn if she had any honey in the house. She received a nod and a puzzled look for a response. She also asked her to bring a small spoon, duct tape, and one of the cloth bandages she had been asked to make for use as wound dressings. Rosalyn resisted the urge to ask questions and immediately turned to go find the things requested of her. She returned with the items moments later and set them on the table next to where Rick lay.

"We're going to change his bandage again, and I'm going to try something with the honey that might help it heal. I know it sounds weird, but I remember hearing that honey can be helpful with healing wounds. I'm not kidding"

One of the doctors who had worked in the ER back when Stephanie used to periodically watch the proceedings there had spent time volunteering in South America. She told Stephanie that raw honey on open wound sites had antibacterial benefits along with additional healing properties. She also remembered the doctor had indicated it was imperative the dressings on honey treated wounds be changed twice a day.

She removed the bandage and looked at the wound. It had actually stopped bleeding, which was good news in itself. Moreover, there was no tell-tale redness outside of the wound site, which meant no infection. As she examined the gash, she made another mental note to check her own first aid supplies in her house to see what kind of infection fighting items it contained.

"Come here and watch me do this, Rosalyn."

She reluctantly approached.

"Looks like you've been doing a good job with this," Stephanie commented as she indicated Rick's injury and nodded her head in approval. Rick, no doubt feeling somewhat better, chimed in, "Oh yeah. She's been taking great care of me." He smiled at his wife.

With her friend watching over her shoulder, Stephanie used the spoon to apply a small amount of honey to the wound. Then she used one of the clean cloth squares as a dressing before taping it to Rick's leg with duct tape.

"You really have to keep up on cleaning those bandages so you can dress his wound with a fresh bandage twice a day. You sure you got all this?"

"Uh-huh; I got it. No problem."

Promising that she would check back in on both of them again the next day, Stephanie grabbed her son and walked out the door, completely drained. Nonetheless, for the first time since she had been made aware of Rick's axe injury, Stephanie felt encouraged that he would come out of this ordeal intact. Maybe.

15

UNINCORPORATED SOUTHEAST LOS ANGELES

If one could describe the afternoon rioters and pillagers on the first day following the EMP as the "junior varsity" thugs, then after dark it was the "varsity" thugs that became active. Some of the store owners remained in their places of business, making futile efforts to protect what amounted to their entire lives' financial investments, only to be brutalized by the violent predators claiming the territory. It was a disgusting sight to behold, but it was the new way of things.

Shop owners, ranging from the young to senior citizens, many of them immigrants from faraway places that had come to America in order to avoid violence and danger in their homelands, now faced a situation even worse than that from which they had fled. Life could be cruel in its irony.

Hardened and experienced gangbangers punched, kicked--and struck with a variety of blunt objects--the storeowners they encountered on the first night following the EMP. Scores of store owners and employees suffered serious injuries that would have required ambulance transportation to local hospitals under normal circumstances, but on this night they had to settle for being carried to locations of relative safety. Locations where, if they were lucky, they could be attended to by loved ones.

Two dozen store owners and half as many gangsters were killed during the first forty eight hours following the EMP incident in the Nadeau Station patrol area. The former were killed by the riotous thugs caught up in the frenzy of unchecked mob violence and the latter were shot by store owners fortunate enough—or smart enough—to be armed. Dozens of residents suffered fatalities from heart attacks and other serious health problems. The number of rapes and other sexual assaults--just in the Nadeau Station venue alone-- exceeded a hundred during this brief time period.

Not a single deputy sheriff or county firefighter/paramedic responded to any of the above incidents. They could not have responded even had they wanted to. And virtually all of the area's residents--innocent victims and predators alike--took notice of this. It had the effect of a powerful accelerant on the chaos of the region, a fact that was borne out by the following twenty four hours producing an even higher body count than the first forty eight.

There were a few stores that were spared from the destruction and theft suffered by most. These exceptions were not based on the vandals' consideration for altruistic store owners who had contributed to the community. Nor were they based on the pillagers' empathy for the financial plight endured by many of the struggling owners. No quarter was given to store owners based on ethnicity either; although some believed they were attacked with extra savagery because of it. It really didn't matter; there was enough violence and mayhem to make everyone's circumstances a living hell.

The simple and brutal fact was that store owners of every ethnic group doing business in the area were beaten and their stores pillaged. The only stores that were spared were those whose owners or employees were providing their own security. And this security was being accomplished by individuals carrying every manner of firearm available to California residents.

Men, and even a few women, could be seen on store roof tops with military look-alike rifles, shotguns of all types, and hunting rifles. Many of these wore handguns holstered in plain view on their hips or shoved into their waist bands. At first store owners had refrained from shooting looters as the mere presence of serious looking armed citizens ready to protect their personal safety and property was sufficient to send the pillagers elsewhere.

However, before long it became a different story.

Alek Bejko, a forty two-year-old Albanian immigrant, stood on the rooftop of a store that represented his family's last and only hope of achieving any semblance of a successful life. The business located beneath where he now paced sold blemished seconds and other grey market entertainment electronics. Many of the store's customers were comprised of undocumented immigrants who still called their mother countries home.

Bejko smoked a cigarette that hung loosely from his lower lip. He used the two remaining fingers of his right hand to periodically reposition the cigarette, its ash inexplicably seeming to defy gravity, growing longer by the second as it burned. The Albanian immigrant store owner, with a rifle slung across his back, watched another store owner being dragged from his retail establishment, a place that sold items varying from ball caps emblazoned with designs or slogans long ago passé to overruns of basic cookware. They dragged him by his feet.

Several thugs took turns kicking him, while yet another struck him with a two foot piece of one inch diameter metal tubing that had been broken off of a clothing rack in the store. The out of control young criminals were delivering their own version of pay back for the man's having dared to physically resist them while they set about destroying his store.

The Albanian immigrant store owner smoking a cigarette on the roof next door had no idea whether the man being dragged and beaten was alive or dead. In truth, he wasn't even certain he could recall his name despite having had several short conversations with him over the last year and a half.

Bejko was the product of a war torn and brutal Eastern European region, which explained his missing fingers as well as a lot of other things about the man. He had learned to use violence decisively when circumstances required it. Friend or not, he wasn't going to let the beating of his fellow store owner continue as long as he had a rifle at his disposal. He unslung his weapon, a Ruger Mini-14, from where it hung across his back.

Taking a knee from a distance of approximately forty yards, Bejko began shooting the thugs one by one. The first round struck the eighteen-year-old doing the dragging. The soft nosed .223 caliber hunting round, travelling at close to three thousand feet per second, hit him high in the chest, sending a spray of pink mist and bone fragments out his back. He was dead within seconds of the bullet's impact.

Not stopping to view the results of his first shot, the Albanian continued firing. He placed the rifle's sights on another man doing the beating, squeezed the trigger, and moved on to the next target to repeat the process. The sound of the Mini-14's four expended brass cartridge casings bouncing on the asphalt papered roof went unheard due to the loud sounds of the chaos, destruction, and carnage taking place below. There were now five dead men on the street twenty feet beneath his elevated position--one store owner and four hoodlums.

Bejko re-activated the safety on the rifle and slung it over his back. He let his depleted cigarette drop to the roof, and used the two remaining fingers on his right hand to remove another smoke from the pack he kept in his shirt pocket. He placed a new cigarette between his lips and lit it. He took a long slow drag, pulling the smoke deep into his lungs before exhaling as he casually looked down from the rooftop at the results of his shooting. He did so with no more concern than if he were viewing someone having difficulty backing into a parking space.

Most of the nihilistic hoods were now aware of the man on the roof who had been shooting looters. Subsequently many had moved to locations where they were out of sight, or at least out of the line of fire, from the rifleman. Some left the area altogether, not wanting to take the chance of being shot, while others, secure in their belief the shooter could not see them or reach them, continued with their stealing and other mayhem-related activities.

On the following day, as the dawn cast its first light on South Los Angeles, there were virtually no products left inside most of the stores in the Nadeau Station jurisdiction. Not only were the shelves and racks devoid of any merchandise, but most of these stores had

had their miscellaneous machines, racks, electrical fixtures, and even copper plumbing removed and stolen.

The non-theft-related destruction and vandalism visited upon these buildings was just as severe. Racks were bent and broken beyond hope of further use, huge holes were made in store walls, permanent lighting devices were destroyed, and windows were broken. It was amazing, even to the gangsters, how much devastation and destruction had taken place during such a short time without a law enforcement presence in the area.

With the exception of touching base with Marino twice a day, the station's captain, Hillary O'Neal, had remained inside of her office with the door locked following the grid crash. Just before noon on the second day, the captain exited her office in civilian attire, and then informed Sgt. Marino she was going to use one of the bicycles taken from the evidence room to ride to her residence.

Uttering a perfunctory promise about finding out why no assistance had been provided to the station, she rode away without looking back. The sergeant didn't share his thoughts with any of the deputies, but privately he felt relieved to have the captain gone. He didn't have a lot of confidence in her ability to contribute meaningful input on how to cope with their growing problems.

He had actually liked the captain when she was a young deputy working in the field because she had been smart, dedicated, and willing to look outside the proverbial box. Yet something had happened as she climbed the ranks. In his view she was no longer invested in doing a good job. Whether due to outside job interests or simply professional burnout, she hadn't been invested for years.

Approximately one hour following the captain's departure, Sergeant Marino instructed the deputy assigned to station jail duty to release all misdemeanor inmates. He also directed him to release all inmates who were in jail for drug arrests or other non-violent felonies. He ordered the jailer to issue citations to the released prisoners, all with future court dates as far into the future as possible given his court calendar guide. He didn't know if this would make any difference if the infrastructure wasn't repaired by the time the court dates arrived, but he figured it couldn't hurt.

Looking for an excuse to get up and move around for the purpose of getting his blood circulating and to take in a little change of scenery, Marino walked out of his office and began to make the rounds to check on his deputies. He found Gattuso and Anderson standing watch in a section of the large parking lot that afforded both of them views of different sides of the station without taking them out of easy hearing distance from each other. Both deputies hat shotguns slung over their shoulders. He motioned them over.

When he asked them how things were going, Gattuso responded without hesitation.

"Looks like we're screwed for who knows how long, doesn't it? All I know is that I've been wearing the same dirty socks and underwear for too many days now. And I'm feeling pretty disgusting too. This whole thing is bullshit. The biggest fuckin' sheriff's department in the country and the house fairies in management can't even get their shit together when we need help. Not to mention all of the residents around us. We can't even protect them at all. We look like complete pussies now Sarge. This whole thing is just totally *unsat* man, completely *unsat*."

Anderson chimed in with a question she hoped would show loyalty to her patrol car partner while at the same time trying to diffuse the growing tension between him and their sergeant.

"Is there any way we can set up some sort of way to do a little laundry by hand? How bout I go look for a big pot in the jail kitchen?"

"Yeah...good idea. If anyone can come up with a way to heat the water in the pot, let me know. I know the natural gas lines have quit on us, so I guess we'll have to build a fire. It would be nice to have some warm water to wash our clothes, not to mention our bodies."

He looked at Anderson and assessed her briefly—not as a woman, but as a patrol cop. He was an old school sergeant, and wasn't known for embracing the relatively new departmental push to infuse patrol ranks with female officers, but he had no problem with women in patrol when they could carry their end of the log. In his view Anderson had proven her right to do so.

Cindy Anderson was in her late twenties. Five years earlier, three months after receiving her bachelor's degree in business administration from USC, she had accepted a position with the LASD. It was accepted over the protests of her parents. She was almost six feet tall, and obviously spent a lot of time in the gym trying to maximize her upper body strength. And she spent just as much time running as she did in the gym lifting weights. The woman was in great athletic shape.

If Deputy Anderson wore makeup she could easily pass for a fledgling Hollywood actress. However, she had no interest in such things--at least not while performing her duties as a patrol deputy. She was all business out in the field, a notion that was supported by her high arrest stats every month.

Anderson was one of the few deputies assigned to Nadeau Station who refused to eat the food from the local restaurants (virtually all of which were greasy and/or fast food joints). She preferred to bring her own carefully selected food to work every day.

She had earned a reputation among her fellow deputies, as well as the habitual criminals and gangsters in much of the Nadeau Station's patrol area, seven months prior. The incident, involving a foot chase through a gang infested neighborhood where she eventually arrested a skinny eighteen-year-old burglar and then marched him handcuffed two blocks back to her patrol car, had left her with the moniker of *Wonder Woman*. It was an affectionate sobriquet used by many of the locals and her fellow deputies alike.

***

Marino reminded himself that he had wanted to check out the old rusted water tank at the back of the parking lot. Seeing Anderson during a rare moment of looking bored, he asked her to go with him to check it out. She shrugged her shoulders and followed.

He approached the hose bib spigot mounted on the tank. The spigot looked to be as old as the tank itself. His first attempt to open it failed. The hose bib seemed to be frozen shut, probably due to not having been used for so long. Taking care not to sever the hose bib from the short length of pipe that connected it to the tank, he eventually managed to open it. Rust tainted water poured out of the spigot, and he immediately shut it off in order to conserve the valuable substance.

Feeling dumb for not having done so initially, the sergeant found a milk crate full of canned motor oil resting against the maintenance area wall and pulled it over next to the water tank. Using the crate to stand on, he gained enough height to remove the sixteen inch diameter tank lid located at the very top of the container. Now afforded an unobstructed view of the tank's interior, he saw the tank was between half and three quarters full. An assortment of dead bugs floated on top of the water, but this failed to diminish the sense of relief that flooded through him. They would have to find a way to filter the precious liquid, but the important thing was they now had enough water to last for a while.

After Marino had shared his discovery with Anderson, she wrinkled her nose and shrugged her shoulders again.

"I dunno Sarge. I saw the water that came out of that faucet just now, and I don't think I want to drink it. Looks pretty nasty."

"Yeah, well, we'll have to figure a way to filter it and make it safe to drink. It'll be okay; you'll see. Do me a favor and see if you can dig up a big cooking pot from the jail section so we can heat up water on the barbeque."

"No problem Sarge." She turned to see if she could find what he wanted. .

Marino re-entered the station and found the deputy in charge of the station jail standing near the sergeant's office. He asked the shorter and younger Cuban-American deputy for a list of the remaining prisoners. As he began to walk away, Marino stopped him.

"Hey, here's another thing. Don't feed any inmates until the ones you're going to release are already gone. And after that, the rest of 'em only get one meal a day from now on until I say otherwise. Okay? Also, I would feed 'em that one meal at lunch time if I were you.".

The deputy nodded to acknowledge the directive and headed off to the jail section.

Fifteen minutes later he returned to Sgt. Marino's office with a list of the remaining inmates. There were three in jail for domestic violence, two parolees for possession of firearms and heroine for sale, and one for strong armed robbery. The sergeant asked to have the paper booking packets for each prisoner brought to him. The packets would include details of the arrest as well as prior arrests. He wanted to know exactly what the risk to the public would be, if, and when, it came time to release them.

The station's natural gas and water supplies had been inoperable for a while now. This required a new protocol for human waste disposal—including that of the jail prisoners. Marino requested the desk deputy bring every single trash bag liner in the building to his office. He planned to use the liners as repositories for human waste when the latrine wasn't available, and they would have to be monitored carefully.

Gattuso had discovered that one of the patrol cars in the lot would start but its engine would not continue to run. None of the others would even start. As a sort of consolation prize, he realized the vehicles' batteries were still providing 12 volt power. This meant they could use their 12 volt flashlight chargers to keep the powerful hand-held lights working--at least for as long as the car batteries held juice.

As an afterthought, Marino collected all of the toilet paper and paper towels in the station and custodial supply room as well. It would have to be rationed somehow. He told the jailer to carefully ration the toilet paper to the remaining handful of inmates as well. The sergeant was beginning, for the first time since the incident had begun, to have serious doubts about how he was going to be able to keep the situation together.

Water was going to become an issue that trumped most of the others. And even with the discovery of the old water tank and its contents, he knew that general awareness of this fact, both within the confines of the sheriff's station, and in the surrounding community, was going to happen soon. And there was a good chance it would bring more trouble.

16

INGLEWOOD, CA

It hadn't even been five minutes since Rob had left the house of human terror, his own personal agony over his decision to walk away only growing in intensity with every passing moment, when he changed his mind. Admitting to himself that he simply could not live with his decision if he continued walking away from the evil taking place in the home, Rob turned and headed back. He had several thoughts running through his head as he broke into a jog, heading toward the place he had just left with a clear purpose.

Am I even a cop anymore? Should I be putting myself in harm's way to help strangers I don't even know when my own family needs me? What's the right thing to do here? If I get myself killed, or even wounded, I won't be able to protect my family. No ambulances are going to be responding for my dumb ass if I get hurt. Yeah, but the right thing to do is what any decent man would do if he had the ability to carry it out. I know what to do, and it's time to saddle up and make it happen!

Changing his thought process on the run, he constructed a basic plan of attack in his head. He realized he would most likely not have time to reload his seventeen round 9mm pistol once the close quarters combat began with the gangbangers, so he removed his tactical folding knife, flicked the blade open, and took a reverse grip with the knife in his non-gun hand.

He gripped the pistol with his right hand in a normal combat grip, safety off with his trigger finger outside of the trigger guard. The knife in his left hand was held point down, with the cutting edge facing away from him. This allowed his thumbs to be touching each other as he held his pistol, utilizing both hands pressed against each other to provide as stable of a shooting platform as possible, even with the knife in his left hand.

He didn't think he would actually need the knife once the situation went hot, but he wanted to be able to use it in case his plan didn't go how he expected. Anything could go wrong. He could run out of ammo before the gunfight was over, his gun could malfunction, or it could be taken away from him if multiple opponents rushed him. And he knew the odds of his being rushed grew as the size of the combat area shrank.

After all was said and done, due to the ultra-close quarters nature of what he was about to do, Rob felt the slight reduction in his shooting stability was a worthwhile trade-off in order to have the knife. The judgment call had been made.

Rob didn't kid himself. He knew that engaging multiple violent armed criminals was not exactly a smart move if self-preservation was a goal. Once again, he questioned his decision. But he pushed ahead regardless. He was still enough of a street cop that he couldn't ignore the situation, no matter how hard he tried. As he unknowingly put his war face on and the battle chemicals were released into his bloodstream, he ran the whole scenario through his mind.

Fuck these guys. They're all going down. Their misery causing lives are going to come to an end right now! Their whole world is about to change and they don't even know it!

Before he reached the front porch, Rob slowed his pace and let his pack slide off of his back and onto the grass of the front yard. He would allow it to remain here for the time being. No sense wearing anything he didn't need that might slow him down or get in his way. He jogged to the window where he had been watching the savagery take place moments earlier. Looking inside, he took in some good news and some bad news.

The bad news was that both the girl and her mother now lay on the floor. The mother appeared to be either dead or comatose, while the daughter lay in a fetal position, body against her mother as though seeking some comfort from her. The girl was sobbing uncontrollably as she lay there. The sight was as pitiful as any he had ever had to view, but pity was not the primary emotion that Rob was experiencing right now. Barely controlled rage surged through his entire body.

The good news was only three of the five gangbangers were present in the front of the house: two in the living room and one in the adjacent kitchen, which had no wall separating it from the living room. While Rob couldn't be certain where the other two thugs were at this very moment, he suspected they were in one of the back rooms trying to locate money or other valuables.

He recognized the situation as giving him a slight tactical advantage—he didn't have to deal with all five in the same room. He tried to conjure up a way to create a diversion of some sort to give him an extra second when he would be entering the front room. Failing to come up with anything workable, he opted for a KISS plan. The *keep it simple stupid* strategy had served him well many times in his life, and he hoped today would be no exception.

His impromptu plan involved entering the house quickly and shooting the bad guys without any preamble or pre-conditions. Hopefully he could do this before he was shot himself. It was all going to be about his employing surprise, aggression, and speed as he hit the group of predators.

Rob softly walked onto the porch with his pistol in his strong hand and his knife in the other. He saw that at some point since he had last been here, all three gangbangers in the front of the home had pulled their bandanas down allowing their faces to be visible. Apparently they weren't worried about leaving any witnesses behind that could identify them. Rob almost expected to see the faces of monsters revealed, but all three looked like run-of-the-mill gangbangers.

He wasn't sure if it was more unsettling, or less, that their faces were so normal in appearance given the evil he had watched them perform only minutes prior. Two of them were standing with their backs at an oblique angle to the front doorway. The third stood at the kitchen counter area about fifteen feet from two of his cohorts. The guy in the kitchen had placed his shotgun on the counter top next to where he stood.

Rob took careful note of the fact the shotgun had its exposed hammer cocked back. All the psychopath had to do was touch that shotgun's trigger and a round would be fired. The men in the living room had their handguns shoved into the front of their waistbands—a medium sized revolver of unknown caliber and a mid-sized Glock.

Reaching the open doorway, Rob stopped only long enough to acquire a quick sight picture with his pistol and then fired twice. One of the rounds struck the closest man in the back of the head, the hollow point bullet shattering his skull and taking a good amount of brain matter with it in the process. Rob's second round missed. It went over the thug's head as he was falling, coming to rest inside the refrigerator after entering through its thin steel door. The gangster was dead before he collapsed onto the floor.

Rob stepped forward, gun firing, as the first man hit the ground. He wasn't here to engage in any fair play "duel at high noon" bullshit or play by any other rules. He was here to kill these sociopathic thugs. And he planned to carry it out as efficiently as possible.

The second gangster had started to turn toward Rob in reaction to the initial shots, reaching for the revolver in his waistband as he did so. It did him no good. Not even bothering to use his sights as he continued firing, Rob stormed forward and almost bowled the man over while sending three more bullets into his chest. His pistol muzzle was so close to touching his chest when he fired the last two rounds, that they were, for all intents and purposes, contact shots. Any of the three hits would have been fatal, and the rapist went down hard for good.

Rob didn't waste any time looking at the men he had killed. He stepped over the torso of the second bad guy without breaking stride, his eyes fixated on the third gunman in the kitchen as he approached him.

He moved through the living room fast, using deliberate high steps, just like he had been trained for tactical building entries. You didn't want to be stumbling over the miscellaneous stuff often encountered on residential floors. On the other hand, he ignored his training as he forced himself *not* to scan the room for any additional threats. He knew exactly who and where the threats were. All except for the last two anyway.

Glancing quickly at the cocked shotgun resting on the kitchen counter, Rob thought about the devastation the shotgun pellets could cause. He had seen the damage to human flesh and bone brought about by buckshot more than a few times--it was no joke. Still approaching at a slow walk, he lined up his pistol's front sight on the gangster's torso and fired twice. Predictably, the now terrified thug grabbed for the shotgun lying on the counter as he watched Rob coming at him. He was able to grasp the weapon just as two 9mm slugs struck him in his abdomen.

The gangbanger, still functioning despite being gut shot, raised the shotgun off the counter. As Rob pressed forward firing his Smith and Wesson, the guy discharged the shotgun. Fortunately for Rob, as the bad guy had realized there was a good chance his own life was about to come to a violent end, he had panicked. And this panic had caused him to pull the shotgun's trigger before he had pointed it at Rob, sending buckshot pellets across the counter top and harmlessly into the wall.

In contrast to the gut shot rapist, Rob controlled his own fear well enough to send four more rounds into his adversary's shoulder, neck, and face. Unfortunately for Rob, the wounds, while fatal, were not instantly so.

Like his cohorts seconds earlier, the mortally wounded man fell to the ground. Yet unlike his friends, he was not dead. He moaned unintelligibly as his badly damaged carotid artery dumped dark arterial blood onto the kitchen floor. Rob knew this guy's time left on Earth was going to be a matter of seconds, not minutes. But he had to focus on finishing the battle. Even more importantly, he had to survive it. He feared the remaining two gangsters, presumably located at another unknown part of the house, were going to come to their crime partners' aid at any moment.

Shit! These last two are going to be coming at me guns blazing. And any second now.

He had already used too much of his valuable ammo, but he needed to shut up the dying thug on the floor. Now.

Rob kicked the thug in the side of his head with all of the force he could muster. Then he immediately repeated this action, his booted foot making a second sickening thud as it impacted the man's skull. The moaning came to an abrupt end.

He tried to scramble to a different location in case the remaining thugs were heading toward the sound of the moaning. He slipped in the slippery blood pool and smacked his knee on the hard floor.

Shit. This doesn't happen in the movies!

At least he hadn't gotten any blood on his hands during the fall.

He wasn't sure exactly how many rounds he had left in his Smith & Wesson. He turned to face the hallway connecting the living room with the house's two bedrooms, eager to finish what he had started. At any moment he expected one or more of the bad guys to come down the short hallway to engage him.

He considered performing a "tactical reload"--dumping his mostly expended magazine and replacing it with a fully loaded one. However, he decided against taking the risk of being caught with an empty gun--or a gun with only one round loaded--even if only for the second or two required to change magazines. When you expected armed assaulters to appear at any second, a second or two could seem like a lifetime.

As it turned out, Rob's fears were unfounded. He heard a sliding window being opened at the other end of the house. He thought he heard the sound of one or more guys exiting through this window in a hurry. Apparently the last two bangers had opted to live to rape and pillage another day rather than risk dying in that house.

Real tough guys, thought Rob.

Now he performed his tactical magazine reload to ensure he had a fully loaded pistol. He shoved the mostly depleted magazine in his jeans pocket, making a mental note to reload it with the ammunition in his pack when time allowed. He exited the living room, retrieved his pack from the front lawn area, and re-entered the house. He opened his pack and found his box of 9mm ammunition. He topped off the magazine in his pocket and put it in the magazine pouch on his belt.

Rob entertained the notion of checking out the bedroom where he was sure he had heard the two gangsters fleeing, but after a moment's thought, he checked himself.

Stop thinking like a damn cop!

The barely audible moaning and sobbing brought his focus to another issue. He had to consider the welfare of the injured and traumatized teenager who was lying on the living room floor. The entire room was a nauseating mess, and he concentrated on breathing through his mouth

He went to attend to the two women on the floor. He failed to find a pulse on the older of the two after trying both her wrist and carotid artery. Upon turning her over to attempt CPR, he saw that the mother's throat had been slashed. He immediately turned his attention to the girl, who had ceased sobbing, and now wore a blank "thousand yard stare" on her face.

Not sure how to attend to her, he put his hand on her shoulder and assured her as best he could. It wasn't very effective. He spoke to her in a low voice, telling her that the bad men were all dead or gone. They would not be able to hurt her any more. She turned her head toward him, still wearing the blank stare.

"Do you have any injuries?" No response.

"Can you walk?" Just a silent nod for an answer.

Rob took her arm to help her to her feet. He was surprised when she reacted with a visceral aversion to his touch. A show of repulsion. Ignoring this reaction, he guided her out through the front door and helped her seat herself on the porch steps where she could get some fresh air.

"Wait here. I'll be back in a minute." Her expression gave no indication she had even heard him.

Rob knew there would probably be little or no investigation as well as no processing of the crime scene. He returned to where the girl's parents lay dead in the living room. He positioned the couple next to each other in a manner he felt was somehow more dignified and respectful than where they had been previously. He wasn't sure why he was taking the time to do this; after all they were dead. Nevertheless, he felt an obligation to this before he left the home. One last act of kindness and respect.

The severity of the tragedy here was inescapable, and it destroyed his ability to hold onto a belief that the world contained any semblance of fairness. A young family, through no fault of their own, had been completely destroyed in a manner of minutes. He wondered if the girl would ever be able to recover from what she had experienced.

Rob had no idea what to do about her. As he considered the magnitude of what had happened here during the last half hour, he was instantly overcome with such grief that he thought he might actually begin to break down and weep right there in the living room. But he fought through his despair. He told himself he had to compartmentalize his emotions if he wanted to have any chance of making it home.

Within a few moments, he had regained his steely determination and was ready to get back to taking care of the business at hand. He looked around and decided he should check the dead gangsters to see if they had any items that might be of value for his journey home.

Rob went to the dead gangbanger in the kitchen. He saw a large kitchen knife in the sink that was covered in blood, and assumed it had been used to slit the mother's throat. He briefly considered taking the knife as an extra tool, but couldn't bring himself to do it.

He picked up the sawed-off shotgun from where it had been dropped on the counter. He hefted its weight, noticing that it was a Harrington & Richardson brand. The overall length of the gun was no more than twenty inches or so, and it was surprisingly light. Rob opened the single-shot action and extracted the shot shell.

The double aught round was a proven man stopper, the impact being similar to nine small to medium caliber handgun rounds impacting at once. He searched the man's pockets and found four additional shells—all double aught.

Rob searched the other dead gangsters. One had a Glock.40 caliber pistol, but he could find no extra ammunition or magazines other than what was loaded in the pistol. The other guy had a .38 caliber revolver along with six extra rounds in a speed loader found in his pocket. Rob wondered if the dead gangster had any idea how to use the speed loader device, or if it had merely been acquired at the same time as the revolver.

Rob considered which, if any, of the newly acquired weapons he should keep. He was disappointed that none of the guns used the same caliber ammunition as his own Smith & Wesson 9mm. He placed all three of the newfound guns into his pack. He would figure out what to do with them later.

Walking back to where the girl was sitting on the porch, Rob showed her his sheriff's department identification, hoping to assuage any fears she might be harboring. She looked at the identification items but said nothing.

"I have some friends who live nearby who are very nice people. They're a good family. The mother is a nurse. I'm going to take you there so they can look after you, Okay?"

Once again, no answer.

"I know you're hurting really bad. I know that. But you have to walk with me or you won't be safe. I'm so sorry that this happened."

He felt the old familiar helplessness that so many cops experienced when trying to comfort the inconsolable following tragedy.

How was a mere cop supposed to help when shit as ugly as this happens? Just another reminder of how close to worthless we are during moments of human tragedy. The badge, gun, and authority given to us doesn't mean a goddamn thing. When it's all said and done, we're as fucking useless as everyone else when the victims need us the most.

Rob forced himself to exit the mentally dark place he had wandered into and redoubled his efforts toward focusing on what needed to be done.

He approached the front window, keeping himself out of view from the street as much as possible. He looked at his surroundings in search of any new threats that might have developed. Nothing he could see.

He noticed how almost all the neighbors had decided to "hole up" inside of their homes now. Not a single person had been seen following all of the gunshots and mayhem that had taken place at this house. Seeing nothing that caused him alarm, he took the girl gently by her arm and urged her out into the small yard and onto the sidewalk.

As they walked to the Browns' house, Rob's head on a virtual swivel looking for danger the whole time, he considered the pros and cons of the little sawed-off single shot shotgun. He was well aware of the limitations and disadvantages of the scattergun. The weapon had a very limited effective range--maybe ten to twenty yards maximum, whereas the pistols recovered from the gangsters would be effective at twice that range at least. Another drawback to the shotgun was that its ammunition was on the bulky and heavy side. But all of the above notwithstanding, with the double aught shells, the little shotgun was undeniably devastating at close distances

He decided he would keep it for himself.

Shortly after they had set out for the Browns' residence, Rob saw there was a large amount of dark smoke climbing into the sky about a mile or two south of their present location. It had not been present when he had entered the house to engage the thugs, or had it? Maybe he had just failed to notice it.

He glanced at the girl. "What's your name?"

"Rochelle," she replied in a voice so low in volume he wasn't even sure he had heard her correctly. He smiled and nodded, deciding not to press her any further for now.

They arrived in front of the Browns' house twenty minutes later. He called out to announce their presence before even setting foot onto the property. Kevin, apparently on security duty, opened the door. After a moment he waived them in, still displaying the family revolver tucked into his belt. It appeared as though the family had decided to continue using the front door despite Rob having suggested otherwise, but it did look like it was at least going to be guarded seriously.

All three of the Brown family stood in the entrance area looking at Rob. Gerald and Eunice wore expressions of curiosity and concern. Kevin looked mostly irritated.

The Browns were now looking at the teenaged girl as well as at Rob, obviously awaiting some sort of explanation. Rob asked to speak to Eunice alone in the front yard. He brought Rochelle with him, and introduced the two women to each other.

Eunice didn't want to wait for Rob—who was clearly in way over his head now—to explain. She addressed Rochelle.

"What happened honey?"

Eunice glanced over at Rob. "Why don't you let us talk alone Rob?"

"Uh, oh yeah. Sure."

Grateful for the chance to separate himself from the uncomfortable situation, he turned and went to join Gerald and Kevin.

He provided the men with a short version of what had happened. Then he looked Gerald in the eye.

"She's been through hell. I think having her stay here with your family would be the best thing for her, but of course that's gonna be up to you. At least I sure can't think of anything better."

Then it struck him. He had essentially brought the Browns another mouth to feed. And he had completely overlooked the possibility that Rochelle's home may have contained valuable food that could be used by the Browns and her. He had screwed up by overlooking that. He had also failed to take down the address in case the Browns wanted to visit the house for supplies.

Well, I guess Rochelle will have to show them her house later on...if it's not too late.

Eunice took charge of looking after Rochelle and guided the traumatized girl inside the house. Rob removed his pack and opened it up on the living room floor. He showed Gerald and Kevin the two handguns taken from the gangsters.

"I come bearing gifts," he said jokingly. But the men were too interested in what he had to say next to respond to the weak humor.

"These two handguns are for you guys. I can't carry all the guns with me, and I'm keepin' the shotgun. I decided to come back here and give 'em to you. I know you'll put 'em to good use".

He pointed at the revolver. "This one's a .38, so it uses the same ammo as the gun you already have."

"The Glock here is a forty cal, and it only has the ammo that's loaded in it right now. I figure your family could use a little extra help in the security department."

"Yeah. I hear you on that. And we appreciate it," Kevin said.

Rob looked at Gerald and then at Kevin. "Do you know how to use the Glock?"

A blank stare from Gerald, and Kevin nodded his head.

Without warning, Rob felt a light-headed sensation wash over him, followed by some difficulty in maintaining his balance. He reached out to get his hand on the living room wall to ensure he didn't fall.

"Hey man....you alright?" Keith looked at Rob with an expression holding as much suspicion as concern.

"Yeah, I think so anyway. Is there any way I can bother you guys for a place to take a nap for an hour or two. I think this whole thing that just happened has hit me pretty hard. Tired me out."

"Sure," Gerald said as he thrust his open hand out to indicate the sofa where Rob had spent the previous night.

Rob shucked his pack and kicked off his boots without fully undoing the laces. Then he let his body hit the couch hard. Less than two minutes later he was asleep.

***

When **Rob awoke**, he was aware he had slept a lot longer than just a short nap, but he wasn't certain just how long that had been. He sat up and looked at his watch. It read eight-oh-seven, and the sun was out. He swung his legs around and sat up on the couch. Then he stretched his arms and slowly but firmly used his hands to pull his neck upward in a stretching movement. It was still sore but there was no sharp pain or spasms.

When Kevin entered the living room a minute later, Rob was almost apologetic as he commented, "I'm sorry--I guess I crashed out all night."

Kevin's retort was an attempt at humor--and in his case--what passed for friendly male interaction. 'Yeah well, you know... you was a little busy yesterday. You needed some good sleep."

Kevin smiled at Rob. It was the first time Rob had ever seen the stern man's teeth.

Rob accepted a small breakfast of oatmeal and honey washed down with a cup of coffee, both of which were made possible by Gerald's propane fueled barbeque. He used the newly dug latrine and drank some water. He accepted a few ibuprofen tablets and downed them immediately. He was thankful his neck was doing better, and wanted to make sure the inflammation didn't flare up on him.

His thoughts went to Stephanie and Charlie Wyatt as he worried about how they were dealing with their situation out in Thousand Oaks. Then he wondered about his pals at Nadeau Station. Finally, he worried about the Brown family and how they would handle the hard times he felt certain were coming.

Shit man; I have to give myself a break here. I can't carry the weight of the whole world on my back! I need to keep my focus on getting home. to Thousand Oaks.

Before taking off he asked Eunice for a piece of paper and a pencil. Rob wrote his name, his wife's name, their address, and phone numbers on the paper. He requested contact information for them as well.

He looked at Eunice, hoping to appeal to her nurturing side.

"I have a favor to ask. If you don't hear from me after all of this craziness is over with, please try to get ahold my wife Stephanie and let her know what was happening here. I would want her to know why I didn't start walking home immediately after the EMP happened".

Eunice gave him a comforting smile and promised that she would.

Rob said his good byes to the Browns for the second time since arriving at their home. He hugged Eunice and gave Gerald an affectionate two-handed hand shake. Kevin, still on watch, presented his closed fist and Rob touched his own fist to his. Kevin said, "Keep it real, and be safe. Thanks for what you did man."

Rob nodded and then slipped into his pack and headed out the door at a fast walk. It was mid-afternoon already, and he wanted to cover some distance before figuring out a place, and a way, to sleep tonight. He allowed himself to think over his situation as he hiked along feeling the comforting weight of his pack.

What are my chances of making it home? Will I have to fight again? Will I be able to protect myself against whatever threats I am likely to encounter along the route home? Am I still a cop, or am I now just a husband and father trying to get home?

He was unable to come up with a single answer to any of the questions he had asked himself.

17

THOUSAND OAKS, CA

The sun rose on the fifth day following the EMP event just like any other beautiful Southern California spring morning, but it belied the status of the situation in the Flynn's Thousand Oaks suburban neighborhood.

After having given it a great deal of thought, Stephanie had seriously considered cutting off any further assistance to the neighbors, but she hadn't finalized her decision as of yet. She had played out the scenario many times in her head while lying in bed the previous night trying to fall asleep.

How long can I help them before they ask, or demand, that I give them some of our supplies? Isn't my first responsibility to our son? What if this thing doesn't get fixed for a long time? Anything I give to my neighbors is something that I can't give to Charlie Wyatt. Or to myself. Maybe things will be back to normal in a couple of days and I won't have to decide.

Realizing the problem with the scenario they faced was that sharing their limited supplies with the neighbors might eventually cause the Flynn family to run out of supplies for themselves, Stephanie began to think about her husband. Once again she began to wonder and worry what situation he might be dealing with at this moment.

Is he trying to get home? Did he stay at work? Did he even make it all the way to the Nadeau Station? What's going on in South L.A.?

Stephanie asked herself these questions for the hundredth time without any hope of answers.

Returning to her quandary of how to handle the issue of the neighbors and their needs, she played devil's advocate with herself. If she refused to share with Rosalynn and Rick, she could pretty well assume she would have severed their friendship forever, possibly even creating a couple of enemies. This could be the case whether the disaster lasted for months or only the next several days. People weren't likely to forget that kind of thing--ever. The unintended consequences stemming from the wrong choice could be serious as well as permanent.

Stephanie and Charlie Wyatt had eaten all of the refrigerator's contents they could before being forced to discard the small amount of remaining food as it began to spoil. She and Rob had discussed how to approach food consumption during a disaster, and it was a "no-brainer" that the refrigerated food would be eaten first, followed by the contents in the freezer. Only then would canned goods be used. The exception to this was when there were no more vegetables or fruit available other than canned goods. The freeze dried food, which claimed a shelf life of twenty five years, was to be saved till all of their other supplies had been exhausted. She hoped that things would be normalized before then.

Stephanie began to let her mind wander.

How long is this mess going to last anyway? Why haven't we seen any emergency response actions taken by the authorities? Are any of the governmental agencies going to get us some relief or what? What about all of the people who need medical attention? How will injured or sick people even be able to communicate their need for help?

She looked over at Charlie Wyatt, now busy with one of his toy trucks, apparently oblivious to the seriousness of what lay before them. She hoped to be able to continue to shield him from the conditions that surrounded them. She felt a little relief in knowing he rarely watched television--a deliberate decision she and Rob had made after he was born.

She wondered if any of her neighbors had heard any news about what had happened to cause the power outage and equipment failures, as well as exactly how wide spread the damage was. She was pretty certain she knew the answer to at least the first question, but she still yearned to hear any news about the situation.

This reminded Stephanie that Rob had included a small AM-FM radio in their emergency supplies. The radio could be powered by turning the small hand crank. Rob had demonstrated how to use it months earlier, but she had thought it close to ridiculous to have to wind the hand crank for a full minute only to get about two minutes of radio operation.

Now she wanted to get that radio out and see if it would work. She would gladly turn the crank for a few minutes to get a news report of some kind. The radio was stored with some of the other supplies inside of a large four-foot by two-foot by two-foot steel tool box positioned against an interior garage wall. It was the type designed to secure tools on a construction job site. Stephanie had no way of knowing that the super-sized steel tool box had unintention-ally served as what is known as a *Faraday Cage.*

The tightly sealed metal box had shielded the contents that were not touching the metal while stored. Sometimes it was better to be lucky than good..

Stephanie brought the radio into the kitchen and prepared to try it out. She read the basic directions taped to the device, and then began winding the small hand crank. She tried the AM and FM fre-quencies, but discovered only static. Well at least the radio itself was working. She told herself she could try again later.

One afternoon her neighbors, Rick and Rosalyn, approached her with a request for some of her emergency water. The couple knocked on her front door and invited themselves into the entrance area under the pretense of "checking in" on her. Stephanie observed with a combination of self-satisfaction and relief that Rick was clearly doing much better. He was now using crutches to walk around, his coloring looked good, and he was in decent spirits considering the predicament they were in.

It was Rick who brought up the subject of water. Stephanie saw Rosalyn had averted her eyes, suddenly finding something interesting to examine on one of the floor's large tiles. Stephanie inferred from this that this was in fact the primary purpose of the visit. Rob had always said that water was at the top of the list in importance during serious disasters. And now here it was: right in her lap for her to deal with by herself.

Stephanie thought she might have detected a trace of aggression on Rick's part when he asked for water. It reminded her of the manner displayed by some of the homeless people who panhandled as a means of obtaining money. Without actually overtly threatening the person being asked for a donation, there was often more than a little bit of insistence contained within the request. Rick was now putting out this very same "vibe". In fact, Stephanie thought she detected the slightest indication of a latent threat that hovered unspoken in the air.

Stephanie feigned a cheerful reaction, hoping to convey to her neighbors that she had arrived at a solution to their problem, despite the fact it was only a temporary one. She advised them to use the water contained in their water heater, adding that they should probably sterilize it before drinking it.

"A couple of drops of unscented bleach mixed into a gallon should do it. Let it sit a couple of hours before drinking it is all. Or, you can just bring it to a boil," Stephanie suggested. Just don't injure yourself," she said with a slight laugh.

Her attempt at humor fell on deaf ears. She had no way of knowing the couple had removed their forty gallon traditional water heater and replaced it with one of the new "tankless" heaters. The kind that required electricity to activate the heating element and had no water storage tank. Rick hadn't explained this to Rosalyn, but he knew he would soon have to. He was now starting to get angry and didn't want to lose his temper in front of Stephanie. It was time to go home. Rosalyn recognized something had happened to create her husband's sudden desire to end the visit, but decided to withhold her questions until they were back in their own house.

"Okay Stephanie; we'll check in with you tomorrow," Rick called out as the couple stepped out of the Flynn's home and onto the front porch.

In addition to the rare and brief gravity shower, Stephanie and Charlie Wyatt were utilizing a large squirt bottle filled with her emergency water with a splash of bleach (to battle the bacteria) for all basic daily hygiene needs. It came nowhere close to replacing the regular showers she had become used to for all of her life, but it was definitely better than suffering without bathing altogether. She figured that she would have to use a bit more water to wash her hair when she could no longer put it off, but that would be reduced to a weekly event according to her plan.

Stephanie and Charlie Wyatt had been using a makeshift latrine she had created with a garden shovel in the back yard. Charlie Wyatt warmed up to the procedure in no time, apparently finding it to be a fun change from using the toilet inside of the house. Kids could oftentimes cope better than adults in this regard.

The capable mother of one had also created a hand washing station using a common plastic bucket. She filled the bucket with a half-gallon of water, and then added a teaspoon of bleach into the contents. They each dipped their hands into the solution and rubbed them together when hygiene required and then allowed them to air dry. It was an effective means of maintaining a health protocol using only a small amount of water. She replaced the bucket's contents every twenty four hours or so.

Other than the growing collection of garbage being placed on the street curbs, including rotten food, plastic bags (some of which Stephanie suspected contained human waste), things were not that different than normal in their quiet suburb.

As mother and son sat in the living room, Stephanie reading a book, and Charlie Wyatt playing a game, she again let her thoughts wander off to Rob and what he was doing. She knew he was more than capable in dealing with emergencies that most would find too daunting to even try to manage, but she nonetheless worried. The truth of the matter was that she was past worrying. Her mind was someplace between worry and despair at this point.

After running too many possible scenarios through her mind, she walked over to Charlie Wyatt and asked him what he was doing. She saw that he was looking out the living room window in the direction of the street in front of their house.

"I'm waiting for Daddy," he answered. His comment about broke her heart right there.

Suppressing her emotions for what seemed like the hundredth time since the grid had gone down, she answered her little boy.

"Well Daddy might not be home for a while Honey," she answered, all the while trying valiantly to hide her own very real concerns, worry, and sadness from her perceptive child.

"I think he needs to come home now Mommy."

Stephanie didn't answer him. She smiled and pulled him toward her, giving him a tight hug, and then kissing him on the forehead.

"Well we'll just have to wait and see when he gets home Charlie Wyatt."

Stephanie let a few moments pass before speaking.

"Hey, how would you like to walk to the store with me?" she asked him.

He responded with a smile that gave her his answer. Then he threw out his little arms and said "Yes!" drawing out the word so that it took twice as long to utter as it normally would.

She doubted the local supermarket would be open but thought they might be conducting business in some manner despite having no electricity. She retrieved several five dollar bills from her purse. She saw no need to overpay for items if the store couldn't make change for larger bills.

The supermarket was located a half mile from their home in a medium sized shopping center housing a dozen other small retail stores. She figured most of the food in the market was probably gone by now, but she was hopeful that she would find something they could use. If nothing else, it would provide the two of them with a little exercise, not to mention a welcomed change of scenery and surroundings. She had Charlie Wyatt carry two large empty grocery bags while she had opted to wear an empty daypack. They both felt their spirits lift as they began walking down their suburban sidewalk. Unfortunately, they wouldn't remain lifted for long.

18

UNINCORPORATED SOUTHEAST LOS ANGELES

By day five after the EMP, Sergeant Marino had ordered the rest of the prisoners in the Nadeau Station jail to be released. He had only six deputy sheriffs who remained with him at the station. The rest of the deputies had individually decided, at different times, to leave the station and attempt to walk to their respective homes. When all was said and done, these deputies couldn't get past their invasive thoughts. Thoughts that involved their suffering families and their inability to help them.

The sergeant was conflicted about how he viewed this latest development. While he had always been big on values like duty and honor for patrol cops, he had a hard time demanding his charges remain at the station to protect the community while leaving their own families to fend for themselves after the entire societal infrastructure had collapsed. He reflected on the situation in the temporary privacy of his office.

The hard truth of the matter is the sheriff's department has failed to function during this entire damn disaster. We haven't seen a single reinforcement, or help of any kind, since this thing happened. How the hell did the department fail so badly? This is just un-fucking-believable!

Even on day one, Marino had harbored little doubt that the power outage and related problems they faced had been caused by an EMP. Now he had no doubt whatsoever. For about the hundredth time, he began wondering just how widespread the EMP event had been.

He surmised the lack of assistance or response of any kind up to this point was indicative of the event being extremely widespread.

This thing might have knocked out the infrastructure of pretty much the whole damn country, depending on how it happened. Not good. Not good at all. I guess it would be too much to ask for someone to figure out a way to let us know what the hell's going on with the country, the state, or L.A. County! Is it possible no one in the whole nation planned for this?

Still trying to reconcile how the entire system had crashed so completely, Marino went out the station's back door and felt the gentle warmth of the mid-morning sun on his face as he leaned against the building's wall, allowing himself a rare moment to partially decompress--relatively speaking anyway. He could even hear a few birds chirping.

Since when do I give a shit about birds singing? I like that I'm hearing it now though.

Under normal circumstances, the sounds of traffic would cover all but the loudest noises and sounds, but not now. It was quiet other than the periodic gun shots in the surrounding neighborhoods or the occasional sounds of yelling or screaming.

What bothered Marino more than the periodic sounds of gunfire was the unique smell of all the structure fires in the area. The unnatural smell of synthetic materials burning along with the wood used to frame the homes decades earlier wasn't exactly a new phenomenon for the cops assigned to this area, but it nonetheless assaulted their collective sense of smell, leaving each with a slightly queasy sensation.

The patrol officers remaining at the station could see at least a hundred dark colored smoke columns in the neighborhoods surrounding the sheriff building every time they went out to the parking lot to look around. Some of these were the result of improvised cooking fires or candles carelessly monitored. Others were caused by seldom used fireplaces whose non-serviced chimneys were full of combustible material.

And some of the burning homes had resulted from arson. Even under normal conditions, the infamous *Molotov Cocktail* fire bombs were a favorite means of retaliation and intimidation in the Southeast Los Angeles neighborhoods. In addition to those who had opted to settle old scores with fire, at least half of the currently burning homes had been caused by local reprobates who had no beef with the victims. They had simply wanted the entertainment value provided by a good old-fashioned arson fire.

So far, Marino's role of leader had not been challenged, and he hoped this would continue to be the case. Yesterday he had assigned two of the deputies, Gattuso and Anderson, to dig a latrine in a section of dirt located at the very rear of the secured parking lot. Of course the term "secured" was now a relative one. What was considered secure during normal times--even in this high crime area--was not so secure under the current conditions. He didn't like the feeling he was having about the security issue, but he had been living with the unease for the past several days. Marino was pretty sure that following the EMP event, the relationship between Gattuso and Anderson had developed into one that was more than that of merely patrol partners. The sergeant had picked up on the slight changes in how they looked at each other, and even the reduction of the previous healthy but rough manner in which they talked to each other. The veteran sergeant was right of course. The two had probably been attracted to each other, whether subliminally or otherwise, for a long time but had never let the relationship develop past that of patrol partners who watched each other's backs. Gattuso was married, trying to hold onto a long since damaged marriage for the purpose of doing what was best for his two kids. Anderson was single.

Given what had transpired at the Nadeau Station and its surroundings over the past several days, it would have almost been unusual if the evolution of Gattuso's and Anderson's relationship had *not* happened. The upshot of the matter was that their newfound romance—and whatever problems that might be attendant to the new relationship--didn't even register on his importance scale under the current conditions. As long as they continued to perform their assignments as well as they had been up till now, the issue would not be addressed.

The sergeant had requested the other deputies push one of the patrol cars in the lot in front of the latrine to provide some privacy. The earlier scavenger hunt around the station had revealed a supply closet containing dozens of rolls of the precious bathroom tissue. One of the deputies came up with a system of putting a roll of toilet paper on the car's antenna when the latrine was not in use. Among the several hand tools discovered during the search of the station was the full-sized shovel used to construct the latrine trench.

While performing one of his now routine perimeter checks, Marino took a good look at the big five gallon cooking pot that had been placed over the wire grill of the charcoal barbeque in the parking lot. He recalled how the station captain had wanted to have the big cooking device removed. Eventually good judgment, and the will to provide a little morale for the patrol officers, had won out. The barbeque had stayed.

Now it was being used as a means to heat water for basic hygiene and laundry.

He stopped and considered their situation. *If it hadn't been for the four hundred gallons of old water in the rusted water tank I found by dumb luck, things would be even worse right now. How the hell did we get hung out to dry in such a bad situation?*

He had summoned the deputies for a quick *sit rep* meeting, and they had now all arrived. As usual, two of the six were responsible for watching for outside threats--each cop covering 180 degrees of the temporary defensive perimeter. It was flawed, but it was the best they could do.

Marino looked at the station's remaining half dozen cops. He felt a mixture of emotions.

I'm not sure we made the right call by deciding to remain here at the station, but it's too late to rethink that now.

The bear-like sergeant took a long swig of water from his water bottle as he prepared to talk with the deputies. He found himself wishing he had something stronger than water to swig as he mulled over the growing problems and potential threats.

"Okay, I just want to discuss the situation and get all of your thoughts and ideas. I figure we should be doing this exchange of ideas thing at least twice a day."

Two of the deputies nodded in acknowledgement. A third deputy, a black man who at 6'3" and a solid 250 pounds, was almost as big as the sergeant, said nothing. His given name at birth was Rupert Kellum, but no one but his mother dared call him by his given first name now that he was a full grown man. He wore his hair razor shaved down to his dark brown scalp. He had shaved his head since he had first started the academy almost sixteen years prior. It was presumed, although no one currently assigned at the station knew for sure, that his shaved head had earned him the name of "Slick" from day one as a deputy sheriff. In any case, that was how all addressed him at the station.

He listened to the sergeant, respectfully keeping eye contact as he removed a can of Copenhagen chaw from his uniform shirt pocket, selected a pinch between his index finger and thumb, and then inserted the concentrated tobacco product behind his lower lip. He went through several cans of the stuff every week, which was why he restocked his locker with a new "log" of Copenhagen, ten full cans, every two weeks.

The powerful tobacco chewing deputy shattered one stereotype as a black man while at the same time fulfilling another one as a Los Angeles County *ghetto station deputy*. Slick was a dedicated amateur rodeo cowboy who participated in many of the police rodeo events all over the state. He was a good amateur steer wrestler, and he had several police rodeo trophy buckles to prove it. It was a hobby or sport that most cared little about, including his two ex-wives. Neither gave a damn how he chose to spend his off time as long as they received their alimony every month.

Slick sported an out of policy mustache that protruded a good inch or more below his mouth, almost reaching his lower jaw line. It was part of his cowboy persona—it was also a clear violation of LASD policy. But his supervisors left him alone.

Like many of the Nadeau Station patrol cops, he had earned a reputation among both the citizens and his fellow deputies. In his case it was a reputation that spoke loudly as soon as the big black cowboy stepped out of his radio car anywhere in the Nadeau Station patrol area. Unless they had only recently moved to the region, pretty much everyone knew who he was.

Even though his large physical size and grim personality had generally resulted in compliance even when he was a rookie patrol deputy, there was one specific incident that had cemented his reputation forever.

The incident was a horrific one by any standards. One of those nightmare scenarios where even a decade later, a patrol cop might wake in the middle of the night, get out of bed to pour himself three fingers of whiskey, and then watch TV in the hopes of forgetting the ugly event.

It involved a three-year-old El Salvadorian boy whose father had decided to hold his hand over a gas stove burner while a big cowboy patrol cop was forced to watch behind a locked steel mesh security door as helpless as if he were watching the horror show on a video screen. Forced to listen to the young boy scream in terror as his arm was held over a burning stove flame, Slick had picked up a hundred fifty pound boulder being used as an inexpensive landscape decoration, and then hoisted the big rock to his chest to mash the security door over and over. He eventually smashed his way through the thick steel screen and made his way into the kitchen. But not until after the sadistic father had caused irreparable burn injuries to the little boy.

Most of his fellow patrol cops complimented Slick on his performance during the ordeal of the burned young kid, making comments like "Good job" and "That was impressive big guy." A few of his co-workers made remarks such as, "I would've just shot the asshole through the screen door" or "I would have shot the lock off the door", but these comments were never made in front of Slick. While they may have been dumb enough to entertain such inane ideas, they weren't stupid enough to voice them where the object of their criticism could overhear them.

The sad truth of the matter was that Slick had begun second guessing himself after the incident. He had worked past his own psychological trauma, but the wounds were always there.

Later that night, long after the post-EMP meeting Marino had called in the station parking lot had broken up and the deputies all returned to their respective assignments, Slick told one of his fellow deputies he would be back in a few minutes. He found a place away from the others, tucked behind a parking lot outbuilding near the gas pumps used for fueling the patrol cars. He would suffer his demons by himself for a little while, the way he preferred it.

19

WESTCHESTER, CA

On **the sixth** day after the EMP hit, Rob trudged along in a northerly direction on a sidewalk currently devoid of people in the Westchester area of Los Angeles. Located only a few miles north of the Los Angeles International Airport, Westchester included older largely residential areas as well as a decent concentration of retail stores. It had taken him a lot longer to get this far than he had anticipated, and he wasn't happy about it. Circumstances just didn't seem to be cooperating.

After leaving the Browns' house in Inglewood, he had made his way to Century Blvd. and then travelled westward several miles, only to once again change direction just before reaching LAX. He began walking northbound on Sepulveda Boulevard, a large multi-lane street that under normal conditions served as a major traffic artery for the greater western Los Angeles area.

Prior to reaching the street he was now hiking on, Rob had come near the site of the airliner crash that he had witnessed several days earlier while standing at the side of the freeway with Gerald. While he had not actually seen the downed aircraft itself, or the remains of it, he had witnessed some of the collateral damage it had caused. And it wasn't pretty. He smelled the terrible consequences of the plane crash and its aftermath before he saw it.

Those who have witnessed fully involved house fires will tell you there is a pungent and unforgettable smell that accosts the senses. It consists of an unnatural combination of natural and synthetic processes that nature never intended to exist at the same time and place.

The extreme heat resulting from burning jet fuel and plastics, polymers, chemically treated woods, and living flesh, created a uniquely ugly smell. And this odor now permeated the areas surrounding the airline crash.

As Rob took in the scene of the burned down homes he estimated the fire had easily reached out a half mile from the crash site, destroying homes, automobiles, and other once valuable items possessed by those that had lived in the affected areas. Since there was currently no operational fire department to respond to the incident, the fire was clearly, and tragically, allowed to burn much longer than would have been the case under normal circumstances.

He found himself wondering about how the conflagration had eventually been put out.

Had it simply burned itself out after running out of fuel to consume due to streets serving as firebreaks, or had residents banded together to defeat the flames somehow?

Then Rob began wondering about how many people had been killed in the crash, not to mention the resultant burning of the surrounding neighborhood.

Hell, how many people were injured and then weren't able to get treatment for their injuries? Who had been forced to witness that kind of suffering, all the while standing by powerless to provide any help?

He willed himself not to think about how much suffering was endured by those who were burned and received no emergency medical assistance afterward. Rob shook his head and considered the random nature of the tragedy.

And to think that every one of these poor bastards had been busily involved in their day-to-day activities until the EMP had happened. Then their whole worlds changed on a fuckin' dime. Life's fair, ain't it though?

Rob contemplated the situation and eventually arrived at the conclusion that the real heroes in this thing were eventually going to be those who could put together the broken pieces of a society badly damaged. It wasn't going to be the military, the first responders, the teachers, or even the medical professionals that would be the heroes who brought America out of this mess. It was going to be the construction workers, the plumbers, the welders, and all those who could *build* things that would be afforded the title of "hero".

It had been 48 hours since Rob had indulged in what passed for a bath, and he was well aware of his own body odor. Two days prior the sweaty and oily lawman (or was he now a civilian?) had soaked his large bandana with the remaining water he had located in a large coiled residential garden hose found along his route in the neighborhood burned out by the airliner crash fire. Using the wet bandana to sponge bathe his most needy body parts, he was able to repeat the process several times before completely depleting the meager water supply contained within the hose. Rob wore his hair short in a style not too different than the style he wore as an active duty Marine, and he was thankful for the minimal amount of effort it required.

Due to the large numbers of people--most in groups of anywhere from three to ten individuals--he had seen roaming about looking for food, water, and who knows what else, two days prior Rob had elected to prolong his trip home in favor of minimizing the chances of contacting anyone. He had subsequently spent a few days in an area alongside the 405 freeway where the land had accumulated a good deal of large overgrown bushes offering him concealment. It just wasn't worth taking the chance of encountering desperate, and presumably violent, people if he could take any measures to avoid it.

The problem was that he only had limited food and water, which meant he could only hide out for so long before he was forced to move on. On the night he left the Browns' house Rob had been pleasantly surprised to discover one of the family (he suspected Eunice of course) had seen fit to put a zip-lock plastic sandwich bag containing crackers and peanut butter in his pack. The peanut butter was a smeared mess inside of the plastic bag, but he couldn't care less about that. He was simply thrilled to have the extra food. He also saw a can of tuna had been thrown into his pack without his knowledge. It was a welcomed surprise and would be put to good use.

He suffered terrible loneliness pangs on that first night, the incessant intrusive thoughts of his wife and son assaulting his mind mercilessly. He tried a whole host of approaches to try to trick his brain into thinking about other things, but the loneliness and yearning for his family never stayed away for long.

He suffered recurrent thoughts about the shooting incident that had gone down in the house near the Brown family. He was hard on himself for having hesitated to get involved initially. And he asked himself over and over if he could have prevented some of the terrible things that had gone down in that house if he had acted sooner. He had no regrets about the violent manner in which he had resolved the matter. The thugs had reaped what they had coming.

He had been averaging less than four hours of sleep every day since he left the Browns' home, but he had at least been able to keep himself minimally fed and hydrated. So far. He tried to harness the misery of the troubling dreams and thoughts to serve as extra motivation to press on and find his way home, telling himself that once he was reunited with his family things would be good again. He was of the opinion that the suburbs would take a little longer to unravel than the densely populated urban areas, but lately he wasn't so sure if he was right.

During one period of sleep while camping next to the freeway, Rob had a particularly vivid dream of a romantic evening he had shared with Stephanie not long after they had been married. The dream ended with a sensual scene of lovemaking in a beautiful luxury hotel. The experience had felt real to him while he slept.

Several minutes after he had awoken from this dream, he had found himself looking around at his miserable and depressing circumstances that made up his new post EMP surroundings. He was overcome with a blanket of despair that was almost too heavy to shake off. He had told himself repeatedly that he could make it home if he simply forced himself to focus on the objective.

The world already has enough pussies in it--I don't need to add myself to the list. I need to focus and get myself switched on. I can do this thing, and Stephanie and Charlie Wyatt need me. Just press on Rob had urged himself, trying to get motivated to carry on with his plan.

Rob looked around his present location carefully and in all directions, reminding himself to take time to focus on possible areas of concealment in an effort to spot anyone that might be hidden there.

Hell, just about every place around here is a possible hiding spot really. Who am I kidding here?

With the exception of a woman in her thirties wearing filthy sweat pants and an even dirtier t-shirt--who appeared to be looking for something in a pile of garbage stacked on the curb line in front of a two story house--he saw no one out in the open.

Unsure as to what accounted for the lack of people around him, he settled for hoping that these conditions would continue. In his judgment, the less chance he had of encountering anyone the lower the likelihood of finding himself involved in a problem. It was all about avoidance now.

The neck pain Rob had been suffering had begun to subside over the past few days. He had stopped taking the anti-inflammatory pills twenty four hours ago. It was now nothing more than a small nuisance that reminded him of its lingering presence every so often, and he was grateful that it would no longer be a significant issue for him.

Just keep marching. I've got to push on and make it home somehow.

Rob had opted to travel at night whenever possible in the hopes of reducing the chance of encountering trouble, but some nights cooperated in terms of natural starlight-- allowing him to see well enough for nocturnal foot travel--while others were too dark to see well enough to walk. He was amazed at how dark it could be with no street lights.

He had a small LED flashlight that used two small lithium batteries, but despite the low power draw, he didn't want to use the light unless absolutely necessary. In addition, he wanted to avoid the possibility of announcing his presence in advance with the light beam. It was amazing how far away even the smallest of light beams could be observed during heavy darkness. And to be seen under these circumstances was to possibly invite trouble.

Looking at his watch, Rob estimated he had approximately two hours left until the arrival of dawn. Over the past several days, he had developed a practice of selecting his sleeping location about an hour before first light. By doing so, he could spend a few minutes setting up his basic short term camp and then begin his fitful sleep while it was still dark out. He had learned a long time ago that trying to sleep when surrounded by sunlight was extremely difficult regardless of whether or not he covered his eyes. Starting one's sleep period when it was still dark improved the chances of getting at least a little sleep; and every bit helped.

The area he was now walking through was a combination of residential and retail storefronts, the former on one side of the street and the latter on the other. Every single one of the storefronts was no longer in possession of its windows; the telltale broken glass scattered all about the sidewalk. The store interiors no longer contained any merchandise, and there had clearly been a good deal of vandalism performed within the structures.

What's the vandalism all about anyway, he asked himself. *The stealing part of this situation makes some semblance of sense, especially if people are desperate and scared about not having what they need, but what the hell is all the pointless destruction all about? Is it just anger, frustration, or what the hell?*

All of the above notwithstanding, Rob had no moral problem with anyone, including himself, who scavenged through the stores at this point in time. Now things had devolved to the point where finding anything to help one's own survival was a definite need. He observed that a group of four or five men, all of them appearing to be homeless, had gathered inside of one of the empty vandalized storefronts. They all lay in various positions on makeshift bedding comprised of scavenged materials that were at least softer than the linoleum tiled floor. Several steel mesh shopping carts had been parked inside next to the new "residents", the contents of these including items ranging from canned food goods to plastic tarps.

Rob could tell the men had been homeless even before the EMP. He thought about whether they, and those like them, would end up handling the new post-EMP circumstances better than those who were used to having all of the western world's luxuries.

Walking thirty yards farther, he noticed one of the retail buildings bore evidence of a bonfire someone had built in the middle of the tile floor. Rob surmised that the genius responsible for the failed camp fire had likely discovered the smoke had nowhere to escape soon after the fire had gotten started, and subsequently had fled the smoke filled location. Once again, he derisively shook his head.

On the residential side of the boulevard, where he was currently walking, Rob saw piles of garbage and miscellaneous bags containing human waste that had been deposited along the curbsides. Some of the human feces wasn't even enclosed in bags, but had simply been wrapped haphazardly in newspaper and other available paper items.

Without working plumbing, people were obviously desperate to get the nastiest by-products of everyday life as far away from their homes as possible. The only problem was that there was no longer any garbage pick-up service. So all of the refuse began to accumulate and pile up. The flies surrounding the garbage and waste were constant, while the rats only showed themselves periodically.

Things are going to be really nice when people run out of toilet paper. No toilet paper and no water. Great fun. He shook his head back and forth at the thought.

When Rob first encountered the piles of refuse, he found himself employing his old trick of breathing through his mouth to avoid the nauseating stench that surrounded him. The combination of garbage, feces, and smoke filled air was one that he found difficult, or at least unpleasant, to endure. He surmised that quite a few residents in the area, now faced with having to cook and heat water without natural gas or electricity, had improvised ways to use wood or charcoal fires to accomplish these basic needs. The result was a heavy presence of smoke that endured throughout the day and night.

Eventually Rob decided to cross the four lane boulevard. By continuing to make his way northward on that side of the street, he created some distance between the source of the stench and himself. It was still unpleasant, but it wasn't as overpowering as it had been on the residential side of the street.

He needed to start thinking about finding a place to make camp for a short while.

Rob swatted his hand at a small cluster of bugs swarming near his face that he couldn't identify. The ubiquitous insects were smaller than flies, but they had not been a part of normal life before the EMP incident.

Wherever the bugs came from, it seems like they're now a permanent part of post-EMP Los Angeles. Just one more mystery related to this goddamn EMP thing.

The discouraged former deputy found himself regretting having not included a simple bug net to wear over his face as part of his disaster pack contents.

At least my feet are holding up to all this hiking, he thought with a degree of gratitude.

He had been distractedly looking down at his hiking boots as he walked along the sidewalk, forcing himself to keep placing one foot in front of the other, despite how tired he was. He knew better than to do this, having been told--as well as telling others—too many times to count how important it was to keep alert and constantly aware of his surroundings. Catching himself, he blamed this lapse on his being tired. He almost stepped on a dead cat lying on the sidewalk, the condition of its remains suggesting it had been there for more than twenty four hours.

When Rob looked up he saw the unmistakable soft glow of a fire possibly a hundred fifty yards in front of him. At this distance the fire looked small, but there was no way he could make an accurate assessment of its actual size. More important, he had no idea of how many people, and what kind of people, might be gathered at the fire. It appeared to be located along the sidewalk, or pretty near the sidewalk, but he couldn't even be sure about this.

When he was approximately a hundred yards from the fire, Rob made a right turn on a perpendicular sidewalk. He wanted to get a closer look at the bonfire scene, but he had to make sure he wouldn't be seen in the process. Even more than before, he was well aware of the pack he wore making him a target for would be robbers.

Rob had taken one of the several pieces of cordage from his pack and cut a piece about two feet in length. It now served as a make-shift sling (referred to as a *single point* sling in tactical circles) that he had clipped to the Carabiner so that the compact little shotgun hung suspended from his pack strap. It was a decent configuration that allowed him to have immediate access to the weapon if needed. All while having both of his hands free.

He didn't give a damn now what others might think about him walking down the sidewalk with the cut down shotgun hanging against his chest in plain view. Circumstances had deteriorated to the point where anyone walking in the public either did so at their own peril, had the security of a group, or they were armed. And of course none of these were necessarily exclusive of each other.

Looking around in virtually all directions as he hiked eastbound down the residential sidewalk, Rob made a left turn at the first inter-secting sidewalk, now heading north again. He made one more left-hand turn, heading west, and toward the bonfire. When he had come to about sixty yards from the blaze he saw that it had in fact been built in a small parking lot adjacent to a gas station. The gas station's retail snack shop had obviously been ransacked and vandalized, its store-front windows smashed and removed to the frames. The gas pumps themselves appeared to have been severely damaged as well, no doubt the result of numerous attempts to retrieve gasoline from the devices. Given the current stripped condition of the retail premises, it was apparent no one had any remaining interest in the location. It had been picked clean.

Rob battled against his fatigue as he carefully worked his way closer to the small bonfire. He saw half a dozen male characters standing as well as seated around the flames. The fire had been built with boards pulled off of wood pallets. A stack of additional pallets, removed from some nearby unknown location, and collectively about half the size of a semi-trailer, lay twenty feet behind the fire. He could see what appeared to be stacks of other smaller boxes not far from the pallets, but he could not identify what he was looking at from this distance.

Four of the men sat in lightweight metal framed patio chairs, no doubt taken from the yard of a local residence, while a couple of guys stood with their hands extended out towards the warmth of the flames. An animal consistent in shape to a medium sized dog hung suspended over a second fire pit located about twenty feet from the first. A six foot long wooden spit, no more than an inch or so in diameter, had been run through the entire length of the skinless animal allowing it to be positioned at the right height over the flames as well as allowing it to be rotated as it cooked. Even at this distance Rob could smell the meat cooking. He acknowledged, with a slight pang of guilt, that the aroma was stimulating his appetite.

All of the men looked like they were Latino, ranging in ages from late teens to early forties. They were of different sizes and builds, as well as being clad in a variety of clothing. One of the men standing in front of the fire, of average height and thickly built, wore oversized baggy jeans cinched in snug around the waist and a flannel shirt buttoned up at the collar but unbuttoned at the point of his navel and south. He looked to be about thirty years old and had a shaved head and a goatee.

Judging from the way he appeared to be holding court with the others situated around the fire, the thickly built man looked to be in charge, or at least like someone who held a good degree of influence over the others. Rob could hear several of the men talking, but couldn't make out enough to ascertain the content of the conversation.

Maybe it was the part of him that was still a cop, or maybe it was because he wanted to assess whether or not he was going to be forced to take a long circuitous path around the men in order to avoid contact. Or maybe he was simply hoping the group might look worthy of asking for some food. Whatever the reason, he suffered a lapse in judgment when he failed to turn around immediately and continue on his way.

He used the trees adjacent to the sidewalk as cover to reduce the odds of being seen as he made his way closer.

He could see well enough to identify some of the items that were stacked next to the pallets by the fire--at least fifty cartons of cigarettes, a hundred or more candy bars of various brands, a few score of various soft drink six packs, and at least this much beer. All of the pillaged loot was stored right there on the parking lot pavement under the direct observation of the hoodlums.

These guys have put together a damn store like some of the guys used to do in the L.A. County Jail. Any way to make a buck, regardless of the circumstances. It sure didn't take these guys long to take advantage of the situation.

Rob could now hear the voice of the stocky leader of the bunch more clearly. It seemed that he was having a debate with one of the others. Rob removed the little monocular from the small pouch where it was housed on the front of his pack strap.

One of the men spoke with the heavy accent and dialect that Rob immediately associated with the Latino gang culture.

"I'm tellin you *Ese*, this shit is gonna be so fuckin' easy it ain't even funny, *Ese*. There ain't any cops or nothing no more, *Homes*. We can just take that shit from them and nobody can do nothin. I'll take their shit and put a fucking cap in their ass; it don't matter to me, *Homes*. We can just hit one house after another and shit *Ese*; just keep going till we get tired of taking all their shit. Maybe we even get to mess with some *chicas* in those houses *Homes*". The gangster let loose with a cruel laugh at his mention of sexually assaulting women in the targeted residences. Some of the others joined in his laughter.

Another of the group, sitting in one of the patio chairs, made short work of a twelve ounce beer in an aluminum can as he listened to his companion making his pitch to the others to commit a home invasion robbery, and possibly a murder. Gazing straight ahead as if transfixed on some imaginary object, he crushed the red and white can into a small clump of metal and threw it fifteen feet across the parking lot where a pile of similar cans had collected. This guy had heard enough. It was time to take action. He broke his gaze and looked at the fellow gangster who had been making the pitch.

"Okay; fuck it then *Ese*; let's just do this shit then. I'm down for it right now *Ese*."

He stood up from his patio chair as he finished his announcement to the other hoodlums.

Listening to, and watching, the conversation, Rob wasn't sure whether the men were seriously planning a criminal caper that was going to happen right now or if they were just throwing out suggestions. Maybe they were merely calling each other's bluff. But one thing he had concluded after listening to the exchange was that this was a predatory group, probably gangbangers judging from the way they were talking. With this in mind, he had decided it would be wise to avoid the group by just about any means available, even if it meant having to take a route that would cost him more time. He had to avoid any conflicts if at all possible. And this one would likely be deadly.

Why the hell am I even watching them? I shouldn't even be here in the first place, Rob thought as he scolded himself for stubbornly holding on to some of his cop's curiosity.

Time to get the hell out of here!

Many years ago, when Rob was participating in Marine Corps field exercises, he learned one of the biggest dangers one faces when trying to watch another from a stationary position in the dark is the possibility of light reflecting off of one's face. A sure position giveaway. Although more often than not a Marine done up in tri-color camouflage face paint was an undeniably intimidating visual transformation, this was not the primary reason for the practice. The primary purpose for the paint was to minimize the odds of being seen by the enemy—a fact he would soon be reminded of.

Within seconds of having decided to haul ass out of there and accept the fact it would cost him some extra effort and time to allow the thugs a wide berth, trouble had arrived. Big time. He hadn't even started to turn around when one of the gangsters looked in his direction and immediately held up both of his hands at shoulder height, wordlessly beckoning the others around him to cease all conversation and movement. Head jutted forward in Rob's direction, and still holding his hands up, it was obvious he was intently focused on something. And Rob knew that the something was him.

Shit!

The man dropped one of his hands, reached behind his back, and pulled out a black pistol that had been tucked into his rear waistband. He quickly and roughly stood up, noisily kicking the flimsy metal chair several feet to the side in the process.

"Hey, check it out *Ese;* somebody's standing over there *Ese.* I just barely saw him right now. Let's go check it out and see what the fuck that *pendejo* is doing," he yelled at the other thug he had been talking to seconds earlier as he broke into a jog, gun outstretched in front of him, and headed toward Rob.

Rob knew right away that he had to move. Now! He turned and started running as fast as he could, all efforts to maintain silence and concealment abandoned. His pack shifted uncomfortably on his shoulders as he pushed his legs as hard as he was able.

There was only one thing in the whole world he cared about. He wanted to keep as much distance as possible between himself and those chasing him. He frantically looked at his surroundings, turning his head from side to side, desperately hoping to find some place offering a chance at escape. He knew the closest pursuer was probably less than fifty yards behind him, but he wasn't confident he could maintain that lead for long.

20

THOUSAND OAKS, CA

As the mother and son came within a half block of the shopping center, Stephanie saw a scene that sent her heart racing. She saw a hundred people or more carrying items in their hands and arms. These people were spread throughout the large parking lot as well as along the sidewalks in every direction leading away from the shopping center. The scene reminded her of one associated with other parts of the country, or other parts of the world: anywhere but this suburb. Yet here it was, right in front of her.

The items being carried away included computer lap-tops, tablets, mobile phones, household appliances, clothing items, and other miscellaneous household devices. She mused briefly over how the thieves expected to use any of the items requiring electricity. It would have been funny were it not so serious, and dangerous.

There were also persons carrying different types of containers, everything from cardboard boxes to plastic storage bins. Judging by the apparent weight these containers held, they were filled with other goods.

Food or beverages maybe, she wondered. *No matter. It's definitely time to turn around and go home.*

Almost at the same time she had made the decision to turn around she saw three men on the sidewalk not far from the edge of the shopping center parking lot. They were less than thirty yards from where she stood with her son. She watched them approach a woman in her early sixties. It didn't look like this was going to be a friendly encounter. The woman held a cardboard box that appeared to require all of the strength her two arms could muster just to hold it up. The woman looked tired, even at the distance from which Stephanie watched her.

All three were white and in their early twenties. Two of the men wore sleeveless t-shirts that displayed the voluminous tattoos on their arms. They were of average height and had thin but muscular builds. Both wore their hair shaved to the scalp. One had a white scalp indicating it had probably only recently been shaved.

The long pony-tail worn by the third man was probably dark blond when it was clean, but it was now a dark greasy color. Stephanie could tell, despite the sweatshirt covering his torso, that this guy was both taller, and more heavily muscled, than the other two. He demonstrated difficulty in holding still. He stepped from place to place and moved his hands incessantly. Stephanie accurately concluded that this creep was wired on something stronger than coffee. Even at this distance, Stephanie could see that pony-tail man had a prominent tattoo on the right side of his neck. It was a large five pointed star done with black and red ink.

All three men wore jeans and boots similar to those commonly used by men working in the construction field. She could tell that the interaction taking place between the woman and these three was full of tension. She saw the guy wearing the sweat shirt take a quick look around in all directions. Then he used both hands to grab the box held by the woman. The woman resisted letting go of the box, and one of the men wearing a sleeveless shirt struck the woman.

Stephanie wasted no time in grabbing Charlie Wyatt by the shoulders and forcefully turning him around so that he was facing away from the brutal scene. At least now his small back was positioned toward what she feared was soon to become a terribly violent scene involving the woman and the three low-lifes. But despite being frightened by what she feared was about to happen, she continued to watch the scene unfold.

It is a common misconception that evil men are also always cowards. In point of fact, the two are separate categories, and they do not always go hand in hand any more than they are mutually exclusive. While most predators will seek out victims that are incapable, or at least less capable, of offering effective resistance, some evil men are not dissuaded by the possibility of engaging an opponent or victim that can hurt them.

To be sure, pony-tail man was a brawler without a properly functioning conscience, but he was not a coward. Over the years he had willingly engaged in many a street fight where his opponent was physically tough, in rare cases even besting him in the hand to hand weaponless battles. No, he was not a coward; but he was definitely a sociopathic brawler who would ply his penchant for violence and cruelty against defenseless victims or capable opponents with equal enthusiasm. Whatever the case, what he was about to do now was ugly stuff, and it sure as hell didn't involve courage.

Continuing to watch the scenario unfolding, Stephanie saw her fears confirmed. The pony-tailed man with the large star tattooed on his neck hit the unsuspecting middle-aged woman without warning, hesitation, or preamble. And he hit her hard, with a closed fist. His fist, toughened over years of brawling, collided with the woman's cheek, shattering her delicate bone structure, causing severe damage to her orbital socket and eye. She was knocked out completely in an instant. Had she survived, the woman would have never used that eye again.

The box she held fell to the ground, spilling the miscellaneous food items that had been contained within the box. The fact that Stephanie's earlier question about the container's contents had just been answered as the items within came spilling out was of no consolation to her as she watched in horror.

The woman fell to the ground, the back of her head bouncing off of the cement sidewalk like a grotesque over-ripe melon. She would never recover, making her one more fatal statistic indirectly attributed to the EMP event. The thug with the sweatshirt picked up the box while the tank-top clad man next to him quickly picked up the food items and tossed them back into the box held by his buddy.

The psychopathic savage with the strong right cross walked over to where the dead or dying woman lay on the ground, looked at her, and then raised his hands up in some sort of a twisted victory gesture.

The other two sociopaths, apparently completely disinterested in the actions of their cohort, simply began walking, one carrying the box of food. Joined by ponytail man, who had given up on his little victory performance, all three walked off together.

Seemingly out of nowhere, two well-intentioned men approached them, yelling at them to stop as they drew near. Both men, having just witnessed the attack and robbery of the late middle aged woman, were intent on holding the thugs accountable. It was too bad that neither of them had figured out exactly how this was going to be accomplished. In fact, neither had the slightest notion of a plan. They just knew they had a moral obligation to stop the three cretins.

One of the two Good Samaritans was in his early forties, the other five years older. Although each of the approaching men was clad in casual clothing, they both had the appearance of men that were in their element when inside of an air conditioned office wearing three piece suits. Perhaps, within the corporate arena, professional protocol demanded that one announce his or her intention before surprising another with a confrontation. But in the arena of the street, and that was clearly what this normally laid back suburb had turned into, telegraphing one's intentions in a potentially violent confrontation was a mistake. And these professional corporate men were soon going to pay for this mistake. And the cost was going to be high.

As they approached the three predators, pony tail man took two short steps toward the younger of the pair and kicked him in the balls without so much as uttering a "fuck you". The injured man's knees buckled, and he fell forward, vomiting on the sidewalk as he lay there in agony intuitively trying to use his arms to protect his face and head. Unfortunately, it was not quickly enough to avoid being kicked in the face by the same foot that had seconds earlier smashed his testicles. While the man with the damaged testicles and broken face writhed on the sidewalk that was quickly becoming covered with his bodily substances, the other two bad guys jumped his shocked friend.

Both accomplices punched the older of the two corporate men a half dozen times each, all of the blows landing with serious impact. The violent punks became immediately cognizant of how soft and defenseless their current victim was compared to those they were accustomed to hitting. The conscienceless brawlers were used to fighting in meat market bars and wild parties, both environs that were full of self-proclaimed tough guys spilling over with testosterone, equally likely to manifest itself in sexual conquest or fist fights.

The second corporate man tried to support himself on his hands and knees after having fallen to the sidewalk next to his friend, imploring through a mouthful of blood for the men to stop beating him. Pony tail man walked over and delivered two snap kicks to the dazed victim. The first of the kicks broke three of his ribs, while the second shattered his jaw, knocked out two teeth, leaving him folded over and seconds away from passing out.

The other people in the area either ignored the incident altogether or quickly walked in the opposite direction, trying to put as much distance between the violent three men as they possibly could in as short a time as possible. Pony-tail man, for reasons unknown, suddenly looked directly at Stephanie and showed her a smile that never reached his eyes. Then he looked away, once again giving his full attention to his accomplices and the situation before them.

The three thugs didn't even bother to wait to get to wherever they were headed before pulling out several food items from the box they had taken from the woman. They discarded the food packaging on the sidewalk and hungrily consumed it as they laughed and walked toward their destination.

Unlike the moral and ethical dilemma her husband had agonized over at the Inglewood house of horrors, Stephanie didn't hesitate for a single second as she decided what she needed to do. She knew immediately, without the slightest reservation, that it was all about protecting her son, and by extension herself. She was not tempted in the least to go render aid to the poor woman, or the two *do-gooders*, who lay on the sidewalk.

Nor did she even consider for a second that she should attempt to notify someone about what she had just witnessed. Her present circumstances constituted a complete paradigm shift from her normal life and she knew it. Stephanie knew the right thing to do, in fact the only thing to do, was to grab Charlie Wyatt and get both of them to the relative safety of their modest home as soon as possible.

The force used to change directions and urge Charlie Wyatt hurriedly in the opposite direction from which they so happily marched just a minute ago communicated much of her anxiety and fear to the now tearful four year old.

What the hell was I thinking? That was really stupid to think we could just walk to the shopping center with all of this craziness going on. No more lazy thinking or wishing things were different than they are Steph. You gotta get yourself together.

As Stephanie walked home as fast as she could with Charlie Wyatt in tow, her mind was working in overdrive. She was making a basic list of priorities that she would address as soon as she cleared the front door of their home.

She had experienced an epiphany while watching the brutal attack and robbery moments earlier. This realization had immediately formed her decision about whether or not she was going to share supplies with her neighbors. They were going to have to fend for themselves from this point on. She had to devote all of her efforts, and make every decision, keeping in mind her top priority—taking care of Charlie Wyatt and herself.

Stephanie flung the front door shut behind her and locked the deadbolt immediately upon walking through the doorway with Charlie Wyatt. She released his hand from her own, told him to wait for her in the kitchen, and went straight to the lock box that housed the revolver. Largely due to her nerves, it took her three attempts to open the simple combination lock mechanism before she was rewarded with access to the contents. She examined the dark colored revolver as though for the first time. It was a .38 caliber Smith & Wesson .model 19 with a four inch barrel, but this was of no importance to her. All she cared about was that it offered her some sort of a chance to protect her son and herself.

She picked up the belt and holster lying next to the lock box. The determined and highly focused housewife threaded the leather belt through her jeans, fiddling with the holster until she was satisfied with where it was positioned on her body. She recalled that Rob had given her some basic instruction about how to wear and use the holster way back when, but now she couldn't remember any of it.

Stephanie recalled Rob instructing her to empty the revolver and familiarize herself with it for a few minutes before reloading it and wearing it in the holster. She felt guilty about the level of resentment that passed through her as she tried to recall what else her husband had said so long ago about using the gun she now held in her hands.

I can't believe it, but I'm actually angry with him for being right about stressing the importance of learning how to use this damn thing!

After spending a minute with the revolver, including ensuring that she could yank it out of its holster quickly if desired, she reloaded the empty cylinder and slid the handgun into its holster. She fastened the holster's retention strap with an audible snap to prevent it from being dislodged accidentally.

Stephanie looked at the two speed loaders that were still in the box where the revolver had been moments earlier. She considered trying to familiarize herself with the small cartridge holding devices constructed of plastic and steel, but gave up on the idea. She had never allowed Rob to show her how to use the damn things, and now wasn't the time to take on a new learning project. So she decided against removing them from the lock box. She did, however, take a dozen cartridges from the full fifty round cardboard ammunition box that was in the lock box. She put these extra cartridges in her jeans pocket. She knew how to reload the revolver's cylinder the slow way (one round at a time) if necessary.

This is good enough, she told herself.

A thought came to her as she finished arming herself. She knew that Rob had a large gun--either a rifle or a shotgun--that he kept locked up in a large steel tool chest in the garage. She briefly considered whether she should try to get access to this firearm as well, but dismissed the idea out of hand. She had no idea how to use it, and she didn't have the combination to the large padlock that secured the tool chest.

No, she told herself, *that will have to wait until Rob comes home. Then he can use it to protect all of us. If only he would just get home.*

After returning to the front door, now wearing her holstered and loaded revolver on her belt, she double-checked the deadbolt. Then she began looking around the house, room by room, conducting a plan in her head for how to begin fortifying the place. She was holding Charlie Wyatt's hand, bringing him with her while she performed her survey of the entire house. She ignored his frightened and confused expression for the time being, intent on finishing her security check of the premises.

God, I wish Rob were here to help us. God, please bring him home to us.

She then lost the battle of wills with herself and began to weep, hugging Charlie Wyatt tightly against her chest as he too began to cry.

21

UNINCORPORATED SOUTHEAST

LOS ANGELES

The **last two** deputies rounding out the six remaining at the post EMP Nadeau Station, not counting Sgt. Marino, were a couple of young cops in their mid-twenties. Mike Mori was a third generation American; Raul Cruz was a second generation American. The former's ancestors were Japanese, while the latter was a Cuban-American whose family had emigrated from a pre-Castro Cuba just before the communist dictator had taken over the beautiful island.

Neither of the two assigned partners and good friends was more than five foot seven inches tall, and while both were reasonably fit, they were merely average in build. Cruz spent minimal time in the gym and Mori spent next to no time there. They were not avid runners either. In this sense the two were a bit unusual for being Nadeau Station patrol deputies, where the average deputy was around two hundred pounds or more, and those that were smaller generally compensated for this by staying in above average physical condition.

The above notwithstanding, Cruz and Mori earned their place in the alpha personality pool of deputies by virtue of their gun handling and related tactical capabilities. The strong and competitive work ethic each possessed, measured mostly by felony arrest numbers, didn't hurt either. They shared a devotion to tactical shooting sports and the police and military world of tactical firearms related training. Each of them had won numerous trophies for various shooting events, in both the law enforcement and civilian worlds of competition. With the possible exception of one deputy assigned to the Nadeau Station, a college linebacker sized patrol cop named John Purnell, who had been involved in several deadly shootings during the previous decade, Mori and Cruz had no equals among their fellow patrol cops when it came to tactical and shooting knowledge.

The partners spent a lot of their off-duty time hanging out together as well. Both made it a habit—whether on duty or not--to dress in a "tactical" manner. This included BDU style trousers, fragment resistant sunglasses, and lightweight *tac boots*. And more. Neither was married, which allowed them to spend all the time they wanted in pursuit of their hobbies. More than a few of the girl-friends over the years had been known to make jokes, or complain about, the many times conversations had been steered into tactical training, shooting, or other work related matters. For them, shop talk was the only talk.

They were also extremely competitive in their monthly arrest statistics. Not only with respect to measuring their performance as a team against other patrol car teams, but against each other. Neither Mori nor Cruz had ever had to shoot his gun in the line of duty, which placed them in the minority category at the Nadeau Station. However, most of their fellow patrol deputies thought it was a safe bet to assume that sooner or later they would find out how much difference existed between the world of shooting competitively and shooting another human being.

Rob Flynn had always thought that the department, and even many of the individual station deputies, had failed to recognize or uti-lize the skill sets these young tactical wizards had to offer. Both Mori and Cruz had proficiency levels that would have landed them training positions at any of the nation's top tactical schools. But they wanted to be patrol cops. Moreover, they wanted to work at what each of them considered the best patrol station in the U.S. Rob had sown the seeds of friendship with these two during their training periods at the station, the whole time being careful not to encroach on the pseudo-sacred relationship that existed between patrol trainee and field training officer. Consequently Rob had gleaned a lot of tactical knowledge and gun handling skills that were not generally made available to patrol cops.

As Sergeant Marino stood with the deputies in the parking lot, they heard over a dozen gun shots in a ten minute period. Some of the shots sounded like they were less than a block away, but it was often difficult to tell. None of the cops present showed any reaction to the gunfire. The sounds had become such a common occurrence that it almost served as a substitute for the absent vehicle traffic noise.

An unusual sound grabbed the deputies' complete attention. The throaty rumble of an old eight cylinder motor, reminiscent of a time when powerful muscle cars were a common sight, could be heard moving at a fast clip not far from the station. Several of the patrolmen wore silly smiles as they listened to the old and powerful car. The sound grew less and less audible as its distance from the station increased until it could no longer be heard at all.

"Well, sounds like someone's got some transportation around here at least," Cruz remarked.

"Yeah; I wonder where he came from, or where he's going," Marino said. "Whoever he is, he better have a damn good way to protect that car or he won't have it for long around here."

After discussion had run out about the old muscle car, Marino raised the issue of the growing number of people sleeping and hanging out by the station's front doors. The decision had been made to lock the doors and tell anyone outside that nobody would be allowed into the building--no matter what. They had tried to order the desperate souls to leave the premises but they had refused. To describe what they were doing as "camping" would have been a poor description, but whatever they were doing, few were leaving. Some were apparently too afraid to even leave the area for the short time required to perform toilet functions. Instead they took care of these needs within sight of the building entrance.

It was one more thing to irritate Marino.

Over the past 48 hours a handful of the hoodlum types had thrown small rocks, bottles, and other miscellaneous items they could find at the front of the building to display their resentment at being denied entrance. It was obvious the crowd was taking on an increasingly hostile tone as time went on.

The deputies were also forced to watch many of the thugs periodically show up in front of the building to taunt them. Not only were they throwing items, they yelled vulgar insults, and a few even pulled out their penises, wagging them at the deputies as a display of absolute contempt. It was all activity the deputies had seen before during periods of "unrest" in the area, but now it portended more serious trouble.

A brutal incident that had taken place the previous afternoon was still fresh in Mori's and Cruz's memories. Three gangsters, all across the street, but in direct line of sight of the station front lobby, had viciously beat a weakened elderly man for over a full minute without stopping. They had presumably picked the front of the sheriff's station to do this for the sole purpose of tormenting the few deputies remaining at the station. It was as if they sought to remind the cops of their impotence and powerlessness under the new conditions.

Two of the punks used sections of galvanized steel pipe, striking the victim repeatedly on his legs and back as he lay curled up in a fetal position. The third kicked the man several times as he lay unconscious on the cement not twenty five yards from the front of the sheriff's station dying. Then he went through his pockets.

Discarding his tactical wisdom due to emotional overload while watching the attack, Cruz ran out of the station with his handgun drawn. All three bad guys saw him way before he was anywhere near approaching them and slowly walked away from the elderly dead man. The oldest thrust his arm up over his head as he gangster-shuffled away, contemptuously displaying his middle finger. Mori knowingly violated the security protocol established by his sergeant when he ran out of the station with his Remington, scanning the crowd for any direct threat to his partner. *You never, ever, let your partner or team member enter into a high risk area by himself!*

Cruz considered shooting the guy making the obscene hand gesture as he walked off—he knew he could make the shot--but he reminded himself he could still be held accountable for his actions after things returned to normal. Also, he told himself he should preserve his ammo for more pressing matters that might be coming. He drew the sad but accurate conclusion that the elderly man whom he had watched being beaten to death would most likely not have survived the post EMP conditions in any case.

Both deputies took notice of the growing number of dead that could be seen on the sidewalks and other places in open view. None of the station people had come up with a plan for that yet. But it was going to need to be addressed pretty soon.

When they had returned to the station, Mori was pissed off.

"So how long does it take for a first world nation to turn into a third world nation," he asked with a strong dose of vitriol.

Cruz responded without humor.

"About forty eight hours based on what we saw during Hurricane Katrina. Looks like L.A. is about the same. Except we got nobody coming to help us so far."

Sergeant Marino took a swig of the orange contents from his plastic water bottle while he stood in the station parking lot. The substance had been created by straining a small portion of the water tank contents through a clean t-shirt and then boiling it. A small amount of orange colored powdered mix, purloined from the jail supplies cupboard, was mixed in to cover the taste. Marino screwed the cap back on the bottle and grabbed the container by its neck as he began talking.

"I'm starting to get a little worried about what's gonna happen with all the people that are collecting in front of the station. We're getting more of them showing up every hour it seems. And some don't look like the nicest folks in the community either. They probably think we have a huge supply of food and water in here...I dunno."

Cruz piped up and said, "Sarge, this thing is gonna eventually go ugly here. At some point they're going to get desperate enough to break out the station windows, and then what?"

Gattuso commented, "There's no question, man; these guys are gonna get to the point where they don't give a shit and we all know how it'll go down as soon as the first one breaks through the glass.

We all know at that point it's gonna go seriously western *inside* the station!"

Mori also had an opinion on the situation. "I hate to break the bad news to everybody here, but we got a serious problem if it goes down like that. From a tactical point of view, we can't secure this place once the front of the building gets compromised--especially if they decide to hit us from the back or the sides after they start coming in through the front. We just don't have enough bodies to defend against that."

Mori looked at Marino and then Cruz anticipating a response from one or both of the other two tactically oriented minds in the group. Cruz held eye contact with his partner, his right hand holding his chin, and then slightly nodded his head several times. He had come to the same conclusion.

Anderson briefly caught her partner's eye before doing the same with Marino. Her searching expression was a clear indication that she was uncomfortable with the scenario they all faced, as well as being at a loss for how to deal with it.

Slick, for his part, appeared to be unconcerned by the whole situation as he propped one of his booted feet on the bumper of a patrol car and then leaned over, resting his forearm over his thigh. As usual, he had his lower lip packed with chaw as he paid silent attention to his fellow deputies while they offered their opinions. The manner in which he watched them suggested, without conveying arrogance, that he already had his mind made up as far as what and how he was going to handle things when the proverbial shit hit the fan inside the station.

Gattuso was also silent when it came to offering an opinion about the likely pending confrontation with the crowd. He and Anderson had both retrieved their *Kevlar* protective helmets from their "war bags" and had kept them handy following the first incident of rocks and bottles being thrown at the front of the station. But it now seemed like a completely inadequate preparation for what possibly lay in store for them.

Marino found himself battling despair while he stood there listening to, and watching, what was left of his patrol force. They only had five deputies at a time to use for station security. This allowed one deputy at a time to sleep for four hours. Every so often, Marino would stand in for one of them to give them a little extra rack time. The deputies slept wearing all of their clothes with the exception of their boots and heavy gun belts. They kept their weapons and flashlights within arm's reach. Not for the first or even tenth time, Marino thought about how they had found themselves in this situation.

I made a mistake by deciding to stay here and protect the station. What the fuck was I thinking? As soon as I realized we weren't going to get any help or supplies the writing was right there on the wall to see. By day two it was obvious we couldn't protect the community anymore, so what was the point of staying to protect the station when the department management didn't even give a shit enough to help us out? The station is just a building in the end. Is the idea of surrendering so unacceptable that I am willing to sacrifice all of us? And how many fuckin' times did I approach the high ranking management types, all but begging them to take station preparation more seriously? They always had some reason to say no. Instead, time and time again they spent money on useless programs. What a bunch of assholes...and now here we are with our butts hanging out unprotected in the wind.

Like the other football player sized cop in the group that now stood around discussing possible scenarios and reaction plans, his inability to let go of his role in the burning of a little boy well over a year prior weighing like an albatross around his neck, Sergeant Dave Marino carried his own personal load of dissatisfaction--or perhaps good old-fashioned guilt--about the decision he had made to remain at the station.

Marino addressed the group again.

"I've been thinking about this. It's going to come down to us being the ones who will handle any hostile entry into the station. By ourselves. We need to view it as a deadly threat, plain and simple. Anybody here see it differently?"

Slick pulled his head up from its position where he had been watching a small bug scurry across the asphalt and looked directly at the other big man who had just made that heavy statement. He seldom offered opinions in discussions like the one going on at present, but he spoke to what he had just heard.

"Is the department gonna be good with us handling it that way--or better yet, is the DA's Office gonna be alright with it? You know how they like to put a case on a cop...cops working in areas the D.A.'s are afraid to even drive through in the daytime. Shit, one a those cops hits a bad guy too hard and they're ready to file charges on the cop. I wouldn't trust them to do the right thing when all this is over. Hell no."

He spat a stream of Copenhagen onto the ground after making his comment, effectively adding punctuation to the remark.

Several of the others began echoing Slick's cynical view, each of them having either experienced, or at least been made aware of, incidents where patrol cops were given a hard way to go over use of force incidents. To a person, every one of the six deputies viewed the concept of "appropriate and lawful" use of force being judged by those who hadn't been in a fistfight since grammar school as being tantamount to virgins giving advice on love making. Or even advising on how to run a brothel.

Harris, who had been silently watching and listening to all of the others in the group, finally gave his own opinion on the subject matter. His silence up to this point was unusual, but his profanity laced language and direct manner of speaking were not.

He looked from face to face at the deputies around him.

"In case anyone here hasn't figured this shit out by now, we got abandoned. So none of that shit fucking matters anymore. Fuck the department brass and especially the D.A.'s Office. They shouldn't even register at this point in our decision making. Period."

Harris half way expected the sergeant next to him to make a request that he dial it back a little, but the rebuke never came, implied or otherwise. After Harris had continued his rant a little longer, Marino stepped in. It was time to get everyone back to their respective posts. Marino held up his big open right hand as he would to halt traffic. Within seconds the group was quiet.

"Here's the way I see it. If we let anyone get into the station who's intent on attacking us, it's an imminent threat to our lives. And if anyone here doesn't see that, let's discuss it right here, right now. As far as I'm concerned, I have to agree with Harris. Screw the D.A. and the department management people. You know you don't ever hear me bad-mouthing my superiors to the troops, but I guess that's about to change."

Marino looked around to see if anyone wanted to interject. Silence.

"They left us out in the open with nothing! And this started way before this EMP thing ever happened. Me and some of the other sergeants on the department tried to warn them about this way back after the World Trade Center attacks went down in 2001. After they started sending us to the terrorism classes and we got made aware of the threats that are actually out there. Shit, they didn't even prepare this station with supplies to handle a major earthquake, which everyone with half a brain agrees is gonna happen at some point. They just didn't give a shit is all. They figured it was going to be someone else's problem!"

Looking at the group to see if anyone wanted to challenge him, he paused for a moment before continuing.

"Look guys, I have to tell you that I feel bad, or maybe responsible at least, for our current situation. I basically convinced all you guys to stay here, telling you that it was our duty and everything. And now we're in a pickle because I got no idea how we're gonna be able to stay here if we don't get any help coming. But I'll tell you this much for damn sure: We ain't letting a bunch of savages come through our station perimeter and overrun us. No fuckin' way. Not on my watch we aren't! So if they get through we shoot them before they overpower us. I know I don't need to tell you how bad it will likely be if they overrun us. We all know how this stuff works in the real world. I also think we might be getting pretty close to having some of them getting desperate enough to make a try at getting through. So take a minute to make sure all your weapons are good to go."

Once again the big old school sergeant stopped and invited any-one to ask questions or challenge his thinking. None of the deputies disagreed with him. Even Slick, who rarely gave any oral or visible acknowledgement to such things, nodded his head in agreement with Marino.

Mori energetically commented "Fuckin' A right Sarge. I'm good to go if it hits the fan here"

"Straight up," replied Cruz.

Gattuso put one arm around Anderson's shoulder as a means of support, the gesture falling somewhere between a platonic pat on the shoulder that one would typically see between patrol partners and a romantic embrace. Each and every one of the patrol cops present caught the significance of the gesture.

Anderson, apparently less than comfortable with the action of her long-time partner but newly acquired lover, removed her Beretta 9mm pistol from its holster and performed a chamber check. As had always been the case, she wanted there to be no doubt among her fel-low patrol cops that her mind was focused on the business at hand.

Marino had one more thing to say, and he wanted to get it done quickly. The meeting was getting to be longer than he wanted.

"You know, the truth is that we all should have taken the responsi-bility on ourselves. Since when have we ever counted on the depart-ment to take care of everything we need to do this job right anyway? Think about it. We work out on our own time because we want to be able to handle that big parolee that we end up facing by ourselves until our partner catches up to us or whatever."

Marino looked at the pair of tactical aficionados.

"Think about how much shooting time you both put in that the department doesn't pay you for. The bottom line is that we should've been putting supplies in our lockers and personal vehicles. I know I will in the future, but that won't help us now. He dismissed the group to go take up their assignments, each of them mulling over what had been discussed.

Later that night, sometime between midnight and dawn, a couple of the larger and harder looking thugs in the crowd made a move to get into the station. It went down a bit differently than any of the deputies had thought it would, but it had nonetheless happened. And it had happened less than twelve hours after the possibility had been discussed. The seasoned patrol sergeant had once again proven that he knew how to read people, and conditions, as a result of his three decades spent as a street cop and sergeant.

When the assault went down, Anderson had been assigned in the parking lot near an eight foot high cinder block wall. She leaned with her back against the wall, shotgun hanging from her shoulder as an insurance policy against her falling asleep. First, the heavy shotgun and its position on her body was uncomfortable enough that she expected it would keep her awake. Second, she knew that if she slumped past a certain point the shotgun would begin to slide down her shoulder, hopefully with enough feeling to jar her awake. And if that failed to wake her, the weapon hitting the parking lot pavement would no doubt do the trick, albeit with all of the subtlety of a freight train smacking a semi-trailer.

There is a mental state for human beings, recognized by most who have ever had to stay up all night pulling guard duty or a similar task, that is called *micro sleep*. In the simplest of terms, it is a mental state where a person is not fully awake, yet has not reached the full condition of sleep. Typically, a person experiencing *micro sleep* will be more attuned to sensual stimuli than one who is fully asleep—the snap of a twig, shuffling of feet, or the slight metallic click of a door latch have all been known to open the eyelids of those engaged in *micro sleep*.

Anderson was in a state of *micro sleep* when she smelled, rather than saw or heard, trouble approaching near her post. Anyone who doubts the level of stench a physically active human being can acquire after a week of not bathing or showering, just hasn't experienced some of the finer things in life. If the unique chemicals of fear induced sweat are added to the mix it worsens.

The odor accosted her nostrils, a putrid smell that brought to mind a combination of dirty socks, old body odor, and unchanged baby diapers. Opening her eyes but remaining perfectly still, Anderson shifted her gaze from side to side in an attempt to take in her sur-roundings under the light of the almost full moon. It was only then that she heard the low volume verbal exchange taking place between two men she had no doubt were bad guys. She overheard one of the voices refer to a gun.

"Yo, I keepin' the *strap* Dawg. I finna get busy with this shit man. These po-leese motha fuckas about to get served bigtime now."

As far as Anderson was concerned, there was now no doubt as to what the assaulters had in mind once they breeched the sheriff sta-tion walls. What Anderson didn't know was how many were actually going to be coming over the wall. She had heard only two involved in the discussion on the other side of the wall, but that didn't mean they were the only two involved in the imminent attack. Another thing she didn't know was what kind of weapon(s) they might have. In her experience the term *strap* referred to a handgun, but how could she be sure that was the case this time?

Stepping away from the wall as quietly as possible, the female deputy grabbed the pistol grip of her shotgun with her right hand, pulling it out in front of her, muzzle facing downward at about a forty five degree angle in what was termed the *low ready* position. She used her right index finger to click off the shotgun's safety, hoping that whoever was on the other side wouldn't hear the "click" and be warned of her immediate presence. It was common practice for dep-uties on the LASD, as well as most police agencies, to carry their long guns with empty chambers. But Mori and Cruz, always seeking the tactical advantage, had convinced the deputies to keep their cham-bers loaded, leaving only the gun's safety as a barrier to discharging the weapon if the trigger was pressed. The deputies had all agreed to follow the advice.

Anderson looked about quickly, assessing her immediate sur-roundings for any place to take cover. Her primary intent in doing so was to conceal her presence long enough for both attackers to get over the wall before she engaged them. She felt the familiar sensation of a heavy dose of adrenaline surging through her body and tried to control her heart rate as best she could.

This is different than other situations I've been in because I can't get on the radio to let the cavalry know where I am and what I'm facing. Besides, they'll all come soon enough when they hear me shooting out here. I have to handle it myself. If I just run them off they will only regroup and come up with a different plan...maybe one that will get some of us hurt or killed. I know what to do here; I've trained for this. I'm the one who insisted on carrying my full share of the load by offering to take my turn at this spot rather than only manning one of the inside positions.

Anderson made the decision to quietly back up twenty five feet and crouch behind the front fender of a squad car. She pointed the muzzle of her shotgun toward the wall. Then she waited.

The first thug came over the wall with a black pistol in his front waistband. She couldn't tell what make or caliber the gun was, and she didn't care. The second guy cleared the top of the concrete block wall seconds after the first guy landed on the ground, his sneaker clad feet making a "smack" as they found purchase on the asphalt. Anderson had caught a glimpse of a third person beginning to scale the wall as well, his hands appearing over the top of the cinder block as he started to pull himself over.

The second man, now dropping himself inside of the parking lot after his cohort, was hurriedly trying to unsling his SKS rifle from his shoulder and bring it up to a firing position. She was well aware that despite the fact that the semi-automatic rifle only had a ten round fixed magazine, it was a powerful weapon that fired the same rounds as its more common AK-47 "cousin". It had killed a lot of Americans during the Viet Nam conflict. But none of this mattered one way or the other to Anderson. He was going down for the count along with his buddies.

Anderson fired the double aught load at the first attacker, all nine of the thirty three caliber lead pellets hitting him in the torso. He went down immediately, the massive tissue destruction ending his rapacious ways forever. She wasted no time confirming her hit with the first target. She charged the slide on the shotgun as soon as she had pulled the trigger, securing another double aught round in the weapon's chamber. She pulled the trigger again as she pointed the barrel at the second man entering the parking lot. He went down as fast as the first guy, his SKS carbine clattering onto the pavement just before he convulsed for a few seconds and then died. The third attacker had somehow dislodged the pistol he was carrying in his waistband or pocket. The distinctive sound of a handgun striking the pavement was one that Anderson had heard many times in her career, and this sounded no different. She chambered yet another round, fired, and watched him follow the fate of his two fellow thugs.

Following her training, she immediately chambered another round, thumbed three more shells into the gun's magazine, and began scanning her surroundings for additional threats. Seconds later, Gattuso and Slick, the two assigned closest to her, came running, gun muzzles and flashlight beams sweeping the entire parking lot.

Slick called out, "I got this side covered; go check on her."

The taller deputy was scanning the lot, including the three downed bodies, while Gattuso made sure that Anderson was okay. He tried to comfort her by hugging her, but she resisted this attempt, apparently still amped up with the adrenaline attendant to what had just happened. The rest of the deputies, as well as Sergeant Marino, maintained their positions as had been agreed upon earlier in the event of such a scenario. It was clear they had nowhere near enough personnel to secure the station properly, but they had to work with what they had. They left the three dead bodies where they were, planning to figure out what to do with them with the help of daylight.

"I would offer you a drink Anderson, but I don't have anything stronger than that funky orange flavored water right now. Of course I could offer you a pinch of Copenhagen, but I don't think you'd appreciate that," Slick laughed as he spat a glob of his own tobacco saturated saliva next to one of the bodies on the ground.

"No way man. Thanks anyway. I'm just a lightweight girl. A glass of white wine with dinner and flavored coffee in the morning is more my speed."

Slick nodded slowly in response, preoccupied with his assessment of the heavy damage the buckshot loads had visited upon all three dead men.

"Whatever you say Anderson, whatever you say," the big cowboy said as he shook his head once back and forth.

Sergeant Marino had Cruz and Mori retrieve the dead assaulters' weapons and any ammunition on their persons before dragging the bodies outside of the station parking lot and dumping them on the sidewalk. The rifle had been loaded with only seven rounds total, and the handguns were inferior to those possessed by the deputies.

Cruz asked the sergeant, "Are you sure we should leave the bodies right here in the open like this?"

"Yeah, I'm sure. It might be good for the assholes in the area to see what happened to these guys when they tried to attack our station. They got nothin' good comin' from us as far as I'm concerned. Screw 'em!"

The next day, while Marino took a walk around the station's exterior perimeter, he was waved over by a guy who couldn't have been more than nineteen or twenty. The clean shaven young man wore glasses and had a neatly trimmed short natural hairstyle. Marino thought it peculiar that the person before him had managed to find a way to maintain what appeared to be top grade hygiene when virtually everyone else around here, including he and his deputies, was unable to do so.

The youngster spoke articulately, and addressed him with respect, even referring to him by his rightful rank of "sergeant". Wary of the possibility of more attacks, Marino looked around carefully before giving his full attention, or almost full attention, to the man before him.

"Please talk to me like you're asking me questions I don't want to answer, sergeant. Just so it will look good to anyone who is watching," the well-groomed man said.

Marino just looked at him blankly for a few seconds, not knowing what the kid (he regarded everyone under twenty five as a kid now) was asking of him or why. Feeling a bit embarrassed for his lack of quick thinking under the circumstances, Marino engaged in the charade and asked him what was going on.

Throwing his hands up, palms out in front of his shoulders, the young man hoped that his theatrical actions would appear to be a less than friendly response to the sergeant's contact. It was a cheap ruse, but he couldn't afford to have any of the numerous onlookers report that he was being cooperative with the authorities. Then the younger man said something that all but stopped the big LASD supervisor's heart cold right where he stood.

"There are some seriously bad individuals that are going to hit your station hard pretty soon. These guys are no joke sergeant; they have weapons that only the military has access to, and they want to kill everyone in the station so they can take it over completely. These people have been waiting for the right time to do this for a very long time--I'm talking since over ten years ago-sergeant. It sounds crazy I know, but I'm as serious as a heart attack."

Playing along with the ruse, Marino accusingly jabbed his index finger at the serious guy standing in front of him with the disconcerting news. He definitely had the sergeant's attention at this point.

"Who exactly are we talking about here?"

"There are some heavy hitters from groups like the *American Communist Workers' Party* and *The Black Resistance Movement* that are involved in this. We're talking serious Marxist political stuff, ya hear what I'm sayin'? They got some hard core gangsters that are on board now too; well actually, they used to be gangbangers, but now they're down for the new cause. Overthrowing the government and all that."

Marino was at a loss for words, but the young man continued.

"These people thought that they were going to make their move after the attacks on September 11th back in 2001. But then they changed their minds. Probably woke up and realized they couldn't pull it off. And please don't ask me for details about how I know about all this. We don't have time for that."

Marino, now finding the information even more disturbing than he had a few minutes ago, asked the kid if he could talk to him again later or the next day. The young man shook his head forcefully back and forth a few times.

"No way. Can't do that. This was too risky at it is, sergeant."

"Well, when is this supposed to happen then? Any idea at all?"

"I don't know. But if I think it's going down I can try to warn you by doing something unusual across the street from the station front door like twelve to twenty four hours before it's supposed to start. That's the best I can do."

Marino just stared at the young man.

"Oh yeah I hate to tell you this, cause I know a lot of the deputies were friends with the old man, but the owner of the liquor store— Phil—well somebody killed him. It was ugly too. I saw his body myself. A couple blocks from his store, over on 63rd. That's seriously fucked up... what they did. I'm sorry man."

22

WESTCHESTER, CA

Three of the men gathered around the fire, including the apparent shot caller, jumped to their feet and joined the initial pursuer. Every one of them produced their own handguns from wherever they had been concealed and joined the pack in pursuit of Rob. To a man, they were all caught up in the frenzy of the hunt. Not only were they caught up in the frenzy of the hunt, every one of them harbored a real fear of suffering the contempt of their compatriots for being weak. This fear was far more powerful than the fear of physical danger. Yet two of the group remained seated around the fire.

Whether it was a display of discipline coupled with the innate recognition that someone had to stick around to guard the valuables, part of a pre-arranged plan, or plain old laziness, two of the men seated around the warm flames remained where they were, watching over the goods that were stacked next to them. They too now held handguns in their laps as they sat in their patio chairs. The fact that the entire group had managed to arm itself in the time it took the average person to stoop and pick up a dropped quarter was testimony to their familiarity with perceived danger and weapons.

Looking around at his surroundings as he ran, Rob glimpsed a two story house enclosed by a six foot high chain link fence with dark green aluminum slats woven into the fencing. It was a feature intended to provide extra privacy for the residents living behind the fence, and it concealed the property from Rob as he ran. The property had a large sliding solid wood gate that separated the driveway from the sidewalk. He could see no latch or locking mechanism on the side of the gate facing the street, so he concluded that it was locked on the inside.

Desperate to find a way to evade his pursuers and thereby avoid a battle he likely wouldn't survive, Rob ran toward the large wood gate, grabbed the top with both hands, and pulled himself over having no idea what he would find on the other side. His shotgun, swinging freely on its cord as he used both hands to hoist himself over the gate, smacked him in the side of the face as he went over.

He identified the fence line on the opposite side of the back yard as his immediate objective. He hit the ground hard and ran for all he was worth in an attempt to cover the thirty yards of back yard and vault his body over the six foot chain link fence. No sooner had he resumed running than he heard a couple of large dogs barking and snarling. Big and mean. Rob could tell by the unique sound of their barking that the dogs were inside of the residence of the property he had just trespassed onto--at least for the time being.

How long are they gonna be inside the house, he asked himself. *It doesn't matter at this point; I have to keep on running. That's all I can do.*

He heard the sound of his closest pursuer landing on the cement driveway after scaling the big gate. Soft soled shoes hitting cement. He had made it over without difficulty.

Shit!

Seconds after he heard his pursuer's feet landing on the driveway behind him, Rob received the answer to his earlier question about how long the dogs would remain inside the house. He heard the sliding glass door being opened just as he got his two tired arms onto the top rail of the chain link fence.

Failing to register the mild pain of the shallow cuts he sustained as he gripped the sharp edges of the twisted wire protruding at the top of the fence, Rob once again pulled himself over a six foot barrier. Descending into the adjacent back yard of still another residence, he landed on a rose bush growing there.

Fuck! Can I just get a simple break here?!

The snarling dogs in the adjacent yard, fortunately now separated from him by the fence he had just scaled, distracted Rob from the painful half dozen thorn punctures in his calf. The dogs sounded like they were serious about protecting their turf, not merely making a good show of it. He wasn't sure exactly why or how he had made this assessment, but his gut told him this was the case.

As it so happened, the couple living in the house had paid close to ten thousand dollars for the pair of the professional guard dogs. They had acquired them after having been robbed months earlier. All of this was bad news for the gangbanger who unexpectedly found himself in the same back yard as the two German Shepherds.

The first canine, weighing slightly more than ninety pounds, hit the running man, muzzle first, with enough force to knock him off of his feet, sending him sprawling to the ground. Within a fraction of a second, the dog clamped down on the man's left hamstring with over two hundred fifty pounds per square inch of bite pressure.

The dog, maintaining its vice-like grip, pulled backward. He dug all four paws into the grass covered ground and determinedly pumped his canine legs for all he was worth, continuously pulling backward in a manner that allowed him to drag the screaming gangster rearward several feet. The progress was halted when a large chunk of flesh had been torn loose from the man's leg, prompting the shepherd to find another bite location and start the process all over again.

While this was taking place, the second shepherd got a solid bite on the man's right calf and similarly pulled rearward, starting a parallel cycle of events almost identical to that of the first dog. It was not a good day for the gangster.

The thug managed to grip his handgun and fire two rounds as more of a reflex than anything else, his ability to accomplish any modicum of accurate fire having come and gone as soon as he found himself being yanked backward by the powerful animals. Several times the canines were forced to find new locations to bite their human prey due to the chunks of flesh being completely torn away from his body.

The pistol was lost early during the attack, and the dogs continued to shred chunks of tissue on the terrified man without an ounce of compassion. The frenzied manner in which the pair repeatedly punctured and tore away flesh from the thrashing man's body elicited screams from him that sent chills down Rob's spine as he continued running through the second yard and out onto the sidewalk in front of the residence.

On more than a few occasions Rob had seen the damage police canines could do to a strong man in the relatively brief period of time it took for the dog handler to call off the animal. The gangbanger in the adjacent yard, rapidly losing blood as well as consciousness and possibly his very life, would receive no such merciful reprieve from a professional dog handler this pre-dawn morning.

Two of the original group had heard the savage canine attack, as well as the unnerving screams of their fellow gangster. However, they were unable to pinpoint where the bloody confrontation was taking place. Apparently unwilling to risk a fate similar to that of their friend, they opted to return to the safety of their bonfire. Despite it being unspoken between them, they each suspected anyone who owned dogs capable of that kind of violence was also likely to be well armed. And like most predators, they weren't interested in even odds. Better to live to prey on the weak another day.

Breathing hard and sweating heavily, Rob made his way on a residential sidewalk in an easterly direction, away from the four lane boulevard. He alternated between jogging and walking at a fast clip. Both the pack straps that dug into his shoulders, and the shotgun that bounced against his chest, were now bugging the hell out of him.

It was his plan to turn left at the next sidewalk, and then press on in a northbound direction, paralleling the large boulevard for several blocks until he was confident that he could return to the big street far enough north of the bonfire to avoid being seen by the men there.

Almost a half hour had passed before Rob felt comfortable enough to look for a place to eat some food, rehydrate his body, and grab a few hours of sleep. He spotted an obviously abandoned residence, its front door wide open and several of its front windows broken. He carefully approached the front doorway and announced his presence. No response. He made a mental note, by habit as a cop who had taken hundreds of burglary reports, of how the initial invader(s) had forced their way into the house. The door jamb was split, leaving the deadbolt useless.

Just prior to entering the residence, he used his flashlight to look around the interior from the doorway. The inside had been ransacked, but the amount of actual damage appeared minimal.

After loosening the slip knot on the improvised sling that looped around the shotgun grip, Rob separated the weapon from his pack. He carefully set the pack on a relatively clean section of the floor. Removing the load from his tired shoulders and back gave him instant relief. He massaged his shoulders and neck for a moment while he glanced around at the surroundings.

Rob grasped the shotgun, cocked the hammer back, and pulled his shirt tail up and tucked it behind his holstered handgun. Having the pistol readily accessible for an unobstructed draw could make the difference between winning and losing. He removed his small tactical flashlight, gripped it in his left hand, and held it tightly against the shotgun's wood fore-end so that the light's beam shone close to where the shotgun barrel was pointing as he moved.

Trying to be as tactically cautious as possible as a lone searcher, he quickly, yet systematically, cleared the entire residence. Secure in the knowledge that no one was inside of the structure, he closed the front door. He barricaded it with a heavy table turned upside-down and then stacked about a hundred pounds of miscellaneous junk on top of it. He only sought to make it difficult for someone to enter the house without making enough noise to warn him of their presence. The back door of the house had a medium sized deadbolt lock that was still intact, eliminating the need to come up with a way to secure it while he looked through the house.

The early sun rays had just started to enter through the windows on the east wall of the attached garage. He was glad he wouldn't have to use his flashlight to see. He located the home's water heater tank.

Looks like a thirty gallon tank, but who knows how much water is left in it?

He opened the relief valve at the top of the tank, followed by the spigot attached to its side near the bottom. He watched the rust tinted water sputter at first, then become almost clear after several seconds. He shut it off, not wanting to waste any.

Rob stopped and strained to listen. He heard the distinctive sound of a Harley Davidson motorcycle motoring up the street in front of the house. He guessed that whoever was riding the bike had maintained the old pre-electronic machine as a source of pride and joy, a true labor of love. Now the old motorcycle was repaying the loyalty by providing her owner with motorized transportation in a world that had damn little of it.

Good for you man. Good for you.

He walked back to where he had left his pack and pulled out two pieces of *Paracord*. Then he retrieved his steel water bottle and returned to the water heater. He put his bandana in the mouth of the bottle to act as a filter for any tank sediment. He opened the spigot, slowly filling the container through the bandana's material. It was a slow process, but eventually he was rewarded with a full bottle. Now he had to purify it.

He walked to the back yard of the house, grateful for being able to see with daylight—or at least the beginning of it. But he thought about his sleep need as well.

So much for the idea of getting to sleep while still dark out.

He could smell the odor of wood smoke, as well as seeing numerous columns of smoke throughout the neighborhood.

A lot of people are learning to make due with old-fashioned fire. Those that were lucky enough to have barbeques with refillable propane tanks are now living in luxury compared to their neighbors who have to build fires for their heating needs.

Returning to the house, he rummaged through the kitchen cupboards and drawers in hopes of finding something edible, but it had definitely been ransacked prior to his arrival. He searched anyway. In the rear of one of the higher cupboards, outside of view from where he stood, he ran his fingers over the interior base. He found two small packets of honey reminding him of what they served in diners with toast. He dropped the packets into his shirt pocket.

A search of the other rooms rewarded him with some old magazines on a living room table. He found a few non-glossy pages that would work better for fire starting, and then picked up his pack and headed out behind the house, looking for a suitable place for his fire. He settled for a spot a few feet away from a galvanized steel fence post.

Rob walked about the spacious yard and gathered a pile of dead sticks and tree branches. They ranged in diameter from a typical pencil to the thickness of his wrist. He deposited the bundle of wood—about the size of a laundry basket--next to where he planned to make his fire.

He used his *Kabar* to split several small pieces of wood into ultra-fine kindling no bigger than match sticks. After whittling a small pile of wood shavings, he arranged the above with magazine paper to start the fire. The flame of his *Bic* lighter provided the final step, bringing the fire to life.

Pleased that he hadn't had to use his *Vaseline* soaked cotton balls to get the fire going, he nursed it, gradually adding increasingly larger pieces of wood. Within fifteen minutes it was a full-fledged, but small, campfire.

Once again using the *Kabar*, he cut off a green branch from a nearby tree. The branch was about six feet long and only slightly thinner than his wrist. He stripped the smaller limbs and leaves from the branch and brought it to the fire, then positioned it diagonally well above the flames. He tied the higher end of the branch to the steel fence post and allowed the lower end to rest on the ground.

The result was a branch secured at a forty five degree angle over the fire that had at least three feet of clearance from the flames at its higher end. He tied one of the lengths of paracord closer to the higher end of the branch, letting the loose end hang well above the blaze.

Rob fished around in his pack until he found a cable the diameter of picture hanging wire that had small loops formed at each end. He created a slip knot and looped it around the rolled steel lip of his water bottle. He tied the *Paracord* hanging from the stick to the loop at the other end of the cable so that he could hang the bottle over the fire with no danger of melting the *Paracord*. He then removed the lid from the bottle so that the pressure wouldn't build up inside as it grew hotter. He added more sticks to the fire, positioning them so that they rested against the side of the steel water container to create more heat.

He had the water at a boil in minutes. Boiling the water was an extra precaution that may not have been necessary, but he wanted to make sure that there were no harmful organisms to contend with. Stomach cramps and diarrhea were not something he needed to deal with in addition to everything else.

Rob sensed the man's presence as he walked into the rear yard. Angry with himself for compromising his night vision in order to treat himself to the comfort of the fire, he turned his head away from the flames and toward the source of his concern. He observed a fifty-ish white male, carrying a bundle--fashioned out of a shirt or similar item of clothing-- over his right shoulder. It reminded him of the kind often depicted in the old portraits of hobos before "homeless" was in the lexicon of most American families.

He was larger than average, but not what most would describe as a 'big" guy. His hands were thick and hardened. For those who knew what to look for, it was clear that he had spent a few years working with these hands in a capacity other than filing papers or punching computer keys behind a desk. He wore a short sleeve grey utility uni-form shirt that had the name of an electrical power company sten-ciled on the back and front, as well as a cloth name tag sewn over his left pocket that read "Don" in cursive writing. The other pocket had a similarly made ensign that read "Field Supervisor".

The man walked slowly and tentatively toward Rob. To say that the man's unexpected appearance surprised him would have been a huge understatement. It almost literally scared the shit out of him, his morning constitutional being behind schedule. But Rob's startle reaction was short-lived. Rob had a positive feeling about the new arrival.

The man came to an abrupt stop twenty feet from Rob, raised his hands to just above navel height, and turned his palms outward.

"I don't mean any harm buddy. I'm just trying to make it home is all. After all the power went off, I spent the first three days in my truck, and then found some nice people who let me stay in their back yard for a couple nights. I've been walking since I left their yard. What a total friggin mess, huh?!"

Rob looked at the unexpected visitor with a poker face, his eyes looking directly at the other man's, hoping to read any indication of ill intention that might be there. Seeing none, Rob did the only thing he could think of under the circumstances.

"Come on in by the campfire and introduce yourself man."

He waived him forward with his left hand. Good vibe or not, he was keeping his gun hand close to his pistol.

"Thanks. Don't mind if I do. Shit, my feet are tired."

He dropped his makeshift pack onto the grass as he approached Rob.

"I'm Don McNair," the man said as he extended his open hand toward Rob.

Rob shook his hand and introduced himself.

23

THOUSAND OAKS, CA

Stephanie forced herself to calm down and take deep breaths. She was pretty sure she remembered hearing somewhere that a person should use a four-count to slow down their breathing when stressed out. Supposedly it could even help to slow one's heart rate.

Inhale-one, two, three, four. Exhale- one, two, three, four.

She walked across the living room and glanced over at Charlie Wyatt, who was playing with one of his toy trucks. She plopped herself down onto the comfortable couch. She just needed to relax for a few minutes and calm down.

The threat is gone for the time being, so there is no immediate need to address this thing right now, she told herself.

The threat that had contributed to her current state of stress had come in the form of three young guys, two of whom were in their late teens to early twenties and one a few years older. She hadn't gotten a good view, but she could see they were Caucasian, tough looking, and did not live on her block. They had made their way down the residential block going door to door, knocking and waiting, presumably to see if the residents were home. All three had looked unrefined to her—she guessed they had been in trouble with the law before, possibly having spent time in jail or even prison.

She watched them approach her neighbors' houses that were within the view afforded from her living room window. Although they didn't appear to be threatening violence directly, she had no doubt that they were casing the homes for potential victims.

Residences that are vacated and those that are "soft targets" will be sought after by opportunistic predators now, she told herself.

The biggest of them wore a bright orange ball cap. Despite the cap, there was something odd about the man's hairstyle, or maybe the shape of his head, that she couldn't quite identify. Like the others, he was muscular, although his build consisted of a heavier musculature-- the type that most young men don't acquire until they are into their twenties, regardless of how hard they lift weights.

Orange hat man wore a t-shirt that looked like it was a size too small for him, and jeans that were a couple of sizes too big. In fact the waistband was cinched in with a non-descript belt to prevent the pants from falling down.

Each of the men walked with his arms slightly held out from the sides as though too muscular to hold them any other way. It was an acquired mannerism she had seen lots of times. Mostly guys who spent a lot of time in the gym—much of it posing before a mirror. They were strutting around like predators in the jungle, completely unconcerned for their safety because all the other creatures had to fear them.

The fact all three wore medium sized backpacks, none of which appeared to have much in the way of contents, only raised her suspicions further. She surmised they were planning to fill the packs with any loot they were able to take from unattended or insufficiently protected homes. She wondered if any of the neighbors on this street would be considered vulnerable enough for these thieves to attack.

The neighbors are not my problem right now. I have to focus on protecting my child and myself--not anyone else.

Stephanie told herself that without any police response it was a completely different world now in this formerly low crime suburban neighborhood. When the three men had approached her front door, she was not taken by surprise. Her Australian Shepherds had alerted her. She stood ten feet from the door, revolver in her hands as they approached. The one closest to the door, apparently the spokesman for the group, called out to any occupant(s) in the house.

"Excuse me, but I'm just wondering if you can spare any water or food for me and my little girl. We haven't had anything to eat or drink in a while and we could use some help."

Stephanie answered while she gripped her revolver, muzzle pointed at the door.

"Sorry, but we don't even have enough for all of us. We can't help you."

There was a pause for a long couple of seconds before the spokesman responded.

"Okay. Thanks anyhow."

She heard a short conversation take place on the other side of the door and then silence. She hoped her response would convey the idea that there were several people in the house. And her car was parked in the driveway. Maybe they would think her husband was home.

It had been ten days since the power grid had gone down, and she had yet to hear any news as to what the situation was or what was being done by the government to address it. The lack of information or communication was taking a toll on her in a way that she would not have thought possible before the EMP. She reminded herself to try the little portable radio again to see if she could find any news reports.

The importance of their two dogs, previously considered to be valuable only in the sense of the companionship they offered, was something that was now abundantly clear. They were a warning system for danger, and this was a top priority in her mind.

You guys are earning every bit of the dog food you're eating--every bit indeed.

After spending over an hour to survey the house and taking inventory of the materials she had available, she gave up on trying to fortify the house. The task was simply too overwhelming given her limited knowledge of construction, available materials, and minimal grasp of security methods. The experience had left her disheartened.

Who the hell has ever spent any time trying to think of ways to fortify their home? Nobody normal--that's who. How can I be expected to know the first thing about how, or what, to do in this regard? Even Rob never brought this up. He never thought this kind of thing would go on this long without help of some kind being available. He pretty much wanted to avoid any of us having to wait in FEMA or RED CROSS lines for food and water is all. He said they were always full of people that were angry and pushy--a situation that begged for trouble. But this situation is a lot worse than what he talked about.

Stephanie once again had to suppress her emotions as she thought about Rob and what he might be enduring now. She then contemplated the weight of her own situation, the combination of the two threatening to push her over the edge she had come perilously close to so many times since the lights had gone out.

Determined not to cry in front of Charlie Wyatt, who for the time being was content, she busied herself with the process of making herself a cup of afternoon tea. They had experienced intermittent light rain today, and she had been battling a slight chill for the past few hours. The hot tea would be a small but welcomed treat.

After making her tea on the camp stove, she walked to the living room window and looked up and down the block. She saw a woman, about three quarters of the way down the street, walking on the sidewalk. Stephanie could not discern much about the woman, being that she was wearing a dark gray rain hat and matching coat.

The rain coat notwithstanding, she could tell the woman was not obviously overweight, nor was she rail thin. Even with the raincoat she appeared to be endowed with a classically attractive figure as best Stephanie could tell from her vantage point. She watched her walk up the cement walkway at the house with the large flagpole mounted in the front yard.

The flag pole flew the American stars and stripes on top and the black and white colored *Amnesty International* flag directly below it, the combination one that both she and Rob had thought unusual the first time they had seen it.

24

UNINCORPORATED SOUTHEAST LOS ANGELES

Sergeant Marino wasn't sure what he should do about the disconcerting information he had just received from the odd young man, but he knew he had to call another meeting with his deputies and fill them in. And he needed to do it immediately. As he walked toward the front door of the station, several of the growing crowd's members taunted him, but none of them dared approach the big serious looking man. He noticed that there were now several dead bodies that lay within a stone's throw of the station, each of them gathering their own swarm of flies. He allowed himself to think for a moment as he reached the front door.

My deputies have got to be getting tired of all these "sit rep" meetings. And it's always just more bad news. Never good news. Shit. When are we gonna get a break here? It's been eight days since this thing happened and still no sign of getting any help.

Deputy Harris, whose security duty involved ensuring the front lobby and entrance area remained uncompromised, opened the front door and let Marino march into the station.

"Hey Lee," the sergeant said to Harris in a clipped and forceful tone, "we need to get everyone together right now. Get everyone to the back door for another meeting-- immediately."

"You got it Boss. What's goin' on?"

"I'll tell you after we get everyone together. It could be serious shit," the sergeant said.

Harris moved at a double time jog to the various security posts around the station facility and notified each of the others.

The deputies gathered for the sit rep meeting, every one of them wearing a shotgun slung over their back--except Gattuso. The sergeant, displaying his temper, looked at Gattuso and threw both of his hands up into the air in frustration.

"Where the hell is your shotgun?"

"I left it on the front seat of the patrol car over near my post. I can get to it fast if I need it. I hate carrying that thing all the time. It slows me down."

Marino was pissed.

"Are you kiddin' me? This isn't about being comfortable. I want everyone to have a fully loaded shotgun on their person at all times unless you're using the damn latrine. And even then it better be within arm's reach. That's it. No debate on the issue. I'm dead serious about this guys!"

Gattuso was fully aware that he had screwed up.

"Okay Sarge. My bad on that."

Marino had a good deal of respect for Gattuso regardless of his present frustration with the fireplug of a cop. Despite his happy-go-lucky personality and signature chuckle, Gattuso was more than capable of doing the kind of physical heavy lifting that was required every once in a while in violent high crime areas. Two years prior he had been involved in a caper that served as a good illustration of this, and Marino had been the field sergeant on duty when it had happened.

At the time Gattuso had fought with a desperate armed robber following a car chase that ended with the bad guy fleeing on foot from his crashed getaway vehicle. It was an unusually long fight as these things went, and it took place following a foot chase that placed the two combatants in a location mostly hidden from public view or timely police assistance. No one who was inclined to help him knew where the hell he was.

After the dust had settled, a badly injured and cognitively impaired Gattuso handcuffed the comatose ex-con. The latter was removed from the scene handcuffed to a paramedic's gurney while the former walked a block and a half back to his patrol car with the assistance of two Nadeau Station deputies. Appearances were important in this tough community, and Gattuso would be damned if he would leave the scene any way other than on his own two feet.

Standing outside the rear door of the post-EMP sheriff's station, Marino told himself to calm down. He knew Gattuso, like the others still here, was a solid cop who could be counted on.

"Alright. I'm a little amped up I guess, but do me a favor and go get your shotgun right now. After I tell you about what I just heard you'll probably want that thing with you twenty four/seven."

The other deputies had been looking down at the ground while their big and now short tempered supervisor scolded their friend and colleague. They all knew it was out of character for Marino, and each wondered what specifically had caused this outburst of anger. Not that all of the shit going down around them, and to them, wasn't enough of an explanation.

When Marino made the comment about keeping their shotguns on their persons "twenty four/seven", all but one of them raised their eyes from the ground and looked up at him. It was clear that something had changed with the situation.

Gattuso returned wearing his shotgun and Marino began talking.

"I just heard something pretty disturbing a few minutes ago. One of the civilians out there told me some stuff that's got me pretty nervous. And we need to come up with a plan on how to deal with it...just in case it's legit info."

Marino related the entire incident, including both the conversation and the young man's unusual appearance. How that kid had managed to remain so well groomed after a week of no utilities or running water was still a mystery to Marino. He asked the deputies if anyone had come across any information in the past that might tie into what the young man had told him.

Harris was the only one who indicated that he had.

"This is weird, but I think I might have some info that could be related to this. It actually goes way back to around the time of the '92 riots. I was a rookie just off training and I stopped a kid, maybe seventeen years old, who had a piece of rock cocaine in his pocket down on Hickory just north of the projects. He offered me some good info if I would cut him a break. It was only a small rock, and I figured it was worth takin' a chance, so I said alright."

He paused and twisted his neck with his hands to stretch the tense muscles.

"So the kid tells me that a railroad boxcar was sitting on the tracks in the hood, and it was full of all kinds of fuckin' military weapons and hand grenades--shit like that. At first I thought he was bullshitting me. I stepped on his rock....ground it into the cement....you know.... wrote his name down in my notebook, then kicked him loose."

Harris glanced around at his audience to gauge their reaction. He didn't see much of one either way.

"The gang unit guys found the kid and talked to him a few days later. Should've been done a few *hours* later, but what the fuck, right? I think it was Leroux who talked to the kid at first; I know he was the one who was keeping in touch with him later anyway. The kid wasn't a gangster, so the other gang guys weren't that interested in him. Thought his story was bullshit. Anyway, he told Leroux that some radical domestic terrorist types were planning on taking over a sheriff or police station in South L.A. if the shit jumped off real bad again. "

This time when he looked around he saw he had the rapt attention of all who were present. Even Slick, who had by now mastered the ability of giving off the calm and cool vibe of disinterest, was looking at Harris with anticipation.

"Sarge, you remember how there was all this talk at the time of a second wave of riots that were gonna jump off—even worse than the first round. Supposed to be shooting a lot of cops and all that, remember?" Marino dipped his head up and down in affirmation, but said nothing.

Harris pressed on.

"I was really interested in this thing at the time and I ran into the kid again a week later. He told me the militants were only going to do the attack on a station if they thought the system was fucked up bad enough to give them a decent shot at pulling it off. We're talking crazy third world revolution shit here. He said these guys were really hot to pull off a station takeover though—gonna kill every cop in the place if it went down. I remember the kid was pretty shook up about it at the time. Really scared. Then, right after the September 11th attacks went down, I got contacted by a couple of our guys working terrorism out of headquarters. They started asking me all about my contact with this kid back in '92. These guys wouldn't tell me shit of course, but I connected the dots."

Several of the deputies, as well as Sergeant Marino, started asking Harris questions at the same time. Harris held up his hand in a halting motion and raised his voice so that he could be heard.

"The whole thing pretty much died off as far as I know. I guess when it came down to it the bad guys didn't have the balls to actually try that shit."

There were nods all around--a subconscious attempt to convince themselves it would be a mistake to attack them. Slick let loose with a stream of saliva and Copenhagen, once again the calm, cool, and disinterested stoic. He had been working at the station after the September 11th attacks when these rumors, and others, were making the rounds. Damn near every vehicle stop and pedestrian contact at the time had been done with the anticipation of something big being imminent. There had been a lot of after-work "choir practice" sessions to ease the tension at the time.

Harris continued. The guy not only loved being in the middle of the action, he also loved to talk about it. And most of the time his audiences liked listening to him. He was a natural entertainer as well as a bona fide bad-ass.

"There was never any case made over that railroad car full of weapons--I know that much. I think the informant said the whole load got unloaded pretty quick in the middle of the first or second night it got there, and he didn't know who unloaded it or where they took it all. And I never heard about any military cache of weapons, or even any individual weapons of that type, that were ever found. None of it being used in gang murders or anything like that."

He shrugged his shoulders as if to say he was stumped by the whole thing.

"The whole thing could be bullshit for all I know. Some of the detectives thought somebody was just floating a bullshit story to see if they had a snitch in their ranks. But there was something about this kid that was really convincing to me. Plus I got contacted again in 2001 after the nine eleven attacks. The whole thing was weird."

It was now Marino's turn to speak, and he was irritated.

"Fucking amazing. I never heard about any boxcar full of military weapons at all back then, and I was assigned to SWAT at the time. Even if it was bullshit they should have at least let us know about the rumor."

He shook his head to emphasize his disgust. Clearly, the veteran sergeant had become more direct in the manner in which he addressed his charges, no longer as concerned about maintaining his loyalty to the department's management ranks.

Harris, for his part, wasn't so sure that sharing the information with the entire LASD SWAT unit would have been all that good of an idea. Deputies had a propensity for talking to other deputies. But he kept his thoughts to himself on the matter.

Marino got down to the business at hand.

"Okay, we need to really get our shit together about this just in case it's legit info. Hey, by the way, did anyone ever find those bolt cutters I asked you guys to look for? We need to get into the rest of the lockers to see if we can get more ammo or anything else we might be able to use."

Cruz spoke up, "Yeah Sarge. I put 'em on your desk a couple of hours ago."

The sergeant, annoyed that he hadn't been told about the bolt cutters and that no one had taken the initiative to use the cutters to get into the remaining lockers, forced himself to hold his temper in check.

"Let's get those bolt cutters into action and open the rest of the lockers ASAP. And if that locker with the heavy duty lock on it can't be cut then figure out some other way to get into it. I don't care if you have to cut the whole door off. Get it done. I want every single car trunk, locker, desk drawer, and whatever else to be searched for anything we can use to defend this place. In the meantime, everyone needs to think about how we might defend the station against a serious attack. I'm going to heat up some water in the big pot, clean up a little, and then grab an hour or two of sleep. Harris is in charge while I'm sleeping, but someone better wake me up if anything looks like it's going down. Let's get moving everyone."

The small group dispersed, returning to their designated security positions. The exception was Harris, who went to retrieve the bolt cutters and begin the search of the secured lockers. Marino stopped Harris and reminded him of what the strange youngster had said about trying to warn the deputies of an imminent assault. Marino reiterated that the kid had mentioned trying to do something unusual directly across the street from the station—for the purpose of serving as a warning--within twelve hours of the attack if possible. It was yet another strange part of a bizarre story, but it was there for the taking.

Fifty feet from where the meeting had taken place, Mori and Cruz had a hurried conversation. Mori double timed it into the station. He went directly to the sergeant's office where he found him deep in a conversation with Harris.

"What's up, Mike" the sergeant asked.

Mori was glad Harris was here. It was no secret that he had done suspension days for carrying an unauthorized weapon during an off-duty shooting a while back. Mori hoped he would offer a sympathetic ear to what he was going to bring up, and maybe even serve as a buffer between an angry sergeant and himself.

"Sarge, I need to bring something to your attention here, and I hope you won't get too pissed off about it. But the situation we're dealing with right now is so serious that I figure I got no choice other than to let you know what's up."

The young deputy looked at the sergeant and waited for some kind of indication as to how this was going to be received. He received nothing but a poker face expression from Marino.

"Uh, you know how I'm into all the shooting sport thing and fire-arms training and all that, right," Mori said before pausing.

The sergeant didn't respond, and just looked at the smaller cop impassively.

"Well", Mori said, his nervousness obvious, "I know we got a directive, back whenever it was, that said we weren't supposed to keep any personal unauthorized weapons in our lockers. The thing is, I've been keeping an unauthorized gun in my locker because I didn't want to take the chance of having it stolen from my house. It cost me a lot of money, and I'm hardly ever at my house. Didn't want some asshole to burg my house and steal it, so I kept it in my locker here till I could save up enough to buy a good safe for the house."

Sergeant Marino was tired of waiting for him to get to the point, and he once again let his temper show.

"Just say whatever you came here for, Mike. We all have a lot of shit that we need to get after. What's the deal? Do you have an unauthorized gun in your locker now or what? And if you do—and I don't give a shit---what kind of gun is it?

"Well actually Sarge, it's a rifle. I got my Springfield Armory M1A Scout rifle in there."

The sergeant froze for a second before allowing a big smile to erupt across his face. He was familiar with the rifle being described. It was a true battle rifle that fired the powerful .308 caliber (7.62 X 51) cartridge, which was similar to the well-known .30-06 round in performance. With its slightly shortened eighteen inch barrel, the weapon was a fairly compact semi-automatic rifle whose design had been literally battle tested over the past several decades. The .308 caliber round was capable of penetrating most improvised barriers encountered in urban environments. This included vehicle doors, house walls, small to medium sized trees, and even cinder block walls.

With the exception of the relatively small and thick armored hard plates that could be inserted into vest "pockets", typical body armor would be incapable of stopping the .308 caliber round. Lastly, the rifle in question, in the hands of even a competent rifleman with a decent platform from which to fire it, should be capable of consistently, or at least regularly, hitting man-sized targets at out to five hundred yards. Simply put, the Springfield Armory rifle could be an extremely effective weapon under their present circumstances.

Marino wasn't angry. On the contrary.

"This is a good thing Mike. And quit worrying about department policy—that's history. How many rounds and magazines do you have for your rifle?"

"I got six of the twenty-round magazines and two ten-rounders. And I have about five hundred rounds--all of it ball ammo." Mori looked at Marino and then at Harris.

Harris interjected with his opinion.

"This rifle could be a game changer if this attack thing goes down like we think it might."

Marino nodded.

"Oh yeah. It definitely could. If they come at us wearing body armor, that rifle will make the armor useless. Plus, we can hit them from a serious distance if we put Mike on the roof on *over-watch* detail. Maybe use a couple of the others to work it in shifts. Use Mike here for twelve hours, and two others—probably Cruz and you—in six hour shifts."

After Mori assured him that the rifle was sighted in, the office grew quiet for a moment as all three digested the information and thought about their circumstances.

"Okay Mike, go get your rifle and load up all of your mags for it. Bring all of your ammo too. Bring it all to my office and we'll work it into whatever our new defense plan is going to be. Get Harris here and Cruz all trained up with the operation of the rifle before we deploy you guys to the roof."

Marino clapped his hand on Mori's back in a gesture of encouragement as the younger deputy prepared to leave the office. Mori was visibly moved forward from the impact. The sergeant picked up the bolt cutters on his desk and thrust them at Harris's chest.

"Why don't you go finish opening up the rest of those lockers as soon as possible?"

Marino hadn't finished his request of Harris when the barely audible sound of a helicopter could be heard by all three cops standing in the sergeant's office.

It was Mori who broke the silence.

"That's a helo!"

He ran from the small office, out through the station's back door, and into the parking lot with the sergeant and Harris right behind him the entire way.

As the three cops arrived in the open parking lot they all craned their necks toward the sky looking for the exact location of the helicopter. It didn't take them long to find it, and they each tracked its movement. The airship flew over the station at an altitude low enough to allow the deputies to see that two guys were seated in the aircraft's open side door. Both men were wearing black military type BDU (battle dress utilities) clothing and load bearing combat vests and helmets. Each was holding what appeared to be an M4 military carbine in his arms.

The helicopter circled around the station for two and a half rotations, before breaking off and flying away to an unknown location. All three uniformed and hopeful cops waived their arms frantically in hopes of getting the attention of the men seated in the aircraft's open doorway, but they received no acknowledgement whatsoever from the helicopter's occupants.

"Motherfuckers," uttered the veteran sergeant over the diminishing sound of the helicopter as it flew away, eventually disappearing from their view altogether. It was stated more as an observation of irrefutable fact than an angry insult.

"Wonder what the hell that was all about," Harris announced to anyone who cared to listen. "That was weird, man. Anyone have a clue what agency that was? Or was it military maybe?"

Marino responded, "I didn't see any insignias or anything. Probably feds of some kind that had access to a helo hardened against EMP. Ain't it great how the government made sure to harden their own equipment but didn't bother to shield the power grid against

EMP? I wonder how long they expect to get fuel for their military vehicles without the civilian power grid working. Guess they think that fuel is going to transport itself, huh? Bunch of morons--just like the brass of the sheriff's department!"

Harris chuckled. Unlike the others around him, he was still having fun.

"Yeah, and it was nice of these assholes to let us know what's going on, huh? They didn't even drop us a courtesy pamphlet like the military does for the civilians in other countries. But you know what? Fuck those guys. We're on our own is all. We don't need their help anyway."

Harris actually meant what he had just said. He had never accepted the idea of having to depend on other agencies' assistance for anything. If the Los Angeles Sheriff's Department couldn't handle a problem, he doubted the assistance of outside agencies would be of much help. He could be stubborn. He hadn't allowed the magnitude of the present situation to change his opinion on this subject. At least not yet.

The deputies around him were a different story. Each of them, to a person, was seriously disappointed when the helicopter left them without so much as a small reason to hope for assistance. It was yet one more setback in a growing chain of them as far as the others were concerned.

Harris went directly to the locker rooms carrying his bolt cutters. The women's locker room, only a fraction of the size of its male counterpart, revealed no padlocked lockers. Apparently the women all thought the small built-in locks from the factory were sufficient. He didn't find anything he wanted to remove from these lockers.

Upon entering the men's section he cut padlocks on seven lockers. After going through them all, he had collected a total of almost three hundred fifty rounds of duty issued 147 grain hollow point 9mm ammunition and over a dozen fifteen round magazines for the Beretta 9mm pistols issued by the department. Three of the lockers actually contained Beretta 9mm pistols, their owners apparently electing not to carry their side arms to and from home every day. It was a large-- and some thought overly bulky—handgun. He placed all of the items into a cardboard box and carried it to the sergeant's office where he deposited it roughly on the floor behind Marino's desk.

He returned to the locker room with his cutters. Two lockers remained secured by high security padlocks. Harris tried again, unsuccessfully, to cut the locks before finally abandoning the effort. Examining the heavy tool, he observed several indentations in the hardened steel cutting surfaces contained within the jaws of the cutters. He rightly concluded the padlocks' shackles were each comprised of steel that was harder than that of the bolt cutter jaws. This wasn't going to work.

He left the bolt cutters by one of the lockers to see if any of the others had any ideas or tools that might help him get through the massive padlocks. He found Cruz standing in the lot performing his security detail. He looked happy to no longer be responsible for jail prisoners. When asked about tools, the young patrolman answered with excitement.

"Yeah, I actually have something that might work. It's a tomahawk designed for cutting through car doors, building walls, or whatever else during emergencies. They call it a *tactical* tomahawk—of course". He chuckled and rolled his eyes. It seemed like damn near everything designed for the law enforcement and military communities was now given the title of 'tactical'.

"Anyway", Cruz added, "the tool is pretty basic, but it should get through a locker door if the user does his part. Let's go find out."

After summoning another deputy to fill in at his post for a few minutes, he turned away from Harris and walked toward his Ford F-150 truck parked in the lot fifty feet away. Cruz dragged a three foot long duffle bag out of the cab, dropped the truck's tailgate, and plopped the bag on top of it.

Cruz pulled out a black tactical load bearing vest with miscellaneous gear pouches –some black and others olive drab--mounted all over the front and a large olive drab pouch holding a flexible water carrier on the rear. His attention was briefly drawn to the medium sized pouch with a small cloth red cross sewn onto it that was mounted just below the water carrier. Harris asked about its contents.

Cruz opened up the medical pouch and showed him the essential first aid contents as he explained how he had selected the items. Referring to the contents as his *blowout kit*, Cruz explained the concept of the kit was to have a few life-saving items that could be applied even during combat conditions. It included a trauma dressing, a rolled up six foot length of duct tape, and a sealed package of a granular substance called *Celox*. The substance was designed to be applied to serious wounds to stem the blood flow. It was a proven performer when it came to quickly clotting heavily bleeding wounds after other methods had failed. He dropped the vest next to the duffle bag and continued sorting through the contents.

"I can reach behind my back with either hand to reach this pouch if I need to," Cruz said as he made a brief show of reaching behind his back with first one hand, and then the other.

Harris took a good look at the load bearing vest and said, "What the fuck man? Why aren't you wearing this thing right now? If you keep that thing for a rainy day, then I guess you haven't received the memo man--but it's fuckin' rainin' cats and dogs now!" Harris laughed good-naturedly after making the smart ass comment.

Embarrassed by the quasi-legendary patrol cop's scolding comments even though wrapped in good humor, Cruz shrugged his shoulders. He was a little bit defensive.

"I dunno. I guess I figured it wasn't authorized equipment. Me and Mike always get a bunch of shit from everyone whenever they see our non-issued tactical gear. That shit gets old after a while is all."

Now Harris was getting irritated and made no attempt to hide it.

"Just put that fuckin' rig on and load it up with as many extra magazines and shotgun shells as you can fit into the thing. I just found some more pistol mags and ammo in the lockers. I put it all in the sergeant's office. As soon as you find that tomahawk for me, just go to the sergeant's office and let Marino know you're going to be using some of your personal gear. I guarantee you he isn't going to have a problem with it, except he's gonna wonder why the hell you haven't been wearing it. Nobody should be worrying about any department policy bullshit rules at this point man; c'mon!"

Harris affectionately clapped Cruz on the shoulder in an effort to assure him he wasn't really angry with him. Cruz shrugged away and answered Harris with some of his own frustration leaking out in his voice.

"Yeah, yeah, I got it. I'll get that handled ASAP."

Yeah; I'm the dumbass for not using my unauthorized gear, but no one else even had any gear just in case the shit ever hit the fan. And we work in the middle of one of the most violent areas in the country—and that's when things are "normal". How smart was it not to have any extra gear for "just in case" insurance?

Cruz went back to rooting around in his duffle and fished out an impressive looking black all steel tomahawk. It was approximately eighteen inches long and sported a narrow blade no more than two inch wide on one side, and a short spike on the other end of the blade. It was emblazoned *ESTWING* in large bold letters on the handle just below the blade. Harris accepted the tomahawk and briefly admired the appearance of the unusual tool.

"What was this thing designed for anyway," Harris asked. "This sucker looks wicked, doesn't it though?"

Cruz answered, "Like I said, it was actually made to break into, or through, stuff when you can only carry the most simple and light weight tools. A guy could chop through a wall or even through the roof of a car--or whatever—with this. You know, it's for whatever you might need to do during a serious *shit hits the fan* situation. Kinda like right now I guess, huh," he added after a few seconds of contemplation.

Harris considered Cruz's comment before responding.

"Yeah, *'kinda like right now'* is exactly right. Hey, do me a favor and tell everybody else to pass the word that if they have any unauthorized gear or guns, they need to go get that shit and start carrying it with them. And I mean like right now! "

Not wanting to beat the proverbial dead horse, Harris changed the conversation.

"I'll go let the sarge know I told you to tell the other guys what I just said. He won't have a problem with it. If I'm wrong I'll eat it and go tell everyone that it was my bad call--but I ain't wrong about this. Trust me on this. Marino lives in the real world when it comes to this shit."

Carrying his recently borrowed tomahawk in a manner reminiscent of a kid with a new toy on Christmas morning, Harris went to the first locker that was still secured. True to form, he was excited about breaking into the locker to find out what was inside of it. The locker had a small sticker on its steel door that read *"Tap Out"*. He knew the deputy the locker belonged to, a forty two year old Irish-American named Adam Treanor. The man was a serious bad ass who had become proficient in several martial arts over the span of three decades. But what interested Harris right now was that he happened to know Treanor had recently expanded his martial interests to firearms other than those issued by the department to patrol cops.

He knew Treanor lived in Orange County somewhere, and he assumed he was sheltering in place at his house like most of the station personnel. In his mind this was unfortunate; Treanor would have been a great asset to have at the station right now. So would Treanor's good pal, Chuck Koffman, as far as that went. Koffman, another tough street cop who also happened to be an Army reservist, was currently serving as a door gunner in Afghanistan. Harris considered the irony of a guy like Koffman serving overseas out of his sense of duty, and then having an event that threatened to implode the entire United States--like this EMP incident--occurring while he was over there.

Harris wasn't sure why, but he began to form a list in his head of some of the deputies he wished were here at the station with the others: guys like Adam Treanor, Chuck Koffman, "Big John" Purnell, and of course Rob Flynn--guys that had proven their capability under fire--quite literally in several instances.

He took a good look at Treanor's locker, and then examined the tomahawk tool in his hand. He adjusted his strong two handed grip and swung the steel device with about ninety percent of his strength.

The two inch section of the tomahawk's blade penetrated the steel door of the locker, the tip protruding through the back by about an inch. He worked the blade back out and then repeated the entire process, this time sacrificing some of the force used in his swing in order to ensure more accuracy in impact. He was able to gradually increase the length of the opening he had cut into the door. It was a labor intensive and time consuming endeavor, but he was eventually able to use the tool to pry open a large section of the sheet metal, affording him a view of the locker's contents.

"Jackpot motherfucker," Harris exclaimed in his typical profanity laced manner of speaking.

Hanging on a steel hook inside the locker was a civilian-legal compact M4 carbine. The weapon fired the common 5.56 mm cartridge. The general weapon platform, although not this specific version, was standard American military issue. The weapon had also become a staple for American police agencies where and when rifles were being deployed in law enforcement capacities. Nadeau Station had several similar weapons—all of them now locked inside of a high security safe whose lock had been ruined by the EMP event.

Using the *Estwing* to make the hole large enough to remove the carbine from the locker, Harris retrieved the newfound prize and examined it. The carbine had a ten round magazine that was locked into the receiver by a device commonly referred to as a *bullet button*, as required by California law. In essence, the *bullet button* restricted the weapon so that it could only fire ten rounds at a time unless a tool of some kind was used to remove the magazine from the rifle. Other magazines would work in the weapon, but changing them out would be slower than how the rifle had originally been designed to do so.

The upside was that the locker contained not only a handful of thirty round magazines for the rifle, but also close to three hundred rounds of ammunition for it. Harris grabbed the shotgun he had been carrying with him and re-slung it across his back. Then he scooped up Treanor's carbine and used the nylon sling to position the weapon over his shoulder.

He grabbed the small duffle bag containing the extra rifle magazines and ammunition, and headed toward the sergeant's office like a hunter returning from a successful hunt. He walked in through the open door of the sergeant's office and proudly announced his findings to Marino.

"Got this from Treanor's locker. Definitely a good score," Harris said as he leaned the newly acquired carbine against the wall and dropped the duffle on Marino's desk. He unzipped the bag to reveal its contents.

"Looks like about three hundred rounds, give or take," Harris offered as he took the tomahawk tool from his belt and hefted it in his hand, admiring it once again.

"I'll tell you what boss, this thing kicked ass on Treanor's locker. The bolt cutters wouldn't cut the padlock, so I used this thing to cut through the locker door itself--sorta like a can opener."

Marino quipped, "Where the hell did you get that thing anyway?"

"Cruz had it in his personal war bag that he had in his truck. It's good shit Sarge."

Harris handed the tomahawk to his supervisor to examine. Harris laughed as he took in the sight of the burly six-foot-four sergeant, who was now well on his way to having a full beard due to his not having shaved since the grid failure. Harris was reminded of a Viking as he watched Marino testing the balance of the tomahawk, slowly raising and lowering the tool in a striking motion.

"What the hell's so funny Lee," the sergeant asked Harris with a touch of irritation. The sergeant wasn't the first one who found himself envious of the stocky deputy's penchant for finding humor in situations where others felt only dread.

"Nothin'. Except that you look like some wild Viking with that thing in your hand."

Harris erupted in a chuckle, and Marino joined him in laughter for a few seconds as he ran a big hand through his developing beard and set the tomahawk on his desk.

"I still got one more locker to get into--it's Flynn's actually," Harris said as he made sure to make eye contact with Marino. "I'll be surprised if there isn't somethin' we can use that's in his locker."

Marino said, "Yeah, I'll bet you find somethin' in there that makes the job of peeling that steel door worth it."

Harris had known from the outset that one of the two lockers with the high security padlocks had belonged to his close buddy-- Rob Flynn. The two friends had discussed many times the wisdom of keeping items in their lockers in preparation for unforeseen and highly unusual incidents, including large scale disasters. After all, they were in the Los Angeles area, where virtually anything could, and many things had, happened.

It was nothing more, or less, than a cruel irony that left Harris without any emergency food stores in his own locker when the EMP occurred. On the last day of work prior to his taking a rare two week vacation, Harris had emptied his locker of the military MRE food rations, as well as a small water filter, that he normally kept there. He reasoned that it was time to rotate the food rations since they were almost seven years old. He had consumed them during the three separate camping outings he had planned for his vacation, and the water filter was sitting on his kitchen sink at home. The well-rested and eager deputy had returned to work only two days prior to the EMP induced grid crash, and unfortunately, he had not yet made time to replace the MRE's when the proverbial shit had hit the fan.

Perfect timing. Goddamn the irony—and that fuckin' little bastard Murphy too!

Harris had saved for last the job of opening Rob Flynn's locker for a couple of reasons. First, he thought his buddy's locker would likely offer the most useful find for the remaining deputies at the station, and therefore wanted to save the best for last so to speak. Of course the M-4 carbine and ammunition retrieved from Treanor's locker had now made that unlikely. But there was also another reason for his waiting until the end to force his way into his friend's locker. Due to his reservist Marine Corps training a decade ago, Harris knew better than most how the consequences of the EMP incident were likely to play out over the next several weeks and months. And he knew there was a significant possibility that either he or his best friend wouldn't survive this thing to the end—however long that turned out to be.

With the above thought in mind, Harris experienced a rare moment of melancholy that temporarily threatened to overrun his eagerness to gain access to whatever was stored in Flynn's locker. The feeling was short-lived however, and once again he hoisted the tomahawk in preparation for penetrating the steel door of the last unopened locker.

When he finally got the sturdy door peeled back sufficiently to view the locker's contents, he was not disappointed. As expected, the contents included items that would be useful for the deputies who remained at Nadeau Station.

Harris pulled out no less than fifteen MRE's, six two-meal foil pouches of *Mountain House* brand freeze dried meals, ten *Millenium* 400 calorie power bars, and two gallons of drinking water. He found a small single burner propane stove along with two small sixteen ounce propane canisters. Flynn had taken to storing very little else in his modest sized locker in order to have room for the above items. Harris quickly estimated the number of cooking hours the two propane canisters would provide. He figured the two bottles would run the little stove somewhere between ten to fourteen hours.

Harris also located Rob's department issued Berettta 9mm pistol in a black nylon shoulder holster that held two extra fifteen round magazines, in addition to the pistol itself, on the shelf of Flynn's locker. Harris allowed himself a smile as he was reminded of a specific day, over a year ago, he had been assigned to work as Flynn's patrol car partner. On this day Rob had arrived at work only to realize that he didn't have his duty sidearm with him. At the time Rob had only recently begun carrying the more concealable Smith and Wesson pistol while off-duty, and had not yet acquired the proper uniform holster required to carry the new weapon while working uniformed patrol.

Rob had inadvertently left the Beretta at home on the day in question, which created a problem. He had his Smith and Wesson, but had no duty holster in which to carry it in uniform. Harris had helped his friend find another deputy that could lend him a Beretta that fit his uniform holster. Rob had been bothered by the embarrassing incident throughout the entire shift that day, and had vowed to make sure it never happened again. From that point on he left his issued Beretta pistol in his locker.

On the top shelf of his locker Flynn stored an extra hundred rounds of duty authorized 9mm cartridges beyond what was loaded in the magazines kept in his gun belt pouches. Harris also found forty eight rounds of department authorized twelve gauge double aught buck shotgun shells, all of which were loaded into an olive drab green nylon bandoleer that was designed to be worn across the chest in the time-proven manner of warriors ranging from nineteenth century bandits to present day soldiers. And last, but not least, Harris discovered a small but significant collection of items that he immediately realized would make life better for him here at the station under the current conditions.

Situated on the top shelf of Rob's locker next to the two boxes of pistol ammo, were four clean and neatly folded changes of underwear, including socks, underwear briefs, and white t-shirts. For reasons not completely known to him at the time Harris felt a little sad about the whole thing, but he took encouragement by thinking of how Rob would be more than happy to know that the items he had stored would be used by his buddy, or by any of the deputies that would be defending the station. Harris, who was not a religious man whatsoever, made a quick request of God to see to it that he would have the opportunity to tell his friend how his preparation items were put to good use.

The patrol deputy and former Marine shifted his mind set from one of sadness and into one of aggression and focused thinking. He examined Flynn's shoulder holster, noting that the pistol was suspended on one side and two extra magazine pouches hung from the opposite side. He slipped the shoulder holster over his uniform shirt and made a few adjustments to the nylon webbing to fit his torso. He checked the Beretta and confirmed that it was loaded with fifteen rounds in the magazine and one more in the chamber. The two extra magazines in the shoulder rig's pouches were loaded with fifteen rounds apiece.

Since Harris routinely carried three extra magazines—all fully loaded--for his own Beretta on his duty belt, he now had a total of five extra magazines for the two identical Beretta pistols he was wearing. By his count he was now armed with one hundred seven rounds of 9mm ammunition, including the sixteen rounds each of the two pistols held.

The last items of significant value Harris found in Rob's locker were a dozen individually packaged *Kerlix* gauze wraps, all contained in a cardboard box that supported his uniform boots on the bottom of the locker. The super absorbent gauze dressings were often used by soldiers on the battle field as trauma sponges to be placed over and pressed against wounds. Harris gave a moment of thought to consider the value of the *Kerlix*. He concluded it couldn't hurt to provide the deputies with the newfound first aid items, despite the fact that the lack of hospital access or medical professionals would most likely render the trauma dressings only minimally effective at best.

Rather than attempt to carry all of the contents retrieved from Flynn's locker to Marino's office, Harris simply walked to the office and informed the sergeant of what he had found. He tapped the second pistol that he now wore in the exposed shoulder holster and addressed Marino.

"You okay with me wearing Flynn's shoulder rig and Beretta?"

The question wasn't asked because he was unclear whether the sergeant approved of his wearing a second exposed side arm but out of a concern that Marino might have another use in mind for the extra pistol. It turned out he didn't.

The bearded supervisor only threw a quick glance at the black shoulder holster and pistol before giving a quick nod, the brevity of which suggested he felt the question wasn't worthy of spending a full sentence on. After several seconds had gone by Marino said, "Whadya say we break out some of those MRE's you just found and share them with the troops now? I figure they could all use a little morale booster about now."

Harris nodded and said, "Sounds like a damn good idea to me."

Harris walked to Rob's locker and removed half of the MRE's and carried them to Marino's office before returning to get the second half. He made a third trip to get the pouches of freeze dried food and the two water jugs. As he loaded up his arms on a fourth trip with energy bars and the small propane stove, he stopped for a second before carrying the last of the food items to the sergeant's office. He set the items down, walked over to the recently destroyed locker, and grabbed a pair of each of the three underwear items. He shoved the folded t-shirt under his uniform shirt, the pair of socks into his left front pocket, and the briefs into his front right pocket.

He removed the bandoleer holding the shotgun shells from the hook inside his friend's locker and threw it over his shoulder before stuffing one box of fifty pistol cartridges in his left rear pocket and the other in his right pocket. He returned once more to the sergeant's office, dropped the bandoleer and boxes of pistol ammunition onto Marino's desk, and the food items and stove onto the floor. He did not remove the clothing items from where he had stashed them on his person. There was no point in mentioning it he figured.

25

WESTCHESTER, CA

Rob felt a shiver run through his body as he moved closer to the small fire in the back yard. The shiver was the result of the combination of a chilly morning and his sweat dampened t-shirt as opposed to any feeling of unease. Seeing as how his shirt was wet with perspiration and all, he reminded himself to monitor his body temperature as best he could. He had learned from his outdoors experience, as well as his Marine Corps basic training, that wearing wet clothes could be an invitation for hypothermia, even when in temperatures no colder than the current fifty eight degrees.

Rob and his new acquaintance both stared at the stainless steel water bottle that hung suspended over the flames waiting to come to a boil. The process took about twenty minutes, plus a few more minutes after that to wait for the steel container to cool down, even with the gloves Rob used for that purpose. Don looked at the set-up Rob had created with the steel bottle, small cable, and the diagonally positioned stick that supported it. He sized up the little system all in a few seconds.

Don had always prided himself with having an aptitude for being able to quickly assess and figure out practical challenges along with being able to improvise solutions on the fly.

"Are you doing that mostly to make the water safe to drink or so you can make up a hot cup of coffee?"

Rob surmised, correctly, that Don was wondering if he had any coffee in his pack that he might be willing to share. The fact of the matter was he didn't have any. He had reached the point where even sipping on hot water in the cool mornings was a treat. In any case, he planned on grabbing a few hours of sleep shortly, and he wouldn't have wanted the caffeine in his system even if he had had it available.

Rob answered the man, "I just want to make sure there's no chance I'll get sick, just in case there were any invisible critters in that water heater tank where I got the water. I strained any big stuff with my bandana as I filled the bottle, and I know boiling it will kill anything that can hurt me. The last thing I need is to have a case of the shits while I'm trying to walk outta here."

Don nodded, and said, "Yeah. Just make sure you don't ever screw the bottle cap on that thing when you boil it."

Picturing the small explosion of scalding hot water that would result from such a move, Rob let a slight chortle escape and said, "Yeah, that would be a problem alright."

Just seconds after the water came to a low boil, Rob reached out with a gloved hand and removed the steel container from its suspension system. Finding a relatively flat spot on the ground to temporarily set the bottle of hot liquid, Rob placed the container there and waited a few minutes in silence before removing one of his gloves and handed it to Don.

"Here, put this on in case this thing's still too hot to handle with bare hands. Be careful sipping it. Better wait a minute or two--that water's still pretty hot."

Rob immediately realized the way his comment must have come across.

"I guess that was pretty obvious wasn't it? Not sure why I said it." He erupted in a smile and decided not to say anything more about it.

"It's been a while since I've talked with anyone."

Don didn't reply, but he still wore a smile on his face. He hadn't been offended. He slipped on the glove Rob had given him and picked up the bottle of hot water from its resting place. It appeared to Rob as though Don was enjoying the comfort of the hot steel container as he held it in his gloved hand. After a few moments had passed, he blew on the edge of the bottle's opening and carefully sipped the hot water. It wasn't coffee, but it was hot and it was liquid. He was grateful for the basic and brief comfort it provided.

"Hold on a second," Rob said as he pulled one of the little honey packets from his shirt pocket. He emptied the honey into the hot water and sat back down, allowing Don to sip the brew when he was ready.

"Shit. I never thought a cup of hot water would taste so damn good," Don said as he looked at Rob and laughed.

Rob asked, "You got anything to eat there in your bundle?"

"All I got is half a Snickers bar and a little fast food packet of mustard," Don said as he laughed again and shook his head.

It was becoming pretty apparent to Rob that Don had an easygoing personality. He seemed to see the humor in a lot of the miserable circumstances he was dealing with. This was in sharp contrast with Rob's own intense personality, and he found the company of the man enjoyable for this very reason. Nothing wrong with taking a little break from the mental pressure cooker Rob had been operating under since this whole electromagnetic pulse thing had happened. Nothing wrong with it at all.

Throughout their marriage, Stephanie had remarked about how Rob was too intense-- and that was under normal circumstances. It was safe to say that nothing associated with the EMP infrastructure crash had eased this tendency for him. Rob looked at Don as he fished the pitiful piece of candy bar out of his makeshift bundle of minimal possessions.

The worn down street cop started to laugh. It started off small, not much more than a polite chuckle really. But soon Don started to laugh with him. And then Rob's laugh started to build in intensity, until it evolved into a full-blown belly laugh that continued for what seemed like a full minute or more, leaving his stomach muscles aching with the effort. Don had laughed right along with him, matching him both in intensity and duration. It was a good feeling. Just like a couple of regular guys hanging out by a camp fire laughing it up over a funny joke or humorous incident being retold.

Finally able to speak coherently following his laughing spell, Rob asked Don where he was headed.

"I'm thinking I should be able to make it home in a full day or so even if I have to stop and hide for a while along the way. I live in Culver City, not more than a few miles from here."

"You got a family, Don?"

"Yeah, I'm married. No kids at home anymore. It's kinda funny actually, but about a month back or so my wife started tellin' me about how we should have a month's worth of food and water stored at the house in case of an earthquake. I pretty much just went along with it, just to make her less stressed out. Never thought we would actually ever need it. Go figure, huh?"

Rob retorted, "Yeah, well, at our house it was the opposite. Being a cop, I've seen too many ugly things I guess. And what I haven't seen first-hand I've heard about from real people that were there to see it, or had it happen to them. Human beings can be some of the ugliest, most brutal, and evil scheming sonsabitches on the planet when they think it serves their needs. Or when they get desperate."

Rob looked at Don to try to get a read on how he was responding to this. If he looked disinterested, he would simply stop talking. Don seemed like he wanted to hear what he had to say, so he continued.

"As if I hadn't lost enough faith in my fellow human beings already, not long after *September Eleventh* I was assigned to this terrorism liaison job at the station--not really much of a job to tell the truth. No top secret stuff or anything like that. Just a contact at the local level for the Feds is all. But they sent us to monthly meetings and a lot of pretty interesting classes. So now I really know how fucked up human beings can be. On a big scale."

He glanced over at Don to see if he was still interested. Either he was being polite and was a good actor, or he wanted to hear what Rob had to say.

"Anyway, I told my wife I wanted to stock up on some supplies at the house--mostly food and water and emergency lights, in case whatever disaster flavor of the month might happen. And she pretty much just went along with it to make me feel better. All good, right? Except now I'm so friggin' far away from our house that I'm no good to them. Some big professional protector I am, huh? Not there when my family needs me the most."

He realized he was getting a little too emotional now as he thought about his present situation and the magnitude of the circumstances he, and now Don, faced.

I'm just tired is all. More like exhausted. Things will look better after a little bit of sleep.

Don asked him, "Where do you live anyway?"

"Thousand Oaks. About forty miles or so from here."

"Oh shit. That's a haul man," Don said.

"Well, I got a plan I want to run by you if you're up to hearing it," Rob replied. "But first let's get some food and a little shut eye under our belts".

Don looked directly at Rob and said, "If it's all the same to you, I'd like to hear your idea before then. If you don't mind that is."

Rob asked Don what he thought of the idea of the two of them sharing some peanut butter and crackers, taking turns getting some sleep, two hours at a time, and then heading out after dark as a team toward Don's house. Rob suggested that he could stay for twenty four hours at Don's house to rest up and then head out on his way toward Thousand Oaks. He knew being rested—and hopefully fed—would help his odds to get home.

Don was silent for a minute. He was clearly mulling over the idea. Rob guessed he was trying to predict how his wife might react to him showing up with a stranger, and then letting her know that he had agreed to let him stay at the house for twenty four hours. Finally, Don agreed to the plan.

"What kinda peanut butter are we talking about in this deal you come up with," Don said with a big smile.

"Hell if I know. I never saw the jar it came out of." Rob laughed with his new friend. He became serious again and gave Don the abbreviated version of how he had met the Brown family, minus the violent details. He ended the story by mentioning how he had discovered the gift of peanut butter and crackers in his pack.

"How about passing me that weak tasting coffee you got there," Rob asked, referring to the hot water and honey in the steel bottle. Don handed it over. Rob found the container warm but not dangerously so. He sipped as though it were good tasting coffee. Maintaining his grasp of the bottle, he reached into his pack and withdrew a zip-lock baggie holding the equivalent of a half dozen tablespoons of peanut butter and a dozen saltine crackers.

They shared the food and polished off the hot water as well.

"I want to go over the sleeping arrangements or whatever, but first let me get some more water in that bottle. I want to make as much drinkable water as I can before we take off from here." With that, Rob grabbed the bottle and started toward the garage. He hadn't walked ten feet before he stopped, suddenly remembering something.

"Hey Don, do you know how to use that little sawed-off shotgun leaning against my pack there?"

Don replied, "Probably, why?"

"Well let me show you real quick anyway. Just in case you need it while I'm getting this water. It takes a little while to filter the water from that water heater tank spigot through my bandana and into the water bottle, so I might be away for a bit."

Rob removed the shotgun from its cord and showed him how to cock back the hammer before firing it.

"It's only one shot, but it packs a serious punch with that double aught load. Just don't use it past twenty five yards," he said. Don responded with a nod and a simple "Okay," taking a quick look around at his surroundings in the process.

Rob added, "Keep it handy, like right next to you, until I get back. And if anyone comes around that you even think might be up to no good, start making some noise so I know what's going on. And don't hesitate to pull the trigger if someone comes closer than you want him to. Twenty feet is plenty close by the way. I'm sorry if I sound like I'm givin' orders and all, but you gotta trust me on this stuff. I've been to this rodeo a few times. We're talkin' some serious shit here."

Once again, Don nodded and said "Okay. I got it." He simultaneously picked up the little shotgun and hefted its weight, familiarizing himself with the feel of the weapon and the location of the features he would need to know how to manipulate should he have to use it. He said, "I think I got this covered Rob. Go ahead and get your water."

Rob returned several minutes later and used the small cable-like wire and a length of *Paracord* to suspend the bottle over the fire. Despite the fact he had made it a point to tell Don he wanted to get some sleep, for some reason he found himself forestalling that activity. Maybe it was because, for the first time in a long while, he was enjoying the basic comfort provided by a camp fire and friendly human contact: companionship. He realized the feeling was going to be brief—after all there were going to be new problems to deal with—but for now he allowed himself the luxury of enjoying the experience in the moment.

Don was staring at the water container hanging over the flame when he asked Rob, "I guess you already looked through the house for pots or pans that could be used for boiling bigger amounts of water, right?"

There was a pregnant pause, and then Rob smiled as he turned his head and looked at his new buddy. "You know what, Don, sometimes I have to admit I'm just not as smart as I like to think I am. I never even thought to do that, but it's a damn good idea."

He allowed himself to enjoy a few more minutes of the tranquil setting before he got up.

"I think I'll go look for that pot you suggested before I hit the rack for a few Z's. Makes more sense, right? Get a big pot of water heating the sooner the better. Stay heads up."

He didn't wait for a response before he took off walking toward the house.

Rob searched all of the kitchen cupboards until he was finally rewarded with two lidded pots, one capable of holding about two quarts of water and the other close to twice as much. He placed them by the back door and went into the living room. There, he removed several magazines from a stack on the coffee table and placed them next to the pots. He searched the two bedrooms, paying particular attention to the closets, but found nothing of value.

Finally, he searched the medicine cabinets, but it was obvious someone had picked them clean prior to his arrival. Rob walked to the back door, picked up all of the items he had placed there and took a quick glance over at where Don was sitting with the shotgun. He noticed his friend had been looking around at his surroundings as Rob exited the house with his arms full of the discovered loot.

That's good. He's paying attention for possible threats. It looks like he's taking things seriously. Definitely a good thing.

Rob approached the fire and set the items on the ground. Don looked at the stuff, his puzzled look indicating he was curious about why Rob had brought the magazines out of the house.

"Okay, here's the deal," Rob said, "I gotta go take care of my morning business, and I'm not going to waste the remaining supply of my toilet paper any more than I have to. I'm gonna use some of the pages of these magazines for the beginning of the paperwork and only use the toilet paper for the very end. Sorry for the details, but it's a system that works and I figure I'd share the knowledge is all."

Don just stared at Rob, his expression not giving up whether he was evaluating the information for its worth, marveling at Rob's knowledge, or pondering how he could separate himself from this lunatic claiming to be a cop.

Rob didn't care too much at this point. He had to take care of his morning constitutional bowel movement. He removed his large camp knife from its sheath that was still secured to his pack strap with duct tape. He used the knife to whittle the end of a stick that was somewhere between the diameter of his thumb and wrist. He stopped when he had transformed the end into a dull point.

"I'm gonna use this to dig my cat hole to crap in. I know I could just dig the hole with my knife, but dirt against a knife edge will dull it quicker than you would believe. Better to sharpen a stick and use that to dig with."

Rob flipped the whittled stick in his hand a few times as he explained his system to Don. He grunted and slightly nodded an acknowledgement. Rob wasn't sure if he thought he was nuts or if he thought the information was worth having, but he figured it didn't cost anything to utter a few words.

Before going to take care of his toilet needs, Rob set his digging stick on the ground and carried the two pots to the garage. Several minutes later he returned with the containers full of water. He used his sharpened stick to push some coals over to the side of the burning wood in the fire and set the pots directly on the coals. The water started to hiss and create steam almost immediately. He added several more of the branches from the pile to the fire as well.

Rob offered that he thought they should sleep in two hour shifts throughout the day if possible.

"We just gotta make sure we purify as much water as we can. I think we should drink as much water as our bodies can handle short of drowning ourselves while we have access to it here, and then fill as many containers as we can for when we head out tonight. Any other thoughts or ideas," Rob asked.

He could see that Don was thinking again.

Walking to the rear of the yard to find partial privacy, Rob used the stick to dig a cat hole, squatted over it and took care of his toilet business, using the stick to fill in the hole when finished. He used a small amount of the hand sanitizer, put it back in the plastic bag, and brought the bag and the stick back to the fire with him. He tossed the stick on the ground and knelt next to his pack in preparation for putting the sandwich bag containing the toilet paper and sanitizer gel back inside. He also wanted to find his toothbrush to brush his teeth, even if only with water.

Perhaps it was the fact Rob was feeling relatively content for the moment, or maybe it was the phenomenon where a guy feels safer when he has a partner to work with, but for whatever reason he had allowed himself to drop his awareness level a few notches. Throughout history, complacency had been responsible for more than one good cop or military operator meeting a bad end—a point emphasized in many a training course.

As fate will often do to those that have made it a habit of keeping themselves vigilant, it turned out that his brief relaxation was about to be rewarded by something bad happening. Murphy, of the infamous *Murphy's Law* notoriety, was a son of a bitch, pure and simple.

Rob didn't see the man with the machete until he picked up the smallest indication of movement with his peripheral vision. Unfortunately, this didn't happen until the guy was less than ten feet away from where Rob knelt next to his pack, and the maniacal cretin was closing in fast, his machete poised above his head in a two-handed grip in preparation for striking.

Holy shit. What the hell?!

The average sized man he saw in front of him had long filthy hair growing out of both his scalp and his face. He wore equally filthy clothes, and most importantly, he was quite clearly intent on slicing him up with the big machete. And he was walking directly toward Rob and covering what little ground separated them. Fast.

The man appeared to be Caucasian, although his skin tone was all but impossible to ascertain due to the layers of dirt and whatever else had accumulated there. The guy had the look of a vagrant- the type that present-day society had collectively decided to refer to as "homeless" over the past couple of decades. Of course there were now a whole bunch of folks that were homeless, not because they chose to live that lifestyle, but because circumstances had thrust it upon them following the EMP. Or at least they no longer had homes that represented a lifestyle that was anything close to what it had been before the infrastructure had shut down without warning.

Rob's split second judgment told him it was too late for him to go for the pistol holstered on his belt. His training had taught him this over and over, but he didn't need any formal training to know he didn't have time to draw his gun. This fucker was damn near on top of him! He had to get something between himself and that machete blade immediately. Not immediately as in within a second or two, but immediately as in right fucking now! It was a matter of milliseconds--not seconds.

Rob yelled out to Don as he grabbed the pack he had been fumbling with and yanked it up in front of him. Managing to get the backpack between his body and the machete wielding lunatic, he rose to his feet, using the pack as a shield in front of him. He could smell the foul odor of the man preparing to kill him. It was a mixture of excrement, old body odor and even older garbage. He raised the machete even higher over his head in a two-handed grip as he closed in on the inches separating the two. Rob, protecting himself with nothing but his pack, once again called out to his friend. This time there was a noticeable trace of panic in his voice. Actually, he was seriously panicked, and he felt no shame that his voice conveyed this.

"Shoot this guy Don; shoot him right now; shoot him godamnit!"

The homicidal psychopath swung his machete at Rob, and he could hear as well as feel the blade's impact as it sliced through the heavy nylon material forming the outer layer of the pack. The big blade's progress was mercifully halted by a heavy metal strap buckle attached to the pack. Rob couldn't actually see the impact of the blade due to how he was holding the pack in front of his body and face, but he felt the considerable force behind the blow. Struggling to maintain his balance and not lose his footing, twice more Rob felt the machete blade striking his pack under the powerful swings of the madman. Strangely, the wild man said nothing at all during the attack. No indication whatsoever as to why the man was trying to slice him up. All Rob heard was an animalistic grunting noise uttered by his assailant as he swung the machete.

Why the fuck is this guy trying to hack me up into pieces? And where the hell did he come from?

After what seemed like an infinitely longer length of time than the mere five seconds that had actually transpired, Rob heard the unmistakable boom of a shotgun being fired at close range. A second later he heard the machete wielding man crumple to the ground.

Not wasting any time, and thinking in the martial manner he was accustomed to, Rob quickly took several steps backward, threw his pack away from him and drew his pistol in one fluid movement. Gripping his pistol with both hands and looking all around them, he half expected to find another attacker. But that didn't happen.

He took a long look at the dead psychopath lying on the ground, paying particular attention to the massive damage caused by the buckshot payload. Still holding the 9mm in a two-handed combat grip, Rob told Don to reload the shotgun and to keep his eyes open for any additional danger.

Rob was about to caution his friend to be careful not to get him in his line of fire. Before he could get the words out he suddenly realized he had never given Don the four extra rounds for the shotgun. They were still in his pocket. He looked over at his friend and saw him fumbling with the shotgun, presumably trying to remove the expended shotgun shell from the breach. He watched the spent shell pop out of the breech end of the barrel and fall to the ground.

Man, I am really starting to slip here. I never showed him how to reload the gun or gave him the extra shells. I've got to make myself focus better, Rob told himself as he stepped toward Don.

"Never mind about reloading. I just remembered I have the extra shells. I'll take care of it," Rob said.

Rob crossed the ten yards to where Don was holding the empty shotgun. He had ceased looking around and was now staring at the massive wound he had inflicted upon the dead man. The buckshot had struck him from the side just below his right armpit, penetrating deep enough to destroy much of the man's heart and at least one lung. Rob surmised the man had died close to instantly, thus ending the attack and saving Rob's ass.

Indicating the shotgun in Don's hand with a jerk of his head, Rob extended his open hand toward his new friend.

"Lemme see that for a second and I'll show you how to load it. By the way, thanks for shooting that asshole. That was crazy. Fuckin' crazy. I wish I had a clean pair of underwear," Rob said as he laughed at his own humor.

Don handed Rob the scatter gun as he asked, "What the hell was that about anyway? Any idea why that guy attacked you like that? It was like somethin' out of a horror movie!"

Rob shook his head and then shrugged his shoulders. "Partner, I got no fuckin' idea why this happened." He stole another glance at the dead man lying less than twenty feet from where they now stood as if the man's appearance might somehow provide an answer to the mystery.

"All I can think of is that all the crazies are no longer gettin' their medications, and now they're runnin' around on the streets."

He showed Don how to reload the shotgun, reminding him that the hammer had to be manually cocked before the gun would fire.

Rob chuckled and said, "Why am I tellin' you that? I guess you figured out how to shoot that thing alright when it counted, huh."

Don responded, "Yeah, I don't think he even saw me. I went over to take a leak when you were messin' around with your pack, and all-of-a-sudden this guy just comes runnin' up on you out of nowhere. Like I said, I don't think he ever even saw me till after I shot him."

Rob listened and thought about the information Don had just given him. He was extremely pissed off at himself for having let the machete wielding maniac get that close to him before noticing what was happening, and he was trying to get his head wrapped around how it had happened. But in the end it really didn't matter he told himself. All that mattered was that the bad guy was no longer a threat and Rob had escaped injury. And only barely at that. It also mattered whether or not the crazy guy had any friends with him, crazy or otherwise. So far--so good.

He was going to hand Don the remaining three shotgun shells he had in his pocket, but after thinking about it, he opted to hang onto them. He would be carrying the shotgun as well as his sidearm when they hiked out of here.

Rob walked over to the dead man and looked at him for a few seconds. He considered going through the man's pockets in case they contained anything of value, but dismissed the idea as not being worth it almost as soon as the thought had come to him. The guy was just too filthy to be worth touching. Not worth the precious water it would take, or the hand sanitizer, to clean off whatever disease the cretin might be carrying. Rob did however walk over and retrieve the machete that had fallen from the assailant's hands. He held the bladed tool in his hand and examined the edge with his finger, being careful not to cut himself. As filthy as the owner of the machete had been, the machete looked like it had been maintained well, which prompted Rob to think that perhaps the crazy man hadn't owned it very long.

"There are a lot of these homeless creeps that are seriously crazy. Learned a long time ago they ain't all family men who are just down on their luck. I wonder if somehow this EMP thing has caused more of 'em to go off the deep end somehow. There was no sane reason for this guy to just attack me out of the blue like that."

Shaking his head, he added, "Stone cold psychopath for sure."

As he looked at the dead man, something caught Rob's eye. It was a bright red plastic wristband riveted to the corpse's left wrist. It was a type of wristband Rob had seen hundreds of times in the past. The kind the Los Angeles County Jail used to label *KEEP AWAY* inmates. These were inmates who were mandated to be separated from the general jail population for any number of reasons. One of these reasons included the need to isolate a psychotic individual given to uncontrollable violent behavior.

Rob looked at Don and said, "Buddy, I think I just figured out what this attack was all about, and it's not good."

Don looked at Rob, anxious to hear what he was going to say.

"That red wristband he's wearing is what the sheriff's department puts on inmates in the county jail—inmates they call *KEEP AWAYS*. Prisoners can be classified as *KEEP AWAYS* for a bunch of different reasons—one of 'em being if a guy is a total lunatic who will attack another inmate without any reason whatsoever."

He gave his friend several seconds to connect the dots before he continued.

"So here's the deal. I think either the jail system has been screwed up by this EMP thing so that some, or even all, of the inmates have escaped, or else the sheriff's department has let a bunch of these guys out of jail because they can't feed or water them—or they don't have enough deputies to watch them all--whatever. Either way it's definitely bad news."

Rob looked over at the dead man after he finished revealing his theory.

"Hey...you want this machete? It might be a good idea for you to have your own weapon on you from now on. I'm planning on taking my shotgun back before we leave here ya know."

Rob smiled as he said this, despite the fact that he was dead serious about what he had just stated.

Don didn't hesitate to answer up.

"Hell yeah I want that thing. After what just happened I figure any crazy fuckin' thing can happen. It ain't like there's any cops that are gonna be comin' to save me."

Don realized the irony of what he had just said in light of what Rob's profession was. "No offense," Don added.

"Hey, I totally agree. I'm not offended. We're all on our own out here--at least for now."

Rob handed the machete to his friend.

"We'll figure a way to rig up some kinda sheath for that with duct tape and whatever else."

Don examined his newly acquired machete, trying out its feel and balance with first a one-handed, and then a double-handed grip. Watching him handling the machete, Rob quipped, "Hell, I think more people have died by machete in Africa and other third world places than they have from AIDS, Ebola, and gunfire together. Yeah, I guess this will work as a weapon if you need it."

"Yeah well, I sure as hell hope we aren't gonna have any more problems till I get home."

Rob raised his hands in a gesture intended to indicate it was out of his control. He looked over at Don, who suddenly appeared to be feeling a little woozy.

"I think I need to sit down for a minute. I just need a second to clear my head here. I almost feel a little sea sick. "

Rob understood that the adrenalized state of his friend, following the shooting of the crazy man and all, was probably responsible for his sudden feeling of light headedness and nausea.

"Okay. Sit down and put your head between your knees for a little while. It should help make sure you don't pass out. What you're feelin' right now is normal stuff man. Totally normal," Rob said.

Don didn't respond.

While he watched his friend continue sitting with his face in his palms trying to clear his head, Rob put his gloves on and dragged the dead man by his heels approximately fifty feet. He pulled the foul smelling mass behind the garage wall where he would be out of view from the sidewalk as well as from Rob and Don. Things were bad enough without having to camp with a damn corpse in their midst.

Rob took off his gloves and began rooting through his pack yet again, this time making sure to look up and around at his surroundings every few seconds. He pulled out the last of his high calorie energy bars, cut it in half with his folding knife, and walked over to where Don was still sitting. Now he had his head positioned forward between his knees.

"If you promise you're not gonna throw up and waste it, I'll give you half of my last energy bar. Plus, I'll go get you some hot water to chase it down with. Nothin' but the best for my buddy who just saved my ass."

Rob laughed as he cracked wise about the situation.

Don held out his hand and took his half of the energy bar, but he didn't eat it. He still seemed to be working past his light-headedness and nausea. After several minutes had passed and he felt better, Don ate the piece of the energy bar and asked Rob for the hot water he had promised. Rob jumped up, happy to see that his pal was feeling better, and brought him the warm stainless steel bottle.

Rob examined the damage that had been done to his pack with the machete. He observed three places where the machete had penetrated the pack's outer heavy nylon material. Each was three to four inches in length. After examining all of the pack's contents, he saw his fleece hoodie had been cut by the machete blade as it had penetrated the pack, but no other items had been damaged that he could see. He got busy with the duct tape he had included in his 'bug out" supplies and repaired the damage as best he could, figuring it would hold up well enough for now.

After making sure Don was doing okay, he asked him if he wanted to take the first sleeping shift. But his friend preferred to wait a couple of hours before trying to sleep.

"Still too wound up about that machete guy I shot," Don said.

Rob nodded in understanding.

"I get it man. I really do. I'll see if I can grab a couple hours now. Wake me up then. And whatever you do, don't fall asleep yourself."

Rob set his pack against a tree so he could use it as a means of support to lean against. He didn't subscribe to the idea of lying down to sleep under high danger conditions. Too difficult to get up and into action quickly.

Rob took off his boots and socks, turning the latter inside-out so that the sun could dry them out and possibly even serve as a low level disinfectant. He realized the springtime sun was not likely to be hot enough, nor the exposure time long enough, to do much good, but it was better than nothing. He had packed an extra pair of socks in his pack, and he had been alternating the two pairs when he could as well as airing out his feet for as long as possible during makeshift camp site rest stops. He wanted to avoid foot problems at all costs.

"You got on a watch that works, right," Rob asked.

"Yeah, why?"

"I want you to be sure to wake me up in two hours...sooner if you start to get sleepy."

"No problem."

"Oh yeah; here," Rob added as he rolled away from the pack he was using to lean against and onto his side so that he could gain access to his front jeans pocket. He withdrew the shotgun shells from his pocket, and held them up in his hand.

"Hang on to these until I take my shotgun back." Don walked over and held out his hand whereupon Rob dropped the shells into his palm.

Rob was unable to sleep at first, and he began talking to Don about the electromagnetic pulse concept, including much of the information he had learned from his terrorism courses. He elaborated on how the sheriff's department powers that be had knowingly failed to prepare the individual stations or emphasize the importance of department employee families to prepare for disasters.

"I guess they preferred the philosophy of ignoring the problem and just hoping it wouldn't happen on their watch," Rob said in a sarcasm filled voice.

Don looked very serious, concerned even, which was not in character with his normal personality--at least from what Rob had seen so far.

"What are you thinking right now," Rob asked him.

Don answered without looking away from the pot of water that was being heated while resting on a bed of coals.

"I used to be a partner in a company that did electric power line construction, and I'm gonna tell you somethin'. Even under normal conditions, when you're talking about large electric transformers, the average wait time to get them built and shipped is anywhere from one to three years. A lot of 'em aren't even made in the U.S—if you can believe that shit."

He looked at Rob to see if he was taking this in.

"Now that's when things are normal, and most times there are a few transformers in supply storage somewhere. But now think about a situation like this mess we have now. If it's as wide spread across the country as you think it is, then how long is it gonna take to get replacements for the thousands of transformers that got fried by this EMP thing?"

Rob replied, "You have got to be fuckin' kiddin' me. One to three years under normal circumstances? That's unbelievable. The news just keeps on gettin' better."

Rob found himself wishing he could have a double shot of whiskey to calm his nerves, but that obviously wasn't going to happen. He tried to think about pleasant things he had done in his life. He thought about some of the good times he had shared with his family growing up, the enjoyable moments spent with Stephanie and Charlie Wyatt, and the serenity he experienced while spending time in the great out of doors.

He was sound asleep within fifteen minutes of leaning against his pack in the shade, barefoot with his bandana covering his eyes. His hand rested on the butt of his handgun secured in his belt holster.

Not very far into his sleep, he began dreaming of fighting with bad guys while working as a uniformed patrol cop. In one dream scene his head was being held against a curb next to his patrol car by a huge thug while his partner in crime prepared to stomp the life out of him. Then he dreamed of walking into a house where a rape victim and her dying parents looked at him with desperately imploring eyes as he stood there paralyzed. And he dreamed of being attacked by a crazy foul smelling man trying to chop him up with a machete.

Later into his sleep, Rob dreamt of his wife Stephanie and their four-year-old little boy, all three sitting at a table full of food and drinks, laughter as plentiful as the food. In the dream, a group of heavily armed thugs forced their way into the house and kidnapped the most precious things in his life while he was beaten and forced to endure the horrific kidnapping in a state of total helplessness. When he awoke he was still badly shaken, the tears on his cheeks bearing evidence to the vividness of the dream.

He looked around to see if his friend had noticed, but it was apparent Don was busy working on the water treatment routine. He rubbed his cheeks dry and worked the stiffness out of his neck as best he could, willing himself to dig in deeper in order to get through the ordeal he was facing.

He was reminded of a saying coined by one of America's top tier special operations military units.

The only easy day was yesterday.

26

THOUSAND OAKS, CA

The owner of the home with the American Stars and Stripes and *Amnesty International* flags presented on his front yard flagpole was a single man in his late forties. He was purportedly a recently retired employee of the human rights organization whose flag was displayed as well as a former U.S. Defense Department employee. The two organizations presented a seemingly incongruous combination for employment, but he had a well-rehearsed story to explain this for those who inquired.

The version Roger Graham tended to share with casual acquaintances was that he had worked twenty years for the Defense Department (D.O.D.) after serving in the U.S. Army. The story went that he so enjoyed travelling to, and assisting, the less fortunate nations across the globe during his career with the D.O.D., that he took a position with the well-known international human rights organization called *Amnesty International* for four years after leaving the Defense Department. So the story went. The truth was a little different.

In actuality, Roger had spent four years with the D.O.D. before it was strongly suggested he resign his position and find employment elsewhere. Although it was never recorded in any official records, those who had access to such information knew he had been involved in numerous intimate, and arguably inappropriate, relationships with women ranging in age between fifteen and fifty during his assignments abroad with the government agency. Numerous as in hundreds. Upon discovering this pattern, the D.O.D. managers collectively decided that Roger was a liability for the organization and subsequently had to go, one way or another.

Roger had the situation explained to him by his superiors in clear and non-negotiable terms. He was given a choice between looking for work somewhere other than the Department of Defense or suffering a scathing and public firing. He chose the former, and it was arranged for him to have an interview with the well-known human rights organization the following week. He was offered a position with the organization shortly thereafter. After resigning from the Defense Department, Roger had worked for *Amnesty International* for twenty years before deciding to retire. Being freshly retired, he was still trying to adjust to his new life.

He religiously ran past the Flynn residence three or four times a week as part of his strict exercise regimen. Rob had been in the front yard a few times as Roger approached on the sidewalk in front of the house. Rob introduced himself and the two had a brief conversation during that initial meeting, the content consisting of not much more than small talk about the neighborhood and the town.

At about six feet tall with a fit but slender build, Roger achieved his exercise by running as opposed to developing his upper body strength. During their second conversation, Rob had answered the man's inquiry about what he did for a living. In turn, Roger had provided Rob with the embellished version about his own background that included a twenty year stint with the D.O.D. He made it a point to go on (a little too much Rob thought) about his running program, stopping just short of asking the heavier muscled patrol cop what kind of running regimen, if any, he followed.

Under the mistaken impression that the man had been a career D.O.D. employee, Rob noted to himself that the man's physical conditioning was simply another illustration of form following function. Contrary to what most Americans might assume about a Defense Department employee who was assigned all over the world to defend America's interests, Rob knew most of these assignments were essentially desk jobs. A government analyst who spent virtually all of his or her time either behind a computer screen or travelling abroad in an observational capacity really didn't have the need to be able to hold their own in physical confrontations with violent sociopaths. No need to build upper body strength. Defending against cardiac arrest was the top objective.

Roger's hair was cut short and parted on the side, with close to equal parts gray and blonde. He looked like he could have been a clothes model for the L.L. Bean catalogue, or maybe even part of a 1970's FBI recruiting bulletin if not for the grey in his hair. Rob had had several conversations with the man in front of their house over the past six months. After Roger had learned Rob was a LASD deputy sheriff, he told him a little bit about what he had done, and where he had been assigned as a government employee. Rob had snorted inwardly at the time. The man's efforts to impress him were nothing more than penis measuring. Rob had encountered this so many times—always after his line of work was revealed—that it had become about as predictable as jokes about doughnut shops and cops.

The topic of conversation had eventually arrived at terrorism, which quickly broached the subject of individual civilian preparation for large scale terrorism incidents within the U.S. Roger, now telling the truth, indicated he was an avid advocate of preparing for protracted disasters, and urged Rob to consider doing the same.

Roger's annoying idiosyncrasies notwithstanding, Rob hadn't written the guy off yet, thinking he might be an interesting acquaintance to have in the neighborhood. He figured the guy had most likely seen a lot of things, as a result of his being stationed abroad at different locations, that most Americans had not had the opportunity to see. Rob had meant to discuss the preparedness issue with him further the next time the two had a conversation, but that follow-up discussion had not yet taken place on the day of the EMP incident.

Over a month ago, while at a neighbors' party, Rob had passed on to Stephanie the fact he had met the new neighbor with the two flags in his front yard. He had mentioned the content of the conversation he shared with the strange and somewhat enigmatic man, but Roger hadn't been discussed since then.

As Stephanie continued peering out the living room window on the post-EMP afternoon, her curiosity over the odd woman in the raincoat growing, she tried to recall what it was that Rob had found interesting about the man called "Roger". Something had prompted her husband to mention his brief discussion with the guy, but she just couldn't remember what it was.

She was suddenly struck by what was odd about the woman she was watching from afar. She was wearing a skirt or dress, as evidenced by the fact she could see the bottom of the lady's legs being exposed below the knee length rain coat she wore. Stephanie also had a complete view of her shoes, which were high-heeled dark colored pumps.

Who would be dressed like that with all that's going on right now? That's just totally ridiculous. Who is she trying to impress out here for God's sake anyway? And where did she come from? Does she live around here? Was she visiting that retired government guy before the grid went down and then just happened to go outside for a minute before going back in or what? This is definitely more than a little strange, Stephanie thought.

Stephanie had no idea why the idea came to her, but as an afterthought, she remembered what Rob had mentioned to her about the former *Amnesty International* employee. He had told her how the man had been very concerned about preparing for major disasters. She wasn't sure how, or even if, that had any relevance to what she was watching, but the thought persisted.

The rain had ceased for the time being, and Stephanie continued to watch what was taking place down the street. She saw the front door open as the rain coat clad woman was only half way up the walkway. She entered the house quickly despite the fact the rain had stopped. Stephanie concluded, based upon the speed in which the woman entered the house, the resident had been expecting her. It appeared as though the retired home owner, if in fact he had been the one opening the door, had been watching the woman's approach. Having difficulty making sense out of what she had just observed, Stephanie decided to watch a bit longer as she drank her warm tea.

Although she could have no way of knowing it from where she stood in her living room, the visit between the homeowner and the woman was a business meeting. Nor could Stephanie have known that the nature of the meeting was a clandestine one that revolved around the availability, and scarcity, of food and water. And the need some men had for sex. The owner of the house in question had plenty of food and water. He also had a sex addiction.

The attractive woman and her husband, who now waited anxiously in the couple's residence less than a block away, had neither food nor water. They had run out of the former over twenty four hours prior and the latter twelve hours ago. Prior to that, the couple had been surviving on bare minimum rations of each, in effect slowly starving and dehydrating their bodies. Now they had nothing, and were past being desperate. It has been said many times that desperate times bring about desperate measures. This was no exception.

As soon as the attractive woman had crossed the threshold of the house, the owner closed the door behind her and locked it. The woman, obviously more than a little nervous about the whole situation, flirtatiously smiled at the middle aged, yet boyishly handsome man standing in front of her. He wore black running sweat pants, running shoes, and a gray t-shirt that was emblazoned with the logo "ARMY STRONG" across the front in large black letters.

"You can call me Roger if you want."

He helped her out of her rain coat and placed it, and her hat, on a hanger inside of a small closet off the entrance room.

"I stuffed a small backpack into the coat pocket for the food items," she said with a smile. Roger opened the closet, reached into her bulging coat pocket, and pulled out a small pink colored pack.

"Thanks." Another smile.

Not for the first time this afternoon, she was aware of how loose fitting her skirt was. Prior to the EMP, she had been frustrated with the fact the skirt had fit too tightly and had promised herself she would lose a few pounds to solve that problem. Now she longed for enough food to allow her body to fill out the skirt again.

The woman, not taking her eyes away from him, smiled and said, "Okay Roger. I guess you can call me Pepper, even though nobody has called me that since back when I was in high school." She wasn't sure what had caused her to provide this stranger with the nickname that had been unused for more than two decades. Was it a subconscious attempt on her part to separate her mind from the situation?

Roger looked briefly into the eyes of the woman called Pepper. He saw not only a sexually attractive woman, but one who seemingly possessed a level of intelligence exceeding that of most of the women he generally kept company with. He also saw a woman who was nervous. Or was it more than that? He sensed that she might be personally conflicted over the transaction about to be arranged between them. Instead of being understanding of her personal conflict, Roger became irritated. But he kept this irritation to himself as he revisited his thoughts on the matter.

Well, that's just too bad, lady.

You and your stupid husband should have thought about that before everything crashed, don't you think?! I bet you were spending lots of money on all kinds of really important things like expensive clothes, eating out every other night, and vacations several times a year while I spent my money on a little insurance for this kind of thing. And now I'm supposed to feel sorry for you and give up my supplies without getting anything in return? I don't think so. It's a tough world, and I've certainly seen my share of it.

The pleasant smile on Roger's face belied his private thoughts. He could barely contain his primal lust as he envisioned what he wanted to do with this woman now standing in his living room. He told himself the first transaction would include a sexual encounter of a mild variety only. After that, things would progress.

Gotta get her to come back for more transactions after all.

Pepper was quite practiced at flirting with the opposite sex, having done so on a regular basis for the past thirty years. As such it was no surprise that even under the stress of her present situation her ability to effectively do so was not noticeably affected. She had been deprived of the luxury of bathing or showering for several days, being forced to settle for once-a-day sponge baths ever since the lights had gone out. More than a little self-conscious about her recent hygiene practices, she had applied slightly more perfume than she normally wore.

Motioning with his hand for her to follow, Roger invited her to accompany him through the living room to the kitchen, and then out through a closed door into the attached garage. She tentatively followed him, her heels clacking on the laminate floor as she walked to the garage.

She looked around and observed with more than a little surprise and awe what the homeowner had done with his garage. Eighteen inch wide shelves had been installed along virtually the full length of one of the walls. The shelves started at about two feet above the ground and continued to the ceiling, leaving approximately twelve inches or so between each shelf. All of the shelves were stocked with miscellaneous food items ranging from regular canned goods such as peaches, pears, soups, beans, vegetables, and canned meats, to large restaurant sized cans of freeze dried and dehydrated foods.

She noticed that one section of the shelving contained a dozen or more large bottles of vodka and whiskey. Another section had several cartons of cigarettes, even though she was certain the man before her was not a smoker. The top shelf was packed with toilet paper, paper towels, and paper plates, along with other miscellaneous bathroom items, including toothpaste, dental floss, and mouthwash. Two flashlights, each suspended by a cord, hung at either end of the well-stocked shelves.

She glanced at the other side of the garage and noticed he had stored a dozen fifty five gallon blue plastic barrels, each labeled with stickers that read "DRINKING WATER". A plastic pump had been inserted into the opening located at the top of one of the barrels. The ten one gallon size plastic water containers resting next to the barrels were all filled with water as well. She noticed a plastic wading pool, easily six feet in diameter and twenty four inches high, emblazoned with crude cartoon-like fish designs around the outside perimeter, had been positioned in the center of the garage. It was also full of water.

The woman had no way of knowing that the childless man, prior to the EMP, had stored the empty children's wading pool suspended from the exposed garage rafters. In keeping with his disaster preparedness plan, Roger had removed the large plastic container from the rafters immediately upon realizing an EMP was the likely cause of the power grid crash.

He had begun filling the kiddie pool with water from a hose bib immediately, fully anticipating his home's water supply would soon be unavailable. By employing his clever plan without delay, Roger had managed to get close to three hundred gallons of water into the kiddie pool before the plumbing lines went dry. He couldn't have cared less that this action had depleted the water supply in the neighborhood all that much faster.

In the garage near the water barrels, "Pepper" took note of a cardboard box that displayed a picture of what she assumed was an improvised shower device. The box had the label *ZODI CAMP SHOWER* emblazoned above the picture. Next to the box was the device itself. Roger was using the large wading pool as the water source for the camp shower and a barbeque size propane tank as the fuel source to heat the water. There was also an empty portable kiddie pool, half the size of the one filled with water, positioned next to the shower device.

She quickly deduced that he had set up the shower in a manner where one could stand in the small pool while showering, allowing the water to collect there rather than make a mess on the garage floor. Someone had plumbed in a garden hose at the bottom of the pool, apparently to facilitate emptying the pool's water by directing it elsewhere with the hose.

Maybe he's figured out some way to reuse that shower water. Who knows? The guy seems to have put a hell of a lot of thought into all of this.

"Does that shower really work," she asked with what she hoped came across as a demure smile. She unwittingly touched her hair, embarrassed about its need of washing.

"Oh yeah. It works great; hot water and everything," he answered with a smile of his own, giving her body a quick once over with his eyes in the process.

He then silently criticized himself for not having thought earlier about the idea that had just come to him. But that was okay. At least he had thought of it now, and it was going to work out for the better in any case. Roger had violated one of his own guidelines by allowing the woman to have a look at his supplies, but he did so with a specific purpose in mind. He hoped that by allowing her to see all of the coveted items in such close proximity that it would whet her appetite for them, thereby ensuring she would not get cold feet about their arrangement.

The day before, when the couple had gone door to door soliciting the residents of virtually every house on the block for food and/or water, Roger had opened the front door wearing a holstered pistol and two extra loaded magazines on his belt. After inviting them into the home's entry way, he had asked the couple to listen to his proposition.

Roger had indicated that he had some canned goods and drinking water he might be willing to trade. When they responded that they had nothing of value to trade, he said he was a lonely man and would consider trading for a little female companionship. Roger had quickly followed up with a comment he hoped would reduce any offense taken by either of the couple.

"Nothing improper or anything like that. Just a little companionship. A half hour to spend in the company of a pretty woman is all. I've been very lonely ever since the power went down. I have no one to talk to or even to listen to on the TV or radio."

The husband had stiffened and tightened his jaws upon hearing the strange man's offer. He had even unknowingly begun to close his hands into fists before he glanced at the pistol on Roger's belt and reconsidered. He had also noticed that Roger had been maintaining a certain distance—enough distance to allow him time to clear the weapon from its holster and bring it into play before the husband could reach him.

Roger made it known that if they were interested in a transaction the wife could return the next day at three PM. He had insisted her husband stay at home while the transaction took place, and that any deviation from the agreement would immediately render the whole deal null and void.

"Just think it over. No hard feelings either way, really," Roger had said as he closed the door and went back inside.

While Roger fantasized about a date with the good looking woman, the couple debated and argued over the proposition most of the night. The husband had come up with a half dozen alternative plans to get the badly needed food and water, most of them involving trying to overpower the man called Roger. But always it came back to the fact the man was armed and the couple was not. Eventually the desire for survival won out, as it nearly always did during times of extreme desperation.

Now the woman was here at the odd man's house out of desperation--a desperation that in her view was quickly approaching life-or-death.

In the garage, standing close enough to her to smell her perfume, Roger touched Pepper on the shoulder as he addressed her.

"I know we talked about the basic transaction yesterday, but we didn't go over the details. What do you say we get down to specifics? Why don't you take a quick look at the stuff on the shelves and get some idea of what you want. Then I'll tell you what I would like out of the deal."

She looked at Roger with a ready smile, still practicing her well-honed flirtation skills. She hoped he hadn't noticed the involuntary chill that had just travelled down her spine.

"Alright Roger. That sounds fine to me."

She wasn't sure if the shiver was the result of her nervousness or something more sinister. She told herself to ignore the uneasy feeling as she walked over to the shelves in a deliberate and practiced walk, her heels once again clacking across the concrete floor of the garage.

After having looked through the food items on the shelves, she walked back to where Roger was standing and crossed her arms across her chest, making it a point to look him directly in the eye. She deluded herself into holding onto the notion that she still possessed enough power to negotiate with this man.

"Okay Roger, what exactly are you expecting out of me to get a few days' worth of food for me and my husband? I'm talking about two cans of tuna, two cans of soup, two of veggies, and two of peaches or pears--eight cans total. And two gallons of water."

"Well, Pepper, I'll be glad to give you what you want if you spend fifteen minutes or so in the bedroom with me. Nothing kinky, just regular sex is all. And I'll even let you use my shower over here when we're done." He pointed his chin toward the camp shower.

Pepper fought the urge to physically recoil at the blunt offer. She had feared this was where the transaction was going, but actually hearing it had hit her hard nonetheless. She had hoped the transaction would somehow fall short of an actual sex act, but reality was now confronting her like a vicious slap to the face.

I already ran this through my head all night and came up with my decision. Why am I having such a hard time with it now? Was I holding out hope that this guy would only want to have a little male-female conversation, a romantic dinner perhaps? Wake up! This is the new situation I have to deal with until things get back to normal.

She let out a sigh and slowly nodded her head in agreement. Roger approached her and slid his hand under her skirt, letting it rest on her nicely shaped buttocks. He gave it a squeeze and gently pushed her toward the doorway separating the garage from the main part of the house, leaving his hand on her ass the entire time.

The bedroom was completely dark, forcing her to stop for fear of colliding with something that might break, or even worse, cause her injury. A bright light beam appeared suddenly from behind her, and Roger walked past her, holding a small but powerful flashlight in his hand. He used its beam to illuminate a small kerosene lamp on top of a nightstand next to the king size bed. He picked up a plastic cigarette lighter that rested next to the oil lamp. He removed the glass chimney from the lamp and lit it with the lighter, its soft flame casting just enough light on the room to see by.

Roger sat on the bed and removed his shoes, gun belt, pants, and underwear, leaving only his shirt and socks on. After he had placed his pants—and pistol—within arms' reach on a chair adjacent to the bed, he sat on the edge of the mattress and patted the neatly made bed with his open hand. It was done in a manner indicative of an order as opposed to an invitation. She reluctantly began to undress, starting with her shoes, followed by her blouse, and finally her skirt. She was thankful for the dim light in the room, as she felt small tears moistening her cheeks.

Forcing herself to put her mind in a different place, she climbed onto the bed and lay on her back on top of the bed spread. Her body never touched the sheets, only the outer bed spread as she allowed Roger to climb on top of her without protest. Despite his public appearance of the refined gentleman, his use of her body was basic and animal like. She endured the intercourse with misery, but she endured it nonetheless.

Roger kept his end of the bargain, limiting his sexual activity to a basic missionary position. But it didn't matter. She was psychologically devastated. Roger rolled off of the attractive but mentally crushed woman, suggesting that she grab a bath towel from the adjacent bathroom and then head over to the camp shower in the garage. He assured her he would get the shower set up for her in a minute.

She tried to hold back her tears as she picked up her discarded clothes next to the bed and walked to the bathroom. With towel in hand she walked to the garage and found Roger already busy setting up the camp shower. She felt embarrassed to be seen naked by this man, despite what he had just done to her moments earlier. Roger gave her basic directions on how to use the camp shower, emphasizing that she only had four minutes before the water would run dry. He then walked over to the shelves to select the items the woman had requested. He placed them into her backpack and set it on the garage floor. He walked over and picked up two gallons of water and carried them to where the backpack lay.

The depressed woman allowed the warm water cascading over her body to provide her with a temporary and partial respite from her misery. She finished her shower and used the towel she had found in the bathroom to dry off. She had opted not to wash her hair, afraid that the four minute allotment wouldn't be enough time to get the shampoo or soap rinsed off. She got dressed quickly and put herself together as best she could.

Roger had waited for her by the backpack and water, deliberately not looking at her until he heard her shoes making their distinctive sound on the garage floor. He handed her the pack, suggesting that she put it on over her coat, and carry one water container in each hand for the walk home. She carried the pack to the closet that held her rain coat and hat, while he carried the two water jugs.

After she put on her coat and hat, she slipped the pack onto her back. As she opened the front door, Roger handed her the two water containers. He was at a loss for words at this juncture of their arrangement, and there was an uncomfortable silence between them. In contrast with the behavior she displayed upon her arrival, all pretense of flirting was now gone. It was all she could do to maintain her composure. She was torn between wanting to break down into a crying jag and rushing at the man to scratch his face until she could muster no more strength. But she successfully fought back both urges.

Roger eventually broke the silence.

"Hey, Pepper, if you want to arrange another transaction, you can come by here day after tomorrow at three PM. I'll be here. No pressure or anything; it's up to you. By the way, don't feel bad about any of this. A lot of the rest of the world has been operating this way for a long time. And it was a real pleasure doing business with you. "

He displayed a lecherous smile. She once again fought back the urge to attack the man. If she had been capable of the deed she would have gladly beat him to death right there inside of the entrance to his house. Instead she bit her lower lip and left his offer unanswered.

He turned around and closed the door, leaving the newly created prostitute to carry her goods home by herself. She had enough food and water for her husband and herself to last about two days. He surmised that she would be back at his door the day after tomorrow. Fighting back tears and struggling with her hard earned items of sustenance, she set the pack with the canned goods down on the sidewalk, looked around for possible threats or witnesses, and then removed her heels and fished around inside of her pack. She pulled out a pair of running shoes she had packed there before leaving her house. She put on the far more comfortable running shoes and stuffed the heels inside of the pack. Then she headed for home.

Stephanie had enjoyed her first cup of tea so much that she had decided to make herself a second cup. She returned to her place by the front window and continued to look at the houses along their residential street. She had almost finished her tea when she saw the woman wearing the rain coat and hat walking on the sidewalk across the street. She was heading her way, but she looked like she was struggling with the weight of the now full pack as well as the two one gallon size water jugs she had in each hand.

Stephanie noticed that she was no longer wearing the ridiculous pumps and was now wearing running shoes. Judging by the way she struggled with the containers, they appeared to be full of water or some other liquid.

What in the world is this woman doing? This is really starting to look strange, Stephanie thought.

As the strange lady came closer to her location, Stephanie thought there was something that looked familiar about her. There was something about her figure, although this woman was thinner than her neighbor and somewhat estranged friend. Nonetheless, she reminded her of Rosalyn. Stephanie watched intently until the woman was almost directly across the street. It was Rosalyn!

Stephanie's first reaction was to run out of the house and call out to her neighbor. Then she thought a second time. The wheels turning rapidly in her head, she connected the dots. Rosalyn had spent twenty minutes or so inside of a strange man's house. She had been dressed to the nine's during circumstances that made no sense to be doing so whatsoever--unless she was intentionally trying to utilize her female attraction toward a specific end. Like acquiring the water jugs and whatever was in her backpack right now.

Stephanie slowly stepped back from her position in front of the living room window and retreated into the center of the room, hopefully escaping the notice of Rosalyn while still maintaining her view of her. Rosalyn's shoulders heaved slightly up and down, and her head hung uncharacteristically low as she walked along staring at the sidewalk. It was obvious that she was sobbing.

Rosalyn crossed the street and walked the last few yards to the front walkway of her house before turning abruptly and disappearing from view. Rick, waiting just outside the front door, let her in and closed the door behind her. She squatted down and dropped the water jugs onto the floor, letting go of the large containers a little bit too soon for safe handling. Although the jugs smacked the ground with a sound that briefly concerned both of them, a quick inspection of the containers revealed their fears were unfounded. Rick hugged his crying wife and helped her out of her back pack and rain coat.

"I'm sorry honey. I'm so sorry this had to be done this way. But we have to survive somehow. There was just no other way. C'mon honey; it's okay. Everything is gonna be okay. Let me go make a fire and I'll warm up some food for us." He attempted to hug his wife, but the effort was unreciprocated.

As Rick hoisted the water jugs he recalled how they had recently replaced their forty gallon water heater with one of the new *on demand* water heater units in order to save energy. He had never considered how the loss of the forty gallon water reserve could be a problem.

Shit. Seems like I pretty much failed to do anything right.

With that, Rick lifted one of the water containers, loosened the cap, and chugged almost a full quart before lowering it. He held it out for Rosalyn who also drank hungrily from the container. Rick grabbed the back pack containing the canned food and limped away toward the back yard, his injured leg still causing him considerable pain as he walked. He headed to the barbeque to burn fire wood. It would be a dinner eaten in a depression filled silence, but it would at least be dinner.

27

UNINCORPORATED SOUTHEAST LOS ANGELES

Marino and Harris had just begun discussing how to best allocate the newfound supplies recovered from Flynn's locker when the loud sound of pounding on the building's window glass distracted them. Harris brought his shotgun out in front of him and went to investigate. Marino followed him.

They observed an underweight yet attractive Hispanic woman, approximately thirty years old, banging away on the glass entrance door. Neither had the slightest idea how the woman came to be in possession of the heavy steel rod, and neither cared. Harris could tell she wasn't trying to break the glass. She only wanted one of the cop's attention.

"Hey, stop hitting the glass! You're gonna break it," Harris yelled as he walked toward the woman.

He opened the door no more than six inches, placing his foot in front of it to serve as a doorstop as he looked the crowd over. He held his shotgun behind the door with the muzzle pointed downward in the *low ready* position. Marino, his shotgun still slung on his back, also visually took in the crowd as he stood several feet behind Harris. He noticed there were now close to a dozen bodies—each of them apparently dead—that had collected around the sheriff's building.

Great. I wonder how many more bodies are around that we can't even see right now. This situation is getting completely out of control. What a total mess. Our department failed us big time on this one.

While looking over the crowd, Marino saw a thug grab a rail thin Hispanic teenaged girl by the hair and pull her to the side of a building across the street, slapping her in the face and head repeatedly as she ineffectively attempted to resist her kidnapping. Another thug type, apparently acting in concert with the first one, followed the girl and her attacker to the partially hidden side of the building. He had already begun to unzip his pants, obviously unable to prolong his sexual appetite that was about to be satiated at the expense of the poor girl.

The sergeant bellowed at Harris, "Let me out, and cover my six! We got two assholes across the street assaulting some girl! I've fuckin' had it Lee. It's high time we start smokin' some a these fuckers!" He swung his shotgun around in front of his chest.

Harris, not hesitating for a second, pulled the door open wide and yelled at the woman still blocking the entrance.

"Get outta the way!" he said as he used his left arm to push the woman out of the doorway. It wasn't forceful but it sent the message that she needed to move, and now. Which was exactly what she did.

A second later Marino bounded through the door, shotgun out in front of him, muzzle at a forty five degree angle. He clicked off the safety and positioned his finger outside the trigger guard.

His massive body clipped the metal doorjamb on his way out, making a crashing noise that startled the woman Harris had addressed. Harris trailed behind his sergeant, doing his best to cover the rear of their path as well as what was in front and beside them. He kept his head on a swivel as he followed Marino across the street.

Marino had come to a halt fifteen yards from where the two miscreants had the teenage girl captive. The apparent leader of the two tuned his head to look at Marino and then refocused his attention on the girl. It was obvious he wasn't super concerned about the arrival of the big lawman. The second low-life zipped up his pants but remained where he was.

The girl, whose back faced Marino, was not aware of him. Her voice was oscillating between pitiful begging and panicked screaming—neither of which had had any effect on her tormenters. He could see they had had ripped her dirty shirt off of her and discarded it on the ground several feet from where she now knelt.

Although the teenaged girl had the body of a woman, there was something about the pitiful scene that made Marino view her as a girl rather than a mature woman. She was wearing only one leg of her filthy jeans. Her underwear, with the exception of her bra, was still intact. The hoodlums had forced her into a kneeling position on the filth covered cement.

Marino was now a man fed up past his limit. He was fed up with the department leadership that had abandoned his deputies and him, he was fed up with the lack of outside help, and he was definitely fed up with the sociopaths who viewed the Nadeau Station deputies as powerless to do anything about what was happening all around them.

These assholes are doin' all of this shit right in front of our station as a way of showing us, and everyone else in the area, that we don't represent order anymore. They think we can't protect the weak from the predators now.

"Step away from her right now, both of you!"

Marino said it with a tone that was strangely devoid of anger given the rage he was feeling. He was all business. The thug standing behind the girl looked up, his eyes taking in the large diameter muzzle of the shotgun and the massive bearded middle-aged cop behind it. He backed up several feet, while the scumbag that stood in front of the half-naked girl hesitated, quickly trying to size up the situation.

Both bad guys rapidly blinked their eyes in confusion as they tried to sort out what they were looking at. The girl had stopped screaming when Marino arrived, but she still sobbed uncontrollably. Marino could see the tears on her face mixing with several days of dirt and who knew what else.

Welcome to the fourth world, he thought.

Suddenly changing tactics, Marino decided to give the girl the orders rather than the bad guys. His plan was simple. He wanted to separate the girl from the two thugs so he could shoot them without the risk of hitting her in the process. She rapidly scrambled to pull the other leg of her pants back on but after failing to accomplish the task, ceased any further efforts. She left her jeans unbuttoned with one leg on and the other dangling on the ground as she looked up at Marino from a seated position on the dirty sidewalk.

The girl continued to cry despite their being a slowing in the tempo of her sobs. She was suddenly hopeful her nightmare might be over, and she tried to focus on what the bearded cop with the shotgun was saying.

"Young lady, get up and walk away from those guys toward me. I'm gonna help you. Do it right now. You guys don't move or I'll shoot you right here." His hard stare remained on them.

"Hey Lee, you still got my six?" He never turned his head as he asked Harris the question. Taking your eyes off the threat could be a huge mistake.

"Yeah, I'm ten yards at your five o'clock Sarge." He continued to look about for any additional danger while he waited for Marino to do whatever he had planned.

Changing tactics, Marino addressed her in Spanish.

"Senorita, benga aqui! Rapido!" The order roughly translated to what he had said earlier in English. The desperate girl started crawling toward Marino. She eventually stood up and ran to him, coming perilously close to tripping over her loose pant leg at one point. She ran to him, and then passed him. The sergeant fought the impulse to turn his head to see where the girl had gone.

Don't take your eyes off these assholes. Focus.

With the girl out of the immediate picture, he now had a clear view of both of the would-be rapists. He was going to take full advantage of this fact.

He shot the thug located farthest from him first, all but one of the discharged pellets catching him high in the chest. He crumpled, experienced a short-lived body spasm, and died on the same filthy cement the girl had been kneeling on less than a minute earlier.

As Marino squeezed the shotgun's trigger, the thought occurred to the sergeant that he should be conserving the relatively scarce buckshot rounds and using his pistol ammo instead. He immediately allowed the shotgun to drop onto its sling across his chest and snatched his Beretta pistol out of its holster.

The second sociopath was still trying to digest what had just happened to his cohort as Marino took an extra second to acquire a basic sight picture with the Beretta. He squeezed off a single round that struck the man an inch to the left of his nose and just below his eye. Marino couldn't say for certain what the last thing was to go through the second thug's mind before he died, but he was pretty sure it was a 9mm 147 grain hollow point bullet.

Fuck you both, he thought. *You both deserve every bit of what I just gave you and worse.*

Marino manipulated the Beretta's de-cocker, and re-holstered the weapon. He chambered a new round into his shotgun and loaded another shell into its magazine. A quick three hundred sixty degree look around at his surroundings revealed nothing that gave him concern. The girl who had been beaten and come so close to being raped was nowhere to be found. Harris was standing in a position where he could watch Marino as well as the front of the station, shotgun still carried in the *low ready* position. He gave Marino a quick but obvious nod to let him know everything was okay, including the shooting that had just gone down.

He kept his eye contact with Marino for another second and called out to him.

"You ready to head back to the station now boss?"

"Yeah, I'm good to go. Just leave these pieces of shit where they are." He took a few seconds to knead his neck muscles before turning back toward the station.

Harris replied, "Sounds good. Go ahead, and I'll bring up the rear."

"Where'd the girl go?"

Harris shrugged his shoulders. "No idea."

The sergeant walked back to the station, taking his time to look around at all of the evidence of the disintegrating society on display all around him. Harris, performing a basic rear guard function, walked slowly backward, taking time to check out where he was going every few steps. Marino was back inside the building, and Harris almost so, when the same woman who had been pounding on the window earlier resumed her conversation with him. He assumed she had just watched what had happened across the street, but she gave no sign of being dissuaded.

She began informing Harris of a whole list of problems, from the growing number of dead people cluttering the sidewalks to the fact fewer and fewer residents had adequate food or water.

"When are they gonna help us Deputy? This is wrong! People out here are hurting!"

He could think of no response.

"The gangbangers are just going into people's houses whenever they want and doing all kinds of things that are really bad like nobody even cares or anything...you guys need to stop them. It's not right!"

He didn't know what to say to the woman. He had never been tolerant of patrol officers who claimed to be unable to help those people who needed it. People they were supposed to be protecting. And he had never hesitated to let those who espoused this sentiment hear his disgust. He viewed it as a dereliction of duty, plain and simple.

Now he found himself in the position of having to convey that very same message to this woman. Given the choice, he would have rather suffered physical pain than have to tell this woman he was powerless to protect her. For the first time since the EMP event had taken place, he was seriously bothered by his circumstances.

"I am so sorry ma'am, but we can't help. The few of us that are still here all want to protect the citizens, but we just can't. We can barely help ourselves."

The woman had tears running down her cheeks but was otherwise quiet. Silent tears and a pained expression. No sobbing, no trembling body, and no pitiful voice. Stoic.

The hardened patrol cop instinctively reached out to comfort her, taking both of her hands in his. He looked at her expression and the toxic cocktail of emotions it contained.

Then it hit him. Hard. Painfully.

"Ma'am, did something bad happen to you that you haven't told me?"

The woman looked at him for a long moment before nodding her head. Then she burst into full-blown, sob-wracked, body heaving crying. Harris, for the first time in his career as a cop, hugged a victim. And not just lightly—he hugged her as if it were the only chance he had of helping her.

After she had stopped sobbing, she told him all about how her door had been kicked in a few days ago, allowing three brutish men—none older than twenty--into her tiny modest home. They had knocked her down, pillaged her house, and then choked her before sexually assaulting her. The bastards took turns with her, using her body as though it were no more than a toy for them to play and experiment with, each one trying to outdo the other with their depraved actions. When finished with her, they walked out through her front door as if nothing unusual had happened. One even taunted her.

She had been left with no choice but to lay on the floor of her trashed home in the filth left behind on, and in her body. There was no water for her to clean up with. After spending twelve hours curled up in a fetal position on the floor, a neighbor had entered through her open front door and offered her a large cup of cloudy water—obtained from a water heater--to drink.

Harris noticed she kept looking over to where Marino had shot the two hoodlums moments earlier. He tossed his head in that direction and asked, "Do you know those two guys, or have you seen them around before?"

She started sobbing again.

"Those...are...two of the...guys that...did...this...to me," she said between sobs as she pulled her long black hair away from her neck to reveal a huge ugly purple bruise.

"Well they're dead now."

He felt his comment was apropos of nothing--or at least inadequate under the circumstances.

"Wait a second," he said and then turned to enter the building.

He waived her forward.

"Come inside here for a second."

He gently grabbed her upper arm and guided her through the front door of the sheriff's building. Once inside, he reached into his pants pocket and pulled out an energy bar and handed it to the woman.

She gratefully accepted and began to turn to leave.

"Wait a second. Hold on a minute," he said.

"You can't let anyone out there see that bar or you'll have big trouble. Hide it somewhere before you leave. Better yet, why don't you eat it right now before you leave—just in case something happens before you can get home. And don't look happy when you leave here either. Pretend to be mad or upset."

The woman looked at Harris and her eyes indicated an understanding of what he had just told her. Then she peeled the plastic wrapper from the bar and began to devour it as she turned back to those outside the station.

28

WESTCHESTER, CA

Having rested as well as could be expected under the conditions, Rob and Don began walking away from the back yard that had been their temporary camp site. Don had done a great job of boiling and purifying water using the two pots they had salvaged from the kitchen of the abandoned house. Both men had intentionally saturated their bodies with as much water as they could hold. They also filled Don's plastic soda bottle and Rob's water containers. While considering their water situation, Rob had come up with the idea to search the kitchen drawers for any plastic zip-lock bags that could be used for short term water transportation. The search had come up empty.

Determined not to be defeated in his effort, Rob took one of the zip-lock bags containing his first aid medications, removed the items and wrapped them in a page he had torn from a magazine found in the house. He then filled the zip-lock with drinking water. He gingerly handed the improvised canteen to Don.

"When you get to the point where you think you can drink it, then drink as much as you can. Otherwise, just keep carrying it until that time. If it comes down to it, you can always toss it or pour some of the water out of it. But tell me before you do that; I might be able to drink some of it by then."

"Don't you worry about that. I'll be drinking it soon enough; trust me."

Don tried to visually take in what was around him. The night offered enough moonlight to see several feet in front of him but not much more.

"Man, everything sure does look different with no lights," Don offered.

"No shit there," Rob said.

"I'll tell ya what," Don joked, "I haven't had a cigarette in two days, and I'd use this fuckin' machete on a convent full of nuns to get one right now."

Rob laughed at the dark humor. Cops talked that way all the time, and the irreverent humor made him wonder about his buddies who might have remained at Nadeau Station. He was certain that at least a few of them had done so. Definitely the guys without families would stay there. He wondered what was going on there right now.

"It so happens I got a little bit of Skoal if you just want some nicotine. Up to you; just let me know," Rob suggested.

Don seemed to be considering the offer. "Yeah, why not? What the hell?"

Rob removed the small circular tin of tobacco from his shirt pocket and tossed it to Don. He caught it mid-air, opened the lid, and stared at the contents for a second or two. He pinched a chunk of the substance no bigger than a small marble with his thumb and index finger and then shoved it behind his lower lip. He rubbed the same two fingers briskly together to discard the tobacco particles sticking to them. He closed up the tin, yelled "Heads up," and threw it back to Rob.

"Thanks. Been a helluva long time since I tried this stuff—like back in high school,"

Rob had made a sheath for the machete Don wore using duct tape wrapped around several sheets of thick magazine covers. It was suspended from his belt with the help of yet more of the magical duct tape, where the huge cutting tool would be immediately accessible if needed. Crude, but good enough for a day or two.

Rob looked around at their surroundings. He glanced at his watch and saw that it was past nine. It was just dark enough to travel on foot in his opinion. He hoisted his pack onto his back and adjusted the straps. He retrieved the shotgun from Don and attached it to his *Paracord* sling that hung from his pack strap. Don handed him the extra shells, which Rob slipped into his pocket.

Rob asked, "You got everything you need, or everything you want?"

"Yep. Let's go."

In addition to his makeshift bundle and the machete, he was carrying the large plastic zip-lock full of water in his hands. It was definitely going to be a pain in the ass to carry it. But he knew this was nowhere near as much of a pain as dehydration. And they had no idea whether they might have to hole up somewhere for a while before reaching Don's house in Culver City. This trek could change from block to block.

"If my knee doesn't decide to act up on me, I should be in good enough shape to get home now," Don said.

"What's wrong with your knee?"

"Oh hell, my knee's been messed up for about four years now. I been meaning to get the damn thing fixed but I just kept putting it off."

"Alright. Well let me know if it starts to bother you and we can rest it up a bit."

Without any further discussion about Don's knee, they headed out. They walked for a half hour or more with only minimal conversation, observing the condition of the residential neighborhoods as best as the limited lighting would allow while they passed through. Their progress was slow, mostly due to Don's knee.

The temperature was close to perfect for this kind of activity. Cool enough to keep the perspiration to a minimum yet not uncomfortably cold. However, the temperature was about the only aspect of their present conditions that was good. They had discussed, and quickly agreed, to avoid the larger streets as much as possible, both of them preferring to walk a little farther in exchange for avoiding people.

As they hiked along the residential sidewalks both men were taken aback by the general appearance of the neighborhoods.

"This looks like something out of another part of the world, doesn't it though," Rob commented.

"It sure does. This is really creepy looking now. I still can't believe it really."

The garbage piled up on the sidewalks and in the street gutters was increasing daily to the point where Rob thought it was going to constitute a health problem before long. Additionally, Rob had noticed every so often unidentified forms that had been deposited among the garbage piles and other locations outside of the homes they passed.

These unidentified objects were covered with a variety of materials, including plastic tarps, old blankets, plastic trash bags taped together, and miscellaneous other items. The smell associated with decaying flesh was certainly present, along with the myriad other malodorous smells in the air, but it was hard to tell whether this was caused by dead animals or people. He suspected there was plenty of each.

To the former street cop, the unidentified objects appeared suspiciously similar to human shapes, but he felt no compunction to investigate further. He had his suspicions confirmed when he saw a foot--shod with a slipper-- protruding from under a blue plastic tarp. The body was in a front yard of a small modest house. Someone had placed the corpse in the farthest portion of the small front yard, just behind a three foot high chain link fence that bordered the public sidewalk where Rob and Don walked.

It was the swarm of flies, so thick they were visible even in the semi-darkness, that prompted Rob to look down through the fence and into the yard. That was when he made the macabre observation of the dead body that had been deposited there.

Rob wondered what had caused the death of the person. He concluded that since it hadn't even been two weeks since the grid crash it couldn't have been the result of starvation. That would still be a while off for most. It could've been dehydration he allowed, but it seemed unlikely.

Not ten yards from the discarded body sat half a dozen or more men and women of varying ages. They were all positioned around a small and obviously makeshift fire pit, their morose faces slightly illuminated by the fire's flames. The group looked like they had been doing without for a while—expressions of desperation displayed by all. It reminded him of another place in the world, or perhaps another time in this nation. A time long before trips to the grocery store and hot showers were available virtually any time they were desired.

Rob kept his pace unchanged as he walked past the small non-threatening group, wondering to himself how long the discarded dead body had been there, and how long it had taken the people around the fire pit to no longer be bothered by its presence. It was a whole new world that he now found himself in.

As they walked onward the stench in the air was strong, an increasingly familiar combination of smells that Rob surmised included old garbage, human waste, rotting flesh, and burning materials that were never intended to be combustible. Even under the minimal lighting conditions, they could see massive swarms of flies collecting everywhere there was refuse. They could also see rats scurrying about the trash piles.

Great. Yet another disease related problem to have to deal with soon.

The occasional discarded dead dog or cat was also observed. Rob concluded that pet owners were in many cases unable to feed their animals.

Some of these people will be eating their pets—or their neighbor's pets--before too much longer. Then again, how many Americans living in the cities even know how to butcher an animal?

He recalled the animal on the spit being cooked over the bonfire just before he had been chased through the yard with the vicious dogs. Poetic justice?

Two blocks ahead they observed a group of several rough looking men standing around a bonfire that looked like it was fueled by broken furniture. The fire was burning in the side yard of what had once been an average sized home. Now it was a mostly burned down house, clearly no longer suitable for normal habitation. The men, about six or seven in number, were all between the ages of twenty and forty by the look of them. To Rob they didn't really look like hard core criminal types. More like blue collar men who were tough but hard working sorts. But he reminded himself that things were different now. People—even good people—were becoming desperate. They had to be coming to the realization that things were not going to be returning to normal anytime soon. And this was dangerous for a guy walking through the neighborhood wearing a backpack—even if it had a shotgun hanging from it.

Rob couldn't see any exposed weapons on anyone in the group, but that didn't mean they weren't present. One of the members of the group, either a Caucasian or light complexioned Latino, was a thick-set man of average height with a square jaw. He wore a bushy mustache that covered much of his face below his lips. His dirty sweatshirt had the sleeves cut off at the shoulders so that his muscular arms were on display, including a large tattoo on his right bicep. Something about him reminded Rob of a pirate.

The guy let his stare remain on Rob several seconds longer than what was comfortable. Rob told himself he should have looked away from the man's stare, but for some reason he held it longer than he should have as well.

Several of the other men also watched them closely as they walked past, each of them paying particular attention to the shotgun hanging from Rob's pack as well as the big machete suspended from Don's belt. Rob had no doubt they were being sized up, both in terms of any valuable loot they might possess, and their ability and willingness to offer resistance to an attack. It was no different than how animals in the wild sized up other creatures crossing their paths.

Don and Rob passed the group without incident. It was a small piece of luck that Rob hoped was a good sign. But Rob had noticed something that gave him concern. Don was now obviously limping.

Shit.

After they had covered another thirty plus yards, Don said, "I felt a bad vibe from those guys. They were thinkin' about jumping us unless I missed my guess. I wasn't sure if I should take my machete out while I had the chance before they actually jumped us or what."

Rob screwed his face into a small frown before answering.

"These situations can be tough calls when it comes to that. I don't think I can actually spell it out as far as exactly when the right time is to take that step. I know I trust my instincts though."

Don's response was merely a grunt.

Ten minutes later, Rob stopped.

"Hold up Don. I gotta take this damn pack off for a minute."

He removed his pack, rolled his neck, and shrugged his shoulders slowly and deeply to loosen his tightening muscles. He watched his friend. Although he didn't share this with Don, half the reason Rob had asked for the break was so that his buddy could rest his knee for a few minutes. In the short time he had been friends with him, Rob had learned that he was from the old school of not complaining unless the situation was absolutely desperate.

Rob caught the movement with his peripheral vision. Just the briefest of changing shapes less than a block behind them. Then he saw it. It was unmistakable. Someone was hurriedly stepping off the sidewalk and into an adjacent yard out of his line of sight. It looked very much like a person trying to avoid being seen by either of them. Someone who was following them.

Shit. Probably a few of those guys from that bunch that were sizing us up a few minutes ago. They probably decided we were too strong to attack from the front when we saw it coming, so they decided to try some kind of a surprise ambush on us. Fuck.

Rob whispered to Don just to make sure his voice wouldn't carry to whoever was following them.

"Heads up. Looks like we spoke too soon about those guys back there. I just saw someone pop off the sidewalk and into a yard like they were trying to make sure we didn't see them."

Don just stared at him.

"Let me think about how to deal with this. And I'm up for any suggestions if you got any."

Don asked, "You sure you saw someone trying to hide?"

"Yeah, I'm pretty sure that's what I was seeing buddy. I got no idea how many are following us, but I'm convinced there's at least one. Probably two or three at least. Remember, they saw we were strapped with knives and my little shotgun, so they're gonna try to take us by surprise....probably hit us pretty hard when they do it too. Won't wanna take a chance of us getting to our weapons."

Don looked at him as he tried to figure out if his cop friend was right about the situation. He was also trying to figure out what he and Rob should do about the problem if Rob had in fact assessed the situation correctly.

By way of emphasizing his earlier comment, Rob added, "All the alarm bells are going off in my head right now, and I learned a long time ago to trust myself when that happens. We got a fuckin' problem on our hands partner. Trust me on this one."

"Let's just keep walking for a little bit while we think about this so it doesn't look like we're onto them," he told Don.

They made a right turn on the sidewalk just before entering the next intersection. Rob was in the lead, walking about six to eight feet in front of his friend.

"Alright, I've been thinkin' about this; and I'm pretty sure you ain't gonna like what I've been thinking. Bottom line is that we gotta set up an ambush on these guys. There's no other way. There's no way we can out-run them. Doubt we could do it even if your knee wasn't in bad shape."

Don stopped walking and looked at Rob, his breath coming in a heavy panting pattern.

The older man said, "Shit. I dunno. What about you getting away and leaving me here. I don't have anything for them to steal anyway. They'll probably just go through my stuff and leave."

Rob's response was short and terse, emphasized by his tight jaw and gritting teeth. "Ain't no fucking way that's happening partner. No way. These guys are operating under the law of the jungle, so that's how we'll play it. Time's wasting here. We gotta pick a spot for an ambush and take care of business. No other way to do this buddy. Wish there was, but there just isn't. Can you get your head around this okay?"

Don replied, "Yeah, yeah. Okay. Let's do it then. Tell me how this works."

Rob slowed just enough to let Don catch up. He looked over at his friend as he shared his simple plan.

"Here's the thing. I don't want to waste any of my ammo if we don't have to. I think we have to use the big blades on this one buddy. There ain't any law out here anymore and we just have to survive this shit. We can't even afford to get injured a little bit. If we get a simple infection it could kill us; ya know what I mean? It isn't like an ambulance will be coming for us, or even like there are any hospitals that can treat us."

Don nodded but said nothing. He didn't like what he was hearing, but couldn't come up with a decent counter argument to Rob's plan. Except that he had never even punched a full grown man, let alone used a machete on one. But he had shot the crazy homeless man at point blank range with a shotgun. That was something, wasn't it?

Rob, thinking about his friend's reluctance to set up an ambush, thought about how simple the solution to their problem was, and yet how harshly they would be judged if their actions were ever found out.

He recalled reading about how several British special ops soldiers had been captured in the first Iraq war after they had opted not to kill, or otherwise disable, a couple of civilian sheep herders that had stumbled upon the covert soldiers in the middle of their mission. In short, the soldiers had found the idea of using extreme violence against the civilians to be unacceptable for a number of reasons—all of them either morally or legally based.

The result of their collective decision to let the sheep herders go rather than kill them was a tragic one. Shortly afterward, the sheep herders had informed the Iraqi Army of the British soldiers' presence in the area. The Brits were subsequently captured and tortured. Over a decade later several American special operations military men encountered an almost identical scenario in Afghanistan. Once again, the collective decision to show mercy ended with catastrophic results for the American operators.

Thinking about the above incidents, the home-bound former deputy sheriff and U.S. Marine reminded himself of how the deck was often stacked against both American law enforcement officers and the military personnel who were sent to dangerous areas in other parts of the world. The rules of engagement had become increasingly restrictive over the past several decades for cops and military operators alike. And violations of these rules often meant criminal prosecution by the powers that be.

Rob and his more contemplative colleagues in the Marine Corps and Sheriff's Department attributed this disturbing phenomenon to the pressure being brought to bear by the agenda driven political forces in the country. And what they didn't create in the way of political pressure, the ranks of the uninformed filled in with pure ignorance.

People who had never even been on a date were giving advice on love-making.

Rob thought over their situation again.

Well, there's no way tonight's scenario is going to serve as another example of how short-sighted compassion brought about the demise of the good guys. I need to get home to my family, and I'm going to do whatever it takes to make sure that happens.

Up ahead about thirty yards Rob found what he was looking for. Or something that would serve his purpose at least. There was a hedge that was about three to four feet in height that ran perpendicular from the sidewalk and the residence that was set back from the street. Rob whispered for his traveling partner to follow him tightly, explaining that it was essential for him to get off of the sidewalk quickly when he saw Rob do the same. Rob walked several houses past the hedge before quickly ducking into a front yard so that he was out of the line of sight of anyone following behind them. Or so he hoped anyway.

Don followed Rob's move, quietly wincing in pain as his knee protested the sudden change in direction. Rob back-tracked through the yards to the hedge he had chosen for their ambush location. He hoped that whoever was pursuing them wouldn't flare wide into the street, or even across the street to the opposite sidewalk, in order to gain a wider vantage point.

Reverting back to some of his Marine Corps training, Rob was concerned about how his pursuers might react to no longer seeing their prey, but he thought it most likely they would simply press forward for a little while in the hopes of once again picking up sight of them.

Rob planned to be waiting behind the hedge with Don as the unsuspecting attackers came walking past them. At that point, knives in hand, Rob and Don would give the would-be-robbers the surprise of their fucking lives.

Sucks to be these guys tonight, he thought.

Rob positioned himself where he could get a decent view of the sidewalk they had walked along after making the last turn before the intersection. He told Don to turn around about ninety degrees so that he could use his peripheral vision to see the area directly behind them as well as being able to see Rob. He saw no need to tempt Murphy (from the infamous "Murphy's Law" notoriety) and have someone exit the house they were crouched in front of, or approach them from anywhere else outside of their view for that matter.

It wasn't long before he saw two men walking along the sidewalk he was surveying. Then a third man came up about twenty five feet behind them. The two in front were looking from side to side up into the yards as they passed them, obviously trying to locate the two intended victims they had been following but could presently no longer see. The third guy was looking all around his surroundings, paying particular attention to the area behind all three of them.

Crouching behind the short hedge, Rob removed his pack and shotgun, setting them on the grass next to the hedge that concealed them. He removed the single shell from the shotgun and dropped it into his pocket—just in case the weapon should find its way into the hands of someone other than Don or him before this was over. He pulled the *Cutlass* machete from its sheath, taking care to make as little noise as possible. He had considered using the smaller folding tactical knife in his pocket, but in the end opted for the longer blade length and superior durability of the stout machete.

The fact his *Kabar*, unlike a typical machete, had a modest point at its blade tip meant he could use it to pierce his target if need be. This removed any doubt as to which knife was the best choice for the job at hand. He told Don to get his own full-sized machete ready as well.

Just as he had experienced before entering the house of horrors in Inglewood, Rob could feel his heart rate begin to accelerate rapidly with the anticipation of what was coming. He recognized the heightened level of his senses he always experienced just prior to engaging in battle or other ultra-high adrenaline situations. He was acutely aware of all manner of sounds and smells around him as the combat related chemicals performed their work on his mind and body.

For about the tenth time, he tried to think of any alternative to what he had planned--anything at all that might offer them a means of avoiding carrying out the brutal ambush. Unable to come up with anything remotely workable, he resolved to go forward.

I can't take the chance of getting hurt, let alone mortally wounded, just because I wanted to play "good guy". It's a whole new ball game now, and I made a promise to myself that nothing would be as important as my getting home. This includes entertaining any bullshit ethical considerations about how I should protect myself. It's all about whatever has the best chance of keeping me safe and nothing else.

He made hard eye contact with Don.

"Okay, it's gonna happen soon now. They're coming down the sidewalk now. Looks like three guys. When I rush 'em, you just follow me. This will be a no-bullshit, full-on, *Brave Heart* kinda deal." He tried to get a read on Don's take. No indication.

"I'm taking out the closest man first. You just walk around me when I start swinging and go directly to the second guy. Don't get too close to me—I don't want you gettin' cut by my Kabar. Make sure you swing your machete full force across his arms so he can't use whatever weapons he has. That goes for all of 'em. Got it?"

Rob looked directly into Don's eyes to drive the point home before continuing.

"No hesitation, no matter what—okay?! Our lives depend on us being totally aggressive with this ambush. We didn't pick this fight, and we can't avoid it. So we win and we do it like we only get one chance. okay?!"

Don nodded his head and removed his machete from its make-shift scabbard with slightly trembling hands. His body was dumping adrenaline into his system. He settled on a two-handed grip. Rob saw his friend's arms shaking but wasn't concerned.

Rob held his own compact machete in his right hand and wound the handle's looped lanyard tightly around his palm so that the knife wouldn't fall from his grasp even if he were to lose his grip. The lanyard would also prevent his hand from sliding forward off the grip and onto the blade, cutting or possibly even severing his fingers, should the handle get slippery from sweat and/or blood.

He continued to focus on the three men as they approached. The straggler had now closed the gap between himself and the two men in front of him so that only a distance of about ten feet was between them. Rob assessed the three men as best he could.

The one in front who was closest to Rob was the man he had seen earlier wearing the sweatshirt with the cut-off sleeves. Rob surmised that he--the obvious leader of the three--was tough and capable with his fists. Probably his idea to do this thing.

This guy definitely looks like he's been around the block a few times. He's got confidence. More like overconfidence actually. Well pride comes before a fall asshole, and you are most certainly going to be falling soon; real soon.

Rob had unwittingly uttered the last two words aloud, although softly. Don looked over at him. Rob just shook his head in dismissal.

The second guy, now walking almost directly next to sweatshirt man, wore a white t-shirt that was so filthy that its original color was not immediately recognizable. He appeared to be Caucasian, or possibly a light complexioned Hispanic. He too was moderately muscular, although not as thickly built as the man in the cut-off sweatshirt. The third man, definitely a Caucasian, was wearing a dark colored tee-shirt. He was stocky but not as muscular as the other two. Rob looked closely but could not discern whether any of them were armed.

Oh well. Doesn't matter anyway. The plan's the same either way.

Rob whispered, "Okay Don, on my *go* we rush 'em. Cut 'em down hard and fast. No rules and no refs here, just winners and losers. Five, four, three, two, one, *GO!*"

Rob sprung up from his position and went at the man in the cut-off sweatshirt at a pace somewhere between a jog and a run. He wanted to reach him fast, but he didn't want to be moving too fast to be able to deliver his machete blows with some level of accuracy. He definitely couldn't afford to trip before he reached his target.

Rob became aware that sweatshirt man was mentally several steps behind the curve in this contest as the ex-marine and former cop presented himself like a maniacal specter out of the dark.

It was too dark for Rob to see the panic in the man's eyes, but it was there. Sweatshirt man instinctively threw up his arms as he saw Rob coming at him with the machete. This would have been a good defensive move had Rob been attacking him by surprise with his fists, or even a blunt object, but it was ineffective for warding off ten inches of sharpened steel swung by a determined and strong man. A desperate man. Rob heard the distinctive clanging of metal striking cement as a fourteen inch length of iron pipe fell out of the robber's waistband and onto the sidewalk.

Bigtime mistake asshole. Should've had the pipe in your hands already, dumb-ass!

Rob had never considered himself much of a sporting man. Unlike many of his buddies, gambling in casinos gave him no pleasure. Just wasn't his idea of a good time. He wasn't about to give these guys anything close to a sporting chance either.

Rob swung his compact machete fast and violently in a right to left motion across the back of the muscular man's exposed forearms. The blade sliced through the skin, muscle, and tendons, hardly slowing the heavy knife's progress at all. When the blade had finished traversing its destructive path, the victim's forearms were essentially disabled. Both arms now hung by his side, each useless as blood gushed from the wounds.

Now fully aware that his survival was dubious at best, the man did his best to press his gushing arms against his body in a futile attempt to slow the blood loss. As a final act of defiance, he began screaming at Rob, "You motherfucker, you motherfucker! I'm gonna kill you!" They both knew it was an impotent threat.

The lead bandit, looking at Rob with pure hatred and alternating between holding his fluid leaking arms against his body and thrusting them out in front of his chest in a defensive gesture, began to show obvious signs of losing his ability to remain standing. Extensive blood loss was a major impediment to performing even the simplest of bodily tasks. Rob continued to move his feet, constantly adjusting his position in relation to the screaming man. His main objective at this point was to avoid, or at least minimize, being sprayed by blood from the badly sliced flailing forearms.

Rob actually considered leaving the would-be bandit to his own devices, recognizing he no longer posed a physical threat to him. Left alone without any medical care, it was doubtful the badly wounded highwayman would survive another hour. But Rob dismissed the idea.

Can't take the chance of this guy somehow telling someone about us or what he thinks we might have. Nothing good can come from letting him live. To Hell with him.

Anxious to put an end to the man's screaming as well as the fight--if it could even be called that--Rob pulled his machete back so that the grip was up against the right side of his chest, ten inches of blade pointing outward away from him at an angle parallel to the ground. For a brief moment he acknowledged the fact he was now crossing a line.

As a cop he was well aware of the distinction between murder and justifiable homicide when it came to taking another's life. The legal justification required a deadly threat to be an *imminent* one. Rob knew that the present conditions would not meet the legal guidelines, but he knew it was his best option. He shifted his thinking to a military mindset rather than a law enforcement one. Hell, it was neither really. It was simply the practical mindset of a man trying to complete an objective. He was committed to doing what he had to in order to make it home.

He used as much power as he could muster from his chest, right shoulder and triceps to thrust the blade straight forward into his target's midsection, feeling the blade penetrate close to six inches. Thankful he had avoided the rib cage and the blade had gone deep, he withdrew the knife immediately, and stepped to the side at the same time, still trying to avoid being sprayed with blood.

The former deputy sheriff, using his left hand to support his right, now wrapped around the *Kabar's* grip, stepped toward the slumping man and swung the large blade across his neck just above the collar bone in a powerful two-handed slashing motion.

Most of what was left of the dying man's blood supply erupted in a spray that had the appearance of black ink under the moonlit night. The man stopped screaming and fell to the sidewalk, no longer of any use to the robbery effort or anything else in this world.

After quickly satisfying himself that sweatshirt man was dead, Rob took a look around at what was happening with the others. He registered that Don had stopped hacking away at the second would-be assailant with his machete. The wounded man bled from numerous wounds on his arms and hands, but he still stood on his feet showing no signs of being ready to fall.

Both men were circling each other. Don was not wounded and was presumably looking for an opportunity to end the attack while the bleeding man sought a way out of the mess he had gotten himself into. Don's intended target held his hands in a defensive position despite the fact they were dripping blood all over the sidewalk. Apparently the post-EMP highwayman had not yet accepted the loss of his life as being inevitable.

"Finish him off Don!"

Rob was worried Don had lost his will to carry through.

He leapt toward the third robber, who now held a small knife in his hand that appeared to be almost comical when compared to the size of the weapons he and Don were using.

Too bad shithead. You should've considered that before you set out to attack us.

The third man had just started to flank Don when he suddenly realized he had a far bigger problem to deal with. Rob was coming straight at him holding his short machete cocked over his right shoulder in a two-handed grip. The panic registered on the man's face as he saw Rob closing in fast with his war face displayed. Unlike his two cohorts, the third bandit was unscathed. He glanced around his present position, giving serious consideration to running away and leaving his friends to suffer whatever fate they had coming.

As the uninjured robber tried to decide whether or not to flee, Rob entertained his own thoughts about tactics. He weighed the idea of dropping his machete and shooting the knife wielding man with his handgun. He had never been one to relish the idea of fighting a knifeman with anything less than a firearm. But the thought was short-lived. Not only was he averse to wasting ammo and making noise that held the potential of bringing more trouble from other sources, he reminded himself he already had an effective weapon in his hands. He was confident he could end this thing quickly with his *Kabar* machete.

Before he could make his decision about staying or going, the third man lost his chance. Rob was closing on him, swinging his big knife as he did so. Vicious blows powered by a resolute man. Using the reach advantage of the ten inch blade, Rob slashed across the man's forearm holding the smaller knife, and then jumped back. Initially there was no blood following the cut, but after a couple seconds, the blood began pouring heavily from the wound, splashing onto the sidewalk as the scenario continued. To his credit, the man retained the grip on his small knife for a while before his damaged arm finally betrayed him despite his will. The desperate knifeman shifted his short blade from his right hand to his left, still not willing to surrender or accept defeat.

Rob sprang forward, using both hands to swing the *Kabar* blade brutally across the man's mid-section, and adroitly jumping back again. This time the bandit dropped the knife altogether, the steel hitting cement a welcome sound, signaling it truly was over now. As the man tried to use his good hand to hold in the blood and intestine oozing through his sliced abdomen, Rob sprang forward again with his machete.

Using a technique he had been taught in basic Marine Corps training, Rob thrust his blade up through the bottom of his victim's jaw and well into his brain, feeling the big blade come to rest as its tip encountered the inside of the top of the man's skull. Rob yanked his blade free and allowed the body to collapse onto the sidewalk, unable to avoid the offensive smell of fresh shit as the man released his bowels in death.

You don't see—or smell—this on the movie screen either, he thought bitterly.

The highwayman occupying Don's efforts was now aware that his two comrades lay dead or dying on the sidewalk. Rob saw that at some point during the ambush he had managed to shed his t-shirt and wrap it around his right hand several times.

Impressive. Give the guy points for being resourceful and collected under high stress conditions. Too bad it isn't going to matter.

The tactic might have actually saved his life had he only had Don to contend with. But it wasn't going to be enough to save him now that Rob was in the game, and he seemed to register this fact in his expression. He looked panic-stricken.

Injured and now desperately worried about his survival, the last of the trio frantically looked at his surroundings. He was trying to gauge whether he could escape the robbery-turned-bad before he too was killed. Don was breathing hard and positioned in a crouch. He was using his machete as a crutch to partially support his fatigued body, the tip of the blade pressed against the sidewalk and the blade slightly bowed as he gripped the handle.

Rob knew at a glance that Don wasn't going to be finishing the task. Whether due to physical or mental exhaustion, or simply a loss of will, it was all irrelevant at this point. All that mattered was that Rob knew he would have to finish this nasty job himself. And he had to do it now.

Rob went to the deepest and darkest regions of his psychic--the place where he stored all of the anger and hate he harbored toward the ugly and evil shit he had seen in his life. He went to this dark place and borrowed from all of the suppressed anger he stored there.

He approached the last of the three robbers as he adjusted his grip on the *Kabar*. With his open left hand in front of him and the machete gripped tightly in his right, its blade protruding straight out in front of him, Rob circled the man. He exploded forward, violently slashing at the arms of the doomed man as he ineffectively tried to protect himself. Rob continued swinging his blade, its sharp edge fileting huge chunks of flesh with every blow. Rob saw nothing more than a virtually shapeless form in front of him as he continued slashing, back and forth, back and forth. It was an exceedingly ugly business he had undertaken, but Rob gave the man no quarter.

The bandit fell to his knees moaning in agony and murmuring for his mother. It was not the first time Rob had observed dying men utter the unanswerable requests for their mothers just moments before succumbing to a violent and lonely death—almost as often as those he had heard addressing God or uttering one last profane curse against their slayer.

In the past, as now, Rob had found these requests for maternal comfort in the midst of death throes disturbing. Anyone who possessed any semblance of a soul would. Yet he also viewed these requests as testament to the unique nature of many mother and child relationships that persisted well into adulthood.

Compelling himself not to dwell on the above, Rob recommitted himself to the objective at hand. He finished the effort with a machete blow to the back of the man's neck, killing him instantly. He used the dead man's shirt to wipe as much of the blood from his *Kabar* as possible. Then he scanned his surroundings.

"Make sure to clean the blood off your machete Don. Find a clean piece of their clothes to do it."

Don gave no sign he had even heard his friend.

As he surveyed the carnage around him, Rob began hyper-ventilating. He opened and closed his fists over and over, his right hand constricting over the flexible soft rubber on the machete's handle as he did so. He felt his heart racing so fast that he feared it would simply explode, leaving him to die on the cement next to those he had just killed.

This was followed by a feeling of light headedness and its cousin nausea. He was overwhelmed by a whole range of cascading emotions spilling over him, momentarily leaving him incapable of forming any rational thought whatsoever. He slumped to a single knee, sucking in as much air as possible using a four count, forcing himself to fight past the urge to simply lie down for a few minutes as he tried to clear his head.

Not ten feet away, Don released the grip on his machete, allowing the weapon to fall to the ground. The loud metallic clanking sound of steel striking cement startled Rob and caused him to glance at his friend. He saw that Don was now leaning forward with his forearms against the front of his thighs, his head turned away from the collection of ruined human bodies positioned in front of him. He retched several times but his stomach had nothing to surrender but bile and water.

Finally getting his own emotions, bodily functions, and thought processes under control, Rob spoke in a voice devoid of emotion.

"C'mon Don. Clean off your blade on their clothes as best you can and then let's get the fuck out of here—*pronto!* We gotta move buddy!"

At first Don didn't respond to Rob's directive. Then he said, "I screwed up. I just couldn't do it I guess."

Recognizing his friend was in a bad mental place, Rob approached Don and put a heavy hand on his shoulder. He left his hand there and squeezed firmly.

"Hey, you did fine." Several seconds went by before Rob continued.

Staring at the last of the men he had slain, Rob addressed Don although he sounded as though he was talking to himself as well.

"We did what we had to here. We didn't look for this fuckin' mess; it came to us, remember? It sucks that we had to do this, but we damn sure had to. These fuckers brought this on themselves. Now we need to get our shit together and move on. And we need to get moving right now, okay!?"

Don nodded in agreement and slowly stood up. It took considerable effort to accomplish the task. He wiped the blade of his machete on the jeans of the man closest to him and slid it back into its improvised sheath, taking care not to cut through the duct tape holding it together.

Scanning all around their present location for any additional threats or other developing problems, Rob walked to the place behind the hedge where he had left his pack and shotgun. He collected all of his gear and adjusted it on his body.

Lastly, he opened the shotgun's action, removed a shell from his shirt pocket, and dropped it into the chamber, closing the weapon's action with an audible metallic click. As he looked at the bloody corpses he was responsible for, Rob decided it was best to move them out of plain view where they currently lay.

"Can you give me a hand moving these guys off the sidewalk? I'd rather not have 'em so obvious to anyone looking down the street."

"Yeah, let's do it."

They pulled all three bodies off of the sidewalk and left them behind several bushes in a front yard. It wasn't ideal, but it was better than where they had been before.

Rob performed another 360 degree survey, this time more slowly than before. He saw nothing that concerned him, but felt a great deal of unease nonetheless. They headed off down the sidewalk, returning to where they had been before making the right turn prior to the ambush that had changed their lives forever.

29

THOUSAND OAKS, CA

It was the day after she had watched Rosalyn walk back from the house down the block that Stephanie had made her decision about her dogs. She had decided to reduce the feedings for the Ausies to just one small meal a day each. She recognized the need to prolong the dog food supply for as long as she could, and she also wanted the dogs to be as alert as possible during the hours of darkness. So the Aussies now got breakfast only.

As for Charlie Wyatt and herself, she was still using the canned goods they had stored to provide their three meals a day. Charlie Wyatt had taken to requesting peanut butter and crackers for his lunch every day. Stephanie really didn't mind accommodating his request seeing as how the peanut butter was full of proteins and fats— a good fuel source. However, she insisted he eat some of the canned vegetables and fruits with her at dinner.

Once again, she silently thanked God he was not a picky eater. They were getting by. She was also thankful they had stored a good supply of emergency water, but she was surprised, and a little worried, at how much the two of them were using every day despite her severe self-imposed rationing.

She was taking a jerry-rigged four gallon shower every three to four days. Charlie Wyatt was getting a similar shower once a week. Today she told herself she would only use the small spray bottle and a wet wash cloth to perform her hygiene tasks. No more four gallon showers for the time being. She also planned on using a five gallon plastic bucket to do a load of laundry.

Rob had mentioned to her when they were establishing their emergency supplies that water would dwindle a lot faster than most realized during a prolonged disaster. She was now being given a firsthand view of just how right he had been. She made a promise to herself that she would never again complain about the space the fifty five gallon barrels took up in their garage. She now wished they had stored more of them.

One afternoon, a few days after her dogs had been reduced to one meal a day, Stephanie heard a terrible squealing. She was pretty certain the source was a dog located several houses away from her own. The pitiful sound suddenly, and without explanation, ceased within several seconds of its beginning. She experienced an inexplicable feeling that the pet had been killed in order to serve as dinner, or dinners, for a desperate neighbor. It depressed her greatly.

She tried to recall who lived at the various homes on her block, as well as where the sound had come from. She could only imagine how the owner had carried out the terrible task. She felt sorry for the dog's owner who most likely had to choose between taking the pet's life and watching his or her family go hungry. The idea literally brought tears to her eyes. Then, her thoughts returned to the recurrent worry she had been dealing with as of late.

Where the hell is Rob right now? What is he doing to survive through all of this? Is he trying to get home now, or is he staying somewhere until he can figure out a way to get home? Why did he insist on working at a sheriff's station that was so far from home? Stupid. And stubborn. Damn him anyway! If I had married a normal man he would probably be here with me right now. And I wouldn't be having to handle all of these problems by myself with no one to help me! It just isn't right!

Stephanie's emotions built up inside of her like an overflowing reservoir whose walls were no longer capable of containing a rising volume of water. She began to cry, shedding tears quietly at first, and eventually sobbing loudly, the tears flowing unabated. She cried for several minutes.

Her first thought after finishing the crying jag was to hope Charlie Wyatt had slept through her emotional episode. Looking toward his bedroom, she noticed with relief that he had remained in his room the entire time.

Later that afternoon, while in her back yard surveying what she could of the neighborhood, Stephanie watched one of her neighbors down the street drawing water from his spa. Two of the adjacent residents stood in front of the spa holding plastic five gallon buckets by their wire handles. Another held an empty plastic milk jug, and still another had what looked like a large empty pickle jar in her hands. Anything handy that could hold water from the looks of it. She tried to estimate how much water the small spa contained—two hundred gallons? Three hundred?

Stephanie and Rob had previously discussed the advisability of drinking residential swimming pool water during times of emergency, even though there were no pools on their block. The problem was that oftentimes pools and spas were treated with chemicals that could be dangerous to ingest. And neither boiling the water nor using the typical camping water filter would remove these chemicals.

At least they can use that water for personal hygiene, she thought. *I only hope they know better than to drink it.*

Out of nowhere and without warning, a flash of orange presented itself in her peripheral vision. She swiveled her head toward the source and felt a surge of adrenaline course through her body. Approximately twenty yards away, at the opposite end of the yard, stood the oldest of the three criminal looking men who had been prowling through the neighborhood, going door to door, earlier. He looked around in all directions, pausing for only the briefest of micro seconds on Stephanie. He had already identified her presence before entering the yard, and now he was checking out the surroundings for any potential intervention with what he had planned. Predator behavior by the numbers.

Unbeknownst to her at the time, the three roaming pillagers had skipped two other streets that were similar to the one she resided on before they decided to see what they could find on her quiet neighborhood block. Unlike the street the Flynn family called home, the other two streets had involved many of the blocks' residents in performing a high visibility security presence three days after the power grid had crashed.

The residents on these two streets--the first serving as a model for the other--had organized a neighborhood watch program following a spate of residential burglaries a year earlier. This had evolved into a basic earthquake preparedness effort in both groups. Immediately following the EMP event, the two streets in question had several men taking turns, working in shifts, keeping an eye on their streets and neighbors' homes. Some were armed and some were not, but to a man, they were intent on protecting their block.

In both cases the ends of the streets on these blocks had been secured against vehicular invasion by pushing inoperable vehicles across the streets from sidewalk to sidewalk. It also sent a clear message to any marauders on foot.

It wasn't a very elaborate plan and it certainly wasn't anywhere near a professional security operation, but it was something—and it was visible. Their efforts had already paid off in one instance for these residents and they didn't even know it. The three predatory marauders who were now mulling about near Stephanie's house had earlier opted to bypass the blocks with the citizen security patrols.

She watched the man's two cohorts scale the five foot high cinderblock wall that formed the rear border of her yard. Now in her back yard, these two looked around at their surroundings as their leader had done seconds earlier. She felt a panic that started in her heart and brain, and then washed over her entire body.

C'mon Steph...think through the panic. Focus!

She wondered if they had realized there was most likely no man in the house when they had spoken to her through the front door days earlier. Apparently all of her attempts at fooling the three criminals had failed. They had clearly sought out her home for a reason, and she feared it was an especially ugly motivation that had brought them here.

As the leader turned his head toward her, she saw a large tattoo on his neck. It was a large five point star. She recognized it at once.

Oh shit. Oh no. That's the same guy with the pony tail who savagely punched the older lady holding the box of food near the super market. And that's why his hair style looked strange to me earlier--he has his pony tail bunched up under that stupid orange ball cap. This can't be happening. What do I do now?!

Stephanie reflexively glanced toward the patio door at the rear of her house--the place where the most important thing in her life was taking a nap...completely vulnerable with nothing and no one to shield him from the looming predators--except her. She choked down the terror that washed over her like a huge wave. All she could think about was the necessity to keep these guys from getting into her house where Charlie Wyatt was now sleeping.

Uh-oh. What if Charlie Wyatt wakes up from his nap and wanders out here looking for me? Then what? Maybe they're just going through back yards to avoid being seen.

Rob had told her long ago that criminals—especially residential burglars--often ran through back yards as a means of avoiding police.

Wait a second...there are no police now!

As she processed all of this, pony tail man began walking toward her. He signaled to the other two with nothing more than a short terse jerk of his head toward her direction. They fell in behind him without hesitation—further confirmation of his role as leader of the trio. It was also clear that, not only was he the leader, he was also used to getting immediate compliance when he gave direction or orders.

The panicked housewife strained her memory as she watched the three men coming toward her, now less than twenty yards away and reducing the distance at a fast rate. She was trying to recall the shooting lessons Rob had given her on a handful of occasions over the years of their marriage. But despite her efforts to recall the instruction and to put the important parts of it together in a way to benefit her now, she just couldn't do it. She felt as though it were all running together and out her ears, like working with watery mud that wouldn't hold its form.

She thought about what the three monsters had done to the woman and the two Good Samaritans the previous week near the super market. She was convinced that regardless of whatever their plans were for her right now, they would enter the house to take whatever they wanted after they had finished with her. And then they would find Charlie Wyatt.

She was going to do what was necessary to protect her son and herself, and she wasn't going to worry about anything. Nothing else mattered in the whole world.

She pulled her thoughts away from what a failed scenario would mean for her little boy, and instead tried to focus on what she was going to do right here and now. Without being too obvious, she tried to adjust her loose fitting blouse so that it concealed her holstered revolver. She took some comfort in feeling the revolver on her belt.

Intuitively she thought she would be in a better position to resist the attack if she made herself look weak rather than strong. The element of surprise. It wasn't that Stephanie kidded herself by thinking she could have looked capable of putting up any real challenge to the powerful young thugs anyway, but she wanted to give the appearance that she was not going to offer any resistance whatsoever. So she sought to exaggerate the appearance of her weakness, hoping it might increase her odds of pulling her gun out to shoot them before they saw it coming.

As pony tail man came closer, Stephanie took in his overall appearance and mannerisms. He walked with a distinctive bounce in his step. It was not the kind of bounce that suggests a positive energy often associated with eager and productive members of society anxious to get about their contribution to the world, however large or small. It was a subtle but nefarious mannerism that—for those who knew what they were looking at—signaled a dangerous and malevolent attitude...a mannerism signaling a latent yet cruel propensity for violence that was merely waiting to unleash itself at the slightest perceived provocation. Or at any opportunity that presented itself. It was the stride of a one hundred percent pure human predator.

He displayed a smirk indicating a combination of arrogance and sinister intention, an especially disconcerting air of not only an evil nature, but a high intellectual capacity--at least in a practical real world sense--to go along with it. An especially bad combination. It was an expression that conveyed a subliminal message of an absolute conviction of his own ability to dominate any circumstance or to use a person for anything he wanted, and then discard them like so much garbage when he was through.

Stephanie was so unnerved by the man's overall persona that she briefly questioned whether she could press on with her plan to defend herself and son. She tried to make a note of the distance between the three targets--she had reduced their human value to zero and now saw them only as targets--as they walked toward her.

The two Aussies exploded into a barking frenzy without warning. The unexpected canine outburst, coupled with the pre-existing stress on her nerves, caused Stephanie to jerk unintentionally. The dogs, having discovered the intruders, yet still enclosed within the house, were now reacting with their version of a full court press. But it made no difference. The human carnivore turned his head no more than forty five degrees toward the dogs and then back again almost immediately. It was just enough to assess the sound and determine that it posed no threat to him. She found the coldly efficient sociopath to be irritating and terrifying all at once as she tried to mentally prepare herself for the fight of her life.

She reached under the tail of her blouse as he came within fifteen feet of her. With her right hand, now shaking so badly that she feared it might compromise her whole effort, she found the butt of the revolver.

Please don't let me screw this up. Not when I am so close to going through with this. I have to make this happen. Let me do this right so that my little boy can be okay. Please God. Please.

She fumbled with the holster's retention strap for what seemed like a minute but in reality was only a split second. The sound of the snap being unfastened sounded as loud as a gunshot to the woman trying so hard to mentally hold it all together. But the man in front of her, if he had heard it at all, showed no reaction to it.

Stephanie pulled the revolver free from its holster. It came out with surprising speed given the fact she had never practiced drawing the revolver from under her clothing. She instantly brought her left hand up and around to help steady the gun, just as she had been taught, although she wasn't even aware of the fact she was doing so. Muscle memory under conditions of high stress was a fascinating thing.

He was within arm's reach when she fired the gun into his chest.

The sinister sneer remained on his face even as he looked at the revolver's muzzle pointing at his chest and saw the muzzle flash twice. Stephanie was surprised by the sound of the shots. The .38 caliber *Plus P Plus* rounds were LASD issue, restricted for law enforcement use due to their having been loaded to ultra-high pressure levels. Yet she heard only popping sounds. No loud explosions like she had anticipated. For a moment she questioned whether the gun was working properly, but her observation of the ponytailed man falling to the ground confirmed that it indeed was.

The first round found its mark, the hollow point bullet having expanded, as it was designed, and almost completely severed the aorta of the muscular thug. Although there was no way she could have known it, the second round, having penetrated the heart itself, was wasted. He was already dead.

Stephanie wasn't going to roll the dice on a hope that the remaining two would leave her alone just because she had killed the alpha of the pack. No way. Not when the stakes were this high. Stephanie continued shooting at the other two men, both of whom were no more than twenty feet from her.

The closer of the remaining two had watched Stephanie as she shot his friend, but the sudden and extreme change in events was too much for his brain to fully process in the brief second before she fired the revolver twice more. The first round struck him in his abdomen, causing a small gore splatter that she failed to register due to her adrenalized state. She was just pulling the trigger, pointing the handgun as she would an accusatory index finger, completely ignoring the weapon's sights.

The second and third shots fired at bad guy number two went wide of their mark and fragmented harmlessly on the cinderblock wall behind him. No matter. He stumbled as he used both hands to grab at his gaping wound, the blood and intestinal shreds turning both of his hands crimson within a few seconds. It is doubtful whether his life could have been saved even if he had been positioned on a trauma center operating room table while he had been shot. He crumpled to the ground as his body endured massive internal hemorrhaging. He died less than a minute later, writhing in agony up to his last breath.

The last of the three, having just watched the sudden and complete destruction of his two cohorts, had the benefit of an extra second or two to process the information he had just witnessed. He started to turn to run from the woman with the revolver and the hate-filled eyes. Before he had completed his turn Stephanie fired at him from a distance of about twelve feet.

She squeezed the heavy trigger twice. The first trigger pull resulted in another popping sound, just like the others. The bullet went high and wide of its intended target by more than two feet. The second trigger pull resulted in a clearly audible *click*. The revolver was empty. The young thug slowed down but continued boogying to get out of there. He vaulted himself over the cinder block wall and into the neighbor's back yard. Having put the cement structure between Stephanie and himself, he stopped and took one last look over the wall at the determined and recently violent housewife. All but his eyes and head were protected by the wall. He saw her arms were still outstretched and supporting the now empty revolver, its muzzle pointed in his general direction. He decided to haul ass.

Stephanie experienced sheer panic. Different from what she had felt moments earlier. This was the kind of panic that accompanies the realization that one is holding an empty gun and yet still has a dangerous threat to contend with. The kind of panic that so called "gun experts" who have made statements such as "if you can't solve the problem with six rounds, your problem isn't the gun" have never experienced.

Life often throws cruel and unfair scenarios at people, and Stephanie feared she might be about to experience one of those. She considered the real possibility that despite how well she had handled the situation up till now, the last of the three pillagers might be coming back to destroy all she cared about—because her gun was empty. She spent a long few seconds thinking this over--and then the third guy was gone.

Stephanie turned away from the sight of the two dead men lying in her yard. Overcome by emotions and a wave of physical weakness she couldn't understand, she fell to her knees, dropping the revolver onto the grass in the process. Leaning forward and using her hands to support herself, she experienced a wave of nausea rolling through her that culminated in her throwing up the modest contents of her stomach. She retched for another several seconds before she willed herself to retrieve the revolver, shove it back into her holster, and walk back into the house. She had to check on Charlie Wyatt before doing anything else.

As she entered the house through the sliding back patio door, Stephanie heard Charlie Wyatt calling out for her. He was standing just outside of his bedroom door looking a bit confused.

"Mommy. Where are you? What was that noise?"

"I'm right here honey. Wait for me. I'll be there in a minute."

Uncharacteristically, she resisted the urge to immediately go over and hug him. She was concerned that small traces of blood and gore may have found their way onto her hands and arms during the close range shooting in the yard. And she feared she might transfer some of this onto Charlie Wyatt if she hugged him before cleaning herself up. Additionally, she was dealing with a powerful psychological need to wash her hands before touching her innocent little boy. Stephanie urged him to go into his room for a minute, promising that she would be right back.

Confirming that Charlie Wyatt had complied with her request, she went to her bedroom, removed her blouse with hands that shook despite her attempts to make them stop, and examined the garment for any signs of blood or other bodily fluid splatter. Finding nothing of concern, she threw the blouse on the foot of her bed. Wearing only jeans and a bra, her holstered revolver on her belt, Stephanie walked quickly to the kitchen, calling out to Charlie Wyatt as she passed his closed door.

"I'll be there in a minute Charlie Wyatt. Just wait there a little while longer for Mommy."

He's been such a good boy through all of this. When I was his age I wouldn't have done as well as he has under these circumstances. No way.

Once in the kitchen, Stephanie used the pot of bleach treated water to wash her hands and arms. The shaking seemed to be less severe now. She rushed through the process, returned to her bedroom, and hurriedly found another blouse to put on.

Suddenly recalling that she had not yet reloaded her revolver, she withdrew the gun from its holster and opened the cylinder. She dumped the expended casings, watching them fall onto her bed spread with a slight tinkling sound. She used the loose cartridges in her pocket to reload the empty cylinder, then closed it and shoved it into her holster. She made a mental note to also replenish the cartridges in her pocket. Right now she wanted to hug her little boy more than anything else in the world. She craved the innocence and kindness he represented after what she had just endured in the back yard.

After hugging Charlie Wyatt longer and harder than usual, the mentally strained mother asked her son if he wanted a special treat. It was a rhetorical question, and Charlie Wyatt's face lit up with delight. He nodded his response with enthusiasm, providing a big smile for emphasis.

"Yesss!"

Stephanie went to the garage and found a large freezer bag containing the dozen *Snickers* candy bars she had stored along with the other food. It had been her idea to store a few "morale boosters" along with their sustenance food. She used a knife to cut the candy bar in half and gave a piece to Charlie Wyatt. It was a rare occurrence for him to be given candy even under normal circumstances, and he was excited to get the treat.

As she and Charlie Wyatt sat in the kitchen, each eating their piece of the *Snickers* bar, Stephanie started to think about what had to be done at this point. She had two dead bodies in her back yard, and she couldn't leave them there. She started to think about the magnitude of what she had just done--taking the lives of two men who had been living breathing human beings less than an hour ago.

Those guys caused their own deaths. They were the ones that made the choice to go out and act like predatory animals, not me. I'll be damned if I'm going to let anyone hurt me or my family just because there is currently nothing in place to keep all the creeps in line.

Stephanie felt herself starting to get worked up again, the anger within her clearly pushing away any feelings of guilt that she had started to entertain. She returned to her thinking about what to do with the corpses in her yard. She had to make sure Charlie Wyatt didn't go out there until they were moved somewhere and somehow. Her first thought was to solicit the assistance of her neighbor Rick. After all, she had spent a great deal of time and effort helping him with his leg wound.

But that had been before she had essentially shut off Rosalyn and her husband in the interest of preserving her limited resources for Charlie Wyatt and herself.

30

UNINCORPORATED SOUTHEAST
LOS ANGELES

Sergeant Dave Marino had reached the point where he tried to avoid having any of the deputies enter his confined office to discuss anything. It wasn't that he was growing tired of their company per se, but rather that the stench of unchecked body odor had become stronger as the days passed by. The cops were periodically making use of the makeshift hygiene accommodations—warm water generated by the barbeque and large cooking pot--although some were clearly making better use of it than others. A few were also using the pot for doing laundry. He was going to have to insist that everyone start doing so pretty soon.

An increasing number of the station's deputies were no longer wearing their uniform shirts-- t-shirts and uniform pants were now the norm. *Kevlar* vests, normally concealed by uniform shirts, were being worn outside of the t-shirts in plain view. To a person, they wore their vests at all times save for the few hours during the day/night they were allowed to sleep.

The vests would only stop handgun rounds and shotgun pellets. Yet, despite the likelihood of an assault on the station involving attackers with rifles, they took some comfort in the vests. One never knew when a ricocheting rifle round, depleted of some of its original power, might be stopped by the *Kevlar*. The same held true for flying debris--de facto shrapnel really--that could be fatal if it found its way into human flesh.

Several of the deputies had managed to maintain a daily shaving routine by one means or another, while others--including the sergeant-- had allowed their facial hair to grow ever since the grid crash. Each of the two young tactical aficionados, Mori and Cruz, had shaved his head down to the scalp. The sergeant didn't know whether this had been done as a hygiene measure or for the purpose of presenting a more martial appearance. Maybe both.

The food supply, for the most part derived from the non-perishable supplies contained in the station jail for prisoners, was almost exhausted. Marino was pleased he had decided relatively early on to empty the station jail of its prisoners, but he now second guessed his early decision to send the deputies to Phil Goldstein's liquor store to load up on supplies. He now regretted not having had them walk the extra half mile to the full sized grocery store that had likely still contained plenty of life sustaining food during the first few hours following the EMP. It seemed so obvious now.

The discovery of the emergency food in Rob Flynn's locker was not only a badly needed source for restoring energy to the deputies' bodies, but also a substantial morale booster. The men—and Anderson---ate in pairs mostly, and Marino took some satisfaction in observing the enjoyment his officers derived from the new food. The food items were being rationed out carefully of course, but he estimated it would be gone in another couple of days regardless.

That night, at about two thirty AM, the station was attacked by a coordinated group of Molotov cocktail wielding assaulters. Four 40 ounce malt liquor bottles filled with gasoline and burning gas soaked rags were thrown over the wall of the parking lot at close to the same time a half dozen of the home made devices were heaved against the station's main front window. Fortunately, none of the little fire-bombs had caused any real damage.

About ten seconds following the attack with the Molotov cocktails, two dozen rounds of 7.62mm rifle rounds were fired into the front of the station window. The rounds, fired by two men armed with AK-47 rifles, had impressive penetrating capabilities, and the slugs traversed through several of the station's internal walls after having made it through the window glass. Due to nothing but sheer luck, no one was hit. None of the deputies had been able to pinpoint where the shots--or the fire-bombs for that matter--had originated. Nobody in the station had returned fire.

The Molotovs thrown into the parking lot shattered on the asphalt surface, their burning gasoline contents making for a lackluster visual display but not much more thanks to Gattuso and Slick extinguishing the flames with a four foot by six foot worn out rug that had been positioned outside the station's rear door. The firebombs impacting the station's front window had failed to break the heavy glass. Had the attackers thought to throw heavier missiles, such as rocks or bricks, through the window just prior to launching the Molotovs, consequently creating an opening for the flaming devices to make their way inside of the building before splattering their burning gasoline, the results could very well have been disastrous. Thankfully, the attackers, whoever they were, weren't that experienced with asymmetrical urban warfare tactics.

Harris and the sergeant had immediately run outside, shotguns sweeping the area, using their flashlights to illuminate their surroundings as they looked for threats. They were still able to keep their flashlights charged, although Harris wondered how long the patrol cars' batteries would last as a power source as he continued his search.

When the time comes where we can't charge our flashlights anymore it's gonna be a fuckin' game changer for sure, he thought.

The usual collection of people in front of the station and on the adjacent sidewalk areas was nowhere to be seen. The window and cement surface in front of it were awash in flames, the gasoline that had splattered on these surfaces burning brightly. They had at first tried to put out the flames, but upon seeing that the fire was not likely to cause any serious damage, along with the fact they had no effective means to accomplish the task, they eventually decided to let it burn it's self out. No need to subject anyone to the possibility of more gunfire.

Marino was incensed by the attack. He was not viewing it as police business. This was personal, and he now wanted to handle it as though it were personal.

"I want some serious payback for this shit if we get the chance, Lee."

"Yep. No question about it," Harris replied, tight jawed.

After discussing it with Harris, Marino had come to the conclusion he wanted to shrink down the defensive perimeter that he and his deputies were manning. It was obvious to him the bad guys surrounding them were now conducting probes to test their ability to resist an attack--or at least he thought that's what was going on.

He instructed the deputies to push some of the disabled squad cars to form an outer perimeter around the station. He hoped the cars would provide cover for those taking up positions to defend the building. Also, by shrinking the size of the perimeter, it allowed for the security detail to be less spread out. In theory, this meant a more effective ability to resist an assault. The down side to the reduced perimeter size was simply that it left much of the rear parking lot not being covered by deputies even though it could still be visually monitored.

It was hard work for the deputies. Having to manually push the cars into their appropriate positions to accomplish the objective was no easy endeavor, and the truth of the matter was they were all experiencing some level of diminished strength and/or endurance as a result of the reduced caloric intake and sleep deprivation.

Marino instructed Harris to gather up all the fire extinguishers he could find in the station so they could be strategically located in positions to best aid fire-fighting in the event of a future Molotov cocktail attack. Mori suggested they fill an empty garbage can or two with water, and drop several large rags in the water filled containers so that they could be used as a fire-fighting system should the building be firebombed. The idea was that anyone could grab one of the water soaked rags from the trash cans and use it to smother flames in a pinch.

Impressed by Mori's idea, Marino and the others began discussing how best to pursue the plan. They all liked the idea of using the garbage cans, water, and rags as a make-do fire-fighting system, but a few objected to using up the diminishing water supply for this purpose.

Gattuso, obviously giving the dilemma some heavy thought as he listened to the others, jumped in with his two cents' worth on the matter.

"What if we use the water from the car radiators to fill the trash cans? As long as we're careful not to puncture the secondary radiators for the tranny fluid coolant, there won't be any problem with the radiator fluid being flammable, so it should work fine to put out fires. It isn't like that radiator fluid can be used for anything else now. So we might as well use it for this."

Marino let the information sink in. Then he looked at Gattuso.

"You know what? That's another good idea. You guys are smarter than I gave you credit for." He laughed.

"I'll have to remember all this when I do your evaluations next time." He laughed again. Louder this time. But the patrol cops only smiled politely.

"Now we just have to figure a way to get that fluid out of the radiators."

Harris, his facial expression telegraphing his enthusiasm, offered his own suggestion.

"Sounds to me like another perfect job for that tomahawk that Cruz has."

Gattuso started laughing.

"You don't need to puncture the friggin' radiators to get the coolant out of 'em. You just wanna use that bad-ass tomahawk to break stuff, man, ya fuckin' crazy redneck," he jokingly told Harris. "I'll find the radiator drain plugs and get it out the smart way."

He shook his head in feigned disgust before following up with more.

"Next thing you're gonna be saying is that you want to shoot holes in the radiators to drain em," Gattuso added as he broke into one of his full-fledged infectious laughs he was so well known for around the station.

Harris, seldom thin-skinned when kidded by his friends, joined him in laughter.

"Yeah, yeah, okay Mr. Gearhead."

He, like most of the other deputies assigned here, was well aware of Gattuso's reputation for playing with, and working on, muscle cars. It was no secret the stocky Italian-American cop had come close to being arrested a few times as a high school kid who had a penchant for racing cars illegally on city streets.

Before darkness fell on the station that night, they had placed three large trash cans in strategic locations, each half full of the liquid contents removed from a couple dozen car radiators. Most were sheriff's department cars, but not all. Each garbage can had several jail towels floating in them as well. Every deputy present hoped and/ or prayed they wouldn't need them, but it was another small insurance policy.

The decision to shrink the size of the perimeter along with implementing some structural improvements--like positioning cars on the perimeter--allowed the deputies to get a little more rest. A smaller perimeter translated to a smaller number of persons needed to provide the same level of security, even if it was only a reduction by a number of two.

Marino sought to use this newfound advantage to provide his people with a little more rest than they had been able to get until now. A couple of mattresses had been removed from the now empty jail bunks and placed inside the station where the deputies slept in four hour shifts. However, a downside of the shrunken perimeter was that anyone needing to use the latrine now required another deputy to travel with them in order to provide security. No one wanted to risk literally being caught with his pants down, momentarily unable to protect himself.

For some it offered a chance to engage in a modicum of normalcy, or at least the promise of it, while others simply found that listening to their fellow cops relaxed them, often helping them get to sleep. To a person, every cop now holding down the station-turned-fortress had come to believe the strange young man who had warned Marino of a pending attack was legitimate. It was an unnerving situation, but they all managed to endure it.

One early morning Slick and Harris found themselves discussing who they most wished were at the station to help deal with the feared imminent attack. It was a pointless conversation, but the two men went on with the debate for several minutes.

Slick opined, "Shit man, we got two of the best tactical patrol boys on the whole damn department here with us. Mori and Cruz ain't no joke man. You ever seen the way those two can run their guns on the range? That's some serious shit right there."

As if to emphasize his point, the big cowboy raised the plastic cup in his hand to his mouth and spit a stream of Copenhagen into the empty container that served as a spittoon. Harris nodded in agreement but offered another perspective to consider.

"I agree with you there Slick, but I still wish 'Big John' was here. John Purnell has definitely seen the elephant. That caper last year where he chased down those two motherfuckers that were strapped with high cap forties and extra mags in their pockets...Purnell knew they were strapped heavy and chased 'em both man! Then he smokes each one of those motherfuckers when it comes to show time. That kinda shit puts him in the major bad-ass category in my book. He earned that medal of valor for that one man. Probably saved more than one innocent life by permanently putting an end to those punks that day too. Yeah, skills are a good thing and all that, but a man who can take care of business even when the shit is comin' at him hard and heavy is my first choice for who I want to cover my back."

Slick, who had continued to maintain a shaved scalp since the day the infrastructure collapsed, slowly ran his hand over his head to wipe away sweat. He shrugged his powerful shoulders.

"All I'm gonna say is that Mori and Cruz can run and gun better than any other cops I've ever seen--that's all. I'm talkin' with both pistols and shotguns. And I'm bettin' they both stand up and use those skills even when they're gettin' shot at too."

Harris kept his last comment on the subject short.

"Hey, don't get me wrong. The truth is I think everyone here can hold their mud when it comes down to the shit flyin'. I'm counting on it in fact. It's just a damn good feeling when you actually know the man at your back has done it before; that's all."

Slick nodded, spat a stream of Copenhagen into his cup, and looked straight ahead without further comment. He checked his shotgun to ensure that the chamber was loaded and the safety was on, followed by a check of his handgun. He then removed his *Kevlar* vest. He carefully placed it next to his mattress where he could quickly put it back on in a hurry if necessary. After removing his gun belt and placing it directly next to his mattress, he adjusted the thick pad beneath him so that it allowed him to rest his back and head against the wall at close to a forty five degree angle. He prepared to get some sleep. Harris followed the same procedure, including the weapons checks. He also positioned his vest so that he could put it on quickly if required.

At mid-day the following morning Harris was posted at his security position, repeatedly fighting off the pull of sleep. While inventing new ways to keep awake until his four hour sleep shift arrived, he suddenly heard Gattuso, Anderson, and Cruz yelling. And they were laughing. Or at least Gattuso was laughing. Harris was listening to the unmistakable sounds of happiness and jubilation—sounds that hadn't been heard in a long time around the Nadeau Station.

"What the hell's going on that could make anyone here happy about anything," Harris asked of nobody specifically in a sleep deprived and cranky voice.

He had just let the words leave his mouth when he saw the answer to his question appear in front of him. He was looking at a big white guy, wearing a medium sized olive drab backpack, pushing a mountain bike through the station parking lot.

Well I'll be damned. If it ain't Big John Purnell. What the fuck?!

Harris ran toward his friend with his left hand behind his lower back gripping the shotgun's barrel to minimize its pounding on him as he moved.

"Hell yeah! About time your little pansy ass showed up here!"

He was laughing with a huge smile on his face.

The six foot tall cop, built like an off-season college linebacker, stopped to look in the direction of the good natured insult and broke into a big ear-to-ear grin as he let his bike fall to the pavement and stepped forward to close the gap between them. Harris almost knocked Purnell over with the force of his impact and hug. He clapped the larger man on the back several times.

"It's great to see you, *brother!*"

"Holy shit! I survived all this shit to get to the station and now I'm gonna get beat to death by my buddy--what the hell man!"

Purnell started laughing, and Harris, still grinning, threw a half speed right cross that fell harmlessly on his friend's thick shoulder.

"So how did you get here anyway?"

Before Purnell could begin with his response, Marino walked up and greeted the new arrival. He told the others to man their positions, adding that he had to get Purnell briefed on everything as soon as possible given the threat they faced. He promised they would all get a chance to hear about how the big bicycle riding deputy had made it to the station from his house in El Segundo at a later time.

Harris had started to walk away but then came to a halt and turned toward Purnell to ask a question he deemed important.

"Hey John, screw all the other stuff. The important question is what did you bring with you as far as weapons are concerned, and how much ammo do you have?"

"I got my M-4 carbine, broken down obviously, in my pack. Brought along five thirty-round mags for it...all of 'em loaded. Plus, I brought another hundred fifty plus rounds still in the boxes."

Purnell then used both hands to pat the front of his waistline, to the left and right of his belt buckle.

"I got my two H&K .45's. Probably got about fifty rounds of ammo for em, plus I got another hundred rounds or so in my locker. I brought a few MRE's with me too in case the food rations here are tight."

Harris wrinkled his nose at the mention of the MRE's. He would rather eat just about anything else.

"No one can say you don't always try to be prepared John."

There was a brief but noticeable pause on Harris's part before he continued talking.

"Uh, about that .45 ammo in your locker...well, we took it out of there a few days ago. We went through all the lockers looking for anything we could use. I think Mori has your ammo. I don't think any of the other deputies here use a .45 except him. Anyway, I got to get back to my position, but I'm glad to see you *brother*. We might have a pretty heavy shit-storm coming our way here pretty soon. I'll let the sarge here get you briefed in on that."

Purnell didn't show any negative reaction to this news. He merely shrugged his shoulders and said, "I'll talk to Mori and get it figured out."

Harris walked over to his friend and slapped him on the shoulder in a parting show of affection. Then he turned and headed back to his post. Purnell had only halfheartedly acknowledged the display. He had been staring at Marino ever since Harris had indicated he would brief him on the pending shit-storm. Purnell, not known for being patient even under normal circumstances, was especially impatient to find out what he had walked into. Meanwhile, the deputies at the station all received the news that big John Purnell had joined their ranks. For each and every one of them, his arrival had the effect of raising their spirits.

Marino spent the better part of fifteen minutes filling Purnell in on the possible pending attack, including the strange manner in which the information had been received, the background that Harris had mentioned, and the recent firebomb and shooting attack. He also gave Purnell the basic rundown on how operations and protocols at the station were being conducted.

When Marino had finished, Purnell stared at the bearded and barbarian looking sergeant for a protracted second before responding.

"Shit Sarge. You're making me think I would've been better off staying home and taking my chances by myself there."

He laughed after making the wisecrack. They both knew it wasn't safety that had motivated him to make the journey to the station.

Marino let loose with a deep laugh befitting his appearance.

"Yeah, but then you'd miss out on all this fun we've been having here. To be real honest, the department fucked us big time on this

John. We're totally on our own here. We can't protect anyone but ourselves--and I'm not even sure about how long we can do that."

Purnell lived by himself in the small city of El Segundo. Located twelve miles, and a whole world, away from the Nadeau Sheriff's Station, it was known for its very low crime rate and small town feel. The little bedroom community with a smattering of large commercial businesses was an attractive place for cops to live for those who could afford it on a cop's income. And if they didn't mind the boredom. The night before, Purnell had decided to load up his pack in preparation for heading out the next morning on his mountain bike. Now that he had completed the trip, he wondered if it had been a smart move.

He stooped to pick up his bicycle by the handle bars. He stood in the station parking lot and began telling the sergeant what he had seen on his journey across town. He gently rocked his bicycle back and forth, watching the knobby tires repeatedly roll eight inches forward and then eight inches back, as he shared the information. Marino listened intently as Purnell began to talk.

***

The bicycle ride had taken Purnell almost three hours, mostly due to his having to take circuitous routes in the interest of avoiding trouble. He mentioned that there was even one episode where he had dismounted his bicycle and concealed himself behind a house for a while to avoid being attacked.

When the sergeant asked John if he was familiar with electromagnetic pulse, he indicated he hadn't been until a few days ago. Purnell went on to explain how he had spoken to a man in his El Segundo neighborhood several days following the grid crash. He drew on his better than average memory to recount the conversation he had had with the HAM radio operator.

Almost a week following the power grid crash, Purnell had elected to perform a walk around his immediate neighborhood just to check out the status of things. While he was doing so, he noticed the HAM radio antenna mounted on the roof of a house on his block. The light bulb went off in his head, and he found himself knocking at the front door of the residence half a minute later.

After a brief introduction, Purnell delved right into his question about the HAM radio. The man answered that the radio transmitter hooked up inside his house had been rendered inoperable, presumably as a direct result of the EMP event. Purnell's disappointment was obvious in his expression. The man explained all about electromagnetic pulse and why he had concluded that EMP was the cause of the widespread power outage and vehicle failures.

The Ham operator, who Purnell estimated to be in his seventies, said he had been concerned about the possibility of an EMP attack by America's enemies ever since the terrorist attacks of 2001 in New York and Washington. As a precaution, he had purchased a small handheld HAM radio, programmed it with the desired frequencies, and then stored it in a manner that he was convinced would withstand an exposure to EMP.

Thinking that his new listener might be interested in the specifics of how he had protected his radio, the man explained to John in detail how he had taken the small device and extra batteries, wrapped them in a couple layers of foam rubber, followed by aluminum foil, and then placed them all in a cardboard lined steel garbage can. Then he had taped the lid with aluminum tape.

"They call these things that protect against EMP and such, *Faraday Cages,*" he had said.

The aging yet mentally acute radio hobbyist had pulled a small handheld device--complete with an antenna that seemed too long for such a small radio--from his pocket and waived it in front of Purnell with pride. He told Purnell how the little radio had worked fine when he pulled it out of its storage container despite the fact the EMP had rendered most of his other electric powered items inoperable.

Purnell didn't understand most of what the man had explained to him, other than he had managed to protect his amateur radio and was therefore still able to communicate with the outside world. He politely acknowledged the man's good planning, but wasted no time before pressing him for any information about what was happening outside of their El Segundo neighborhood.

"Well, on a national level, the country has been dealt one serious goddamn blow from the bits and pieces I've been hearing. Sounds like every major city in the whole country has been devastated."

Purnell had looked at him with his jaws agape.

"Well hell," the man had continued, "None of the city infrastructures were set up to resist an EMP attack—even though the stupid shits were warned for years about the threat."

He had glanced at John to see if there was any reaction to his comment. Seeing none, he went on.

"And worse, apparently none of the country's city or county managers had any plans to deal with the effects of an EMP either."

Purnell had asked the man, "Just how bad is it in the cities?"

"Well, there's lots of talk about heavy looting and violence going on in the cities all across the country. No surprise there I guess. One radio operator said the city of Philadelphia was having trouble dealing with all of the dead bodies. Cops aren't around to help with any of it either. Same with the fire departments--I'm a retired Cleveland Fireman by the way. There are reports of fires burning out of control in most of the cities--at least according to what's being said over HAM radio. You never know for sure, but generally the HAM operators are a pretty solid bunch when it comes to getting the facts right--or at least trying to get 'em right."

Purnell had been shocked by the news the retired fireman had given him. To him it wasn't so much the kind of trouble that was occurring but rather the fact that the damage was so wide spread. He couldn't recall any other disaster that had impacted such a wide section of the country. After he had digested the information, he had asked the man what he had heard about the status of the Los Angeles area specifically.

"Heard a few guys talking over the radio--this morning actually--about what was happening in downtown L.A. I guess there were a few police cars that were parked in the underground structures near the big court building that still worked after the EMP happened. Must've been shielded from the EMP by all that concrete," he had said, shrugging his shoulders in a manner suggesting he was unsure.

"Nobody on the radios had any idea of who was using the police cars. I guess it would have been policemen. Anyway, they were seen driving away from the area. Of course there are lots of people destroying buildings and cars down there. You know, rioting. Sounds like a lot of people have been killed too. One of the HAM operators said he had to stop broadcasting so he could protect his house from the mobs rampaging through the streets where he lived. I think he said he was in the Echo Park area."

The last comment the senior neighbor had made to Purnell involved police officers being killed.

Somewhere north of downtown Los Angeles a small group of police officers had made an effort to patrol the neighborhoods using motorcycles of some kind.

"From what they were sayin' over HAM frequencies, they shot and killed all of those cops. Probably gangs. Set up an ambush or some such thing." He shook his head.

"And then the bastards dragged the dead cops through the streets... goddamn animals."

After Purnell had gleaned whatever information he could from the man, he had returned to his small modest house and started to ponder his situation. He had stocked his residence with a month's worth of essentials in preparation for a major earthquake, so he was in decent shape as far as that was concerned. At least for the time being. But he couldn't stop thinking about his sense of duty. Less than forty eight hours later, he was wearing a backpack stuffed with what he thought he would need most, including his civilian legal M4 carbine and ammunition, and preparing to head off to the Nadeau Sheriff's Station.

He plied Sergeant Marino with other information about what he had seen along the route to the sheriff's station, including roaming bands of young criminal looking men carrying weapons ranging from baseball bats and knives to shotguns and military looking rifles. He told the sergeant he had taken great efforts to minimize the chances of encountering hostile contacts, elaborating how he had successfully fled from a group of four gangbangers, riding his mountain bike in a zig-zag pattern as fast as he could, all the while expecting to be shot at as he fled from the thugs.

For whatever reason, the shots had never come his way. Purnell said that at the time he had debated with himself whether he should shoot the gangbangers or try to avoid contact. In the end he had opted to flee on his bicycle for all he was worth.

"My take-away from that incident is that saving ammo is usually a good thing, but don't get so stingy with it that you don't use it when you have to. I got lucky is all," Purnell offered by way of advice.

Finally, he told of how he had heard a whole host of terrible and agonizing sounds during different parts of his twelve mile bike ride, adding that he could only imagine what horrible incidents had been responsible for these sounds.

"Sarge, there are a helluva lot of dead bodies being stacked up out there. And that includes neighborhoods in this area. A shit load of dead bodies man."

Marino held the younger cop's gaze but didn't answer for a while.

"John, I'm gonna say this because it's the truth and you need to hear it. And I hope I don't make you regret making that trip over here, because we're all glad to have you here with us."

He waited for John to react, but he only dipped his head and rotated his palms partially upward, urging the sergeant to hurry up with the information.

Marino obliged him.

"Here's the deal. We're not likely going to be trying to help anyone in any of these neighborhoods we usually police. We couldn't do it even if we wanted to. We have to try to save our own asses now, and we're probably gonna have our hands full just pulling that off unless we get some help here pretty soon. But it looks like there isn't going to be any help for a while. Our own department left us hanging out to dry as far as I'm concerned. All the money, time, and effort spent on the politically correct bullshit over the years, and nothing was spent on preparing for this kind of thing. And the bastards had been warned about the possibility of it happening many a time too."

Purnell, obviously disgusted by what he had just heard, shook his head and merely muttered, "Unbelievable. Un-fucking-believable."

31

WESTCHESTER, CA

The two tired and emotionally shaken men hiked on for another low mileage producing hour—mostly due to Don's bad knee--before they saw any people in close proximity. While walking on a residential sidewalk doing their best to keep in the shadows, their attention was drawn to a sight that took them both aback. They saw two women, both sitting in folding lawn chairs that had been placed on a brown colored dying lawn behind a three foot high tan picket fence. A few children's tricycles and other pedal vehicle toys were scattered throughout the yard. It was difficult to estimate the age of either woman, but Rob's best guess was they were both between the ages of twenty five and thirty five. Both sat next to a hand drawn cardboard sign that had been propped up haphazardly against a cheap looking bicycle supported by its kickstand. The sign read:

*WILL DO **ANYTHING** FOR FOOD OR WATER.*

PLEASE HELP HAVE CHILDREN TO FEED

One of the women was wearing bright red lipstick and a low cut top that exposed much of her breasts. He thought it bordered on the ridiculous. Even under the limited lighting conditions, it appeared as though she hadn't bathed or showered since the EMP had occurred. She looked Rob directly in the eye, followed by Don. She displayed her version of a lascivious smile to both men as she pushed up her ample breasts, and then uncrossed and re-crossed her legs. Her actions removed any doubt as to what was meant by the term *"ANYTHYING"* that had been written and underlined on the sign. For Rob, what shone through the feigned expression of lust was the unmistakable look of complete and utter desperation and despair. She wore the look of a woman who was near the end of her rope and running out of options.

It was an extremely disturbing sight for Rob. He wondered if he found it so disturbing because he was reminded of his own family to whom he was trying so hard to return, or if it was simply the hopelessness of the women's predicament. Maybe it was the growing hopelessness of the region--and maybe even the nation--as a whole. He wondered if either of the women had been successful in getting food or water in exchange for the use of their bodies. He also wondered if either of them had husbands or boyfriends that were waiting behind the walls of the houses.

Maybe the men are lying in wait to attack and rob anyone stepping into the house to use the women for their sexual services. It wouldn't surprise me. All is fair in love and war--and during post EMP conditions.

Rob's thoughts returned to Stephanie and Charlie Wyatt. He asked himself what Stephanie would be willing to do if it came down to making sure their little boy could get what he needed to survive. He supposed that she, like the two sad women sitting in the lawn chairs, would do whatever it took to see that her son had what he needed to survive.

He monitored his watch to keep track of their progress. Not long after walking past the two women sitting in the patio chairs, they heard a volley of gunshots from what sounded like less than a quarter mile from their location. Eight to ten rounds maximum. Rob thought they sounded like handgun rounds, but it was sometimes difficult to tell.

The sound of the shots prompted Rob of the need to go over a procedural matter with Don.

"Hey Don, we should go over a few things about silently communicating. You know...a couple simple hand signals or whatever."

He showed him a raised closed fist, which indicated the command for "stop", forked fingers almost touching the eyes which indicated "to watch or look for", a bladed open hand which indicated "threat or bad guy", and the touching of the ears with a cupped hand which indicated "listen for". He figured it was enough.

At one point, they passed a modest house with a small but obviously well-maintained yard. The owners' pride in the place could be seen even though it had been almost two weeks since the power had gone down. Rob saw an elderly woman, wearing a modest dress with her hair up in a bun, using a broom to sweep off her front porch. Regardless of what was happening, she had responsibilities. Had to keep the house looking respectable. It was her obligation.

Something about the scene affected him emotionally. He instinctively wanted to comfort the elderly woman--wanted to give her the meager food rations contained in his pack and offer to assist her in any way he could. She deserved better than the conditions she now found herself dealing with. Yet he looked away.

Rob did his best to ignore his exhaustion as he continued walking in a northerly direction one block parallel to the main boulevard. He was mentally sorting through all the things he had encountered following the EMP. Lost in his thoughts, he realized he was looking at four young hard cases walking along the sidewalk half a block in front of him. Two of them were carrying what looked like sticks or metal pipes. He wondered if the other two were carrying smaller but more dangerous weapons. Pretty damn easy to hide a pistol under a shirt or inside a pocket.

He and Don watched the group disappear into a front yard, only to return half a minute later. This process was repeated several times as they watched. It was pretty obvious they were scouting out potential victims, looking for something—or someone--worth taking.

Just a pack of wolves sniffing around for something to kill. Now we have yet another detour to make.

Rob was angry, but he knew the value of avoiding trouble, even if it meant further delay.

They took a detour by retreating back to the nearest intersection behind them and heading one block to their east. Another middle class residential neighborhood. Everyone locked up inside their houses. They continued heading north.

They walked for twenty minutes before Rob heard the odd sound. It was little more than a humming noise at first, but as they continued hiking the noise evolved into what was an unmistakable and wholly unexpected sound--the sound of an electricity generator. Rob was puzzled by what he heard, and he mentioned it to Don.

"I thought that after an EMP happened even generators were probably not gonna work--unless they were really old ones. Am I right?"

Don replied with something between a whisper and a low volume voice.

"Well, I can't remember much about that EMP stuff. We had a guy come and talk to a bunch of us linemen years ago, but I forget most of what he said. I thought it was all bullshit doomsday stuff at the time. I think he said some generators might still work after an EMP though. Shit, I can't remember."

Rob spoke in a low tone matching Don's.

"Well someone around here has one that's working. That's definitely a generator we're hearing."

"Oh yeah; that's a generator alright. I hope whoever has that thing running is a friendly type. My knee is starting to really hurt. I think I need to rest it for a while. It would be nice to be able to rest up somewhere where we don't have to fight off these damn crazies and other assholes that are all over the place."

"Okay, let's go see what we can find out."

As the two friends cautiously approached the sound of the generator, Rob threw up a clenched fist in the established signal for stopping, and then came to an abrupt stop. He removed the small monocular from its pouch and tried to get a look at the property housing the generator.

Before them, approximately a half block distant, was a sight that reminded Rob of a third world country some place where the people lived without rule of law. Some place where people survived based on their own practical skill sets, instincts, and established working relationships with others with similar capabilities. What it did *not* look like was any place inside of the United States of America. Yet here it was.

He was looking at what had probably been a fairly normal two-story home prior to the EMP having changed everything. The home had been transformed into a fortress of sorts. It was positioned fifty feet back from the sidewalk. A now dying lawn, absent any trees, took up the land that separated the home from the sidewalk. All of it was surrounded by a six foot high chain link fence.

The owners of the house, or whoever had engineered their security arrangements, had fashioned vertical metal extensions at every fence post that protruded two feet above the fence along its entire length. Someone had strung three strands of barbed wire between each of the steel extensions, so that the end result was a six foot high chain link fence with another two feet of barbed wire on top of that. The now eight foot high security fencing appeared to encircle the entire perimeter of the property, or at least all the property Rob could see from his present position.

He told Don what he was seeing, and then the two of them began walking slowly closer, ever mindful of the two armed men that were positioned at the front corners of the house. It didn't appear either of the guards at the location had seen them yet. They stopped again, and Rob heard Don gulping down the water he had been carrying in the zip-lock bag.

Rob whispered loud enough for his partner to hear, although he was really just thinking out loud.

"Look at all the security measures these guys have, will ya? Crazy. Of course with that generator makin' all that noise like that they're gonna need it. It's gonna attract all the assholes around here like moths to a flame."

Don grunted his acknowledgment as he raised his water filled zip-lock bag.

"You want some of this water before I toss it," he asked, still whispering.

"No. Go ahead and get rid of whatever you can't drink right now. You definitely want to have both of your hands free. Who knows what's going to happen now."

"Yeah, I know. That's why I'm getting ready to throw it out," Don replied with a little bit of irritation.

"I think I'll take a piss though while I have time," Rob said. "I suggest you do the same. Keep an eye on the place and I'll be right back."

While Rob walked off to find a suitable location for his task, Don dumped the water from the zip-lock, folded the empty bag, and stuffed it into his shirt pocket. Rob returned a minute later and Don decided to follow his suggestion.

After both men were back from emptying their bladders, they took another long look at the place with all of the security. The flood lights on the property had been positioned so that most of the light was directed at the outside edges of the property, allowing only a small amount to reach the two guards positioned at the front of the house. However, Rob could still see from where he stood that both of the sentries wore combat gear on their upper bodies and held military-type compact carbines. As he and Don crept closer, he held up a closed fist and stopped, then used the monocular to take another look.

He could see the man at the closer of the two corners of the house was wearing what was often referred to as a *chest rig*. He scrutinized the equipment in the hopes it would tell him something about the man wearing it. The heavy duty nylon olive drab and black colored chest rig contained numerous pouches in the front panel, most of which were designed for carrying extra military style rifle magazines. The magazine pouches all appeared to be full, meaning the guy was packing one hell of a lot of extra ammunition. The guy looked professional too.

The guard's chest rig also had a sheathed fixed blade knife attached to one of the padded shoulder straps. Attached just above the knife was what appeared to be a handheld two-way radio, its small telltale antenna protruding from its pouch. The shoulder strap on the opposite side had what looked like a flashlight pouch attached to it. The sentry appeared to be of average size and build, and fit. On his right thigh, he wore a pistol in a combat holster. On his opposite side was a triple pistol magazine pouch.

He grasped a dark colored carbine with a large magazine protruding from its underside, probably an M4 or similar rifle from what he could tell. The manner in which this guy handled the weapon was not lost on Rob either. He held and manipulated his rifle in a manner indicative of one who has spent a lot of hours training with, and/or using, the thing. Like a framing carpenter with twenty years in the trade handles his hammer.

The second man performing guard duty wore a mostly black tactical vest that contained numerous pouches on it, including a holster that housed a dark colored handgun. Looked physically fit—just like the other one. He, too, had a hand held two-way radio mounted on his vest. This sentry wore a second handgun holstered on his right leg in a similar manner as the other guard. Rob could not make out whether he had additional gear on his left thigh, but he assumed that he did. This guard held a weapon in his hands that looked to be similar, if not identical to, the one held by the first sentry. He, too, handled his rifle like he knew how to use it.

Several feet in front of both of the front corners of the house, Rob saw two plywood structures—boxes really--that had been constructed into "L" shapes. At first he thought they were unfinished planter boxes, but he dismissed this conclusion as he thought about their placement and how they were built.

Rob suspected these boxes were intended to serve as some sort of defensive positions of cover. Probably filled with sand or dirt to help stop bullets.

Rob took in the sight and tried to mentally digest what it all meant.

Wow. These guys, whoever the hell they are, are some serious sonsabitches. No doubt about that. There's no way these guys improvised all of this on the fly after the EMP attack went down. No way. These guys prepared for this way before the EMP hit. The question is whether they're friendly or not. Are they paranoid, or are they just the type that believes in preparing for any possible scenario?

Rob motioned for Don to bring his ear closer to his face before he started talking. Still whispering, Rob turned his head just slightly as he spoke. He didn't want to lose his view of the guards or the property by turning his head completely to look at Don. Don didn't need to see him—only to hear him.

After a brief discussion about the pros and cons of contacting the guards of the place they were looking at, Don made it clear he had little choice given the condition of his knee. If he failed to get some rest pretty soon he was going to have a problem. If this place was a bust then he would have to risk finding a spot out in public—with or without Rob--where even a low level of security would be tough to accomplish.

It wasn't exactly a hard sell for Rob. He wasn't going to abandon his friend, and he badly longed for a place to have a full night's rest where he wasn't trying to sleep with one eye open, ready to use heavy violence against whatever threat might appear. So, without argument or debate, they decided to approach the sentries posted at the house. Sporting man or not, sometimes one just had to roll the dice.

"I need you to follow my lead on this Don. Pretty much just keep your hands up and don't say anything. I'll do the talking."

"Okay buddy. I hope you know what you're doing."

"Yeah, so do I," Rob commented without enthusiasm.

The two nervous friends walked toward the fenced off property with their hands held high. Making a fist to signal a halt, Rob stopped just after he began walking. He crouched down, untied his shotgun from the pack strap's "D" ring, and then removed the pack. He tied the cut-down shotgun to the rear of his backpack so that it would be obvious to the men guarding the property that the weapon was not immediately accessible to him.

Of course the pistol concealed by his untucked shirt was still immediately accessible, but he was pretty sure it would not be visible to the sentries. Rob was convinced the machete taped to his front pack strap would not cause them concern. These guys would surely realize Rob was too far away from them to pose a threat with a knife.

Still leading the way and holding his hands high, Rob called out to the closest of the men pulling guard duty as he approached the fence line.

"We're friendlies. Can we talk to you for a second? We mean you no harm. We are no threat to you."

There was no response at first. Both of the posted guards shouldered their carbines and pointed the muzzles of their weapons in the general direction of Rob and Don. The more he watched these guys, the more he was convinced they were professional gun handlers of some kind.

He decided to gamble again and announce that he was a cop. Both of the sentries were clearly pro's of some kind, but this didn't necessarily make them less dangerous given the post EMP situation. At worst, he reasoned, it would have no impact--good or bad--on their willingness to help him and his friend. Very little to lose, and the possibility of something to gain here. So he made his decision.

"I'm a deputy sheriff and I'm just trying to get to my friend here's house up the way a couple of miles. In Culver City. He's got an injured knee and he's hoping to rest it up for a few hours. We have our own food and water, so we aren't asking for anything but some safety for a few hours, or a day at the most"

The farther away of the two well-armed men was constantly scanning his surroundings, as well as watching Rob and Don. He had been doing so since the two had made their presence known. His carbine remained in the *modified low ready* position, and its muzzle never ventured too far away from Rob and Don.

The closer of the two guards didn't scan his surroundings, at least not noticeably, but he watched them with an intensity that was slightly unsetting.

Jeez. These guys aren't slackers—that's for sure, Rob thought.

The man with the intense stare finally spoke up.

"You say you're a deputy sheriff? What division are you assigned to?"

Rob immediately recognized the subtlety in the man's choice of words and guessed that he was talking to an LAPD cop, either active or retired. The Los Angeles Police Department referred to their patrol areas as *divisions*, whereas the Los Angeles County Sheriff's Department used the term *stations* to identify their patrol areas.

None of this mattered. All that mattered was that he was now almost certain he was dealing with another cop.

Rob answered the question and offered to show him his sheriff identification.

"No. Don't move at all!"

The man seemed to be thinking about something.

"Hey, answer this question for me Mr. Deputy Sheriff. Who is the most respected patrol sergeant there at Nadeau Station right now?"

Rob was now convinced he was right. Nobody other than a fellow cop would ask that question.

"I would have to say Dave Marino," Rob responded in a loud and calm voice that belied the nervousness he felt surging through his body.

32

THOUSAND OAKS, CA

It was almost dark and Stephanie still hadn't come up with a plan for how she was going to deal with the bodies in the back yard. It wasn't until she had made a simple dinner of canned goods, and then put Charlie Wyatt to bed that the idea occurred to her. Stephanie knew Rob kept a wheel barrow somewhere on the side of the house to be used for miscellaneous chores. She was pretty sure she could move a large human body into the contraption, but it would take an effort to do so by herself.

She waited a half hour to make sure that Charlie Wyatt was asleep before using her flashlight and going outside to find the wheelbarrow. She found the sturdy plastic single-wheeled cart leaning against the far exterior wall of the house. Fumbling to find a position that allowed her to hold her flashlight as she took a firm grip of the wheelbarrow's handles, she pushed the cart over to the largest of the bodies. The fact that she was doing this in the dark made the task--creepy under even the best of conditions--seem even more so.

Stephanie was pondering where she wanted to move the body when a bizarre thought crossed her mind. She wondered about the possibility of using the dead bodies for food. Not for herself, but for her two Ausies. She wondered how to slice off the meat so that it could be used. She also pondered the morality of such a decision. She dismissed the thought immediately, ashamed of herself for even considering such a ghastly idea in the first place.

Is this what happens to people after they live in dire conditions long enough? Only two weeks into this disaster and I'm thinking crazy thoughts? And I haven't even been suffering like so many others. This whole situation is crazy. Here I am getting ready to move a dead body in the middle of the night like some character in a B grade horror movie for Christ's sake.

Stephanie parked the wheelbarrow next to the larger of the two bodies and considered the situation. She squatted down, cognizant of maintaining as safe of a lifting position as she could to avoid injuring her back. She grabbed the body, noting that rigor had set in. It was as stiff as a board. And heavy. She struggled determinedly to get it into the cart, but the sheer mass and weight was more than she could manage.

Not giving up, she tipped the large cart on its side so that the wheelbarrow's side wall was flat against the ground. No longer having a height obstacle to deal with, she pushed the body into the plastic box of the cart as one would push detritus over the edge of a dustpan.

Remembering to bend her knees and squat as opposed to bending her back, Stephanie tried to right the wheelbarrow—now weighted with two hundred pounds of flesh--from its side. Mustering more strength and effort than she thought she had, she was able to get the big cart up into its normal position.

Okay...I've got the hard part done now.

The exhausted mother adjusted the position of the body as best she could so that it was not protruding out to the sides any more than necessary. She pushed the wheelbarrow and its heavy load to the gate and let it rest there while she tried to figure out her next step. She walked to the other side of the yard and removed the tarp that covered their large barbeque. Bunching the heavy plastic cover up in her arms, she brought it over to the wheelbarrow and covered the body.

She was suddenly overcome with the urge to laugh. The more she thought about the absurdity of the task she was involved in, the funnier she found it. She started to laugh, and continued to do so for a full minute. She had read somewhere that an increased sense of humor was a common response during super high stress situations, and she wondered if that was what was happening with her. She hoped her neighbors wouldn't see her, but that really wasn't a huge concern the more she considered it.

What are they gonna do, call the police on me? I would be glad to explain to the police what happened and why I did what I did if only they would show up. It would be worth the stress of being questioned just to have some help from the authorities.

More than anything, she wanted to move the bodies out of her yard to protect Charlie Wyatt. She did not want him to see the carnage. She also realized that it wouldn't be long before the bodies would start to stink. And she wasn't sure whether or not there was a serious risk of disease that could accompany rotting bodies.

Stephanie had opted to move the largest and heaviest body first, knowing that she would be physically drained by the time she had to move the second one. It was a slow and laborious process that required her to stop and rest frequently before she reached the intended destination located almost fifty yards from the Flynn's front yard.

She eventually carted both bodies to an empty lot, overgrown with weeds, that was on the corner of her block. The effort took her more than two hours, and she was past being exhausted. She returned the wheelbarrow to the back yard and quietly re-entered the house through the sliding patio door. One of the Aussies started to growl as she entered, immediately stopping upon recognizing Stephanie. Stooping down to gently pat the dog on the head and rub her ears, she felt her leg muscles starting to stiffen up.

Well, what did I expect after all that hard work?

Stephanie submerged her hands in the pot of bleach treated water on the kitchen counter, wiped them on a towel, and then went to check on Charlie Wyatt. She spent a few extra seconds to watch him sleeping peacefully. Following up on an idea she had earlier, she stopped in the hallway bathroom to retrieve an old-fashioned rubber hot water bottle. Compelling herself to move her tired body back to the kitchen, she lit the camping stove and heated water in the coffee pot. She filled the hot water bottle and carried it back to her bedroom. Skipping her normal flossing routine, she quickly brushed her teeth before going to bed.

The worn out mother slid under the covers with her hot water bottle and luxuriated in the soft warmth of the low-tech warming device as she pressed it against her body.

Nothing wrong with simple comforts, she reminded herself.

Stephanie thought about what she had done earlier in the day. Tomorrow would be another day, and perhaps help was soon to arrive in some form or another. She decided to have another look at how she might improve the security of the house. First thing tomorrow. She allowed herself to think about how good things would be once Rob returned and the three of them were together as a complete family unit again. She was sound asleep within two minutes of her head hitting the pillow.

Next door to the Flynn house, Rick and Rosalyn had serious problems. Despite the fact that Rick had managed to stave off starvation--thanks to Rosalyn's arrangement with the former Amnesty International man--he had entered a severe state of mental depression that was punctuated by periods of extreme anger. He had destroyed much of their home's living room wall by kicking and punching the drywall board during fits of rage. Rosalyn, having to deal with her own emotional issues stemming from their situation, was scared and confused when her husband acted out during these episodes.

The couple had tried to talk about the rational reasons behind the decision to barter her body for food and water. But the discussions had failed to ameliorate the guilt and resentment that now consumed Rick. Prior to having reached that decision, Rick had entertained the possibility of trying to rob the man of some of his food storage. Not everything, but just enough to have what they needed for several days.

Rick was sure he could take the guy in a hand-to-hand fight. The self-proclaimed worldly man with the supplies was tall and slender, and nowhere near as powerfully built as Rick. Yeah, he could take him, even with his injured leg. But there was a problem. The guy was armed with a Glock 9mm pistol. So, after much consideration, the plan to let Rosalyn do the hard thing was the plan they went with. And now Rick couldn't make it right in his head. If anything, it was getting worse as each day went by.

Three days after Rosalyn had endured the act of prostitution, the couple once again found themselves with nothing to eat or drink. Rick told his wife they had to come up with a different idea this time, adding that he had already started to put together a plan. He thought back to the couple of times his friend Rob Flynn had suggested he buy a gun. Rob had indicated just a simple shotgun would suffice. Rick had dismissed the idea, insisting that it was a solution to a non-existent problem, or words to that effect anyway.

Rick could still see his friend's smile and hear the last words Rob had uttered on the subject.

"Besides, man, we're only talking about three hundred bucks or so. Plus another thirty or forty bucks for some ammo. And you can always sell it for close to what you paid for it—maybe even more than you paid for it--if you really need the money later on. It's a no-brainer!"

Rick had not followed his friend's advice. Using the vantage point of twenty-twenty hindsight, Rick now realized what a huge mistake he had made. He couldn't help but feel stupid about the whole thing. But it was too late now. That conversation had taken place in another lifetime.

The guilt ridden husband summoned Rosalyn to sit with him on the living room sofa for a discussion. Prefacing the discussion by telling his wife he never again wanted her to have to endure what she had several days ago, he indicated he wanted to run a new plan by her. But first he needed to get as much information from her as she could provide.

Rick addressed his wife with a serious expression that left her a little bit uneasy. This level of intensity was outside his normal personality. He was obviously on a mission now, and she hoped it wasn't going to take them out of the proverbial pan and into the fire.

"Okay Rosalyn, I'm going to need to get every single bit of information you can give me about this guy and his house. And I mean in full detail."

33

UNINCORPORATED SOUTHEAST

LOS ANGELES

The group of urban revolutionaries who were gathered in the one bedroom apartment unit less than a full block from the Nadeau Sheriff's Station numbered somewhere between a dozen and two dozen men. The apartment, as well as the unit directly adjacent, had been selected years earlier for one reason. The distance between the Sheriff's Station and the apartment, and the field of fire it afforded the apartment's occupants, provided excellent strategic and tactical value to the terrorists.

There were three women among the revolutionaries as well. However, they, unlike their male counterparts, were not outfitted in combat gear—other than the loose fitting BDU trousers and tactical boots they wore. The group was not assembled under any particular name, but all save one of the persons present embraced a political ideology that was, for all intents and purposes, Marxism. And like many committed Marxist revolutionaries all over the world, these revolutionaries were more than willing to use whatever violent means were necessary to further their cause. The ends had always justified the means for followers of their shared ideology.

The reason all of the terrorists were crammed uncomfortably into one small apartment unit was twofold. First, they had come to try on all of the combat gear that had been stored for more than a decade in a few residences in the neighborhood. Attendant to this was a basic review and re-familiarization with the Kalashnikov rifles that had been similarly stored. They were expected to use these items in the imminent attack on the Nadeau Sheriff's Station. Two of the men, and one of the women, had also been trained to use the two RPG launchers that currently leaned against the back wall of the apartment's bedroom.

The second reason for the meeting was to brief all of the assaulters on the action plan that, if it succeeded, would give them unprecedented and complete control of a major American local law enforcement headquarters. It was an idea that had been entertained, in one form or another, by Marxist or similarly influenced revolutionaries since way back in the 1960's. But it was not until the EMP incident had rendered the nation's infrastructure too weak to effectively resist such an attack that it had reached its current maturation phase.

The two Caucasian terrorists in the apartment were not Americans. One was a German national, and the other was from Chechnya. Despite the vastly different political ideologies of the two men (the former was a Marxist while the latter was a Jihadist), each had been trained with the same tactics and weapon systems.

It was nothing new for terrorists sharing different political ideologies to discard their differences for the purpose of furthering their terrorist training. *The enemy of my enemy is my friend—for now anyway.* Even the U.S. had been known to subscribe to this thinking from time to time. Perhaps the capable and experienced player in this game was The People's Republic of China, whose propensity for using third party proxies to achieve their dirty deeds was legendary within the intelligence community. And it was China's intelligence apparatus and their surrogates that had found a way to deliver, by a circuitous route, the various weapons that were now in the two apartments

All of the above would have been considered mildly interesting to the deputies who remained at the sheriff's station. But what would have been of far greater interest was the fact the terrorists making plans and checking weapons a few hundred yards away from the local sheriff's building were intent on killing every single deputy inside the station. Soon.

The organizers of the pending attack had selected the Nadeau Sheriff's Station for one reason. Although there was evidence that the station's historical reputation was now beginning to wane, it was nonetheless one that had carried more than a small element of intimidation--as well as respect--among the South Los Angeles region's miscellaneous criminals, thugs, and upstanding citizens alike for more than half a century.

Nadeau Station had been targeted for its psychological impact. The terrorists hadn't determined how long they would occupy the actual building after they had seized it. For those organizing the attack it really didn't matter. It only mattered that they be able to demonstrate their capability to take over the station at will. It was psychological warfare, pure and simple.

Toward this end, several members of the terrorist assault force would carry flags displaying the iconic symbol for Communism—the hammer and sickle. Back-up through redundancy. The odds were good that at least one of the terrorists would survive the attack and be able to hoist the new flag over the conquered station. And the assault on the station was only the beginning of a much larger plan.

34

WESTCHESTER, CA

The intense man outfitted for close quarters combat visibly relaxed upon hearing Rob's response, but clearly he was not ready to completely let his guard down. The man began walking toward the fence, weapon still held in the modified low ready position, trigger finger indexed outside of the trigger guard.

"Don't reach for it now, but tell me where your sheriff ID card is at," the hard core sentry said to Rob as he used the weapon mounted flashlight to shine a powerful beam into Rob's face and then Don's.

Despite the disorienting and uncomfortable effects of the light beam in his eyes, Rob answered the man without moving his hands or turning his head. He merely squinted against the light and did what he was told. He had been on the other side of this drill hundreds of times and understood its purpose. Disorienting an adversary in this manner could often place them at a severe enough disadvantage to avoid physical conflict altogether. And if that wasn't possible, at least it helped the odds for the guy holding the flashlight.

The sentry, still covering the two new arrivals with his carbine, directed both of them to turn around so that they were facing away from him. He then told them to walk twenty feet away from the fence. They complied without uttering a word.

The hard-assed sentry maintained a strong hand grip on his rifle's pistol grip and used his left to insert a key into the gate's padlock and opened the gate. He quickly stepped through the opening and reiterated for Rob and Don to remain where they were. As soon as he had ordered Rob to slowly remove his identification card and show it to him without turning around, the guard took several silent steps to his left. Another quick scan of his surroundings and then intense focus on Rob and Don.

The two guards were now aligned in a basic "L" configuration with respect to Rob and Don, allowing for triangulation of fire if it became necessary. Plus, by quietly stepping to a new position while Rob and Don were facing away from him, the guard not only allowed the second sentry to have a clear field of fire without much risk of hitting his partner, he had changed his position from where Rob and Don had last seen him. This would make it harder--or slower--for either of the "visitors" to deliver accurate fire if they opted to make a surprise move.

Rob complied with the man's request, holding his identification card with his left hand over his shoulder facing behind him. He did this without turning or lowering his hands. Rob heard the man speak in a much quieter voice, in a manner that suggested he was communicating to another guard via hand-held radio transmission. Rob strained to hear the contents of the communication.

"Mike, relieve Chris at his post and I need Chris to come to my location."

The response that came back over the walkie-talkie confirmed Rob's guess.

"Roger that. Moving now."

Moments later, the second sentry, a trim and athletic looking middle-aged Hispanic man, joined the first guard, twenty feet behind Rob and Don. A third man had taken over at the second sentry's post. Following orders, the newly arriving guard slung his carbine and approached Rob from the rear. In keeping with the professional manner exhibited by the first sentry, he made sure to maintain a clear line of fire for the others during his approach. He stepped toward Rob, snatched the identification card from his hand and stepped back several feet. The entire action was accomplished in no more than a second.

Looking at the six digit number displayed in small print on Rob's identification card, he asked him to recite his county employee number. Rob gave it to him from memory without so much as a second's hesitation. Apparently satisfied after looking at the card and then stepping to Rob's side to get a look at his face, the guard announced, "ID looks good."

Realizing it didn't appear that either of them was going to be subjected to a tedious search for weapons, Rob concluded that the guards considered it a moot point. They were only concerned with determining whether or not their visitors were "good guys" and whether they could be trusted. Or at least trusted enough to allow them onto the premises.

"You guys can go ahead and put your hands down and turn around," the first sentry--the one apparently in charge here--announced to Rob and Don. The middle-aged guard allowed his carbine to hang on its sling as he motioned for his visitors to approach him. The second guard unceremoniously returned Rob's identification card as he walked past and then fell in behind them. The head man turned and walked back through the gate, followed by the new arrivals. The intense Hispanic sentry brought up the rear of the foursome and locked the gate behind him.

Rob took a better look at the lead sentry, the man whom he had initially engaged in conversation. He was a fit looking fiftyish Caucasian man with greying blond hair, a whether lined face, and a thick grey mustache. He stopped, and leaning slightly forward, stuck out his hand, pinning his carbine against his chest with his left hand in a practiced movement to prevent the weapon from falling forward, as he did so. First Rob, and then Don, shook his hand firmly.

"I'm Danny Smith, and this is Chris Gutierrez," he said as he jerked a thumb in the direction of his fellow guard.

"Most people just call me 'Smitty'," he added without much expression.

Gutierrez, after being introduced, gave an almost imperceptible nod, but made no further gesture.

Rob noticed that although the second sentry seemed to be less interested in them than he had been moments earlier, he was still performing his periodic scans of the area, letting his gaze rest upon the new guests every so often.

One serious dude for sure, Rob noted.

The man who had introduced himself as "Smitty" continued talking.

Looking directly at Rob, he said, "I assume you're armed with something other than the shotgun tied to your pack, right?"

"Yeah, I got a nine mil handgun with an extra mag on my belt. Don's only got that machete he's wearing."

Smitty nodded in response, not showing much of a reaction one way or the other.

"We have a few other guys on the property, but you probably won't meet them," Smitty commented.

He assumed Smitty didn't want to elaborate on this information or he would have, so he acknowledged the statement with a slight nod and let it go.

Smitty continued, "We're both LAPD. retired. I would apologize for the tough reception, but I'm sure you know why we're doing it this way. There's been a shit load of people getting wacked around here starting about a week after the grid went down. Not to mention all the robberies going on. Some of these assholes have been doing sexual assaults too—pieces of shit. It doesn't take long for things to come apart when the police are no longer available, huh?"

Smitty took a long and careful look at Rob. He asked Rob about Don. It was a somewhat odd way of approaching the subject, asking Rob rather than Don himself. Rob had seen patrol cops do it this way a few times, although he rarely did.

Rob gave Smitty a ten second explanation of how they had linked up. He didn't go into how Don had saved his life by shooting the homeless machete wielding maniac, nor did he mention the hasty ambush the two of them had performed on the would-be robbers. All Rob said was that Don could be counted on when things got tough.

Smitty changed subjects.

"I did some training with Dave Marino back a few years ago. Both of our units—LAPD and SHERIFF SWAT-- were doing some training with the Israelis at the time. You know, showing each other how our teams do stuff. All that sorta shit. So how's that big bruiser Marino doing these days anyway?"

Rob smiled, obviously preferring the new more relaxed relationship, however tenuous it might be. He was patient with Smitty's distraction despite his wanting to hear what the man had started to explain.

"He's doing alright. All things considered anyway. Haven't seen him since the world shut down though."

Smitty nodded and got back to the earlier subject.

"So these Israelis liked to have a few drinks when the training was done for the day. Good male bonding and all that...you know. Well, one guy starts talking about a bunch of stuff and makes the case for being able to live on your own for a couple months if need be. A few of us started thinking about what he had said and did something about it."

"I can see how that would make sense. Those guys have seen things most of us haven't...even in law enforcement," Rob said.

"Yep. So four families in this neighborhood made plans to deal with any major disaster scenarios a few years ago. Me and one of the others are police families, another one's a military family--an ex-Marine lifer who finished twenty years just over a year ago. The fourth family is a couple with no kids. She's an ER nurse and he's a hot shot financial advisor. We all started comparing notes after we got comfortable socializing with each other. Basically all good people who were a little worried about the dangers facing this country and just wanted to be responsible in taking care of our families."

He looked at Smitty, noticing the guy had a face that looked like it belonged in a tobacco commercial where a rugged cowboy was enjoying the company's product.

Rob asked, "By the way, are you guys up to speed on what EMP is and all that?"

"Yeah, we know a little bit about EMP. One of the things the Israeli guys were mentioning in fact. I suspected EMP pretty much right away when all the cars shut down, and then had it confirmed a few days later after listening to a news report out of London on our short wave radio."

"I got a question for you Smitty. How is it that your generator still works after the EMP? And your short wave radio you listened to the London radio broadcast with. The walkie-talkies? EMP is supposed to fry all that stuff."

"I had all that gear stored inside a steel box that I made. Called a *Faraday Cage*. It prevents any of the pulse waves, or whatever they're called, from contacting the electronics that are stored inside the box. Just have to make sure that nothing stored inside the box is touching the metal of the cage. We waited till the day after everything shut down and then took the gear out of the box. All the gear survived."

Rob thought about this and, not for the first time, realized how much research and effort these guys had put into their preparations.

Motioning with his outstretched arms to indicate the property surrounding him, he asked Smitty, "So how did this come about? I mean who came up with the idea for all of this? It's impressive. No doubt there."

He answered Rob with a tone that straddled the often difficult to determine line between condescension and an earnest desire to make sure his listener was grasping his message.

"We made plans a few years ago—like I said. It started with discussions at neighborhood get-togethers. The country's piling up debt like the money is toilet paper-- like that isn't beggin' for a financial crash eventually. The terrorism threats are gettin' worse, and then there's the earthquake risk. The borders are wide open so diseases we've never had on this continent can now come in. And we all know L.A. will riot at the drop of a hat. Shit... not having a plan would be like drivin' without car insurance."

Another glance toward Rob to gauge his reaction. Nothing. Poker face.

"We recognized there were so many problems that could end up being totally catastrophic, that we started thinking we should plan on how we could prepare and help each other if it ever went down. Basically a self-insured mentality is all we're talking about here."

Smitty cleared his throat and spat a piece of phlegm onto the ground. He took another glance at Rob to make sure he was listening.

"We knew the law enforcement structure was vulnerable to any major infrastructure collapse and figured the other first responders— like fire and paramedics--were even more vulnerable than us. Less para-military in their cultures-right? Anyway, a guy would have to be a dumbass not to think we could have some serious shit happening at some point, dontcha think?"

Rob thought about what he had just heard, while Don, following his friend's earlier instructions, remained quiet. Truth be told, Don looked as though he were giving serious thought to what the man had said...getting a whole new perspective.

"Are all four of the families you mentioned living here on your property now? I mean I guess I just can't imagine being willing to leave my house knowing that all these desperate savages around here are looking for anything to steal and destroy."

Rob had heard of survivalist types that often entertained what he considered to be bizarre views of the world. His impression had been that they were generally wing-nuts and the like. But these guys were cops. Not only were they cops, but based on what Smitty had said moments ago, they were apparently retired members of LAPD's SWAT unit--an elite group by any standard.

Smitty answered Rob's question.

"Yeah, they're all here now. We all made a contingency plan to have the four families hook up at one place--my place--if the scenario was bad enough. It's gotta be done that way. Two people just aren't enough to protect a place when it comes down to it. Think about it. So on the fifth day after the grid crashed we decided that it had gotten bad enough to all link up. I started getting this place set up to house this number of people over a year ago, believe it or not. Let me show you guys what we've done here."

Smitty motioned for Rob and Don to follow him. He said a few words into his hand-held radio, apparently letting the other sentries know what he was doing. Looking at the gate where they had entered,

Rob saw a third guard—the guy who had filled in at Gutierrez's post when he left to assist Smitty.

Rob also got the impression that Gutierrez was less than approving of their having been invited into the compound. However, the stern sentry, clearly conditioned to operating under para-military conditions, held his silence. Rob and Don followed their host, Rob not missing the fact the seemingly amiable guard was walking in a manner affording him a strong peripheral view of both of them as he led them away.

As Rob walked past one of the plywood "L" shaped structures, he confirmed they were filled with sand or dirt. Definitely designed to stop bullets. The windows of the house had been covered with a steel wire mesh, the small half inch squares adequate to prevent hand thrown objects from crashing through the window glass.

Don't need rocks or Molotov cocktails coming into the house if the outer perimeter fence gets compromised and the sentries can't stop the assaulters.

"This is really impressive," Rob commented.

"If you look around at what we've done, most of the investment was a matter of thinking about what we might need, planning on how to get that done, and then just doing the physical work to make it happen. We didn't spend a whole lot on our *comms* for instance--simple two way radios is all; no fancy headsets or the like. Most of the guys have ear pieces, but mine broke." He tapped the radio attached to his chest rig.

"The only thing that cost a lot of money really was the food, and that didn't really cost much when you think about it, because it all gets used anyway. A lot of it is just extra canned goods that we eat in normal everyday life. Just takes a little extra planning."

The retired policeman walked to the house's detached garage, opened the large roll-up steel door, and entered. He encouraged his two slightly reluctant guests to enter. Rob was yet again impressed with what he saw. The garage was approximately twenty four feet wide by thirty two feet long. In the far corners of the garage were two huge dark green plastic water tanks, close to ten feet in diameter by about the same height. By his estimate, each tank held over two thousand gallons of water.

The walls of the garage were lined with steel industrial type heavy-duty shelving, all of which housed close to a hundred boxes of what Rob presumed was canned food. The boxes were approximately twenty four-by- twelve-by-twelve inches and had factory installed product labels affixed to them that depicted canned food in full color. Rob also noticed that there were another three dozen or more plastic five gallon size buckets that had been stacked next to the shelves. Most of the buckets were marked "BEANS", "RICE", "PASTA", and "OATMEAL". He saw one such container that was labeled "POWDERED MILK".

Another section of shelving was stocked with a wide variety of medical supplies ranging from bandages to eye wash. Yet another section housed paper towels and toilet paper.

Perhaps even more impressive to Rob than any of the above storage items was the improvised hygiene facility that had been set up in the garage. Three portable toilets that had been configured from hardware store five gallon plastic buckets and snap on toilet seats were positioned along one of the garage walls. The buckets' plastic liners were folded over the edges of the containers, indicating they were ready for use.

Holy shit! These people were really worried something like this might happen, Rob thought.

Fifteen large bags of cat litter were located next to the portable toilets, as were several boxes containing plastic trash can liners. Several gallon-sized bottles of bleach were stacked nearby also. Rob deduced that the cat litter had been purchased for use with the buckets as an inexpensive yet effective means of controlling odor.

Pretty smart thinking on someone's part, Rob mused. *Wonder what they're going to do with all the bagged human waste?*

A cheap looking plastic double sink had been installed against the garage wall as well. A platform built from common lumber was positioned adjacent to the double sinks. It supported a large plastic garbage can with a garden hose spigot plumbed into its side a couple of inches from the bottom. A two-foot long section of garden hose was attached to it, its end hanging over the sink. Next to the garbage can, Rob noticed a large aluminum stock pot resting on top of a single burner camp stove.

Rob looked at the other, larger, wooden platform located against the far wall. Two large plastic garbage cans, identical in appearance to the one next to the sink basins, rested on the platform eight feet above the ground. Both of these garbage cans had ten foot long garden hoses protruding from where they had been affixed to their sides near the bottom. He noticed they both had on-off valves attached to their ends. Another camp stove, with two more large aluminum pots resting on its burners, sat next to the two garbage cans being used as water reservoirs. A ladder was positioned against the platform to allow a person access to al of the above.

A small three foot square and six foot high cubicle, made from cheap plastic pipe and blue tarps stood below the platform next to the ladder. Rob stepped forward and pushed a section of tarp aside. A heavy-duty plastic tub with a drain hose configured from a garden hose ran out of the tub and outside of the garage.

Watching Rob as he examined everything, Smitty said,

"Shower system. Garbage cans were a cheap way to make warm water tanks. We use the camp stoves to heat the water in the pots and pour it into the tanks. Uses simple gravity to flow down from the platform is all."

Pointing at the tub inside the little three foot square cubicle, he said, "The water drains out of the tub and outside through that hose. Probably should figure a way to save and re-use the shower water for something. Same system works at the sink over there—washing dishes, doing laundry, or whatever."

Rob nodded in a gesture intended to communicate both his understanding and his approval.

Cheap, simple, and effective. The KISS philosophy demonstrating its value once again, he thought with appreciation.

Smitty finished his water system tutorial by stating the set-up only required a willingness on the part of the residents to do a little physical labor to be able to use the primitive plumbing system.

The one thing that was conspicuously missing among all of the impressive collection of disaster preparations was any weapons or other related equipment. Rob guessed these guys probably had one hell of an armory set up—wherever that was. He felt no urge to inquire about this, nor did he take any offense at the fact Smitty hadn't brought it up. Need to know only he guessed.

"Let's get you set up somewhere where you can grab some sleep. We don't have any ice to set you up with for that knee, but we might have some over the counter pain relievers to help you out a little."

Don thanked him, but remembering Rob's earlier advice, said nothing more.

Rob chimed in, "I got him covered for tonight anyway, but my supply is almost out."

Smitty gave a quick nod and brought them to a large storage shed that had been outfitted with two sets of bunk beds, a couple of cots, a small table with two chairs, camping stove, and three kerosene lanterns that hung from the two-by-four rafters.

"It ain't *The Four Seasons*, but it ought to be good enough to let you get some sleep. By the way, how many extra shells do you have for that thing," their host asked as he pointed to the shotgun lashed to Rob's pack.

"Actually, I only have three extra shells for it, but it's better than nothing. I figure it can still be used to get me out of a jam if I need it."

Rob realized he probably came off as being a bit defensive. He was slightly embarrassed by the simple little single shot after seeing how well-armed these guys were.

Smitty seemed to be thinking something over.

"Well, gentlemen, get some sleep. And you can use the bucket toilets I showed you."

He turned and began walking out of the converted bunkroom.

Prior to passing through the doorway, he abruptly stopped, turned, and said, "I'm surprised neither of you has asked me if I've heard any news about what's going on in L.A.—or the country for that matter."

"Have you heard anything," Rob asked.

"I heard a little bit of news this morning on the shortwave radio coming out of London. Sounds like pretty much the whole country has been hit hard by this EMP. I think there might've been more than one of 'em that went off. But I don't know. The radio guy in England was only speculating. He also said that Europe's and Asia's financial markets are crashing...bad."

"You said the whole country was 'hit hard'. How hard are we talkin' here?"

"All the major cities' power grids are down and they aren't expecting to get 'em back up any time soon. Lots of violence and lots of deaths. People need medical attention but can't get it--no surprise there. No food or water available, and no police or emergency response. The London radio announcer said a few of the countries in Europe sent over supplies, but that isn't going so well at the distribution locations. Not enough security personnel from what they were saying. Turned into riots in New York, Boston, Atlanta, and Chicago. And those were only the cities they could get any info from. I turned it off after that. Not much more point in using the batteries--for today anyway."

The hard-nosed sentry leaked only the smallest amount of emotion as he shared this news, but Rob caught it. The man's expression showed worry and concern for the briefest of moments before returning to the all-business poker face that was the man's default expression. Pinning his carbine against his chest with his hand again, he stood up.

"You boys try to get some sleep now."

With that, he walked out of the room.

Rob called out to the retreating host, "Hey Smitty, would it be okay if we used your camp stove here for a few minutes? I know we said we had our own food and water, but it would be nice to be able to heat our water if that's okay with you. If not, I understand."

"I guess that would be alright, as long as you don't use it for more than fifteen minutes or so. We got a fair amount of propane stored here, but who knows when we'll be able to get any more, right? Oh, and I'll come back and get you in...what...six hours?"

Smitty glanced at his watch.

"Sounds good. We appreciate all this."

"Oh yeah, almost forgot," Smitty added, "I'll announce myself and knock good and loud before I come in to avoid any *blue on blue* problems. And if anything should go hot outside while you two are in here, make sure to announce yourselves by name before you run up on any of us to help out. The problem with having a place all set up like this is that it attracts a lot of attention we don't want. We had to shoot three guys two nights ago in fact."

"Okay. Got it," Rob replied.

Rob had one more request for their host. "Uh, Don here doesn't complain much, but his knee is hurting him pretty bad. Any way I could get a good sized stick that I can whittle into a walking stick for him?"

Smitty looked at Don's knee from a distance.

"I'll see what I can dig up. Get some sleep." Having put an obvious end to the conversation, he walked out of the storage shed/bunkroom and closed the door behind him.

Rob gave Don some ibuprofen tablets to help with his knee. Within minutes they were both asleep, wearing all of their clothes with the exception of their shoes.

They were awakened in the middle of their sleep by a volley of gunshots. The popping sounds were close by. Really close. After about five seconds and a half dozen shots or more, Rob was awake and attentive enough to recognize the last few gunshots as being those of a high-powered rifle. One of the rounds was noticeably louder than the others, a fact that piqued his curiosity.

He slipped his feet into his boots without lacing them and drew his handgun. He bolted toward the shed door when Smitty's words suddenly came back to him. He dropped to the floor, slithered on his belly to the entrance with his gun in his hand, and then slowly cracked the door.

Rob saw the yard was now lit up by early morning daylight, the hum of the generator no longer present. He heard a short broadcast over a two-way radio, but couldn't make out the words. The shooting had stopped, but he still couldn't see Smitty or Gutierrez.

Again, the distinctive crackle of walkie-talkie communication could be heard.

Where the hell are Smitty and Gutierrez, or whoever is supposed to be on guard duty right now? And where are the bad guys? Keep looking. Keep scanning.

His efforts were unrewarded.

Wait. There by the front corner of the security fence next to that tree. Looks like our guys just shot somebody over there.

He considered getting his monocular from the pouch on his pack but didn't want to risk missing something important happening where he was now looking. Too many things could happen in the few seconds it would take to retrieve the looking glass.

He could see the form of a human body crumpled on the ground several feet outside of the front fence line next to a tree with a trunk about a foot in diameter.

No, those are two bodies!

Without taking his eyes away from the field of view in front of him, he called out in as low of a voice as he felt he could use and still be heard by Don.

"I think our friends just shot a couple guys outside the fence line. Sucks to be those stupid sonsabitches, huh? You get the dumb-ass of the year award for trying to attack this place unless you have a tank or a small army."

Rob yelled out the slightly ajar door.

"Hey Smitty, Gutierrez. Rob here. You need any help? You guys alright?"

A voice Rob thought belonged to Gutierrez answered him.

"We're good for now. Hang tight for a sec. Stay where you're at till we tell you to leave your location."

"Okay. Copy that," Rob replied. He quietly closed the door and went back into the bunk room. Rob looked over to the other side of the shed where Don was sitting on his cot with his feet on the floor rubbing his knee. There was just enough light to see his friend, so complete was the blocking of any outside light source because of the window coverings.

Rob asked Don, "How's your knee feeling; any better?"

He grumbled his response.

"Yeah, I think it's probably good enough to get home anyway. Of course I think it would be feelin' even better if I didn't roll off my damn cot in the middle of the night onto the floor because we're now livin' in a country that sounds like fuckin' Afghanistan."

For some reason, Rob found the remark really funny, and he laughed good and loud for at least ten seconds.

"Glad to amuse you Rob. Now whadya say we get some hot water and a little food in us, and then take off for my place. I had a great time at this party and all, but I'm ready to go home if it's alright with you."

Rob agreed. Even though they had previously agreed that moving at night was preferable to daytime travel, Rob wanted to get moving. The whole journey seemed like it was taking forever with all of the delays he had encountered along the way.

After the two had heated their water and ate some of their meager rations, they heard a loud knock on the outside of the shed door, followed by Smitty announcing himself. Rob jumped up from where he was sitting on his cot and opened the door. The retired SWAT cop, once again, or possibly *still*, wearing his combat harness, explained what had happened earlier.

"Some white shit-bird approached the gate and tried to start up a conversation with me. Said he wanted to make a trade for some food. Gutierrez was at his post, and he sees two other guys--one with a shotgun and the other with a rifle--settin' up behind a tree off the sidewalk. Gutierrez gets cover behind the big planter box and communicates what he sees to the other guards. Then he opens up on 'em."

Rob was listening without saying a word.

"By this time I've found my own cover and I smoke the dude who tried to get me to go for the old 'okie doke'. Bad day for the assholes."

A rare smile from Smitty.

"All three bad guys are dead. No good guys hurt."

Rob interjected, "I heard one round that was noticeably louder than the rest."

Smitty looked at Rob with a hard stare for a few seconds before responding.

"Our man on the roof with a .308 rifle put an end to the asshole flopping around on the ground trying to reload his rifle. That was the louder shot you heard. Guess it's all fun and games till a sub-moa shooter with a scoped bolt rifle sends a 168 grain bullet through your head, eh?!"

Holy shit, Rob thought, not caring that his facial expression gave away his surprise.

These guys have a damn sniper on the roof I didn't even know about. Never saw anything to even suggest that when we first arrived at this place. I guess that's the whole point though.

Rob recognized the term "sub-MOA" as a reference to a marksman capable of placing several rounds in a grouping size of less than an inch at a hundred yards, and less than two inches at two hundred yards, etcetera. Definitely someone deserving of your attention and respect. Or your absolute fear if you happen to be planning an assault on the property the guy is protecting on over-watch duty.

Listening to him as he recounted the incident, Rob was struck by a thought. A simple hope really.

Gesturing toward his little shotgun still tied to his pack, Rob said, "Since I only have three extra rounds for that thing, any chance that guy you shot had some twelve gauge shells in his pockets? You said he was armed with a shotgun, right?"

For the second time this morning, Smitty flashed a quick smile. He reached behind his combat rig to access his shirt pocket. He spent a few seconds fumbling in this position and then pulled out four red shotgun shells.

"Double aught," he said as he thrust the bright colored shells out toward Rob. "Take 'em; they're yours."

"Great. Much appreciated Smitty."

He stuffed the shells into his own shirt pocket.

As the three of them exited the bunkroom, Smitty suddenly reached over and picked up a stick that was leaning against the exterior wall of the shed. It was almost five feet long and looked as though it had recently had its bark whittled away with a knife. He handed the stick to Don, who received it with a smile demonstrating his gratitude as well as any words could have.

"Where did this come from," Don asked.

"Oh hell. I had to do something to stay awake until we could find someone to have a gunfight with. You know how it is around here." For the first time since they had made his acquaintance, they saw the tough-as-nails sentry actually laugh. He was apparently human after all.

"Hey guys," the tough but tired looking sentry said to Rob and Don with a voice that had dropped a few decibels all-of-a-sudden, "I got some bad news for you. Let's go back inside for a minute."

They followed him back into the bunk room without comment. Smitty took a quick glance at Rob, followed by an even briefer look at Don. He tried to get a rough read on their present state(s) of mind. Both men showed interest and concern. A strained silence enveloped the room.

Smitty pulled out one of the inexpensive folding chairs that had been stacked against the wall in the bunk room. He expelled a large amount of air and the slightest indication of a groan escaped from him as his buttocks made contact with the chair. The subtle incident revealed the man's exhaustion despite his stoic attempts at hiding it from his guests.

Looking Rob in the eye and holding it for emphasis, Smitty rolled his palms upward in a gesture of supplication as he began.

"Look, I'm pretty sure you understand why I can't tell you everything we have goin' on here regarding our security measures. It's not anything against you--hell, as it is we pretty much broke with our protocol when we allowed you two inside our perimeter—but I still can't let you in on all we have in place here. It's *need to know* and all that sorta thing."

A quick glance at Don before looking back at Rob.

"So here's the thing--the bad news. Part of our perimeter security involves eyes on the outside. You know--a scout. And we know right now there are several bands of bad guys out roaming the neighborhoods surrounding us. We're talkin' at least four separate groups that our scouts have got eyes on. I think they're hangin' around this area trying to figure a way to penetrate our defenses. I underestimated how much of an attraction this place would be I guess."

Fuck. I can't believe my bad luck. Always some delay, and now this, Rob thought.

"So how big are these groups? You think we could get past 'em at night-- if we're careful?"

Smitty shook his head.

"Our scout says it looks like the groups vary in size from five to eight. Mostly males in their late teens to early thirties—combinations of hard looking types and then losers that are probably just followin' the leaders. Some of 'em are armed with various firearms and other weapons."

He shrugged his shoulders. Another quick glance at Don and back to Rob.

"The bottom line here is that it's not a good time for you two to be heading out. You'll be into a shooting with these assholes before you get a block or two away from this place—no doubt about it."

Rob looked away from the grizzled former SWAT cop and stared at his boots.

"Shit," was all he said. Then he was quiet for several more seconds as he considered in greater detail what this news meant for Don and him.

Rob asked Smitty, "Is everyone here good with us staying here for a few more days if need be?"

"Well, let's just say some of us here are a little more *good with it* than others. But it's all been worked out—not your worry."

"Besides," Smitty went on, "to be honest, I actually like the fact we have a couple of extra trigger pullers to add to our security force over the next few days you two stay on here--or for however long till it looks better out there at least. To me you guys are going to be worth the little bit of rice and beans you'll be eating. But I'm gonna tell you that we expect you to be *heads up* when you're doing your security details while you're here."

He made sure to stare at each man for a brief moment to stress this point.

"I'll fill you in on the details later," he said as he rose from his chair and exited the room without waiting for a response.

Later than night, when Rob prepared to get a few hours of sleep before serving his turn on security duty, he was beset with a heavy blanket of depression as he once again considered his situation. He missed his family terribly and had to draw upon all the mental strength he could muster just to hold it together.

Rob tried to add up the days that had gone by since the grid crash. He couldn't come up with a number. He tried in vain to recall exactly how many days he had spent at the Brown family's house and how many days he had spent camped out next to the freeway waiting for conditions that were safe enough to travel under while he existed in a semi-dehydrated state nibbling on small food rations. Walking during the night and sleeping in the daytime--as he had done so many times--made tracking the days even more difficult.

As luck, or the lack thereof, would have it, Rob and Don had to spend the better part of a week in the Westchester compound. These days of delay created a huge mental strain on Rob, and he was tempted on numerous occasions to throw caution to the wind by resuming his hike home and taking his chances with the packs of predatory marauders outside the compound's perimeter. But whenever he entertained these notions, either one of the sentries and/or Don would talk him down from this thinking.

During their stay Rob and Don were given two modest daily meals of rice and beans as well as a half-gallon of water apiece. The security functions they performed were varied—but always in three hour shifts to reduce the chances of falling asleep. Neither of the two was used in place of the regular guards, but rather as supplements to the others. Given his knee condition, Don's duties were limited.

The days spent inside the safety of the security perimeter were essentially uneventful, with the exception of the frequent sounds of gunfire outside the compound. Another thing that happened during the long boring hours spent at the compound was that Gutierrez softened up a bit. Rob and he actually found they had quite a bit in common, and the two shared dozens of stories about their experiences, philosophies on police work, and life in general.

When the security scout's report finally arrived indicating only one of the numerous roaming predatory groups were visible in the surrounding area (presumably to search for opportunities elsewhere), Rob was encouraged. He smiled and looked at Don, who appeared to be feeling the same way.

"We can figure out a way to avoid that one pack of bad guys. Let's get packed and get on the road partner," Rob intoned as he walked over to where his pack and shotgun were propped against the interior wall of the sleeping quarters.

"You know you don't have to ask me twice," Don replied as he began moving hurriedly.

They quickly prepared to leave. Then they waited. And then they waited some more.

A security team scout from the compound had been tracking the location of the remaining group of four pillagers. It was hoped this might help Rob and Don minimize their chances of encountering the pack. Almost three hours later, when he saw the group was several blocks south of the compound (Rob and Don were going to be heading north), this information was related to Smitty. It was time for Rob and Don to make their move.

By the time they had expressed their thanks and said their goodbyes to Smitty and Gutierrez, it was late afternoon.

***

The journey to Don's house in Culver City was an uneventful one until they had almost arrived at the residence. The walking stick, combined with the ibuprofen, had allowed Don to walk with a pain level that was bearable.

The one thing Rob and Don both found interesting, as well as somewhat disconcerting, was the fact there were quite a few people walking northbound on the sidewalks out of the Westchester area of Los Angeles and into the city of Culver City. The people could be seen walking as individuals, in pairs, small groups of three to five, and even larger groups in some cases. They saw one group of people that numbered fourteen.

This group, despite its size, was not comprised of anyone who appeared to be threatening in any way, but it was unsettling to observe. Each of the fourteen appeared to be carrying their life's possessions. The scene reminded Rob of some old movie where persons in another part of the world carried their meager possessions on their backs while they fled some dangerous place.

For some, their belongings were carried with the aid of a backpack, while others carried shopping bags or plastic garbage bags. One, a thin and unhealthy looking man of sixty years or more, wore formal business attire—minus the tie--that looked ill-suited and uncomfortable for the journey at hand. He also carried a suitcase.

Early that evening as they neared the residential block where Don's house was located, Rob looked at his watch and saw that it was just past six o'clock. They had a quick discussion about how best to let Don's wife know they were approaching the house. He didn't want to scare her any more than was necessary.

Under normal circumstances Don would have used his cell phone to call her, but that was obviously out of the question. After neither was able to come up with a better solution to the problem, Don decided it would be best for him to simply walk up to the front door by himself. Rob would wait out at the sidewalk until he was summoned.

When they came to the cul-de-sac that included Don's home and seven others, they were surprised to see that the small residential street's entrance had been blocked off by several cars positioned across the street. Two men, obviously sentries, were standing behind the cars comprising the barricade. A third guard was walking on the sidewalk fifteen yards farther down the cul-de-sac.

One of the men, a gruff looking and powerfully built clean shaven Hispanic man in his early sixties, wore his hair in a grey crew cut that looked like it was ready for a touch-up. He also wore a Colt .45 automatic, with two extra magazine pouches on his belt, and a red ball cap that sported a *USMC* logo on the front.

Another of the three sentries, a clean shaven white guy in his late-twenties, had a Marlin lever action .30-30 rifle slung over his shoulder with an additional half dozen cartridges attached to the rifle's butt stock. He wore a ball cap that advertised a common brand of work boots. The third man was a clean shaven black guy that looked to be in his mid-forties. He carried a Mossberg twelve gauge pump shotgun in both hands with the muzzle pointed up in the air. He wore a blue windbreaker that was emblazoned with a logo that read *Culver City Kiwanis Club* in large print on the back.

Rob arrived at the cul-de-sac twenty feet in front of Don. He came to a stop to wait for his friend so he could verify he belonged here and then show him the way to his house. The block watchman with the *USMC* cap came out from behind the barricade and began walking toward Rob. The younger man with the deer rifle moved his position so that he was about ten feet to the rear and right of the man with the *USMC* cap. He unslung his .30-30 and held the muzzle pointed at the ground, obviously wanting to be ready to bring the rifle into action without much delay if required. The older man authoritatively thrust his hand out, palm outward, indicating he wanted Rob to stop.

Rob stopped right where he was.

The man looked at the machete attached to Rob's shoulder strap as well as the short shotgun that hung suspended from the cord.

"I'd appreciate you not moving your hands," the gruff man with the thick arms and the holstered .45 said in a voice that sounded like it had been exposed to regular sessions of cigar smoke for half a century.

"No problem, sir."

The man asked him what business he had on this street. Careful to keep both of his hands in plain sight and not to make any sudden moves with them, Rob jerked his head toward Don, who was now quickly approaching.

"My friend Don lives here."

As if on cue, Don stepped up to join the conversation.

"I live at 709. Name's Don Mcnair. My wife is Vangie McNair."

Don had seen each of the three men now performing sentry duty on his street from time to time in the past and recognized all of them as residents on the block. Unfortunately, not only was his appearance different than it had been before the EMP, he had never taken the time to get to know any of them other than to exchange perfunctory hand waives or head nods. It was emblematic of twenty first century American life in the cities and suburbs.

The man with the *USMC* cap and cigar voice recognized Don. He looked past Rob and directly at Don as he said, "We're just trying to keep things safe and under control as you probably figured. There isn't any police response or anything else right now. You probably know that too."

"Yeah, we know," Don responded.

Rob made no move to proceed forward. He asked the man what had been happening in this particular area since the power had gone off.

"We actually haven't had any real problems yet, but we don't want any either. A week ago or so a couple of cops came by here on bicycles because none of their patrol cars were running. They told us that we needed to watch over our own streets and to look out for our neighbors. So now we're taking shifts."

Then, apparently having decided to press forward with the issue he had been debating with himself, cigar man asked Rob who he was and why he was accompanying Don.

"We want to know exactly what business anybody has on this block."

Perhaps Rob would have reacted to the demand more reasonably if he had had anything close to a full night's sleep over the past ten days or more. Maybe having had more than a third of the daily caloric intake his body required would have helped too. And maybe he would have been just a little more tolerant of the man demanding he justify his presence had he not had to kill several people in order to defend his own or other innocent persons' lives during the past week.

But none of these things were the case, and he lost his cool when he answered the gruff man performing security duty. His jaw muscles tightened visibly as he took a half step forward and looked cigar man in the eye.

"Hey look sir, I appreciate you're doing a good service here by protecting your neighbors and all, but you're not in a position to be demanding anything more than you've already been told. I'm here with my friend who has identified himself and is known to you and the other guys doing guard duty here. So I'm going to thank you to back off and let us go to Don's house. Fair enough?"

Before cigar man could respond, Rob added, "Not that it matters much at this time, seeing how things are going, but I happen to be a cop. I can show you my identification if you want to see it. I'm not here to do anybody harm I promise you."

The man was now clearly offended and more than a little pissed off at Rob. He wanted to re-assert his authority.

"Yeah well, the police are pretty much worthless right now, so you're right. You're being a cop doesn't mean much at this point."

Rob had had enough of this guy. He opened his hands and rotated his palms upward in a show of being empty handed. It was also intended to present the opportunity for the man to escalate the confrontation to the next level if he desired. Rob would later regret letting his emotions get the better of him at this moment, but he sensed this guy, despite his performing an important function, was a little bit of a bully-boy. And Rob had never suffered bullies very well.

Rob lowered his voice a few decibels so he would only be heard by the man he was addressing.

"Well this cop standing in front of you sure as hell ain't worthless. If you want to test that yourself then don't let anything stop you. Now's your chance."

The sentry remained quiet, and held perfectly still. But he stared at Rob with daggers in his eyes. Rob held the thick man's stare for several prolonged seconds. Don, who hadn't heard Rob's comment, but could definitely sense that there was a great deal of tension between the two men, broke the silence.

"Let's get going and see how things are going at the house."

Rob, already starting to regret the way he had bristled at the pushy cigar-voiced man, welcomed the distraction and fell in behind his friend without uttering another word or giving another look at the man.

He stopped when he reached the younger man with the lever action deer rifle. He nodded slightly at the man by way of greeting and said, "We just walked up here from the Westchester area. Saw a lot of people walking up this way. Some in groups and some by themselves. Not sure why they were headed this way exactly, but thought you should know. Didn't look particularly dangerous or anything, but can't figure out why they would want to come this way. Thought you might want to know is all."

"Yeah, we're hearing a lot of folks are leaving that area because of all the damage caused by the plane crash and the fires. Some think the people there just figure there might be food and water available outside their own neighborhoods."

The sentry then scoffed and added, "Don't know what they think they're gonna find up here in Culver City. Things ain't working up here either. Guess they'll find that out after they get here."

"Probably so," Rob said. "Oh well. You take care--and be safe. Lots of predators out and about as you know I'm sure." The man grunted in response, ending the brief conversation.

Don began walking again with Rob following. As he turned off the sidewalk and started up the walkway to his house, Rob asked him to stop for a second.

"Hey Don, take however much time you need to talk to your wife and handle that reunion stuff. I don't mind waiting out here for a while. I'm gonna hang back."

Rob gave his friend a double "thumbs up" sign to emphasize his offer.

He made sure his attention was focused on someplace other than the front door of the house so as to offer some level of privacy for the moment of reunion between the couple. After Don reached the door Rob heard a brief emotional exchange. A few seconds later he heard the door being closed with conviction.

Looking around Rob admired the home. It was a spacious single story house that had no fence around it. Despite the fact the lawn and some of the yard plants were dying due to lack of water, it was evident the landscaping was well designed.

After about ten minutes had gone by, Rob made his way over to a wooden bench positioned next to an expensive looking stone bird bath in the front yard and sat down. He removed his pack, setting it on the bench next to him, and then rolled his neck in an effort to release some of the tension that had built up there.

Don came out the front door and called him over.

As Rob climbed the steps to the front porch, he saw a woman standing next to Don in the open doorway. The first thing about her that struck Rob was the fact that the attractive middle-aged Hispanic woman was smiling broadly. And it was a smile that was warm and genuine, a smile that revealed a personality that enjoyed life. Rob was impressed with the fact the lady was capable of such a warm expression in light of all that had happened since the EMP event.

The second thing to strike Rob about the woman was that she appeared to be very clean. Under normal conditions this would have gone unnoticed. But now her appearance contrasted sharply with all the people he had encountered along his journey. Don had his hand around the woman's shoulder, pulling her tightly against him as he introduced Rob. As Rob looked closer at her eyes, he thought he saw evidence suggesting she had been crying.

Well yeah, I bet she cried when her husband came home. I bet Stephanie will cry when I get home too. Hell, I bet I'll cry. No, on second thought, I won't. But my eyeballs will probably sweat a little. Isn't that what they used to say in the Marine Corps?

Don smiled and said, "This is my wife Vangie. And this is Rob. Come on inside, buddy."

Rob was reluctant to get too close to Vangie. He feared his body odor and dirty clothes would be offensive. Rather than endure the awkwardness of trying to maneuver around the issue, he simply put it out there.

"It's really nice to meet you; I just don't want to get too close because I'm so dirty and all. Probably don't smell very good either."

She maintained her smile, but Rob thought he detected the slightest of tells in her expression as he uttered the words of warning. He bet she had suddenly realized that his warning was real and worth heeding. She had probably computed the way he had been living with limited hygiene and drawn the right conclusion. If there had been any doubt, it was removed when she wrinkled her nose, looked at Don, and said, "We need to get you washed up and into some clean clothes."

35

THOUSAND OAKS, CA

Rosalyn and her husband Rick sat in the living room of their home, both exhausted after having spent most of the night planning and scheming with nothing but the light of a single candle placed on their living room coffee table. They had finished the last of the food Rosalyn had traded for sex seventy two hours after the transaction. This meant they hadn't had any food for almost twelve hours now. The meager volume of water that had been acquired from the same transaction had vanished even before all the food was eaten.

Rick was frustrated with himself for not having come up with a way to salvage any of the meager rain water that had come down in their neighborhood two nights earlier. Other than putting out a few pots and a bucket, the rain had gone un-harvested. They had collected little more than a few quarts of water using this method.

Rosalyn had gone to Roger's front door on the day and time he had indicated to set up another transaction. She hadn't made herself available to him at that second meeting. Instead, she had offered to return to his house at three o'clock the following day. At first, he had displayed his disappointment in a brief fit of anger. He had told her it was "now or never", and that he might not even be interested in another sex for food and water transaction on the following day.

However, he had cooled down after his brief show of temper and asked Rosalyn to return at the time she had indicated. Relieved at his willingness to postpone the deal for another twenty four hours, she had flashed what she hoped was a sexy smile and told him that he wouldn't be sorry when she returned. She promised to make the wait worth his while, and hiked up her skirt a few inches as she turned and walked back toward her house.

Roger stood watching her from his doorway as she walked away with a slight swaying of her hips. He thought she looked like she had lost weight since he had bedded her. Too skinny now, he thought—but she would do anyway. He told himself that until she returned he would simply have to settle for thinking about all the things he would do with her when she finally came back to complete the deal.

Rick, who had watched the brief contact between his wife and Roger from the concealment of a tree in his front yard, felt his own sense of relief as he watched Rosalyn turn away from the door and begin walking back to the house. Neither he nor Rosalyn had thought the stranger would attempt to force her into his home against her will, but they had agreed that Rick would run to the front door and somehow get Rosalyn out of the house if he pulled her into the residence. Fortunately, it hadn't come to that.

Now, almost sixteen hours after that short second meeting, Rick and Rosalyn sat in their living room with the harsh realization that either Rosalyn would have to go back and prostitute herself again, or they were going to have to figure out a way to overpower the man. The problem was that they didn't have a lot of time to formulate a good plan to accomplish this. They had until three PM on today's date. If she didn't show who knew what Roger's reaction might be.

Not only was Rick aware of the inflexible time schedule, he was aware that the more time that went by without benefit of food and water, the less physically and mentally capable he would be to execute his plan. So, in essence, it was now or never if they wanted to have any chance at overpowering Roger and getting access to his stored supplies.

The husband and wife team had created, and verbally worked through, a half dozen different plans addressing how to take out Roger and get access to his supplies. In the end, all of these plans had been dismissed as not being workable. They had to come up with a plan that would at least give them a fighting chance at success.

It was agreed the best chances at defeating Roger would be to use a simple plan that utilized surprise, speed, and aggression. Nothing too complicated and nothing that required a firearm--because Rick didn't have one to use. And this, unfortunately, was going to be one helluva big problem. Because Roger, unlike Rick, had a gun. And the man had been wearing the 9mm Glock pistol on every occasion Rosalynn had seen him since the grid went down, including the time she had climbed into his bed.

The plan they eventually settled on involved Rosalynn showing up at Roger's house at the arranged time for the transaction. Rick planned on being hidden somewhere near the front door of Roger's home prior to her arrival. Upon making her presence known to Roger, and prior to entering his house, she would feign some sort of injury—a twisted ankle or something similar. She would do this near the front entrance in the hopes of drawing him out of the doorway where he would be more accessible. This would be the cue for Rick to attack him.

It was about as simple a plan as either of the couple could imagine, and it was in all likelihood a plan that offered a better chance of success than any other. All of the above notwithstanding, the chances of success were still only fifty-fifty at best in Rick's judgment. But he felt he simply didn't have a choice in the matter.

Rick had no doubt either of the two plausible alternatives--going without food and water while hoping relief would arrive or having Rosalynn go to bed with the guy again-- would be catastrophic. The former would probably contribute to their deaths, and the latter would not only ruin their relationship but quite possibly cause irreparable psychological damage to both of them. And the transaction would have to occur again and again until either food and water were once again available or Roger ran out of his stores. And what would happen if and when Roger was no longer willing to engage in the transaction? At that point they would be forced to plan an attack against him in any case.

Rick had thought it over and decided that he would rather lose his life trying to defeat Roger than to live with the knowledge he had pimped out his wife to get food for them. He had also figured out that, with the possible exception of his leg wound, the sooner he made his move against Roger the better his chances would be.

He had considered the different ways in which he could attack the amoral man living down the street. The pig had used his wife like a whore, and he had a lot of payback coming his way as far as Rick was concerned.

Rick was aware that the lynch pin in making his plan work would be whether he could be sufficiently mobile—and quick enough—to reach Roger and disable him before he was able to use his pistol effectively. Rick's leg wound was making progress, but it was far from being healed. The scab had formed and was preventing any bleeding, and so far there were no signs of infection present. However, he still limped when he walked, and the wound caused him discomfort most of the time and outright pain every so often.

Eventually he arrived at the idea of using a steel fireplace poker as his primary weapon to defeat Roger. He entertained a fleeting thought of an old *Flinstone's* cartoon comedy episode he had watched as a kid where one of the characters was using a hand powered sharpening stone wheel to put an edge on a tool.

Smiling to himself at the ridiculous memory, Rick entered his garage and began rooting through a medium sized tool box that sat on his wooden work bench. He retrieved a steel bastard file, clamped the fireplace poker in a vice mounted to his workbench, and set to work on creating a sharp point on the thing. As he worked on this he also reduced the curve of the hook, seeking to create as straight of a point as possible in case he actually drove the tip into Roger's flesh.

He had no experience in combat whatsoever, but Rick was a reasonably intelligent man who had a basic understanding of day-to-day real world physics. He knew that it might be important to pull the sharp spike out of Roger's flesh in a hurry in order to be able to use the weapon for repeated blows in a fight. By straightening the spike as best he could he reduced the odds of getting the improvised weapon stuck in such a scenario.

Rick hefted the newly created weapon in his hands, enjoying the feel of the solid steel tool. He eventually let his eyes come to rest on his forearms. Despite the fact that the previous couple of years had primarily been spent doing paperwork and supervisory work in the construction business, his muscular forearms and thick hands—byproducts of twenty plus years of doing physically demanding work--were still evident.

Rick was confident enough in the power he could muster from his upper body, even under his currently partially diminished capacity, to be convinced that if he could land even a single blow with the medieval looking weapon, he stood a solid chance of ending the deadly contest in his favor. He thought about this another minute and concluded that even if this "Roger" asshole was able to shoot him after he had landed the blow, without medical attention he would probably eventually die from the wound. He told himself that under such a scenario at least Rosalynn would be able to access the creep's food and water supplies, even if she no longer had a husband.

Rick allowed himself to think back on how much their lives had changed since the grid had crashed. It was difficult to wrap his head around the idea of how different their world now was.

If I could only get another chance to do things differently.

He rejoined Rosalyn who had fallen asleep on the living room couch. Rick glanced at his watch, which had survived the EMP incident, and saw that it was already eleven o'clock. Four hours away from game time. He decided to let her get some badly needed rest. In just a few short hours she would probably need all the strength and energy she could manage.

Rick considered how well his wife would be able to hold up under the stress of the violent attack to take place later today.

Can she handle this? Will she telegraph the pending attack to Roger without even knowing she's doing so? Will she somehow get in the way of what I have to do? This thing can't afford to have any little thing go wrong in the plan or it won't work.

He woke his sleeping wife at noon and allowed her a few minutes to become alert enough to comprehend what he needed to share with her about the plan of attack.

Rick addressed her in a slow and clear voice. He didn't want to sound condescending, but he knew it was imperative he have her complete attention while he went over the plan. Even the slightest misunderstanding was not an option if this thing was to have any chance. The balance between condescension and assurance of clarity was a tightrope act he had yet to master after all their years of marriage.

"Honey, we need to go over this plan a little bit more. I'm sorry to put you through this plan over and over but we both know this thing has to be close to perfect. I need you to focus as hard as you can. Now here's what I'm thinking..."

Rosalyn interrupted him, her fierce expression of anger giving her low and even voice all of the emphasis that was needed to convey her emotions.

"I already showed I can focus when the stakes are high. Don't forget that I'm the one who had to keep it together while that pig fucked me in his bedroom! Compared to having to do that, this will be a walk in the park, so don't tell me how I have to focus and keep it together. You just focus on making sure you kill that son of a bitch!"

Her outburst surprised him. He was silent for several seconds as he just looked at his wife. There was now a hardness to her that had not been there prior to the grid crash, and he wondered briefly if their relationship would ever recover from all that had happened.

Rick approached his wife, still seated on the couch, and extended his hands in a gesture to indicate he wanted to pull her to her feet. She looked away at first and then finally took his hands in hers and allowed Rick to help her stand. He hugged her firmly, hoping to let her feel his heartfelt concern and empathy. He loved this woman, and what she had been forced to endure had resulted in his suffering emotional agony ever since she had returned home from the nasty deed. He couldn't imagine how she must feel.

He said, "I know you did the heavy lifting to save us. And now it's my turn. I won't let you down Rosalyn. I love you."

She wept quietly while he stared into space. Neither of them said a word, their mutual embrace providing all of the communication, for the moment, that was necessary.

Rosalyn broke free of the hug and used the tips of her fingers to push away her tears.

"Okay," she said, "We need to get back to working on our plan. We don't have that much time."

Rick endeavored to hide his irritation as he thought

Yeah—no shit. I've been trying to tell you that.

Instead, he replied, "You're right. Okay, here's the deal. I need to find a location where I can get close enough to rush him when the time comes. I'm going to go by his house in a little while and scout out the place to see if I can pick out a decent spot. Then I'll come back here. I want to get set up in position before you get there, but not too early because it might increase the odds of shit-head seeing me. Why take that chance, right?"

He stopped for a few seconds to gather his thoughts before continuing.

"So you'll be walking down the street by yourself to go meet him at his front door, just like last time. Don't look around to see where I am. We can't let him think there might be a trap set for him, and if he thinks you're looking for someone that would be the worst thing that could happen to our plan. Make sense?"

Rosalyn nodded her head, but avoided eye contact. Rick got the distinct impression she was thinking about something else.

"What are you thinking," he asked.

She answered him without looking at him.

"I'm thinking I hope I can look at that goddamn pig without crying or somehow messing up the plan because I hate him so much. I really don't know if I can hold it together when he opens his front door, Rick--I just don't know."

Once again he struggled to control his own emotions before saying anything.

"Honey, it will be alright." A long pause.

"You know, Rosalyn, even if you start to cry a little when you see him, the plan will still work. He'll just think you're upset because of the shitty deal you have to do. And this piece of shit won't care. He's still gonna want to have what he wants—your feelings won't mean shit to him."

He was starting to let his emotions get the better of him so he stopped talking for a short while.

"He's a total asshole. We both know that. So if you get upset, just try to control it the best you can and continue with the plan. Remember this time he isn't getting what he wants. He's gettin' the surprise of his fuckin' life is what he's gonna get!"

Rosalyn looked at her husband, searching for some assurance in his expression or body language to convince her that what he said was in fact true.

Having wrested control of his anger—at least for the moment—he continued.

"What I need you to do is to somehow try to get him to come out of his doorway and away from the house as much as possible. Doesn't have to be that far; just enough to let me get to him before he can run back into his house. If he gets back into the house the plan won't work. You understand that, right?"

She nodded again without speaking.

Rick went on to further explain the plan.

"Unless you can think of something better, I think you should go to the front of his house, and then, before you get up to the front door, drop something on the ground. Whatever you drop is going to be your reason for walking back away from the front door to get what you dropped. You have to get back away from the door for the plan to work. So you need to knock on his door first to make sure he knows you're there so he'll open the door to begin with."

Rick stopped to makes sure he had his wife's full attention before continuing.

"After he opens the door, act like you suddenly notice you dropped something and walk back to get it. It doesn't have to be very far away from the door-maybe ten feet or so. But don't worry about getting the distance part perfect. I would announce it out loud when you pretend to notice what you dropped. Try to get him to look at whatever you dropped too, and then just walk back to get it. Are you good with the plan so far?"

Rosalyn said "Yeah, I got it." Rick was encouraged to see that she appeared to be concentrating.

Rick went on.

"Okay, good. When you get to where you dropped whatever it is, you need to pretend to twist your ankle or something that makes you fall. If you don't want to fall, then at least slump to the ground or something like that. You want him to walk over to help you up without thinking about it. Got it?"

Rosalyn asked, "Is that when you're going to attack him?"

He answered, "Yep. That's when I'm going to come at him. Now here's the deal with that part. This is probably gonna be the hardest part of the whole plan for you. Since we're pretty sure he's gonna be wearing that pistol, I want you to grab onto his arm on whichever side he's wearing the gun. Do you remember where he wears his gun?"

She closed her eyes and drew on her memory of the miserable experience she had endured two days prior.

"He wears it on his right side," she said as she patted the right side of her own waist.

Rick said, "Alright then. So you need to picture in your head how you'll be grabbing his right arm when he comes to help you up. Grab it somewhere around here if you can."

He took his left hand and wrapped it around his lower right forearm, just above his wrist to demonstrate his directions.

"The whole idea of you grabbing his arm is to make it harder for him to get to his gun. If you can't grab his arm the way I just showed you, don't give up. All we need to do is to slow him down. That's all. So anything you can do to make it harder for him to get to that gun when I come at him will help my chances a lot. Okay?"

She nodded her head and made direct eye contact with her husband.

"I'm thinking," Rick added, "that you should use both of your hands when you grab his arm. C'mere a second," he said as he held out his own forearm for her to practice on.

Rick used his left hand to position Rosalyn's hands around his lower right forearm in demonstration of how he wanted her to take hold of Roger's arm when the time came. Satisfied that she knew what to do, he asked Rosalyn to go over the whole plan step by step while they sat in their living room. Then he asked her to do it again. After the third time she had explained the plan in detail, including demonstrating how she would grab Roger's arm, he decided to stop pressing her any further. There really weren't very many moving parts in the entire plan, which was the whole point he had in mind when forming the concept. KISS.

Rick told Rosalyn that she should probably start to get dressed up for her contact with Roger. He indicated he was going to take a walk and scout out a suitable location to conceal himself and still be close enough to spring from hiding to successfully conduct the attack.

As Rick walked down the sidewalk he noticed how all of the residents had opted to retreat within their houses and stay there. It was an eerie situation. The entire residential block had the appearance of a neighborhood like those depicted on the news to illustrate some place where virtually an entire town's population had lost their jobs and been forced to vacate their homes. A neighborhood that had, in essence, died.

Without warning, he saw something that made him momentarily forget about his ambush plan.

A group of six men were now walking up the sidewalk on the other side of the street about sixty yards from where he stood on in his front yard. He could tell that they were trouble as soon as he laid eyes on them. Then again, he realized that just about anybody who was walking about in a group under the present conditions should be considered trouble. But these guys were obvious.

Several of them were carrying some sort of improvised weapons--either pipes or wooden clubs-- from what he could tell. He retreated back into his yard and positioned himself behind a tree he figured would sufficiently conceal him from the group of men down the block. Then he watched.

This is all we need. Great. How are we gonna deal with this now?

He watched three of the group break off and walk to the rear yard of one of the homes across the street. It looked to be only a couple of houses away from Roger's house. The remaining three remained on the sidewalk and began looking up and down the street. They weren't very sneaky about what they were doing. Just blatantly performing their look-out function. They looked as though they were brazenly daring anyone to try to confront them.

Rick had a brief thought that was as close to a glimmer of hope as he had entertained in quite a while. If these guys would only break into Roger's house, the ambush he and Rosalyn had cooked up might not even be necessary. However, not long after the thought had entered his mind he realized that if the pillagers entered Roger's house they would in all likelihood set up residency in the house for a while, leaving Rosalyn and him with an even tougher problem to deal with.

While Rick stood behind the large Oak tree contemplating his situation, he heard a strange sound. It was a sound that wouldn't have seemed strange a few weeks ago. In fact he may not have even noticed it at all then. But the sound of a motorized vehicle of any kind was now odd indeed. And what he was listening to was definitely a vehicle engine of some sort. No doubt about it.

Rick turned to look down the other end of the street in the direction he thought the motor was coming from. After several seconds he saw two persons (he assumed they were men), wearing what appeared to be police uniforms. They were both on an all-terrain *four wheeler* off-road vehicle. It was the type of vehicle that hunters and other outdoorsmen favored when traveling significant distances in the back country with loads that made walking on foot too difficult, or simply because the vehicles were more comfortable than walking. One officer was driving the machine while the second officer was seated on a steel rack affixed to the back of the vehicle. It was pretty clear the rack wasn't designed for human transportation, but things were different now to be sure.

He took his eyes away from the two policemen on the four-wheeler and looked back toward the house where the half dozen marauding men had been. He heard a terror-laden scream and then saw the three men running from the side of the house out to the sidewalk to rejoin their three cohorts. One was carrying a plastic bag filled with unknown items—the rest were empty handed save for the stick-like objects they had been carrying before they had gone to the rear of the residence. Then Rick watched all six pound feet in a hurry, fleeing on the sidewalk in the direction from which they had come until they were around the corner and out of view. He found it curious that the guy with the plastic bag held onto it during his flight.

The frustrated construction worker concealed behind the tree in his front yard felt a sense of relief as he watched the group fleeing from his residential block, but he was even more pleased to see the two cops.

Maybe we can finally get some help here. It would sure as hell be nice to get a break for a change.

He ran to the front door and stepped inside no more than a few feet, yelling out to Rosalyn.

"Hey honey, you gotta get out here. Looks like there are a couple of cops out here. Seriously; come on out here right now!"

He suddenly had another thought. Even though Stephanie Flynn had made it pretty clear that she couldn't help them anymore, he hadn't harbored any hard feelings toward her. Well, maybe he had a few hard feelings, but he did understand that she was going to place the welfare of her son and herself above that of her neighbors. Besides that, she may very well have saved his leg from becoming infected and possibly resulting in his death. Certainly he couldn't forget that.

He made his decision to run to Stephanie's front door and let her know there were a couple of police officers in the neighborhood. He arrived at the front door and after banging on it a few seconds without getting a response, he yelled through the door.

"Stephanie, it's Rick. Just want to let you know there are a couple of police officers on the block in case you want to ask them anything. I'm leaving now to go talk to them."

He walked back to his house and asked Rosalyn if she was going to go with him to talk to the policemen. She told him to go ahead without her and that she would catch up with him in a minute.

36

UNINCORPORATED SOUTHEAST

LOS ANGELES

The bottle that sailed past the patrol cars positioned in front of the Nadeau Station and shattered against the building's front door did not contain gasoline or any other flammable liquid; nor was it set on fire before it was thrown by the young man as he rode his bicycle past the quasi-fortified sheriff's department building.

The simple glass container originally built to house soda pop contained a hand written note. The note was simple and to the point--an urgent warning. It was a primitive delivery system to be sure, but it nonetheless provided a crucial "heads up" for the few that still occupied the Nadeau Sheriff's Station.

There was a bit of irony surrounding the incident. Marino had almost failed to recognize the warning altogether. Hearing the breaking glass of the bottle, he had grabbed a soaking wet towel—one of several floating in the plastic garbage can filled with anti-freeze and water that sat in the entrance area of the station as a fire-fighting measure. After running out of the building to confront what he thought would be a gasoline enhanced fire, he could find no flames to combat. And he had almost failed to spot the crumpled paper that lay on the concrete in front of the station door surrounded by shattered bottle glass.

The now almost barbaric looking sergeant was looking at the broken bottle glass in an effort to deduce what kind—if any—accelerant had been housed in the bottle, and why it had failed to ignite, when he noticed the crumpled note and picked it up. He looked all around him for any indication of the source of the bottle and note. He couldn't come up with even the slightest suspicion of who had thrown the object. Not wishing to remain outside the relative protection of the building for any longer than necessary, Marino re-entered before reading the hand printed note.

TODAY IS THURSDAY, MAY 02. TOMORROW NIGHT OR EARLY SATURDAY MORNING THEY ARE GOING TO ATTACK YOUR STATION. HARD. REALLY DAMN HARD. YOU GUYS HAVE TO GET READY EVEN THOUGH YOU MIGHT NOT BE ABLE TO BEAT THEM EVEN IF YOU ARE. WHATEVER HAPPENS, AT LEAST I CAN NOW SAY THAT I TRIED TO WARN YOU ALL. THESE GUYS ARE SERIOUS AND THEY HAVE SERIOUS WEAPONS.

Marino noticed that the author of the note had taken the time to make sure the deputies knew when the warning had been written. It appeared as though the messenger wanted to ensure there was no mistaking when the attack was planned. The sergeant looked at the calendar on his desk to make sure today was in fact Thursday. It was.

Marino was reminded that he had circled the date of April 29th, which was the previous Monday. He had marked the date in order to keep track of when the Nadeau Station had received the visit from the Department of Homeland Security team. Each member of the six man team (including the pilot) was wearing virtually identical clothing and gear. Each displayed olive drab BDU's and tactical shirts, black nylon combat web gear, M4 carbines, and leg holstered Sig Sauer pistols. The DHS team had landed in a helicopter in the middle of the street in a spot that happened to be vacant of any stalled cars. The pilot had remained at the controls while two of the team stood outside of the aircraft, carbines at the ready. The remaining three team members contacted the sheriff station's personnel.

Unfortunately, the hopes of assistance that initially arrived with the team evaporated almost as quickly as the helo had appeared from the sky.

Marino shook his head in disgust as he recalled the visit. What a bunch of bullshit that whole meeting turned out to be after all was said and done. He had brought to their attention the strange warning about a pending attack on the station, as well as the possibly related intel Harris had mentioned. The agents weren't impressed. In fact they were outright apathetic from what he could glean from their reaction.

In the end, the DHS guys couldn't, or wouldn't, tell him when they could expect help. Nor could they tell them when the power was going to be back on, if and when any supplies would be delivered, or how other cities in the country were handling the disaster. And they had no idea what—or who--had caused the EMP.

When asked, they couldn't even tell the deputy sheriffs what was happening in other parts of the state There was no information to be had about death tolls, medical treatment locations, water and food supplies, or anything else that was asked of them. They wouldn't even confirm that the cause of the problem had been EMP related.

"I'm sorry, but you don't have the clearance for that information sergeant," the DHS team leader had told him in response to his inquiry about the EMP angle.

At the time it was pretty clear to Marino and his deputies who were present that the DHS team was only there to make an assessment and report their findings to whoever had requested it. With this in mind, not long after the meeting had started, the frustrated sergeant had come to the conclusion that his visitors weren't going to bring them any relief, supplies, or other assistance. And Marino didn't bother to make the slightest attempt to hide his disgust. He no longer gave a shit. It wasn't merely their inability to help the embattled patrol cops that pissed off the sergeant, it was the cavalier and condescending manner in which they addressed the local cops' plight that drove Marino over the edge of civility.

The sergeant smacked his palms against his thighs and blurted out, "Well, if you guys can't help us or get us any supplies, I guess we're done here. We've got work to do. You guys can get back to flying around and making your visits."

The brooding sergeant emphasized the term "flying" by holding his thick arms against his ribs and then quickly moving his elbows in an up and down motion. The visual message was not lost on anyone present. Marino, for a brief moment, looked like he was mimicking the fairy tale image of a winged fairy.

While this type of irreverent behavior was unusual for Marino, it was not particularly so for Lee Harris. He was an intelligent but not always long-term consequence oriented patrol cop. His penchant for making clever but disrespectful comments to not only his peers, but also occasionally to those who outranked him, was well known. Harris, intent on making absolutely certain there was no doubt about his intended insult, laughed loudly at Marino's gesture. Not *with* the federal DHS men, but quite obviously *at* them. It was intended to convey the message that despite the fact the DHS agents had the resources and the physical means to do things that the local cops didn't, the deputies viewed their federal counterparts with contempt.

Enjoying the advantage of being on his home turf as well as what he believed to be his physical superiority (even his tattooed fore-arms were bigger than the biceps of the largest of the DHS men that were present), Harris had decided to make sure these condescending agents were well aware of how he viewed them. So he did his very best to send an unequivocal message to the federal prima-donnas standing before him.

Although he would have been well advised to leave the matter alone at that point, discretion was not one of Deputy Harris's virtues. Boldness, on the other hand, was a category where he regularly scored high marks. Love him or hate him, no one could say that Lee Harris lacked balls.

It was a commonly held belief within the ranks of federal law enforcement that local cops all viewed their federal counterparts with a certain amount of awe, respect, and envy, as well as an unspoken deference. Of course the truth of the matter, at least among alpha male patrol cops working in high crime areas, was nothing close to that. In fact it was often the opposite.

Generally, tough patrol cops viewed the feds as administrative types who essentially worked as detectives. Detectives with very little street experience. None of the deputies now occupying the

Nadeau Station viewed themselves as the equals of the DHS men. To a person, they viewed themselves as being better.

Like most seasoned patrol cops, they were convinced the lion's share of federal police work was done behind a computer screen or from a safe distance using high tech surveillance equipment, working cases that often made headlines due to the size of the criminal operations they often targeted. In contrast, they knew urban patrol cops were tasked with less glamorous work--like fighting violent parolees into handcuffs in alleys and housing projects.

Whether or not this perspective was an accurate one was certainly far from being a settled matter, but it was undeniably the dominant view of not only the Nadeau Station cops but that of local law enforcement worker bees all over the country.

Deputy Lee Harris personified this belief, and he made no attempt whatsoever to hide this in his attitude. Moreover, he had no qualms about sharing his opinions explicitly with anyone who cared to listen, including the federal agents themselves. "Devil may care...fuck 'em anyway" was how he tended to view it.

The comparatively crude but effective manner in which Harris was outfitted sharply contrasted with that of the DHS men and their state-of-the-art tactical gear. He carried only traditional standard issue police firearms but was heavily loaded down with extra ammunition. His appearance stated, "extra heavy on the ammo please, and you can skip the extra trimmings."

Moreover, the contrast in equipment was apropos of the contrast between the men themselves, and somehow all three of the federal agents sensed that they were looking at law enforcement operators that were more effective and capable than themselves as they took the measure of Harris and Marino. Despite their less sophisticated gear and lack of access to operable vehicles, this difference emanated from the very pores of the LASD cops.

Noticing that Slick had walked into the building with his shotgun hanging across his massive chest and ever-present chaw stuffed into his lower lip, Harris used a slight nod of his head to motion the big deputy to the sergeant's office. His penchant for showing off for his fellow deputies was not exactly a secret, and he now wanted an audience other than the sergeant. Slick figured it might provide a laugh, so he obliged the stocky deputy.

Harris looked at Marino and said, "Hey Sarge, I think I saw a little bottle of fairy dust in your desk in case anyone wants to use some while they're flying around." He gave a habitual tug at his shotgun sling as he looked into the eyes of all three of the DHS members and displayed a big "fuck you very much" smile. He was clearly daring any of the feds to engage him in verbal combat. It was standard Harris behavior.

The sound of Slick forcing out a large volume of air from his lungs through his nostrils as he tried not to expel the Copenhagen from his lip while laughing at the "fairy dust" remark startled Harris. Soon he joined the big cowboy in laughter. It was mutually infectious. The two were then joined in laughter by Marino, and after several seconds of full-blown unbridled guffawing, the three of them had to force themselves to regain their composure and wait for whatever response the "elite" DHS men would offer. There was only silence.

The team leader of the DHS crew, a thirty seven-year-old who looked like he would be at home behind a desk on Wall Street despite his tactical combat gear, didn't like what he had heard. He didn't like the obviously derisive tone and gesture the powerful bearded sergeant had addressed him with moments earlier, and he certainly didn't like the comments that had been uttered by the stocky deputy with the tattooed forearms. And he didn't much like the fact the newly arriving big black deputy with the chewing tobacco and the shotgun had found the comment to be hilarious.

By the time Harris had finished with his insults, the face of the federal supervisor was close to being crimson. The meeting was now perilously close to being irrevocably finished.

Marino realized that if the DHS visit ended without any positive result it would be detrimental for all parties involved. Actually, it would mostly be detrimental for the LASD deputies, because they probably wouldn't receive any aid or supplies. Or if they did, they could count on being last in line. The federal agents, on the other hand, would in all likelihood suffer nothing more than a further damaged reputation within the ranks of the nation's largest sheriff's department.

In any case, the sergeant decided to put a stop to it all. Despite the fact he had been largely responsible for starting the whole disrespectful tone of the exchange occurring within his office, Marino resolved to make an effort to rehabilitate the meeting. He addressed Harris and Slick.

"Hey guys, how about you let me talk to the DHS guys by myself for a few minutes. Just go ahead and return to your posts. I'll catch up with you both in a little while."

Harris avoided eye contact with his sergeant and abruptly rolled his head from side to side to stretch his neck muscles. Deliberate stalling that was not lost on Marino. He didn't want to let go of the conflict, but he also didn't want to have a beef with Marino. He walked out of the office without saying a word, leaving Marino alone with the three DHS agents.

Slick had not moved from where he was standing just outside the sergeant's office in the hallway, its large window affording all present an unrestricted view of him from inside the office. The big cowboy patrolman spat dark colored tobacco juice into the cup serving as his spittoon and looked straight ahead with a thousand yard stare before he walked back to his post.

Now alone with the agents, Marino threw up his hands, palms open in a "surrender" gesture, and expelled a long breath before he started to speak. The gesture was intended to convey a message of *what a mess we have here. Where do I start?* But the impassive response by the feds told him his attempt had fallen short. Part of him felt apologetic, and part of him wanted to ask the DHS men, *"What did you expect?"* But above all, the sergeant had a desire to salvage whatever positive results he could from the meeting.

He reminded himself that while they were clearly not suffering to the same extent he and his deputies were, the agents were probably overwhelmed by the mission they had taken on. At his core he believed these were decent men who had honorable intentions. It was simply that tensions were high everywhere under the circumstances.

Marino gave his best shot at re-opening the communication. He wasn't going to apologize outright, for that wasn't in his nature. But he would give his best shot at re-establishing the lines of communication.

Looking the DHS team boss in the eye, Marino said, "You have to understand my guys feel like they've pretty much been abandoned and left out to dry by all the people who should be trying to give them support. After all, they're only asking for a little help so they can do some small part of their job around here--that's all. But I don't like the way they were talking to you, or laughing, whatever. I'll handle that later. It was mostly my doing for starting off with the smart-ass stuff. Let's just get past it. We know you guys are doing your best in all of this mess—just like us—and I'm sure it isn't exactly a picnic for you either."

He looked at the other DHS men briefly before returning his eye contact with the team leader and continuing.

"Can we give this meeting another try now?"

The DHS supervisor was quiet for a long moment before responding.

"Okay Sergeant; you're right. But I gotta tell you that wasn't the best way to get our help if you think about it."

Marino offered no rejoinder to the comment. It was now his turn to be quiet. He held eye contact with the federal team leader, maintaining an impassive expression. He waited for the DHS man to continue.

"Alright, let's get past that nonsense; like you said. Our objective in coming here was to take down info so that we can possibly get some supplies to you later. Can't promise when that will be though. They gave us a long list of local police and sheriff agencies to contact. You guys are only the third law enforcement station we've visited, and I hope it goes better with the rest of them."

The DHS man gave Marino a brief and uneasy smile when he made the last comment. The sergeant returned his gesture with a perfunctory smile that never reached his eyes.

Marino was struck by a thought that elicited a strong dose of self-criticism on his part.

We never went to check out the status of the fire stations in our patrol area! How the hell did I forget about that?

Having made a mental note to address this as soon as the opportunity presented itself, he asked the DHS man if they had made contact with any of the local fire stations. He responded with a negative head shake, stating they had not personally contacted any fire facilities yet. The agent added, "Actually it's funny you mentioned that. From what we've been told, there hasn't been any fire personnel that have remained at any of the fire houses our people have contacted so far. From what they've seen so far all the firehouses have been completely abandoned."

Marino noted the agent's use of the term *fire houses* and deduced that the man hailed from the east coast somewhere despite the fact he could not detect an obvious accent on the man.

"Well that's not surprising I guess. They have no way to defend themselves most likely, so they probably realized they would be doomed if they stayed there."

The DHS agent nodded in agreement as he considered Marino's take on the matter. Apparently realizing that he needed to push the business part of the meeting along, he removed a notebook and a small pen from his tactical shirt pocket. The agent asked, "So what are the most important things you guys could use right now? By the way, let's assume we're talking about one large helicopter load, not a semi-trailer or anything like that."

The sergeant responded in a low voice devoid of any enthusiasm.

"Food and water naturally. We have one small propane stove but not much propane for it. Any kind of fuel we can use to heat water would be nice--even barbeque charcoal, kerosene, or whatever you can give us. Toilet paper or paper towels would be much appreciated too. Hand sanitizer gel would be good. Of course ammunition for our weapons--mostly 9mm and twelve gauge shells is what we need."

The federal man was busy writing down all the information in his notebook as Marino spoke. The other two agents stood quietly with their arms folded across their chests. They attempted to match the poker face expression worn by the big Viking looking sheriff's sergeant in front of them, but they couldn't even come close.

Modern man has evolved to the point where a man's physical size and power mean nothing in most negotiations in the current business world, but the fact that Marino was six inches taller than the tallest of the agents, and weighed almost as much as any two of them combined, was something that couldn't be ignored. It was almost literally the elephant in the room that none of the federal agents wanted to acknowledge--to themselves or each other--but all were uncomfortably aware of it. Even more relevant was the latent propensity for violence that emanated from the huge sergeant.

The discussion ceased for a moment, and Marino ran his hand through his developing full beard and clapped his hands together. Clapping his hands in that manner was a gesture that he often did without thought when he was through speaking about a topic, and he meant nothing by it. But the gesture visibly startled the agents. Marino was slightly embarrassed by what had happened, and the agents were more than slightly embarrassed by their reactions.

Marino said, "Let's cut to the chase guys. Should we expect any relief to be coming our way here or not? What do you think we should expect, and how about a ball park estimate of when?"

Before the agent could respond, Marino suddenly remembered the large thick walled safe in the station armory. "You guys don't happen to have any way to cut into a heavy-duty safe do you? The EMP ruined the electronic lock on the damn thing, and we can't get access to the rifles locked inside."

The DHS team boss merely shook his head and then responded to the sergeant's earlier question.

"I can't promise for sure when or what kind of supplies we can get you. That goes without saying. I'm not supposed to tell you this, but things are not looking good for the country right now. What I can promise is that I'll do what I can. It's impressive what you've done here, and I would really like to see you get some supplies at least. Hopefully some actual federal personnel to relieve you guys too. But as things look right now I think it might be at least another week or two before we can get anything to happen for you."

Marino looked at the DHS team leader with a blank expression as he considered one of the comments he had made seconds earlier.

"Did you say the *country* is in bad shape," Marino asked. "Just how far reaching is this fucking thing, anyway?"

The DHS agent didn't answer right away, clearly taking a few extra seconds to consider what, and how much, he should confide in the sheriff's sergeant.

"Basically, the whole lower forty eight states are fucked for the most part--in the major cities anyway. It's actually kinda interesting that the rural areas seem to be coping a lot better with this mess than the cities are." He looked at Marino for his reaction, got nothing more than a slightly quizzical look, and continued.

"From what we're hearing the rural folks are maintaining order in most of their communities--neighbors looking after each other and all that. Course it helps that most of 'em have guns and other outdoor equipment as part of their lifestyle. I'm sure they're suffering too but they seem to be getting by so far. Of course they don't know it, but they're at the end of the line for getting help from the government. We're putting all our resources into assisting the cities first."

After letting that sink in for a moment, he continued. "You didn't ask, but the first police station we stopped at has also ceased to function. A handful of their officers are essentially just camping out in the building--same as you." The agent made brief eye contact with Marino to gauge whether or not the big man had taken offense at the comment. He hadn't considered it might be construed that way until after the words had left his mouth.

"The federal government has even come up with a term for this phenomenon," the agent added.

"They're calling it *the cocoon effect*. The cops stop working to protect the communities and simply focus on protecting themselves in the police stations. Totally understandable under the circumstances of course."

Marino wasn't sure whether or not the man's comments were intended as verbal payback for the earlier derisive remarks made by he and his deputies, but he responded defensively anyway.

"Yeah well, this area can be a goddamn war zone even when things are so-called *normal*. I'm not gonna send my deputies out there under these conditions, and I don't give a fuck who doesn't like it. I have a responsibility to not put them in harm's way to the point where it'd be a long shot for them to survive. And it's just tough shit if someone doesn't like that! The decision would be different if this were a low crime area."

The agent allowed a few seconds to go by before he responded in a low and measured voice. "Well I got news for you sergeant. I don't think there are any places that have been impacted by this event that are going to be 'low crime areas'—at least not for long. We expected things to get bad and then worse. And so far we haven't seen any indication that we were wrong about that." The agent took in a deep breath and then let it out. "Okay; we'll see what we can do to get you guys some help," he offered.

The federal supervisor stood and adjusted his combat belt and holstered pistol. He used his arms to motion to his men that the meeting was over. He and Marino shook hands in a perfunctory manner and exchanged polite comments of thanks and encouragement with each other—just like things were normal and they were simply planning a joint agency drug bust or some similar police endeavor.

The federal man in charge had originally planned on requesting a couple of the deputies' assistance to provide extra security as the three agents went back to their helo, but he had changed his mind following the insulting humor that had taken place at their expense. As he exited the building, the agent signaled to one of the other feds who had remained in a security position at the helo. A second or two later the aircraft's powerful engine came to life, and the three agents began walking toward the big aircraft at a brisk pace, maintaining an obviously well practiced security formation the entire distance.

Dramatically ducking their heads to ensure that there were no accidental decapitations involving the prop of the large mechanical bird, the three DHS men who had just exited the sheriff's station entered the helo first, followed by the two men who had been guarding the aircraft.

Two significant events took place as the DHS helicopter took off. The first was unsettling. The second absolutely scared the living shit out of the deputies who were there to observe it.

Less than ten seconds after the helicopter began to ascend, a volley of gunfire exploded. It was difficult for Marino or any of the deputies watching to determine exactly where the rounds had come from, but there was no question as to what the shooters were trying to hit. The unmistakable sound of fully automatic weapons fire and bullets striking the metal skin of the rapidly departing helo could be heard as the aircraft accelerated upward and forward.

It was by far the most intense gunfire volley any of the station deputies had heard since the EMP had taken place. The sheer volume of fire, despite the fact that it was fairly short-lived, gripped the worn out and defeated feeling patrol cops and left them with a sense of unease. Each deputy who was present to watch and listen to the gunshots being fired at the departing helicopter found it strange that no return gunfire came from the aircraft.

The first event was unsettling to the patrol officers because it involved automatic weapons in the hands of those that quite possibly were planning to assault the station in the near future. Despite the wholesale level of gun violence that took place in this patrol area on a regular basis, fully automatic gunfire was actually a rare phenomenon.

Upon hearing the fully automatic gunfire, every deputy present thought about the information Harris had shared with them earlier regarding the old rumors of military small arms being possessed by militant anti-American radicals in the area. But that wasn't the worst of it.

The second event created a whole new level of fear for the deputies watching the departing helo that soon had all of them questioning whether their decision to remain at the Nadeau Station had been a wise one. Just as the helo had completed its ascent and began accelerating forward, the distinctive light colored contrail of a rocket propelled grenade could be seen arcing through the air and traveling, without effect, just to the rear of the helo. Close but no cigar as the saying went.

The RPG round had originated from somewhere on the ground on the right, or starboard, side of the aircraft, but that was about all that any of them could determine. Watching the grenade's contrail, Harris unslung his shotgun, presented the weapon in the *low ready* position against his shoulder, and clicked off the safety in preparation for firing. It was largely an instinctive action, done mostly to serve as some small source of psychological comfort while facing a superior enemy preparing to attack. The other patrol cops present followed his example, although they too recognized it was little more than a symbolic gesture at this point.

As the deputies tried to wrap their minds around what they had just seen, a second RPG round screamed through the air. Like the grenade preceding it, it missed the DHS helicopter, its contrail outlining an arc just below the climbing airship. The deputies weren't sure if the helo pilot had avoided disaster by virtue of his skill or if it had just been sheer luck.

Heavy doses of fear-induced chemicals began releasing themselves through the bodies of the deputies witnessing the RPG attack. All of them were familiar with the adrenaline associated with fear, and each of these deputies had learned to work past such physical reactions during exposure to danger on the job. This time it was harder than usual.

Reeling his thoughts in from the memory of the brief DHS visit and dramatic departure to the present situation, Marino began to make the rounds to let the remaining deputies know about the most recent warning that had been delivered to the station in the form of a bottle and note. He showed them the note without making much conversation. He was convinced that the note was self-explanatory. In spite of how hard he tried not to, he couldn't help but think of the RPG attack on the DHS helicopter and the warning note's mention of the bad guys having "serious weapons".

How the hell are we supposed to defend against a fuckin' RPG attack?

Unable to come up with any kind of an answer to his own nagging question, Marino simply let the note speak for itself as he showed it around. The only thing he added was a direct order for everyone to fill their pockets and pouches with as many extra loaded magazines and shotgun shells as they could stuff into them. He also directed each of them to keep a Kevlar helmet within arm's reach at all times as well as having their shotguns on their persons.

Mori and Cruz were alternating taking sentry duty on the station's roof with the Springfield Armory .30 caliber rifle. John Purnell was allowed to keep his M-4 carbine with him at all times whether at a defensive position or resting/sleeping. The similar rifle retrieved from Treanor's locker was rotated according to post assignment and the individual deputy's familiarity with that weapon system. So far the protocol was proving to be amenable to all of the deputies.

Marino pulled in his deputies for yet another briefing/meeting, directing several of the patrol cops to face outward watching for threats in what passed for a defensive perimeter. In fact it was really only a defensive perimeter in the nominal sense, being as how the edges of the building were left unattended for the time being. But at least the deputies were facing in the direction any threat would come from, and there was little doubt they were locked on and ready to engage any attackers to the best of their ability. He viewed the momentary decrease in perimeter security as being subordinate to the importance of the group meeting.

Marino started off the meeting by announcing his reason for calling it.

"You all saw the warning note, and you all heard Harris talk about the information he had a few years ago that might be related to this. And some of us saw those RPG rounds that were fired at the Homeland Security helo when it was leaving. This whole situation could go really bad for some of us. Shit, for all of us even. Who knows?"

The sergeant stopped and looked at the deputies present. Some of them weren't sure if he had stopped because he was trying to control his emotions or if he was simply gathering his thoughts before going on.

"The point here is that I want to hear all of your thoughts on this thing. If someone here wants to argue the case that we should leave the station and try to survive the odds of making it on foot to some-where else, then I want to hear that opinion. And I don't want to hear anyone being disrespectful of that opinion. You can disagree, but everyone gets a voice on this. This is Goddamn important, so I want to hear it all now."

No one spoke. Some of the deputies looked at their boots; some looked at miscellaneous objects in their vicinity. Harris tried to make eye contact with the big supervisor, while Slick took the opportunity to remove the Copenhagen tin from his pocket and load up his lip, all the while looking straight ahead impassively.

Marino continued, "I'm going to be honest with all of you right now. I'm starting to have second thoughts about whether I have the right to make you all stay here to defend the station--or whether I should even be pressuring you to stay here."

Harris, predictably, spoke up first.

"Boss, I look at this in a pretty simple way. We can't let these fuck-sticks get away with whatever they have planned. We damn sure can't let them run us out of here. No fucking way. Not ever. I'm down for the cause till the very end. Period. I'll stay here and shoot those motherfuckers till my guns are all empty. Straight up. That's the way it is for me."

Gattuso, somewhat irritated by the matter-of-fact way his friend had presented his case, took it upon himself to represent the other side of the argument.

"The way I see this thing is that we aren't even capable of helping the residents around here anymore. We're now at the point where it's all about saving our own lives. We can't do shit for these citizens now. Haven't been able to for a while now, right? So my point is that there ain't any question of doing the honorable thing—we're only operat-ing from the point of how to have the best chance at saving our own asses now. Let's be fuckin' honest about this whole thing." He looked around for any reaction to his comments before wrapping it up.

"We need to take a good hard look at whether we can figure out a way to make a plan to get out of here and live. It's pretty obvious that nobody else gives a shit about what happens to us. I guess that's all I got to say about it."

Marino made eye contact with Anderson and pushed his chin out at her as he asked her to give her opinion. She began to tear up with the emotion of the moment, but she quickly brought herself under control and waited a few seconds before speaking.

"I think we're now at a point where we need to make our decision all about how we can survive this mess. If anyone can come up with a plan to survive this--and I don't care how we do it or where we have to go—I'm all for that. That's just where I am at this point. We already did our duty and then some—we have no more duty to stay here the way I see it."

The sergeant looked at Mori, his expression inviting his opinion.

"Well, you guys have a lot more time on the job than I do, but the way I see it is that I'm down for the cause. I trained the best part of my adult life for a major CQB scenario. So I pretty much say *fuck these guys if they wanna attack our station. Bring it on I say!* I think we should dig in deep and get ready for 'em."

When it was clear that Mori had nothing more to say, Marino looked at Cruz.

"Sarge, you've always been a great leader as far as I'm concerned. I'm not brown nosing here because this situation has gone way past that. Obviously. you got a helluva lot of experience, and I know you and Harris are always talking about what we should do and considering our options. I doubt I'm gonna come up with a better idea than the two of you have figured out, so I'll go whatever way you say we should Sarge. I trust your judgment."

When it was clear that Cruz wasn't going to offer any further opinion on the matter, Marino moved his gaze to Slick. Like most men who don't talk a lot, his response was eagerly awaited by everyone present. All of the deputies looked toward the big cowboy cop to hear what he had to say.

"The way I see it is that if we wanted to leave we all missed our chance way back. Fuck it man. I'm thinkin' I'm ready to cowboy up and fight till the end on this thing. They can make their move, but I ain't gonna lay down for them. I say it's time to cowboy up and make a stand."

Harris couldn't contain his pleasure over what he had just heard, first from Mori, and now from Slick. "Fuck yeah, Slick," Harris exclaimed as he pumped his fist into the air and gave Mori a nod of affirmation.

Marino looked at Harris and shook his head just enough to communicate to his friend that he didn't want him trying to influence anyone by making outbursts. He finally asked Purnell for his contribution.

Purnell grabbed his head in his hands and twisted his neck in an effort to crack it. Then he weighed in with his own opinion. He didn't bother trying to make eye contact with any of his peers, instead he looked only at the sergeant. He took an extra few seconds to gather his thoughts before speaking.

"Hey, I sat at home for over a week before I decided I had to get over here to do something. Turns out we can't do much for the citizens around here, but I didn't come all of the way over here just to turn around and leave. I say we make a stand here and defend this fucking place. If we bug out of here we'll have to hear about that for a long time from these fucking gangbanger savages—and you all know it." Now he took a few seconds to make eye contact with his fellow deputies.

"Oh yeah; one more thing," he added. "I saw how out of control things have gotten everywhere--or at least everywhere between here and where I live--and it ain't no fuckin' joke. I almost got taken out while trying to get here by some gangster assholes. Bottom line is that I think it would be more dangerous to try to leave here than it would be to stick it out here. I'm just sayin'..."

Marino, trying to think if there was anything else he should be bringing up to the group before ending the meeting, took the time to look directly at everyone present, one cop at a time.

"Alright then, is there anything else that anyone wants to say about any of this?"

Seeing no response, Marino rendered the verdict as though he were announcing information no more important than tomorrow's weather report. "Everybody here got the chance to make their case. Looks like we're staying put. If you haven't already done so, make sure you have your pockets, or whatever, loaded up with as much ammo as you can hold. I got no doubt whatsoever that we got one serious shit-storm headed our way."

Nobody said a word. Anderson blinked rapidly and forced her eyes open wide in an effort to ward off her nascent tears as she began walking away from the gathering. No sooner had she placed her back to her fellow cops than she was forced to accept defeat in her efforts to hold back her tears. She used the side of her index finger to brush away the wetness from her cheeks while making her way to her security post. But she held herself erect and otherwise showed no weakness.

"Fuck," Gattuso said to no one in particular. No chuckle this time.

The normally happy-go-lucky patrolman was pissed off. He looked at the ground and first cracked his knuckles, followed by his neck, before following Anderson without uttering a sound to her or the others. The group had all voiced their opinions and the informal vote would stand for all of them. As far as he was concerned, they didn't have to like it, they just had to do it. It was a fact of paramilitary life he had become accustomed to long ago as an LASD deputy sheriff.

37

CULVER CITY, CA

The first thing Vangie did after telling her husband how glad she was to see him and have him safely back at home was to address the travel weary men's needs. She didn't press Don for information about what had happened or where he had been over the past few weeks. There would be plenty of time for all of that later. It was illustrative of her kind nature, which had won Don over and culminated in marriage decades earlier.

Don considered himself a lucky man to have found such a truly kind woman to spend the rest of his life with. Of course it was a reciprocal relationship. Don had been a conscientious husband and diligent provider for his family throughout the marriage. This was not to suggest that the couple had enjoyed a marriage completely free of turbulence. Like most matrimonial arrangements, it had contained a few stretches of rough road, but the couple had always cared about each other, and looked out for each other, no matter what.

Don mentioned that he and Rob had been traveling together for the past several days and that it hadn't been easy for them. He added that Rob was a policeman trying to make it home to his family out in Thousand Oaks. He promised to give Vangie more details about everything in a few minutes after they had settled inside the house.

"You guys go and sit down at the counter while I go find some food to heat up. I know you both have to be starving. C'mon and sit down. You both need to rest. Do either of you want water? Of course you do. That was a dumb question I guess," Vangie said.

She provided them both with a pleasant smile that made Rob feel comfortable. He knew there would be a few things to address here to help the couple out before he got on his way and continued with his journey to his own home, but for the time being he was thankful for the respite the home offered.

Rob untied the shotgun from his pack and leaned the weapon against the corner wall where he could get to it quickly. He dropped his pack onto the tile hallway floor after getting approval from his friend. He took in a breath and exhaled audibly. Don placed his walking stick against the wall in the foyer, and then removed the makeshift sheath and machete from his belt. As he placed the machete next to his walking stick, his wife took a long look at it. Then she let her eyes wonder over to where Rob had set down his pack inside of the front door seconds earlier. She took in the *Kabar* machete taped to the pack's shoulder strap and then glanced at the shotgun in the corner.

Don limped over to a granite counter top that was located opposite of the kitchen's electric cooking range and pulled out a stool that was tucked beneath it. He sat down on the stool and pointed to an identical stool next to his and said to Rob, "Have a seat buddy. Take a load off."

Rob tentatively followed suit. He was a little apprehensive about using any of the food supplies of the McNair household given the scarcity of food everywhere, but his hunger won out over his manners and altruism.

Vangie picked up a clear glass carafe from the kitchen counter and filled two glasses with water. She set one in front of Rob and the other in front of Don. Both men lifted their respective glasses and chugged down the quenching substance without stopping for air. Don's wife watched them and then retrieved the carafe and refilled their glasses. This time they took a little more time to drink the water. Rob finished his completely and Don left a small amount.

Don asked Vangie, "How are we doing on our water supply by the way?"

She answered, "We're doing okay I guess. You know how you always tease me about storing water. Well I'm sure glad I kept those extra big bottles of drinking water in the garage now. I always thought it would be good to have in case of an earthquake, but I never thought we would have no water--and a power outage--that lasted this long."

Don and Rob exchanged a look. Both were sure she wasn't aware of the magnitude of the grid crash. Rob decided to take a back seat and do whatever Don thought was best. He kept quiet, waiting for his friend to indicate how he wanted to play this. Don said nothing.

He eventually felt the need to address his wife.

"Honey, there's a whole bunch of stuff we need to talk about. I don't even know where to start really. But here's as good a place as any I guess. But before I start in on this stuff, can I get some Advil or Motrin? I could use four of them for my knee if you wouldn't mind getting 'em for me."

"What happened to your knee?"

A frown appeared as she asked the question.

"Oh it's just sore from all the walking I've been doing I guess. It'll be okay. Don't worry."

While she went into the bathroom to look for the ibuprofen, Don looked at Rob without speaking, looking to get a quick read on his friend.

"Well, I guess we can relax a little bit now, huh?"

Rob rolled his shoulders and tilted his head side to side to stretch his neck before answering his friend.

"I'm not so sure we can afford to relax too much right now to tell you the truth. First thing in the morning we should probably get busy looking around here to see what your situation is--after we get a good night's sleep." He looked at his watch and saw that it would be dark in about an hour.

Don's wife returned and gave Don the ibuprofen. He downed them with the remaining water in his glass. He decided to forge ahead with his questions.

"Hey honey, have there been any problems since all the power went out besides none of the electrical stuff working? I'm talking about criminal things or any other serious stuff like that. Has anyone that doesn't live here been hanging around the house or the yard? Anyone coming to the door asking for stuff--anything like that?"

She shrugged her shoulders and said, "No; not that I know of. I talked to Jerry next door the day after the power went out, and he's checked on me every few days since then. On the second and third day after the power went off there were a couple of times where someone came and knocked on the door, but I didn't answer it. Why are you asking about that? Have there been a lot of criminal things going on? I know the neighbors are guarding the street now, but I figured they were just being extra careful."

Don stole a quick glance at Rob and said, "Vangie, this isn't just a normal power outage. You already figured out that your car won't start and your cell phone doesn't work, right?"

She nodded.

"Yeah, I was wondering about that. And the regular phone doesn't work either. Jerry was asking me about that too. What does it mean?"

She looked at Rob and said, "Jerry's been our neighbor for ten years or more. He's an engineer of some kind."

"He's an electrical engineer," Don interjected.

"Yeah. Anyway, he had a funny look on his face when I told him my car wouldn't start and my cell phone wouldn't work. He looked kinda worried I'd say."

Don explained to Vangie what he knew about EMP, including why he—and Rob—were convinced the current situation had been caused by an electromagnetic pulse. He also explained why he feared the infrastructure repair might take a very long time. He decided to hold back what he knew to be true about the absence of police, and how this was contributing to the lawlessness permeating the region.

Rubbing his knee in an effort to alleviate some of the discomfort, Don told Vangie how he and Rob had linked up with each other. He mentioned they had encountered a few run-ins with bad guys along the way, but the savvy husband intentionally avoided providing any specific detail. He wasn't sure if he would ever feel comfortable sharing certain specifics with her, but he damn well knew he didn't want to do so now. No way. This whole thing was going to be stressful enough for her.

"Well I'm sure as hell glad nothing happened here at our place anyway. I can say this much: there's a lot of ugly stuff going on out there right now. We're all on our own for the time being."

After a quick glance to read his wife's reaction, he went on.

"We need to think about that in everything we do now until things get back to normal. We're gonna have to start doing a whole security routine around here from now on too. Rob can help us out with getting set up for some of that."

He looked at Rob for a little support.

Rob responded without hesitation. "Oh yeah. Of course. We can take a look at everything first thing tomorrow morning if that works okay with both of you."

Vangie offered encouragement.

"At least we have the neighbors out there making sure no strangers come down our block, right?"

It was now her turn to seek affirmation of her point as she looked at Don and then Rob. The two men exchanged looks, both of them recalling the conflict that had taken place between Rob and the one block security man. Rob promised himself to make it a point to find the man and try to smooth over any hard feelings. He realized he was performing a valuable function and that Rob, as a visitor to the block, should have been a bit more passive.

"Yeah, that's definitely a good thing they're doing," Don said.

Rob brought up the issue of water usage and availability. He looked at Vangie and said, "I hope this doesn't come across as offensive, or too personal, but I have a question for you."

She encouraged him to go ahead.

"Almost everyone we've seen lately has looked like you'd expect them to after no running water for hygiene for weeks. You seem like you've been able to avoid that. So I'm curious; you don't have running water here, do you?"

"I've been using the water in the spa to wash up with and the *Sparkletts* water in the garage for drinking and brushing my teeth.

Sitting in the bathtub and pouring warm water over myself with a bucket." She pointed to the plastic bucket on the counter.

Rob wrinkled his nose upon hearing this. The method she had described was not the most efficient way to use the precious water. He made a mental note to see if he could come up with a better system using items commonly kept in the garages of men who were handy.

"Let's talk about this after I get you two some food. You must be starving, right?"

Don laughed.

"I think it's safe to say we've been pretty close to starving for the past two weeks." He patted his stomach, now much smaller than when he had left his house to go to work weeks ago. He guessed that he had lost close to twenty pounds since he had last seen his wife.

Vangie disappeared for a minute and came back out to the kitchen with two large cans of stew. She had set up a two burner *Coleman* camping stove on the kitchen counter top that used a small propane bottle for fuel. She poured the contents of both cans into a medium sized cooking pot and placed it onto one of the stove's burners.

"You guys don't mind eating your stew from the cans that it came out of do you? I want to save water by not having to clean soup bowls."

"No problem at all. I'm just grateful to have a warm meal. It's nice of you to feed me the way I see it. By the way, that's a pretty nice little camp stove you got there. Do you have extra propane bottles for it?"

Don answered the question for her.

"We have a half dozen or so in the garage but I don't know if they're still good. They're probably twenty years old or more."

Rob said, "Propane doesn't go bad. The stuff stores indefinitely-- as long as it doesn't leak anyway. Those propane bottles will be usable long after we're all dead."

Rob forced himself to eat the warm stew slowly. It required all of his discipline not to wolf it down like some wild animal. He thought of an old saying he had first heard from a buddy of his while eating a simple meal seated beside a campfire in the back country a decade earlier: *Hunger is the best spice.*

Vangie picked up a plastic bucket from the kitchen counter that she had partially filled with water from the spa. She had created a simple system for cleaning cookware. As long as she had the camp stove to make hot water, the rest was really pretty easy.

As soon as both men had finished eating, Vangie suggested they all go into the living room. Rob selected a wooden chair so as not to soil the furniture. As the natural light began to fade, Vangie lit two candles on the coffee table

All three watched the small flames, enjoying the prehistoric source of comfort. Vangie broke the silence.

"How do you think the kids are doing? I'm pretty worried about them."

The couple had a single son living in Reno, Nevada, as well as two married daughters in Denver and Miami. Don shrugged his shoulders.

"I have no idea honey. We'll just have to wait till some sort of communication is back up and then we'll find out how they're doing. But there's no point in stressing about it now. There's nothing we can do."

His response did little to ameliorate her concerns, and it was pretty obvious.

After spending some more time discussing the dire situation they all faced, as well as outlining what they wanted to address the next day, it was decided it was time to call it a night.

"Do you have a flashlight, Rob?"

"Oh yeah; I'm good in that department."

He tapped his shirt pocket holding the little LED light to make sure it was still there.

Using a flashlight to illuminate her path, Vangie gathered some bedding from a closet and handed it to Rob.

"I have a favor to ask. I don't want to get this blanket dirty. Or the couch either. So can you please use the sheet under your blanket? I can wash the sheet a lot easier than the blanket. I'm sure you understand, right?"

Rob gave her a sheepish smile and said, "I got it. I was hoping to use a little of that spa water tomorrow in fact. I know I'm pretty ripe. I'll be careful of what I touch tonight."

"Don's going to use some of that spa water tonight before he gets into bed. I don't care how tired he is," she said.

They both laughed. Don, who was still seated in the living room, retorted, "Yeah, yeah. Whatever. I don't give a shit." He laughed too.

They agreed to get up at dawn to get an early start. Rob said he had been waking up at dawn every day since the EMP, so he promised to wake the couple as soon as he was up.

Rob retrieved his shotgun and ensured that it was loaded. Handing it to Don, he said, "I'm sure you still remember how to use this right?" He regretted saying that as soon as the words left his mouth. He hoped Vangie didn't catch the reference and start asking questions.

"Yeah; I know how to use that thing. Learned in the Boy Scouts."

Rob thrust the sawed-off twelve gauge, muzzle pointed at the floor, toward Don. He grasped it firmly, and as he took it from Rob's hand said, "Thanks buddy. I hope I don't need this tonight."

"You won't, but just in the off-chance that I'm wrong, I figure you should have it handy. I still got my handgun to keep me company. If anything does happen, just call out so I know it's you."

"Alright. By the way, there's another job I need to add to tomorrow's list. Got a hunting shotgun that needs to be modified. We can check it out tomorrow, like I said. G'night buddy. By the way, thanks for helpin' me get home."

"Hey man, you helped me get this far too. G'night."

All through the night Rob tossed and turned in his temporary bed. In his dreams he relived the bloody ambush he had orchestrated and carried out. As strange dreams are often wont to do, his vivid nightmares included a nonsensical combination and juxtaposition of people and events. In this case it involved an intermingling of the would-be robbers he and Don had slain and the faces of violence victims he had encountered over the last decade as part of his job. He woke up sweat drenched and in mental agony several times before the merciful arrival of dawn.

38

UNINCORPORATED SOUTHEAST

LOS ANGELES

Following the decision to remain at the sheriff's station despite the certainty of an imminent attack, Marino asked Mori and Cruz to spend some time reviewing weapons familiarization and tactical skills with all of the deputies. Both eagerly agreed and spent the next hour and a half going over the basics with each cop, including Marino.

This review and familiarization included combat loading, malfunction clearing procedures, and handgun transition drills. They spent some time reviewing basic emergency medical procedures for combat wounds as well. Each and every one of the patrol deputies was willing to go over the refresher training without complaint. In fact, both Mori and Cruz thought the intensity of the attention given to them by their fellow patrol cops was unprecedented. Nothing like being made aware of an impending shit storm to motivate a guy.

That evening Gattuso and Anderson were performing guard duty at the front of the station. The stocky man and tall athletic woman were positioned behind the improvised barricade of patrol cars. Marino had been reluctant to assign the two deputies together at the same post given the recent development of their personal relationship. He soon changed his mind after realizing that by assigning the couple together, each of them could focus on the duties without being distracted with worry about the other's well-being. It wasn't ideal, but it was better than the alternative.

Regardless of the fact both were experienced street cops--and that each had more than proven themselves--they were now a recognized couple. And as such, Marino preferred not to have them posted at a possible breach location for an attack. He would've been hard pressed to explain why he had this reluctance, but the fact was that he did.

Marino had used the practice of rotating sentry positions every day in an attempt to minimize complacency, and he was satisfied with the way this system seemed to be working. In assigning the couple to the front of the station tonight, Marino had taken into consideration that the warning note in the bottle had specified the attack would occur on Friday night or early Saturday morning. Tonight was only Thursday. Not only that, the sergeant suspected the attack, if it materialized, would likely target the back of the building simply because it would likely be considered more vulnerable.

Gattuso, who was feeling somewhat irritable this evening for a number of reasons--not the least of which was the way the recent meeting had gone down--began complaining to his girlfriend and fellow deputy about the latest attack warning.

"I mean what the hell is this so-called big threat all about anyway? I think the whole thing might be just bullshit meant to try to get us to leave the station, ya know? Like when a kid in high school calls in a bomb threat."

Anderson suspected that he was mostly trying to convince himself that the threat against the station, and all of the ugly possibilities it presented, was nothing to get overly worried about. He probably wanted to assuage her concerns as well. Both he and Anderson had weighed in with their preference to at least consider making a plan to leave the station and to head out for a safer location, but they had been out-voted. And they had to accept it.

Anderson responded to Gattuso with a voice close to a monotone, and a facial expression to match. It conveyed a deep resignation. An acceptance of the inevitable.

"I don't think the threat is bullshit at all. Remember that automatic weapons fire and those RPG rounds that were fired at the helicopter when it took off? That was as real as it gets. That wasn't bullshit at all."

Gattuso looked at Anderson. The late spring Southern California early evening was going to provide enough natural light for him to visually enjoy his statuesque girlfriend for another hour at least. He considered himself a lucky man, despite the current circumstances.

"Yeah, I guess you're right," he said.

"I guess I'm just tired of all this threat shit, and how the sarge is making us carry all of this extra stuff." He emphasized his complaint by reaching back with his open hand and lightly tapping the barrel of the shotgun that hung suspended behind him with its muzzle just below his left buttocks.

He changed the subject.

"Cindy, I was thinking. When things get back to normal again, let's get a place together that's not far from the beach. With both of our salaries combined we could afford a place in the South Bay somewhere--no problem."

Anderson--whose love for the ocean and its related sports was well known--revealed a broad smile that practically removed all traces of her boyfriend's bad mood.

"You know what? I think you're right. We could do that, couldn't we?"

The two of them began working out the numbers of the estimated rent and their monthly incomes. This evolved into a discussion about what shifts they would work, the days off they would be able to get, and even the possibility of transferring to a sheriff's station that had lower levels of activity, even if it meant less overtime income. Love was an interesting thing indeed.

The discussion served as a temporary respite from the ugliness that surrounded them. They were enjoying the distraction when the first RPG round struck the hood of one of the patrol cars serv-ing as a barricade, bounced off without detonating, and then struck the cinderblock wall that formed the front wall of the station. The grenade had failed to explode, either because it was faulty from the time of its manufacture or because it had been compromised over time somehow.

Anderson had asked Harris, a former Marine, all about RPG's after witnessing the failed attack on the DHS helo several days earlier. After listening to Harris's patient explanation, she had gained enough knowledge about the RPG weapon system to immediately recognize the rocket propelled grenade's white contrail when she first saw it screaming toward their location. She also immediately figured out that the grenade had failed to detonate for some reason. Anderson yelled out "RPG attack" as she headed for the station's entrance hoping to reach relative safety.

Gattuso didn't immediately recognize the significance of what had just happened. He stared at the grenade lying on the ground for a full second or two as he sought to connect the dots in his mind. This was a hell of a long time in a combat scenario. He now realized that the threatened attack was in fact underway.

To make matters even worse, as he turned to follow Anderson, now only feet from the front door of the building, a second rocket propelled grenade was inbound. It exploded with its full payload into the external front wall of the station, not ten feet from Anderson.

The violent explosion killed the statuesque female deputy sheriff instantly and therefore painlessly, but it nonetheless did so in an extremely ugly manner. Chunks of what had been her beautiful body, sheriff's uniform, and miscellaneous equipment were sent in many directions following the explosive blast. Some of this debris found its way to Gattuso, showering him with the physical evidence of her murder. Gattuso suffered non-debilitating injuries to his face and both legs, much of which was the result of small chunks of steel from Anderson's weapons, concrete, and bone matter, all of which served as shrapnel.

Mori, instantly reacting to the RPG attack from his rooftop position after concluding the first grenade had struck the station without detonating, dropped to the rooftop and flattened himself out. He quickly crawled over to the fighting position he had concocted out of doubled up plastic garbage can liners filled with dirt and stacked in a U-shaped configuration. He arranged himself in a prone position behind his sandbagged fighting position, his rifle barrel protruding through a gun port he had designed with his placement of dirt filled bags. He now busied himself with trying to pin-point the source of the RPG attack.

C'mon motherfuckers—show me a sign as to where you are. I got somethin' for your ass.

He wanted badly to see the asshole who had fired the damn thing and to take him out, but that didn't happen. He had to settle for what he could get. And what he got was about a ninety percent certainty that he had seen the apartment building from where the grenade had been launched. The wiry deputy told himself that he simply couldn't take the chance of allowing the grenadier to continue launching grenades. He had to do whatever he could to shut down that capability. So he began firing the powerful .30 caliber rounds from his Springfield Armory M1-A rifle at the apartment where he believed the grenade's vapor trail had originated.

Mori fired the rifle at a rate of about one round every three to four seconds, using just enough time to get a decent sight picture before firing again at the apartment located approximately two hundred yards away. He fired at the apartment in question in this manner for approximately a full minute, trying his best to place his rounds on the lower third of the wall in hopes of hitting the grenadier. Due to the distance, he was unaware that he had decorated the apartment's exterior wall with numerous bullet-caused pock marks.

By the time Gattuso had processed what had happened to Anderson, another five seconds had elapsed. Pure red anger and pitch black hate enveloped him. The short powerful cop bellowed his rage and emotional pain like a wounded bull elephant as he swung his shotgun, until now only carried reluctantly, around from his back so that he could make use of it. Pushing the safety off with his trigger finger, he threw the tactical scattergun up to his shoulder in preparation for firing. He, like the rest of the deputies remaining at the station, carried the weapon with the chamber hot and the six round magazine fully loaded. Now he frantically looked for a target to engage as he scanned the area in front of the building.

A couple of skinny African-American teenagers in t-shirts looking in his direction with shocked expressions. They looked confused and scared shitless. No good as targets. A middle-aged Hispanic woman with a torn plastic garbage bag. No good. Scan, man, scan. Gotta find a fucking target! Someone has to pay for this shit! Gimme a fuckin' target is all I ask!

Unlike his friend and fellow patrol cop below him, Mori was not in a near blind state of rage. In fact, he was operating in a very business-like manner. Just doing what he did during lots of his spare time, except now it was for real. When the powerful rifle's magazine was empty, he rapidly and expertly swapped it out with a fresh one and got back to work.

Not more than several seconds after the second grenade blast had killed Anderson, Gattuso saw the attackers heading straight for the front of the sheriff's station at a run. At a glance he estimated there were at least a dozen of them, mostly black and Hispanic men in their twenties and thirties. A white guy with a full beard was in the group as well. Gattuso found that odd, but only spent a fraction of a second acknowledging the fact.

Each of the men carried a Kalashnikov rifle with the trademark curved thirty round magazine protruding from its underside. The men wore the battle dress uniform trousers that were similar in appearance to the standard issue for both military field units and police tactical teams. Each of the BDU trousers had the older woodland camouflage pattern comprised of green, brown, and black colors. The cargo pockets of the pants all appeared to be packed full with unknown items. Some of them wore boots and others wore black sneakers.

They also wore basic combat chest rigs that were secured against their bodies with flat two inch wide straps that went over their shoulders and crossed over in the back making an "X" pattern. They were the simple battle rigs that are ubiquitous among second and third world soldiers and revolutionaries. They housed multiple rifle magazines, and not much else. Everything they needed and nothing they didn't need.

As he watched the assaulters approach at a run from a distance of about thirty five to forty yards, Gattuso waited behind one of the cars being used as part of the barricade. He wanted to let them get close enough so that he could really get full effect from the buck shot blasts. He tried to keep his bubbling rage from erupting prematurely as he waited for the attacking men to get within twenty five yards of him..

The attack force had begun using a variation of a basic *leap frog* technique as they approached the station. Some of the group knelt on one knee and took up firing positions before unleashing cover fire for their comrades, while the others went forward at a pace approximating a slow jog. Then they swapped roles with the latter group providing cover for the former as they pressed forward. It was somewhat slow but it was proving itself to be effective as it forced Gattuso to hunker down behind his barricade much of the time while rounds were coming at him.

The deputy-turned-berserker began firing at the assaulters as they came within range. He aligned the front bead of his shotgun barrel on the middle of an attacker's chest, fired, racked a new round into the chamber, aimed and fired, and then racked another round in before aligning the bead again and firing. He was possessed with the desire to destroy as many of the assaulters as possible, no matter the risk to himself. He didn't give a flying fuck about cover—he only wanted to inflict maximum lethal damage in as short a time as possible. He used a method of shooting three rounds, then loading three more shells into the weapon's magazine tube to replace the fired rounds before repeating the cycle. His plan was simply to continue this drill till he ran out of ammo for the shotgun.

The Italian-American cop was actually amazed at how undramatic the shotgun rounds were as they struck the men running toward him. Four of the assaulters fell hard to the pavement as he shot them, while one seemed to shirk off the visible impact and continued to charge.

Body armor, he thought. *Son of a fucking bitch whore!*

He also noticed the man wearing the body armor was the white guy with the beard. He had no time to ponder the significance of this, if there was any. His state of rage wouldn't allow him to spend any thought on the issue in any case. He only wanted to destroy everything and everyone he could at this point. He was operating in a mental condition close to a semi-blind fury. In his revenge seeking and frenzied state, coupled with the fact he was convinced he was going to spend the last minutes of his life right where he stood, he began yelling at the terrorists as he fired his shotgun as fast as he could.

"Come try to take me you fucking savages! C'mon you sonsabitches; come get me! I'm gonna kill every one of you! C'mon!"

He continued to shoot his shotgun at the assaulters while yelling at the top of his lungs. Shooting, working the shotgun's slide, shooting, thumbing more shells into the magazine, shooting again. It was all muscle memory, somehow working despite the blind rage that engulfed the brain providing the memory.

A .30 caliber bullet fired from one of the Kalashnikov rifles struck Gattuso in the left forearm, completely shattering the bones and turning the deputy into a single-armed combatant. The impact felt like a sledge hammer hitting him. He quickly looked down at his seriously damaged forearm and the thick blood pumping out of the wound. It was a painful wound to be sure, but more than that it was frustrating for the broken hearted modern day berserker. He bellowed out his rage and frustration to not only the attackers but to the world in general.

He saw his wrist and hand were now swinging unsupported in a bizarre manner that would have turned his stomach under normal circumstances. His forearm was attached to the rest of his arm by nothing more than skin and a few mangled tendons. More importantly, he could no longer operate his shotgun's slide. Gattuso was operating on nothing but sheer rage at this point. He had accepted he was going to die and only wanted to wreak as much damage as possible upon those responsible for his pain.

He awkwardly reloaded his shotgun with the six extra shells stored along the side of the weapon's receiver. He was forced to use his uninjured right arm to operate the shotgun's slide by slamming the butt of the weapon against the ground as he held the slide. He fired three more rounds using this method before concluding that it was just too slow. The assaulters would be at his barricade any second now. He dropped the shotgun and yanked his Beretta 9mm pistol from its holster and began shooting with his good arm.

At least nine of the original terrorist attack force reached the patrol cars forming the barricade. Gattuso shot one more of them with multiple rounds from his pistol a fraction of a second before he himself was shot again. The shot terrorist hit the cement hard, never to rejoin the battle. Three of the attackers fired at the collapsing deputy, fingers holding down the triggers of their fully automatic rifles as he continued to curse them and fire his Beretta. Only a few of the rounds actually struck Gattuso due to the muzzle climb associated with the terrorists' uncontrolled fire. But, unfortunately, it was enough.

The seriously wounded deputy, now slumping to the ground as his body pumped out valuable life sustaining blood, was no longer bothering with trying to acquire a sight picture. In fact he wasn't even bothering with placing his front sight on his targets. He simply pointed his pistol muzzle at one last bad guy and continued to shoot as fast as he was able, the expended brass casings bouncing off the ground serving as testimony to the desperate yet inadequate effort of the dying deputy.

The slide of Gattuso's handgun locked open on the weapon's empty chamber as he absorbed five rounds that penetrated his body armor and then his lungs. Then four more rounds also passed through his vest before tearing a large chunk out of his heart and ending his life as he curled into a fetal position on the ground, less than ten feet from what remained of his dead girlfriend.

While this was happening, the third RPG round was launched at the station. This time it came from a different apartment unit that was located adjacent to the unit where the first two RPG rounds had originated.

Gattuso spent the last few seconds of his life on the pavement watching the distinctive contrail that signaled the arrival of another devastating grenade. Unable to actually see where the grenade was going to impact, he heard the grenade detonate somewhere above the building's roof behind him just before he died.

Mori's outstanding rifle work had delivered impressive results in the beginning stages of the attack. Although he had no way of knowing it, his well-disciplined and accurate fire had actually killed the grenadier who had begun the attack on the Nadeau Sheriff's Station, as well as damaged the grenade launcher itself, rendering it inoperable. He similarly had no way of knowing that as the original grenadier lay dead on the apartment floor with a sizable portion of his thoracic cavity destroyed, another RPG trained grenadier armed himself with the second of the two RPG launchers and prepared to take over the deadly attack from the adjacent apartment unit. What Mori did know was that a well-armed assault force of bad guys was going to be breaching his sheriff's station any second now.

Forced to make a decision to either continue firing at the apartment unit hiding the RPG grenadier or start firing at the attackers rushing the station with Kalashnikovs, Mori did what one would expect of a man who had made tactical thinking a major part of his professional life.

Mori had been taught, and had in fact instructed many others, to address the most immediate threats--or largest threats--first when engaged in a combat scenario. Given the fact the assault force of Kalashnikov bearing men was going to reach the station entrance in a matter of seconds, he responded to his training and shifted his attention from the grenadier's apartment to the attackers below him. It was a judgment call.

In a split second the LASD rifleman climbed out from behind his sand-bagged fighting position, went down to one knee, and swung the muzzle of his rifle toward the ground below him in preparation to start dropping as many of the assaulters as possible before they breached the building.

Mori observed one of the men--a bearded white guy at the front of the assault force-- throw his arm forward and command the others to hurry up and breach the station. The attackers were almost at the barricade of inoperable patrol cars when Mori began firing his Springfield M1-A. He acquired a fast sight picture, fired, then immediately acquired another sight picture, and fired again. The devastating impact of the high velocity .30 caliber rifle rounds dropped both of the assaulters immediately in their tracks, spraying an ugly wet cloud of human debris several feet beyond each of the targets in the process.

The destructive consequences of Mori's rounds on the terrorists were so severe that several of the slain men's comrades considered halting their attack, turning, and fleeing for their own safety. However, the bearded man with the body armor, sensing the possibility of a collective loss of will among the attackers, made it clear he would shoot anyone who wavered from pressing forward with the attack. The assault proceeded as planned despite the casualties suffered by their ranks.

The intensely focused Mori spent another second and a half trying to find his third target among the assault force before once again establishing a quick sight picture and firing. This time he hammered the attacker in the hip, sending bone fragments, blood, and miscellaneous tissue into an explosive mist beyond where he fell. He went down hard, his rifle clanging along the pavement as he did so. He screamed and moaned for close to a half minute before finally passing out and eventually succumbing once and for all to the massive blood loss and trauma caused by the large high velocity bullet.

Mori had fired fourteen rounds from the latest magazine he had loaded into his rifle when he saw the tell-tale contrail of the third RPG round screaming toward the station.

"Shit," was all he said. In a fraction of a second, from his rooftop position, his mind began registering events that were happening in front of him. It was all playing out in slow motion for him. Gattuso had been hit hard by numerous rounds as more than a half dozen bad guys, each wearing chest rigs and carrying AK-47 rifles, cleared the makeshift barricade. He also registered that Gattuso was falling to the ground and folding into a fetal position. But what really impacted Mori the most was the fact he could find no more targets to shoot. In that split second the remaining assaulters had passed through his field of fire due to the angle of the roof. Although he had depleted their numbers, he had failed to stop them.

In this instance, the protocol established by Mori's training had, in a sense, betrayed him. He had only been able to lessen the number of assaulters entering the station by a few and yet when he ceased firing his rifle at the apartment unit he had unwittingly allowed the second RPG grenadier to get comfortable enough to fire the well-aimed round that would take his life.

This time the RPG grenadier aimed his weapon at the rooftop location where the deadly rifleman who had killed his fellow grenadier, and almost killed him, was located. Once again the familiar contrail of the RPG arced through the air and then the grenade exploded eight feet from where Mori knelt as he unsuccessfully tried to find another terrorist to shoot. The grenade killed him instantly with its violent explosion.

The first assaulter to reach the station violently kicked what was left of Anderson's body out of the way to allow easier access for the others streaming up behind him. Six determined men stormed the sheriff's station with weapon muzzles pointed forward, fingers on the triggers, and looking for deputies to shoot.

A second group of assaulters, five in number, and each armed similarly to the men who had attacked from the front, entered the rear parking lot of the station and ran toward the back door. Taking advantage of the distraction caused by all of the gunfire and other combat related noise that had taken place in front of the station, the assaulters attacking from the rear encountered no resistance before reaching the station's back door. They ran past the makeshift barricade outside the rear door without so much as seeing a single deputy sheriff.

Upon realizing the sound of the grenades and close gunfire meant the attack they had been dreading for days was happening tonight--not Friday night--Sergeant Marino ran out of his office with his shotgun muzzle pointed in front of him. He saw the first man enter the station before the assaulter saw him.

The gunman paid for his being slower than the sergeant when Marino's shotgun blast tore a hole in his chest, dropping him onto the floor. Marino chambered a new round before the recoiling muzzle had returned to its original position.

Receiving full benefit from a flood of adrenaline, Marino fired at the second man entering the station, striking him in the chest and neck. He too went down hard. But the next two terrorists, forced to stop in order to get past their dead comrades on the deck, opened up on the big sergeant with their fully automatic Kalashnikovs.

A third blast from Marino's shotgun sent a load of heavy pellets into one of the assaulter's neck and face. The dead man's full auto burst tore up several chunks of linoleum tile but never reached Marino. But the second bad guy's fusillade put a dozen .30 caliber bullets traveling at over two thousand feet per second through Marino's abdomen and chest before the determined sergeant could get off a fourth round. The giant lawman remained on his feet for a few seconds despite being technically dead. He managed to get that fourth round off, achieving gruesome results as it took off half of his killer's face. Marino crashed to the floor.

And that was how quickly the legendary cop's life was taken from him. Just like fucking that. No salutary exit, no good-byes from a grateful citizenry, and no loved ones holding his hand at the side of his bed. Just dead is all.

Harris, in yet another illustration of life's cruel irony, had his pants around his ankles while sitting on the station's garbage bag lined toilet when all hell broke loose at the building's entrance. He frantically secured his trousers, fastened his gun belt, and grabbed his shotgun as two assaulters came through the station's front entrance. The veteran cop came running into the front lobby area with his scattergun pointed in front of him. He was just in time to see his sergeant and good friend crumble to the floor in front of him. His brain blazed with rage.

He fired, cycled, and fired his Remington as fast as he was able while standing over the body of his sergeant. He killed one of the assaulters crouched next to the faceless dead man who had taken his friend's life. But Harris refused to slow down. He thumbed more shells into the tactical scattergun.

Harris was intent on sending as much lead downrange in as short a period of time as possible. He had little concern for accuracy at the moment. From a distance of thirty feet, he pulled the shotgun's trigger six times in less than three seconds, launching fifty four potentially lethal lead balls in the general direction of the bulk of the assault force. He watched two more fall with satisfaction.

Good night motherfuckers. Have a nice ride to hell. Hope to send you some more company shortly.

More attackers poured through the front doors. Harris pulled the extra shells from his weapon's *Sidesaddle*, thumbing them into the magazine as fast as possible, and continued the drill. A couple of pellets from his lead maelstrom struck a terrorist in the lobby, inflicting an arterial leg wound. Unable to tie off the femoral bleeder, the wound cost him his life, and the man's last minutes were pent crawling out of the station trying to find cover away from the battle. Harris found satisfaction in this as well.

End of the road Jack. Fuck you anyway.

He emptied his shotgun as the last three men came rushing through the front door and sought out positions of cover behind counter foundations, steel knee high garbage cans, and whatever else was available. Two of the assaulters sprayed the inside of the lobby with fully automatic fire, while the last to enter was firing in semi-auto mode. He experienced a pain in his left lower leg that was both sharp and heavy at the same time. Felt like a sledgehammer had been used to smash his leg.

God damn it!

He buckled and hit the floor, his leg having betrayed him despite his will to keep on his feet to continue shooting bad guys. He allowed his empty shotgun to hang on its sling as he fought to stand up. He instinctively transitioned to his pistol, forgoing his sights and using only the pistol's slide to line up his targets. No time to even acquire a front sight picture. The unique odor of discharged gunpowder that permeated this part of the building was strong now. He continued shooting. He dropped an empty magazine, pulled a fresh one from a pouch on his belt and slammed it home. He hit the slide release and fired some more rounds as he pulled his body across the floor to a hallway corner wall. It offered virtually nothing in terms of cover, but it did provide some concealment.

The tough and experienced patrol cop had always figured he wouldn't feel much pain if he were ever shot in combat due to the fact that he would be in a highly adrenalized state. He now knew this was bullshit. His leg hurt worse than anything he had ever felt in his life. But it didn't hurt enough to reduce his will to fight. He continued using his pistol to make it rain 9mm bullets all over the barricaded positions of the terrorists.

Time to reevaluate the situation.

He was pondering how much longer the natural lighting provided by the sun would be available when he heard the voices of Big John Purnell and Cruz announce themselves from somewhere behind him. Immediately following their announcements, he heard one or both of their M-4 carbines firing 5.56 mm rounds at a rate of about a round per second as each of the deputies sought to kill, wound, or dislodge the attackers occupying the station's lobby.

Harris took advantage of the cover fire. After removing the empty shotgun slung across his chest and laying it on the floor, he performed a combat magazine change with his Beretta so that it was fully loaded again.

He noticed with his peripheral vision that Slick had entered the fight as well. But Slick was firing his shotgun in the opposite direction from the others. Then he saw why. There were multiple bad guys pushing forward from the rear of the station. And they were firing their Kalashnikov carbines as they pushed forward.

Fuck. Shit-fuck.

Slick was performing a rear guard function, doing his best to literally protect the backs of his fellow deputies as he fired several rounds from his shotgun at the rear of the station. Harris noted with some satisfaction that Slick was now wearing the shotgun shell bandoleer found earlier in Rob Flynn's locker.

Deterred from advancing their attack due to Slick's work with the shotgun, the gunmen who had entered the rear of the building had all taken cover by entering a room off the side of the hallway approximately ten feet inside the back door.

Harris turned his attention back to the front of the station as he rushed to reload his Remington. He saw one of the frontal assaulters had been injured, although he had managed to position himself behind a metal desk, leaving a small blood streak marking his path. He was wondering where the two unaccounted for bad guys were when his question was answered. Both terrorists stood up from behind the same desk their wounded comrade had just crawled behind and began firing in full automatic mode.

Harris heard the Kalashnikov rifles, their bolts making that distinctive "clacking" sound as they travelled rapidly back and forth. It was a sound that, for those who had ever heard it, would never be forgotten. He also heard the sound of Purnell's and Cruz's M-4 carbines firing their semi-auto 5.56mm rounds. He watched as two of the remaining three frontal assaulters were shot in the head at virtually the same time. Small explosions of pink mist and grey matter erupted from the backs of their skulls, bearing undeniable testament to the outstanding shooting capability of both Cruz and Purnell even under these extreme conditions.

What happened next was the kind of event that an atheist would offer as proof of there being no God. At least no God that maintains benevolence and omnipotence as two of His unalterable characteristics. On the other hand, a God fearing man might insist it merely proved that Satan is more than a symbolic character.

The last gunman from the frontal assault group remaining on his feet thrust the barrel of his Kalashnikov around the side of the wall that concealed him. Without aiming whatsoever, he held the trigger down and emptied a thirty round magazine. In the space of a second or two, both Purnell and Cruz were fatally wounded, bullets from the

Soviet designed rifle having smashed through the skull of the latter and the torso of the former.

Purnell refused to give up the ghost for a few more seconds, as he squeezed off several rounds at the man who had taken everything from him. Even in death the big lawman had the discipline to focus on a sight picture. He was rewarded with watching the top of his killer's skull come apart in fragments just before he, like Big John, fell to the ground.

The two well trained and disciplined tactical deputies had just been killed by a man who hadn't even bothered to aim his weapon while holding the trigger down.

Another display of cruel irony, and another shitty break.

Harris, once again in possession of a fully loaded shotgun, fired several shotgun rounds in the direction of the terrorist behind the desk without observable effect. It wasn't until several long moments had passed that he realized the sound of both M-4's had stopped. He looked over and saw that both Purnell and Cruz were dead. Harris also saw that the gunmen who had entered from the rear of the station had stopped their forward movement and presumably taken cover somewhere. He couldn't see Slick.

Having once again run his shotgun dry, Harris flipped the sling over his head and dropped the heavy weapon on the linoleum tiled floor. His leg wound was now bleeding badly. He removed a *Kerlix* medical dressing from his shirt pocket, tore off the plastic covering, and began stuffing pieces of the rolled gauze mesh into the wound. It was ugly. He saw a large chuck of flesh had been torn away from his calf.

When he could fit no more of the gauze material into the wound he reached under his shirt and yanked free the *Becker-Necker* knife from its thermo-plastic necklace sheath, all the while holding his palm against the *Kerlix* stuffed wound. He used the knife to cut the excess gauze protruding from the wound and used the rest of the gauze roll to wrap around his leg several times before tying it off.

Lee Harris, breathing hard and grunting with pain, had little expectation of surviving this gunfight, especially knowing there would be no professional medical help even if he prevailed in the battle itself. But that wasn't why he wanted to stop--or at least slow down--the blood loss from his leg wound. He simply wanted to hold onto his ability to press the trigger for as long as possible. He was determined to kill as many of these sons of bitches as he could.

Keeping his focus on the threats in front of him, he reached into his pocket and began removing shotgun shells. He picked up the shotgun and topped off the magazine.

Harris yelled out, "Hey Slick, where you at?"

Slick, who had moved his position to behind the door jamb in the sergeant's office, thought for a second before responding.

"I'm at Marino's place." Whether it actually provided any tactical advantage or not, he didn't want to spell out exactly where he was by referring to it as "the sergeant's office" for the remaining terrorists to hear.

Harris yelled back, "Copy that. We're the only two left man. Let's just kill as many of these pieces of shit as we can. Make 'em suffer. This is a fuckin' modern day Alamo scenario Slick. Let's go out right on this!"

Harris had spent his entire childhood in Texas. Having listened to many a story detailing the brave last stand of men like James Bowie and Davie Crocket at the historic Alamo Mission, he considered how apropos his reference to the famous battle of 1836 actually was in the here and now. Slick spat a glob of Copenhagen and saliva onto the sergeant's office floor and thumbed several shells into his shotgun as he yelled out in his deep voice.

"You got that right Harris. You got that right for damn sure! Fuck all these punk motherfuckers! We're gonna kill 'em all!"

One of the gunmen from the group who had assaulted through the back of the station began taunting the big African-American deputy from behind wherever he was taking cover. He accused Slick of being an "Uncle Tom" and told him he was a traitor to his people. All the typical baseless bullshit. Slick wasn't affected in the least. But Harris was.

Harris, who heard the taunt clearly from his position, couldn't help but respond with a taunt of his own.

"You know what, shithead, on your very best day you wouldn't rate high enough to wipe that man's ass, you little pussy. You bought into a bunch of bullshit that a ten year old should know better than to believe! That goes for all you sonsabitches here. You just killed some good men and you're gonna pay for that. I'm gonna personally make you pay for it--bad. And I'm gonna piss on you after I kill you too."

With that, Harris silently crawled over to the desk concealing the wounded terrorist, taking extra care to ensure his shotgun barrel was directed at the desk in case the shooter should pop up around his cover. If he accomplished nothing else from this point on, he was determined to kill the bastard behind that desk.

The wounded deputy fought back the nausea that threatened to overpower him as he made his way slowly toward the desk. He dragged his wounded body toward his destination, forcing himself to focus. The terrible combination of freshly burnt gunpowder, blood, and miscellaneous bodily fluids expelled by the wounded and dying now permeated the confined space of the sheriff's station entrance area. The uglier side of close quarters battle.

As most patrol cops assigned to Nadeau Station knew all too well, this was not a pleasant smell under any circumstance, but coupled with the queasiness caused by the pain of his leg wound, the mal-odorous conditions made Harris fight to keep from vomiting. At one point he retched while on route to the barricaded terrorist's position, but he was able to use his rage to regain control of his nausea and continue forward. Anger could be an extremely effective motivating force, and Harris used it to full advantage.

When he reached the desk, he gradually stood, trying his best to ensure his shotgun muzzle would appear at the same time his eyes picked up the terrorist. He didn't want the guy to be aware of his presence until he could shoot. The pain from his wound and the effort of crawling to the barricade elicited an involuntary sound from Harris--something between a grunt and a groan--and he fought back another wave of nausea.

As the Marxist assaulter came into view Harris saw that he was lying supine on the floor bleeding from a small wound to his right hand presumably caused by a shotgun pellet. The gunman also had a leg wound that looked to be less severe than the one Harris had sustained—probably also inflicted by a single shotgun pellet. Neither wound was bleeding very badly despite the fact neither had been bandaged. The man's Kalashnikov rifle was lying on the floor next to him, obviously of no immediate combat value. Apparently the wound to his hand, small as it appeared to be, had rendered the terrorist incapable of operating his rifle. He appeared to have lost his will to fight.

This guy's a fuckin' pussy, Harris concluded. *Well, too fuckin' bad for him.*

He instantly formed a plan. He hoped to take advantage of the terrorist's low pain threshold and lack of commitment in a way that would lure at least one of his comrades from their position of cover. For Harris, at this point it was all about killing as many of these assholes as possible—nothing more.

Abject terror revealed itself in the wounded gunman's eyes as Harris glared at him for a split second. The anger-stoked and resolute deputy held eye contact as he lowered his shotgun's muzzle away from the man's face and shot him in his right thigh, just below the belt line. He knew the leg wound he had just inflicted would likely be fatal within the next few minutes due to massive blood loss. He also knew it would be excruciatingly painful. His only fear was that the man might lose consciousness too quickly. But it was the only plan he could come up with at the time.

The man's screams could be heard throughout the station. The devastating wound had created the desired effect. Harris wasn't moved in the least by the man's agonizing. After having witnessed the murder of several of his friends and having become fully aware he was probably going to die here, he didn't give a damn about the man's suffering. He was in a sort of hell, and he was pretty damn close to being in his element.

Harris yelled out to whomever he had been trading insults with earlier.

"Hey fuckhead, I want you to remember this screaming for the rest of your life in case me or my friend don't get to kill you for some reason, you piece of shit! Since you're too much of a pussy to come help your friend here you can just listen to him scream. If you don't tie off his leg wound he'll be dead in a minute from now. Fuck you and him both, you piece of shit coward!"

Harris left the dying man to deal with his agony alone, his screams and moans a haunting and constant reminder of the hell the sheriff's station had turned into on this day. He waited for a comrade to come and help the agonizing man, but none of them even tried.

Well, so much for this part of the plan, Harris thought. *Doesn't look like I'll be getting a chance to shoot one of the other assholes coming to help him. It was worth a try.*

Frustrated over his failed plan, he yelled again.

"That's what I thought, you cowardly pieces of shit. You're all fucking cowards who let your friend die screaming. Now you all know that when your time comes, your fuckin' pussy friends won't help you!"

Slick, still positioned behind the door jamb of the sergeant's office, couldn't help but crack a smile. Harris was inflicting as much damage on these motherfuckers as he could, right up to the very end. Including psychological damage.

Good for him. Yeah, good for him, Slick thought.

The cowboy stuck his shotgun barrel outside of the sergeant's office and rapidly emptied six rounds in the direction of the bad guys who had entered through the back door and were now taking temporary cover wherever they could find it. He couldn't tell whether any of the fifty plus shotgun pellets he had just launched downrange had done any real damage. He could only hope so at this point.

Slick tugged six more shells out from his bandoleer. The first round went into the shotgun's chamber and he slammed the slide closed before he began refilling the shotgun's magazine, spilling one of the rounds onto the floor in his haste. He quickly took a knee and retrieved the dropped round, making certain to only glance at the floor for the micro second it took to locate the shell. He knew that it was essential for him to keep his eyes on the threat in front of him. He fed the shell into the magazine and prepared to re-engage the bad guys.

Harris looked around at the station floor and saw human bodies, large blood smears, red plastic expended shotgun shells, and other brass ammo casings from weapons fired during the attack on the station. The smells that permeated the building were every bit as ugly. Vomit, feces, urine, and the coppery smell that accompanies large volumes of blood all mixed together to create an evil potpourri that has been associated with battlefields since man first waged war.

He tried to make his way to the sergeant's office, thirty feet away, dragging his damaged leg behind the rest of his prone body, leaving yet one more blood smear to serve as evidence of his heroic effort and path. As he cleared the hallway, less than twenty feet from the sergeant's office, two of the remaining attackers opened up on him with their rifles. He was struck several times, but he returned fire with his shotgun as he was forced to stop all forward movement. He fought hard to avoid blacking out.

I only need a few more seconds...just enough to take out at least one or two more of them. That's all I ask. He pleaded to God, and perhaps to himself, trying to gain extra help from that part of his brain that comprised his will—anyone or anything that would hear and grant his last request.

After firing the last round in his shotgun, rather than attempting to reload it, the dying patrol cop used his left hand to pull the sling over his head and unleash it from his body, leaving it on the floor where it lay.

In an amazingly fast motion given the fact he was dying, Harris used his right hand to pull his Beretta from his belt holster while removing an extra magazine from a pouch with his left. He rapidly emptied the pistol as he fired it in the direction of the remaining gunmen, hit the magazine release allowing the empty magazine to fall free, and then slammed the fresh magazine into the weapon. He released the slide release, picked up a front sight picture only, and continued firing fifteen more rounds as fast as he could pull the trigger.

Harris roughly aimed his shots about a foot to eighteen inches above the floor and into the wall that separated the terrorists from his location in case the assaulters were lying close to the ground. If they were standing, leg wounds would still detract from their ability to fight well. He knew this first hand as he struggled with his own leg wound.

He was also familiar with how the 147 grain 9mm slugs he was firing from his Beretta would perform against two pieces of sheetrock that formed the wall now being used as a barricade by the terrorists. He knew the rounds would penetrate the wall with enough lethality remaining to maim or kill the bad guys. And the more rounds he fired at the approximate area where they were concealed the better the chances of hitting them. So the dying deputy continued firing his pistol as fast as he could, emptying several of the numerous extra magazines he wore on his body at an impressive rate.

Slick, firing from the doorway of the sergeant's office, fired all of the rounds in his shotgun in the direction of the assaulters, dropped the empty weapon, and pulled his Beretta. Grasping an extra pistol magazine in his left hand, he rushed forward from the sergeant's office and continued shooting his pistol at a rate of about one round every second.

Upon reaching Harris, Slick dumped his pistol's empty magazine and slammed the fresh one home. He used his left hand to grab Harris by his shoulder holster harness and began dragging him backward toward the sergeant's office, all the while continuing to fire his pistol with his right hand. Slick was hit twice by rifle fire, but he continued to pull Harris toward the office. But it was too late.

Half way back to the doorway, his body having now absorbed another half dozen rounds, Slick dropped his fellow deputy and friend onto the cheap tile floor. It was nothing short of amazing that he was still alive and able to continue fighting. With a collapsed lung, perforated liver, shattered femur, and a neck wound that was rapidly pumping out vital arterial blood, Slick still managed to empty the last remaining rounds in his pistol in the direction of the men who had taken his life.

Harris also continued to fire his pistol, managing to go through two more full magazines before succumbing to the numerous gunshots that had penetrated his body. Harris and Slick killed two more of the remaining five terrorists before they, like their friends moments earlier, died defending Nadeau Station.

The last three terrorists had now gained complete control of the station, but it was a bitter sweet victory for them at best. Not only had they sacrificed the majority of their assault force to gain control of the sheriff's station, they had acquired a building whose interior now looked and smelled like it belonged in Hell, in a special section reserved for those that deserved the very worst for their evil deeds performed on earth.

39

THOUSAND OAKS, CA

Having gone several days with only enough water to keep marginally hydrated, Rosalyn had been forced to forego using water for hygiene purposes. She wasn't sure how she was going to pull off getting cleaned up for her feigned date later today, but she told herself that she would figure something out.

Upon hearing Rick's announcement about a couple of patrol cops being in the neighborhood, she jumped at the opportunity to forestall her "cleaning up" for the dreaded contact with that scumbag Roger. This was so despite the fact that this time her "cleaning up" was part of the plan to get her revenge. She threw on a simple sweatshirt and a pair of jeans before joining her husband outside. She briefly thought back to when she was a kid and had jumped at any opportunity that would allow her to put off doing her homework.

Rosalyn had exited her front door just as Stephanie and Charlie Wyatt were walking by on the sidewalk. Any discomfort remaining from Stephanie's earlier refusal to share resources evaporated immediately between them. The two women hugged, the mutual embrace providing temporary relief from the present circumstances.

Rosalyn made a decision to confide in Stephanie by sharing everything with her that had happened with Roger. She grasped Stephanie's upper arm with both of her hands and whispered in her ear to ensure that Charlie Wyatt was spared any details he shouldn't hear. Rosalyn told her friend everything except for any mention of the plan to rob Roger. All she said was that sooner or later she was going to take revenge against Roger for what he had done.

It was clear to Stephanie that there weren't a whole lot of avenues of opportunity for revenge in the current situation. She assumed the revenge her friend spoke of would include physical violence. After all, what else was there at this point? Stephanie listened to her, the pain and anger linked to what she had endured obviously still affecting her greatly. She then told Rosalyn that she had watched her leaving the man's house on that day, adding that later that same evening she had surmised what had probably happened.

Without letting go of Charlie Wyatt's hand, Stephanie reached her other arm around Rosalyn's shoulder and pulled the woman into her as they walked. It was a gesture of empathy, but to Stephanie, it felt like her efforts were too little and too late. The truth of the matter was that Stephanie felt a pang of guilt as she reflected on her recent refusal to share her food supplies.

But I had to think of my little boy first. I did the right thing. Why do I feel so bad about my decision?

Stephanie said, "This whole situation is just really bad. You're a survivor. You only did what you had to. You did the hard thing Rosalyn. Don't you ever let anyone tell you that what you did was wrong--not ever. And that includes telling yourself that."

Rosalyn began to get teary-eyed, and she used the tips of her fingers to wipe away the small droplets. Stephanie couldn't help but notice her fingernails were now cut short. It was the first time the woman hadn't had long manicured nails since the two had met.

"Thank you Stephanie," she said in a soft and low voice. The two women and the little boy walked on in silence for a little while, but then Charlie Wyatt began asking questions about the two policemen and their all-terrain four-wheeler he was looking at down the block. It was a welcomed distraction for both women, and Stephanie began to answer her young son's questions with more enthusiasm than was typical for the circumstances.

The two law enforcement officers had come to a stop on the ATV four-wheeler and were dismounting when Rick approached them. He remembered Rob had once told him that cops didn't like it when people got too close to them in public settings. He used this information and stopped when he was about ten feet away from the policemen. Rick looked the four-wheeler over. It looked like it was an older ATV that had seen its share of use over the years. He noticed that it had a five gallon gas can that had been tied to the steel cargo rack located at the rear of the machine.

One of the officers--the older of the pair--was well over six feet tall and lanky. The other, no more than five foot nine, had the appearance of a man who visited the weight pile regularly. Both of the policemen began looking up and down the street and at the houses lining the block. Neither made any effort to hide the fact that they were sizing up the residential street for any possible threats or other information that might prove important. It was obvious both were nervous.

Another neighbor, a rail thin fifty-something year-old white guy who looked like he hadn't showered in a month and had just crawled out from a cave, had also exited his house and was approaching the two uniformed men. He noticed the man smelled of a combination of body odor, booze, and nicotine. He figured the guy had somehow been drinking enough water to survive but had not been using it for hygiene purposes.

Whatever....staying inside and drinking booze and smoking ciga-rettes all day was one way to deal with this catastrophe.

As he waited for the officers to finish performing their cursory check of the neighborhood, Rick spent a few seconds to take the mea-sure of the men. Both of them wore black tactical uniforms similar to those often worn by SWAT teams or other specialty law enforcement team members. Their pants were the loose fitting BDU trousers with large cargo pockets on them, and their shirts were a long sleeved but-ton type made of a material that was the same, or similar to, that of their trousers.

The uniform shirts, both of which were rolled up to the patrol-men's elbows, displayed multi-colored patches on the shoulders that were embroidered with "THOUSAND OAKS POLICE" and some sort of design that was difficult to identify. In addition to their pistols, the cops both had long guns slung across their backs. The taller officer had an M4 carbine and the other carried a pump shotgun with a tactical flashlight.

Rick took in the appearance of the patrol officers. They each wore handguns on their legs and had extra ammunition for their weapons. Looking at the cops and their weapons, he was again reminded of how foolish he had been not to heed Rob Flynn's advice long ago about buying a gun to defend Rosalyn and himself.

Oh well. That's all old history at this point. Just stick with what lies in the road up ahead, not what's in the rearview mirror.

Rick began peppering the officers with questions ranging from what the best estimate was for getting some relief and essential supplies, to finding out about the extent of the damage--both locally and in adjacent cities.

Screwing up his courage, he asked the closer of the partners, "What exactly caused this whole problem anyway? I mean not only did all the power go out, but none of the cars will even start, and the cell phones don't work either. What caused that?"

The officers had been specifically briefed with a directive not to say anything to the public that might increase their apprehension. Like law enforcement personnel anywhere who still had services in place--no matter how minimal--these officers knew that keeping the public as calm as possible was paramount.

Rick noticed the look exchanged between the patrolmen when he asked the question. It was a look that revealed uncertainty as to how best to respond. It was also a look that belied the response.

"We're not really sure how it happened. The power grids can do weird things sometimes. It's taking them longer than usual to repair things."

Rick thought about bringing up the fact they were making their rounds on an all-terrain vehicle that had never been used by the police department before, and the fact it bore no department decals or similar official markings. But he knew enough to leave the ridiculous answer alone.

The reeking neighbor interjected and began to explain to the officers how he had been drinking the water from his house water heater.

He also observed that the policemen clearly felt more comfortable with this neighbor's questions than they had with his. Both were pretending to be interested in the man's inquiries. Rick was listening to the inane questions and wondering how some people had survived in the world as long as they had—even under normal conditions-- when he saw his wife and Stephanie Flynn walking toward him with Charlie Wyatt in tow.

He greeted Stephanie and her son as though everything were fine and there hadn't been an uncomfortable exchange a week earlier. Stephanie addressed the shorter officer and didn't waste any time before identifying herself as the wife of a LASD deputy sheriff. She quickly added that her husband was assigned to the Nadeau Station in South L.A., adding that he hadn't come home since the power had gone out. She tried to hold back her emotions but the mention of Rob's absence for over two weeks had her misting up.

At the mention of Rob's station assignment, the younger officer immediately looked at his senior partner. The younger man didn't have enough experience to have acquired even the most basic ability to conceal his non-verbal communication with his partner. Stephanie caught the look and recognized it immediately for what it was.

"What? What's wrong? Did something happen in South LA?"

The officer brought his discussion with the foul-smelling neighbor to an end and asked him to go home so that he could speak to Stephanie alone. The man looked surprised at first, looking at Stephanie and back again at the tall policeman. He affected being stung by the insult and returned to his home. The same officer asked Rick and Rosalyn to return home, but Stephanie reached out for Rosalyn's hand and told the officers she wanted the couple to remain with her.

Stephanie looked at the senior officer and again asked him what it was that he knew.

"I don't know anything for certain. You need to remember that a lot of the information that's going around now is not exactly accurate. We have a HAM radio operator who brought his portable radio and antenna to the police station and has been set up there for the past week. He gives us updates when he hears information. It's pretty sketchy really. But it's the only way we get any news at all."

The officer stopped for a second to let Stephanie soak in the information before continuing. He reached out and took hold of her arm with both of his hands. He bent his knees to bring his face closer to being eye-to-eye. He slowed the pace of his speech as he continued.

"The HAM operator heard that the Nadeau Sheriff's Station was attacked by a bunch of bad guys several days ago and that most of the deputies there were killed."

Stephanie experienced the blood leaving her head and she felt dizzy all-of-a-sudden. The shorter cop must have seen what she was experiencing and recognized that she was in danger of falling, because he lurched forward and grabbed her free arm to steady her. Both cops assisted her with sitting down on the curb. She looked over at Charlie Wyatt, who was now holding Rosalyn's hand, standing on the sidewalk a few feet away. Stephanie, suddenly visited by a wave of nausea, leaned forward and retched into the gutter. After emptying what little she had in her stomach, she leaned forward and let her head rest on her palms as she sat there and tried to wrestle control of her body.

The senior cop pulled a small notebook from one of the large cargo pockets of his pants and opened it up. He removed a pencil from his shirt pocket and prepared to write in the notebook.

He took down Stephanie's name and address as well as Rob's name. After asking her a few basic questions about what shift Rob had been assigned to and when he had left for work the day of the EMP incident, he closed his notebook and shoved it back in his pocket with one hand while using the other to put the pencil back in his shirt pocket.

"I'll see if I can find out any more info about your husband. No promises as to if I can learn anything more or when we'll be back here next. Obviously everything is still really out of control here and everywhere else, so we just don't know. But I have your address. I'll let you know when I can either way."

Stephanie nodded her understanding, and thanked him, even though she had only comprehended half of what he had said. Her head was buzzing. Then another question came to her.

"Okay, when you say things are bad 'everywhere else', just exactly where are you talking about? How many other areas are affected by this power outage?"

The shorter officer answered her question before the senior man could respond.

"Our HAM radio guy is getting reports from all over the country about cities that are completely shut down. No power, no cars, and no cell phones. None of that. Almost no police or other first responder services either. And the hospitals are pretty much out of service too. It's lookin' pretty ugly."

The three neighbors were taken aback by this revelation. None of them said a word in response. At first there was bewilderment as to how the devastation could have affected such a wide portion of the nation. Then they each tried to figure out what this information meant with respect to their own situations. They were crestfallen as they digested the news and what it meant for their future—immediate and possibly longer.

Stephanie slowly climbed back to her feet with the assistance of the stocky officer. She forced herself to consider the fact that Rob was possibly still alive. He had once indicated in the event of a major earthquake or similar disaster he would turn around and head toward home if he was closer to their house than the sheriff's station. If he was closer to the station, he had told her, he would have to make the judgment call at the time.

Stephanie had no way of knowing what her husband had decided at the time of the major grid crash but she convinced herself that she would have to hold on to hope. If there was any possibility for a guy to figure out a way to survive in this mess, Rob was the man to do it. She held onto that thought like it was a life vest in a stormy ocean surrounding a capsized ship.

Aware that all eyes were now on her, she said, "Rob's okay. I can just feel it. I really think he's alright."

She looked over at the empty lot on the corner with the over-grown weeds and low growing brush where she had dumped the bodies after carrying them in the wheelbarrow. It occurred to her that neither of the officers was even aware of the two dead bodies that she had dumped there. After thinking about it, it was no surprise the corpses had gone unnoticed. The unpleasant and distinctive odor of decaying flesh was something that wafted through the air periodically almost everywhere now. So that wouldn't have aroused their suspicions. And the plant growth in the field holding the bodies easily concealed them from view of the casual passerby.

Stephanie hadn't noticed anyone standing outside of their houses on the night she had dumped the corpses, nor had she observed any windows that didn't have curtains closed behind them. But none of this provided her with any certainty as to whether anyone had been watching her that night. She felt a little nervous now as she stood in the presence of the two uniformed patrol cops.

What if one of the neighbors on the block saw me that night moving the bodies and they decide to come out and tell these police officers about what they observed?

"Are you guys arresting people under the current situation, or are you just driving around checking things out or what? It must be hard for you guys in all this mess."

The senior man looked around briefly before answering, signaling to Stephanie that she was about to hear something that was probably not going to be shared with the general public.

He looked at Rick and Rosalyn, making sure that he had their attention before continuing.

"Okay, here's the situation folks. What I'm going to tell you is not for public information. Understood?"

After getting nods from all three adults present, he went on.

"We were sent out here to make observations and take notes about the condition of things in the city. We're pretty much just cruising through the town--neighborhood by neighborhood--and taking notes so some kind of plan can be made."

He jerked his thumb at the little four-wheeler and said, "This is my own ATV, and I rode it into the station from my house. None of the police vehicles are running. This ATV is an old one and I think that has something to do with why it's still working. I'm not really sure why. I just know that the few vehicles we've seen running have all been old ones."

He went on to answer the rest of Stephanie's original question.

"The only crimes we're making arrests for are the really serious things like murder, serious injury causing assault, and rape. Maybe house burglary. That's pretty much it right now."

"That's kinda what I thought," she replied.

"There's a guy who will probably die from an infected arm wound on the next street over," he said as he pointed behind where he was standing, "but we can't bring him anywhere and there's no help to bring to him. No antibiotics around. Things are really bad right now. Nothing we can do about it."

The patrolman looked at his civilian audience briefly and added, "The other thing we're supposed to take notes on is anyone or any place that has a large amount of food storage. Oh yeah, and swimming pool locations."

He glanced at his partner as if to remind him of the need to identify houses with pools.

Looking at all three of them, he asked which houses on the block had swimming pools. Stephanie held her tongue, not sure why she felt hesitant to answer. No one on her block had pools anyway. It didn't matter.

"You don't happen to know of anyone who has a large amount of food storage in their house, do you?"

Stephanie shook her head back and forth, probably a little too soon and a little too adamantly. She felt a small dose of adrenaline course through her body upon hearing the question. She hoped neither Rosalyn nor Rick was going to mention anything to the policemen about her food storage. And then she thought about the food storage held by the jerk down the block that had traded food for sex with Rosalyn. Stephanie wondered for a moment if either of her neighbors would give that information to the two officers, but neither said a word.

Now that's interesting, she thought. *Why would they conceal the fact that Roger has all that food?*

The idea came to Stephanie like the proverbial bolt from the blue. She began working through the mental process, considering the feasibility of her plan as she stood there watching Rick and Rosalyn chat with the officers. Charlie Wyatt had let go of her hand so that he could get a close up view of the neat and strange looking vehicle the officers had used to get here.

Despite the fact she stood only a few feet from them, Stephanie had no idea what her next door neighbors were discussing with the cops because she was far too busy considering her plan. Finally, she convinced herself that it would work. All she had to do was come up with the courage to go forward with it. And now was the time.

Stephanie approached Rosalyn first. She whispered into her ear, smiling as she did so in the hopes of making her effort at private conversation appear as though it were only girl talk.

"Rosalyn, you gotta trust me on this. No questions till later. First of all, smile like you're almost laughing while you're listening to me so the officers don't get suspicious. Now, think back. What kind of gun was Roger wearing when you saw him last time? Whisper in my ear."

She smiled and spoke into Stephanie's ear, offering a mildly flirtatious look to the cop closest to them.

"I don't know anything about guns, but Rick said it looked like it might have been a Glock."

Stephanie smiled and once again spoke into Rosalyn's ear.

"I need you two to go home. Get Rick to leave with you now. Tell him whatever you need to, just get him home with you. I'll stop by your place in a few minutes."

Rosalyn spoke in Rick's ear, telling him they had to leave immediately. He looked at her with a "what the hell?" expression. She smiled in a way that Rick recognized as being phony and incongruous with what she had just told him. She grabbed his hand and headed off toward their house. Rick thanked the patrolman and smiled, leaving him bewildered as to what had just happened.

Stephanie looked around to see if anyone other than the patrol officers were within earshot. She did this in a manner similar to how the taller policeman had moments earlier, but the irony went unnoticed by either of them. Assured that no one was around, she pressed forward with her plan.

"Those two love birds were in the middle of some romance when you guys rode up. They act like teenagers at times."

She rolled her eyes in an effort to add veracity to her comments.

"It's probably better anyway, because I want to tell you guys about something I saw the other night."

Seeing that she now had the undivided attention of both patrolmen, she continued.

"I saw this man who lives down the street--I think his name is 'Roger'--shoot these two men for no reason in front of his house a few nights ago. Then I watched him drag the bodies up the sidewalk and dump them over there in that empty lot. They're probably still there."

He just stood there and looked at her. Then he glanced at his partner.

"Can you show us exactly where you saw him put the bodies?"

"Well, maybe. Pretty close anyway. I think."

Stephanie began to walk toward the lot but stopped after taking only a couple of steps.

"Uh, I really don't want to walk over there with my son."

Charlie Wyatt looked at her with a puzzled expression.

"It's okay honey. I'll be back in a minute."

The tall patrolman looked at Charlie Wyatt and smiled as he crouched down so that he was almost at eye level with him. He pointed at the four-wheeler.

"Hey big guy, do you want to take a ride on that machine with the other policeman for a few minutes?"

Charlie Wyatt's face lit up in a big smile and then he looked at his mother for her reaction to the offer.

"Yeah, I want to ride on it. Can I Mommy?"

The cop off-handedly mentioned that the large gasoline storage tank in the police station parking lot had plenty of gas but he feared it would go bad because there were no cars running to use the fuel.

"Might as well use the gas up before it goes bad on us. Why don't you take a little ride here son," he said to Charlie Wyatt before looking at Stephanie for her answer.

Stephanie forced a smile that never reached her eyes and agreed to let Charlie Wyatt take a ride with the young officer.

She said, "Please drive slow with him," and then everyone except Charlie Wyatt laughed at the irony of the housewife telling the patrol cop to drive slowly.

Stephanie walked to the empty lot while her son took a ride on a machine unlike any other he had ever seen. She allowed herself a brief moment of happiness as she watched her boy display a wide open smile while riding on the ATV. She stopped short of bringing the uniformed officer all the way to where she had dumped the bodies, instead opting to point her finger and move it over the general area.

"I'm not sure, but I think he put them somewhere around this area," she said.

The officer walked over and began searching the area. He began scanning the lot, moving his head left to right, while Stephanie stayed back about fifty feet and watched him perform his search. It took him less than a minute to locate the bodies.

Stephanie made a show of being disgusted at the officer's discovery and turned to walk back to where the younger officer was pulling up on the four-wheeler. Charlie Wyatt was all smiles and laughter as the patrolman helped him down from the machine. He ran up to Stephanie and began telling her all about his grand adventure in run-on sentences. For the time being he was just a normal little boy experiencing the normal joys attendant to his age.

Noticing that the younger police officer was watching his partner in the empty lot, she began telling him where the man called Roger lived. He asked her to hold on while he pulled out a notebook from his trousers pocket. When he was ready she provided him with Roger's physical description, and that of the gun he wore on his belt. She told him she thought it might be a Glock or something similar.

"My husband has told me a little bit about guns and what some of 'em look like, but I'm really not an expert or anything."

"I understand. Do you know how many shots were fired? And I need you to try to show me where everyone was standing."

It was all basic stuff. Basic as in the level of detail typically documented for a misdemeanor assault, not a murder. Welcome to the post EMP world of criminal investigation.

The policeman was busy writing down everything Stephanie told him, at times asking her to repeat what she had said. He made frequent glances toward his partner in the empty lot. He, too, was busy writing notes. And the junior patrolman was now certain his partner was looking at a dead body. Or two dead bodies.

As he looked over his notes, Stephanie asked the stocky patrolman how they were going to investigate the murder she had observed. His response was borderline dismissive in its tone, but Stephanie realized it was unlikely he had intended it that way. He simply hadn't yet developed the communication skills of a more seasoned officer.

"Well, considering how messed up everything is, I know for a fact there isn't going to be any CSI stuff happening at this crime scene."

She nodded.

"We don't even have a crime scene tech now. Actually, we don't have any detectives around that I know of anyway. The sergeant in charge now told us to just take down whatever notes we can about what we see and whatever the witnesses tell us, and to not worry about doing things the way we normally do. It's the best we can do. They pretty much told us that we should focus on saving as many lives as we can and not to spend a whole lot of time on trying to solve crimes that have already happened."

He looked at Stephanie to see how she was responding to this information. She felt a sense of relief upon hearing that her assumptions were accurate, but tried not to allow her relief to show. She made a frown as she listened to the policeman.

"I guess that makes sense when you think about it. You guys have to prioritize under these conditions. Just handle the most important stuff, right?"

"Yep. That's the way it is now for sure." He was apparently pleased with himself for having convinced Stephanie as to why they were handling things this way.

Stephanie, despite her pretending to be disappointedly accepting of the situation, became even more pleased as she considered the circumstances. The area had been doused with light rainfall a few nights prior, which would make any evidence collection even more difficult—not that much of this would be happening anyway. She felt confident she would be okay as far as any criminal repercussions were concerned.

She also realized that in all probability, Roger would not be convicted of a crime by the time the dust settled on this matter. However, she hoped he would be arrested now and held for a while at least. With any luck he would be locked up until things returned to normal. She—and her neighbors—could deal with him at that time.

The lanky policeman was now walking back toward his partner and Stephanie. He didn't look happy. In fact he looked depressed. Or pissed off even--she wasn't sure.

As he came within conversational distance of his younger partner, he briefly informed him of his findings. Two bodies indeed. The junior partner filled in the more experienced patrolman about what Stephanie had told him. The tall cop asked Stephanie to go over everything for him once again, and she did so without protest. He asked for specific details regarding the house where Roger resided and the gun she had seen him use on the night of the murder. He also asked her if she knew whether Roger lived alone as well as what kind of weapons he owned other than the pistol he regularly wore on his belt.

"On our way to his house, let's take a look around the area where she described this thing happening to see if we can find any shell casings," the senior officer said to his partner.

The tall policeman looked directly at Stephanie once again.

"Are you sure there was no way that this 'Roger' shot the two guys in self-defense? There've been a lot of self-defense shootings since the grid went down, and under those circumstances we're just documenting the incident as best we can in our notebooks and moving on."

She shook her head back and forth emphatically.

"No way that was self-defense when he shot them. No way. He just walked up to those guys and shot them. Then he took the backpack the one guy was wearing. Seemed pretty obvious he wanted the backpack for some reason. It didn't even look like they saw him till right before he started shooting. He said something to them, and then they turned around and saw him. Then he shot 'em."

He continued looking directly at Stephanie as if he hoped she would change her answer. Displaying a scowl on his face, he asked her how she was able to see the face of the man doing the shooting during the dark. She told him that the moonlight offered enough light for her to recognize the man as the neighbor who had identified himself as "Roger" a long time ago.

Stephanie asked the two patrolmen if they were going to arrest the guy who did the murder. The senior officer wore an expression suggesting he wanted to find a way to say no, but was resigned to having to make the arrest.

He told her they were going to contact Roger at his house. If he came out they would arrest him. If he didn't answer the door they would wait until another time to take action. Though he didn't voice it, the veteran patrol officer didn't want to enter the house with only his partner and himself. Too dangerous. It was well known to most police officers that even a minimally trained combatant had an inherent advantage when inside his own house. Trying to contact Roger at the front door was going to have to be good enough.

"How long will you keep him in jail if you arrest him?"

"We'll most likely keep him locked up until we get some sort of court up and operating. Who knows how long that might take? Or until we don't have any food to feed the few prisoners we have."

The lawman in charge looked over to where he had seen Rosalyn and Rick enter their home and pointed his chin in that direction for a second as he spoke.

"If we arrest this guy, we'll need you to do a field show-up when we walk him by here. You can stand over there in your friends' front yard if you want."

He looked at her, and she nodded her head in understanding. Rob had talked about field show-ups several times over the years when sharing some of his work experiences with her. She knew he only shared the milder stories with her—usually ones containing an element of humor--but early in their marriage she had wanted to hear them anyway.

"Okay," he said. "We'll have him face a couple of different directions so you can get a good look at him. All you have to do when we're done is either give us a thumbs up sign if it's him for sure or a thumbs down if it's definitely not him. If you aren't sure, just put your hands out to your side like this," he demonstrated by extending his hands out to his side with his palms up.

"This is a serious charge Stephanie, so you have to be sure about him being the right guy. It's just as important to make sure an innocent person doesn't get arrested."

She acknowledged the patrolman's directions before taking Charlie Wyatt by the hand and walking back toward her neighbors' house. She knocked on the front door and Rick immediately opened it and invited them inside.

"I think they're going to arrest Roger right now," she said.

"I need to go in your front yard and identify him for the officers when they come by."

Before she could turn around and walk out to the yard, Rosalyn walked into the living room and grabbed Stephanie's hand with both of her own.

"Tell me what's going on Stephanie. What are they going to arrest him for?"

Stephanie shook her head as she stole a quick glance at Charlie Wyatt.

"I can't go over it right now. I'll explain it all later," she said.

Upon considering the situation for a quick moment, she asked Rosalyn to keep an eye on Charlie Wyatt while she waited in the front yard to make the field identification of Roger. Stephanie bent down and told her son to stay with Rosalyn for just a little while until she came back from outside. Rosalyn took the little boy's hand and took him into the living room. He turned around to see what Stephanie was doing. He looked worried and confused.

"As soon as you get done identifying him we have to talk."

Stephanie didn't respond to the comment and walked out to the front yard. She observed the pair of officers looking around at the ground in the general area where she had indicated the shooting had taken place. To her it seemed more like they were simply going through the motions than actually trying to find any shell casings.

They approached Roger's house with their long guns trained on the front door. When they knocked on the door he answered without any delay or resistance. He also walked out of the house and onto the porch with his hands raised over his head when ordered to do so. Roger may have been without a conscience, but his brain worked fine. Both officers immediately noted that he was wearing a Glock pistol on his belt.

After disarming Roger of his Glock, they told him he was under arrest. Neither of the officers indicated what he was being arrested for. And Roger hadn't asked--a fact that wasn't lost on the two police officers. After they handcuffed him, Roger spontaneously said, in a voice dripping with anger, "I don't know what that bitch told you, but she's lying to you!"

The officers presumed he was referring to Stephanie and her role of murder witness, while Roger was speaking with the assumption that Rosalyn had accused him of sexual assault or some similar offense. He was finding it hard to believe these two cops were going to waste their limited time and resources on arresting him for this low grade crime—even if they believed the woman. Prostitution was a misdemeanor. Not to mention that the whole thing was nothing more than the woman's word against his own.

The two policemen, convinced that Roger's spontaneous comment supported Stephanie's statement, were now certain that at the very least they had a man who had performed a homicide. Whether or not it was a murder or self-defense was yet to be determined. They surmised this guy had been aware of Stephanie witnessing the shooting of the two men, but hadn't done anything about it. Now he was accusing her of being a liar before he had even been advised of the reason for his arrest.

The stocky officer, preparing to question Roger about the accusation, advised him of his legal rights.

"I think I'm done talking to anyone with a badge until I have my lawyer with me."

"Fine by us," the taller patrolman said.

From the vantage point of Rick and Rosalyn's front yard, Stephanie watched what was happening on the opposite side of the street. The two lawmen were riding slowly on the ATV while Roger walked handcuffed in front of them. He was secured with a small rope that connected his cuffed wrists to a welded steel tow ring on the four-wheeler. Roger didn't look happy about his predicament, but the three neighbors watching the event from the front yard and living room were more than pleased with what they saw.

The officers had Roger stop and face three different directs for several seconds at a time to afford Stephanie a view of his face as well as a left and right profile view. As soon as the taller officer looked at her she gave him the thumbs up gesture. Then she turned and headed for the front door of her neighbors' house.

She let herself in without knocking. Stephanie saw that both Rosalyn and Rick were intently watching the event with their faces only inches from the large living room window. She pulled Charlie Wyatt to her and hugged him.

Here I am using my four-year-old for emotional support. I should be supporting him.

As the handcuffed man began to start walking again, Rosalyn suddenly bolted toward the front door with the intent of telling Roger what an asshole he was. Just one last string of obscenities for the man as he was carted off to jail for who knew how long. But Rick, who suspected what his wife was about to do, intercepted her and wrapped his arms around her waist, pulling her back from the door.

"It's okay Rosalyn; it's okay honey. We beat him. We won. You don't want the cops to think there is anything happening that involves us in any way."

The problem appeared to have been solved--at least for now. But he wondered what had led to the arrest of the man they both hated so much. He knew Stephanie was responsible somehow, but not much more than that.

From within the confines of the living room, Rosalyn began yelling, "You fucking pig. I hope you stay in jail forever, you asshole." She broke into sobs and Rick hugged her tightly, telling her that everything was going to be okay now. Charlie Wyatt looked at Stephanie with the wide eyes of a child who wasn't able to keep up with all that was happening. He sought the comfort of his mother. She hugged him tighter.

"Mommy loves you Charlie Wyatt," was all that she said as she affectionately rubbed his back.

Several minutes later, Stephanie brought Rosalyn into another room and then confided in her how she had told the patrol officers about seeing Roger shoot two people several nights ago. She didn't elaborate on the details, nor did she indicate whether or not this statement had been truthful. And Rosalyn didn't ask. Something told Rosalyn not to push the issue at this point.

"You need to tell me the long version of this later sometime when everything is over."

For the second time in the last half hour, Stephanie let her friend's demanding comment go unanswered. She was tempted to tell Rosalyn that she didn't feel compelled to follow directives from her friend, but decided to leave the matter alone for now.

Stephanie brushed a sweaty clump of her hair away from her face and held out her hand.

"Okay Charlie Wyatt—time to go home now."

They headed for the front door. As she reached the door Rick told her that he and Rosalyn wanted to come by in the morning to discuss something with her.

"You're going to like what we have to say I'm pretty sure," he said. "We'll see you tomorrow. And Stephanie," he added, "Thanks for what you did today."

She forced a smile that held no real emotion in it and went through the doorway with her son back to their house.

Stephanie lay in bed that night for hours without getting to sleep, despite the fact that she was physically exhausted. She replayed her actions of the day over and over in her mind, or more specifically, her decision to carry out the scheme to have Roger arrested. She questioned herself as to whether what she had done was a morally good thing or a bad thing. She tormented herself with the question repeatedly that night while lying in her bed until she thought she might have a nervous breakdown.

She weighed the ethical and moral aspects of her having lied to the patrol officers against the benefit of having Roger removed from the neighborhood. On the one hand, she remembered hearing Rob tell her that it was never worth lying about material facts to make an arrest. They could always get the bad guy another day he used to say.

On the other hand, by fabricating the story to have Roger arrested, she had accomplished a couple of good results. First, he deserved to go to jail for what he did to Rosalyn. Under the life or death circumstances surrounding the so-called "transaction" the scenario was for all intents and purposes a rape in her view. Secondly, she convinced herself, she had probably saved Roger from being badly beaten or killed based on what Rosalyn had intimated earlier. Either that or Rick would have been injured or killed. She shuddered to think about where that would have left Rosalyn.

Eventually Stephanie made peace with herself about what she had done. The current situation, with society hardly functioning and all, had created a whole new moral paradigm as far as she was concerned. Roger was a low-life who deserved to be in jail. Who really cared how that was accomplished?

As promised, Rick and Rosalyn showed up at Stephanie's front door at around eight the next morning. They informed Stephanie about the plan they had made to overpower Roger and then take over his house so that they could get access to his food and water stores. They added that now that Roger was gone for the foreseeable future, they were going to follow up with the second part of their plan. They were going to enter his house and avail themselves of his supplies. Rick put his hand on her shoulder.

"We might even decide to stay there in his house, Stephanie. We're not sure at this point. But we want you to know that if you need something, don't hesitate to ask us. I'm sure we can break loose with a few things here and there. That guy has a whole boatload of stuff stored at his place."

Rosalyn nodded her head decisively to affirm this fact.

Stephanie had a lot to say by way of response.

"Well, I hate to break this to you, but the way I see it is all three of us are going to be sharing the supplies that are in Roger's house. I figure I'm the one who came up with the plan that worked. Your plan might have worked, and then again maybe he would have shot you while you tried to overpower him. I guess we'll never know at this point. What we do know is that he's gone because I made it happen."

The impact of Stephanie's statement had a staggering effect on the couple. Rick and Rosalyn just stared at her without either of them uttering a single word. Clearly, neither of them had anticipated what had just happened. Nor did either of them know how to respond.

Stephanie continued, "I think we should start out by removing as much of the food and water from his house as we can--and do it as soon as we can. Who knows when he'll be back? I'm not counting on anything being predictable any more. You heard what the one cop said about cities all over the country being shut down. The local police here might have to let Roger loose before too long. Who knows? And don't forget what he said about trying to locate anyone who has food storage. I think we can all figure out what that's all about, right? So we need to move fast on this."

Rosalyn broke the silence first.

"Stephanie's right Rick. Staying inside his house would be a big mistake. And I don't think I could stand living in that place for even a day after what happened there. We should get as much stuff out of his house as we can as soon as possible."

"Okay," Rick conceded. "Let's wait until after dark and then start removing stuff from his house. We can take suitcases, backpacks, or whatever. Maybe big trash bags?"

Stephanie thought about the plan for a few seconds before answering.

"Alright. Why don't you two come by here tonight at about nine? Does that sound good?"

The couple agreed.

Rick said, "We won't take any of the food out of there till we're all three together, but I want you to know that I'm going to go in there by myself in a little while to look for one thing first—a gun. I know the police took his Glock, but he might have another gun in there somewhere. And I really need one."

Stephanie indicated she understood and that she had no problem with Rick doing this. She was simply glad for the opportunity to obtain more food and water at this point. Despite her severe rationing of her own water supply, between she and Charlie Wyatt—and the two Aussies—they had used up over half of their water. And with no end to the present situation in sight, she was worried.

As the couple walked out the door Stephanie thought they both looked happier than she had seen them since the grid had crashed. She was happy for them, and it made her think of Rob. But for some reason Stephanie had the unshakable feeling that things were going to work out. Rob would find his way back home.

Stephanie felt the nausea visiting her again. It reminded her of when she had been pregnant. Then she did the mental calculations about when she had last had her period. She was almost five weeks late. It was almost exactly the same time that she had started to experience morning sickness when she had been pregnant with Charlie Wyatt.

40

CULVER CITY, CA

The next morning Rob was surprised to wake to the smell of coffee being made on the kitchen camp stove in an old-fashioned percolator. Vangie and Don had used the percolator on camping trips many years ago when their kids were growing up. The aromatic smell of the coffee alone served as a stimulant to get Rob up and started with the day's chores.

Looking forward to the coffee with great anticipation, he jumped up and put his boots on. Like every night following the grid crash, he had slept in his jeans so that he would be better able to deal with an unexpected problem if woken from a sound sleep. He was hoping to be able to use some of the couple's spa water for his own personal hygiene, but he told himself that he would address that later after other things had been handled. More important things.

He began walking toward the kitchen to say good morning to Vangie when he saw Don walking down the hallway toward him carrying his cut-down twelve gauge. Rob jokingly threw up his hands in a mock surrender gesture. Don smiled and said, "Hey, some habits die hard man. I figure I should keep this handy till we get my pump gun modified. In fact, I want that to be our first job this morning--if you don't mind."

Rob retorted, "Well, I'm gonna say that it can be our second job. The first job is to drink some of this great smelling coffee and eat a little breakfast--my own power bar that is. I found a couple more bars in my pack. Don't worry; I'm not planning to use up all of your food stores before I leave."

Rob punctuated his comment with a polite laugh, but the unfortunate truth was that they both knew there were only limited food supplies in the house. Vangie had done better than most by keeping her pantry fully stocked with the food they normally consumed, but who knew how long until food availability in the supermarkets, or anywhere else, would return to some semblance of normalcy? He figured the first food availability would arrive in the form of government provided rations, probably to be dispersed by national guard soldiers.

Now that won't be a fun time, he thought.

Rob had a thought and walked over to his pack by the front door. He removed his steel water bottle, unscrewed the cap, and lifted it to his lips. He drained the little water that remained and carried the empty container to the kitchen.

"Good morning Vangie," he said. "If I can beg a cup of coffee off of you I'll just pour it in here. No need for a cup." Rob held his steel bottle out in front of him to indicate what he was talking about.

She took the percolator pot from the *Coleman* and poured the equivalent of a cup or more into his stainless steel container. Of course she was smiling as though the world was a wonderful place and everything was just fine.

Vangie made Don some oatmeal on the camp stove while her husband and Rob sat at the counter sipping hot coffee. Vangie drank her coffee from the opposite side of the counter near the camp stove. For the men it was the first time they had enjoyed the hot beverage in a long time.

"At least we still have some creature comforts during this damn mess we're living with, huh," Don said to the others as he savored his coffee.

"That's true," Rob said.

Vangie placed the pot of cooked oatmeal in front of Don and gave him a large spoon. In keeping with the practice of not using any dishes that were not absolutely essential, he ate directly from the pot.

Rob ate his power bar slowly in an attempt to pace his breakfast with that of his friend. He watched Vangie open a can of peaches with a manual can opener and begin eating them from the can with a spoon as she stood at the kitchen counter. He watched her put several vitamins into her mouth and chase them with water. Rob let his mind drift to his own home.

Did Stephanie stock up on vitamins as part of our emergency preparations? If that was overlooked, it was a big oversight on our parts. With limited types of food, and less of it, vitamins are going to be important.

"Let's go have a look at that shotgun you're talking about Don," Rob said as he returned his empty water bottle to his pack.

Don motioned for Rob to follow him into the house's attached two car garage. He used a key on his key ring to open a padlock that secured a large steel tool cabinet that was situated next to the garage wall next to a full sized work bench. Don removed a canvas gun case from the cabinet and unzipped it. It held a Remington model 870 twelve gauge pump shotgun. He looked at the shotgun and hefted its weight. Then he threw the stock up to his shoulder and cycled the action twice. He left the action open and offered the gun to Rob to examine.

Rob had handled a hundred or more model 870 shotguns in his life, and this one offered nothing that surprised him. Unlike the model 870's that he used at work or the one he had locked up in his garage at home, this one was a hunting shotgun. It had a long ribbed barrel as well as a nicely finished checkered wood stock and fore end.

Rob said, "Okay, here's the deal as I see it. This is a good solid shotgun, but the way it is now is way too bulky and clumsy for what you need for protection. But we can do a couple of things here to convert it into a decent self-defense shotgun. You'll just need to buy a new barrel for it if you ever want to use it for hunting again is all."

"Okay, let's get busy and make that happen then," Don replied.

They performed two modifications. The first involved using a hacksaw to cut the barrel down so that it just cleared the magazine tube, followed by using a steel file and then sandpaper to remove any burrs from the muzzle of the barrel that were caused by the hacksaw cut. The second modification was so easy that it was done without any tools. Rob simply removed the factory installed magazine plug that limited the gun's capacity to three rounds in order to comply with bird hunting regulations.

The end result, accomplished in little more than a half hour, was a shotgun with an overall length of less than that of a yardstick that held five rounds--four in the magazine and one in the chamber.

Don hefted the newly transformed shotgun with satisfaction. He removed a box of twenty five shotgun shells from the same cabinet that had housed the shotgun moments earlier. Using the method favored by most hunters, he turned the gun up-side-down and began to load the bright red shells into the firearm. Don commented, "These are bird shot rounds. Wish I had buckshot for this thing, but I guess these will work better than nothing, right?"

Rob nodded.

"Yep. Helluva lot better than nothing. Just remember you're maximum effective range for putting down bad guys is probably going to be about fifteen feet--that's all. It'll still hurt 'em plenty past that distance, but I'm talking about putting 'em *down*."

Rob furrowed his eyebrows as he considered something. Don, by now familiar with the signs of deep thought on his friend's part, was curious.

"Tell you what," Rob said as he looked at Don's boxes of shotgun shells.

"You got, what, three boxes of twenty five birdshot shells...which makes seventy five altogether, right?"

Don nodded and said, "Yeah, and?"

"Well, I'd be willing to trade you two of my buckshot rounds for five of your birdshot shells. Works out good for both of us I figure. I get over twice as many rounds, even if they're only good for close up use, and you get two rounds of buckshot in case you need something that hits hard at a little farther out."

Rob shrugged his shoulders as if to say that it was no big deal if Don didn't want to make the trade. But his friend, eager to make the deal, said, "Sounds like a good deal to me." The two friends agreed and the trade was made.

"I already know that you have the good habit of keeping the shot-gun close by at all times, so no need to go over that," Rob said by way of introduction to the impromptu lesson he was going to provide his buddy.

Shifting from a fairly easy going tone to one of a no-nonsense instructor, Rob addressed the issue of how best to use the newly mod-ified weapon.

"The best way to use a pump shotgun in a defensive combat situa-tion is to never let the thing go empty. It's harder than it seems. The way to do that is to try to focus on how many rounds you shoot. And that in itself is a lot harder than you think."

Rob also knew that Don had already showed he could pull the trigger when necessary—something more important than the most advanced *high speed low drag* tactical training.

Rob spent close to twenty minutes showing Don how to use the shotgun as a combat weapon as opposed to a hunting firearm like he was used to. After he was finished with the tutorial, he watched Don go through the motions with his shotgun several times. As expected, he was a little clumsy in his movements, but he had nonetheless grasped the concepts.

"Let me just add one last thing", Rob said, "If you're in the middle of a shit storm and you can't remember all the stuff I just showed you, just do whatever you can to shoot your shotgun. That stuff I taught you is all about trying to shave off seconds, or even fractions of sec-onds, but don't let it stall out your brain if you forget some of it. Make sense?"

Don nodded his head and said, "Right. Gotcha."

Satisfied that his buddy had a basic grasp of the few basics he had shown him, Rob decided to move on to another task. He started look-ing around the garage as he commented, "Enough of the gun stuff for now. How 'bout we try to put together some sort of water system for taking quick showers that works better than using a pitcher of water. Something that doesn't waste so much water and also works better, ya know?"

"Whadya have in mind for that?"

"I was looking at the water system those retired LAPD guys had set up in Westchester. It was pretty simple really. Do you have a plastic trash can that's clean, or one of those plastic storage bins about this big," he asked as he moved his hands back and forth, then up and down, to outline a box about twenty inches long by twelve inches wide and twelve inches deep.

Don rooted around in the back corner of his garage, pulled out a plastic storage bin, and then dumped the miscellaneous contents onto the garage floor in a fairly neat pile.

"How 'bout this," he asked Rob as he held out the plastic bin.

"Perfect," he responded. "Now we need some shower tub caulking or even roofing tar—anything that we can seal out water with. And a piece of garden hose that's about six feet long or so. We can just cut a section to that length. Now, do you have a hand drill and a hole saw or spade bit about the size of the garden hose?"

Don located the items requested and placed them on the big work bench. Rob drilled a hole on the side of the bin near the bottom and shoved one end of the length of hose through the new opening. Don used bathtub sealant caulking to seal the gap where the hose passed through the hole. It really required a simple plumbing fitting, but they made do with what they had.

Vangie arrived in the garage to watch the progress of their latest project, her curiosity having gotten the best of her for the moment. After the men had assembled it, they brought the water dispensing device to the spa so the three of them could test it. The spa was located outside of the master bathroom on an attractive redwood deck that was accessed through French doors separating the bathroom and the deck.

It was a larger than average hot tub, and Rob noted that the spa's water level was still almost three quarters full. He estimated that it contained more than three hundred gallons of water at this time. Ever mindful of not wasting any water, Don and Rob held the bin over the spa while Vangie used the plastic bucket she kept on the kitchen counter to fill it. If it leaked badly at least the water would go back into the hot tub and not onto the deck never to be retrieved.

It turned out the device did in fact leak after being filled with water, but only slightly. The water loss would be insignificant during a typical three minute period of use. It was more than adequate for taking a two minute shower. The three of them entered the master bathroom with Rob carrying his invention. He set the empty and newly created shower box on the bathroom counter top and ran the end of the hose over to the adjacent bathtub.

"Here's your new shower system," Rob announced with more than a little pride in his voice. "Just fill the bin with warm water and make sure to hold the end of the hose above the water level or else keep your thumb tight over the end to hold the water in until you want it. And be gentle with the hose. Don't yank on it."

"I can't wait to try it out," Vangie said.

Rob added, "Remember that water runs downhill, so you have to have the end of your hose lower than the water level in the box to make it work. Just start showering at the highest level of your body first. It's simple gravity."

"I knew I should've paid more attention to my high school physics teacher instead of the cute brunette that sat in front of me," Don joked.

Vangie gave him a well-practiced look that feigned irritation.

The three of them spent the rest of the day going through the house figuring out ways to make the premises more difficult to be compromised by assaulters should things get more desperate in the future days, weeks, or months. Most of these approaches involved serious alterations to the interior of their nice home, including damaging large and expensive pieces of furniture, removing interior doors to be used to board up windows, and miscellaneous other measures.

So, while they came up with detailed plans for fortifying the house, they held off on actually implementing the modifications. Don believed the modifications might be visually severe enough to run the risk of causing unnecessary emotional trauma to his wife. Removing interior doors and nailing/screwing them over window openings--along with expensive table tops—wasn't something she would suffer lightly he feared. Yet if the neighborhood watch guys patrolling their block were overrun by mobs looking for food and water, the fortifications could very well make the difference between surviving an attack and being at the pillagers' mercy. In the end he settled for jotting down specific notes about what to use, but held off on actually doing it.

Rob helped Don modify his tool belt so that the open leather pouch designed to hold nails could be used to hold a large quantity of shotgun shells. This would greatly aid him in being able to effectively use the combat reloading techniques Rob had shown him. Using pieces of garden hose and duct tape, they also constructed a better sheath for the machete Don had acquired, and then attached it to the same tool belt.

Vangie watched some of the modifications the men were making, and listened to their discussions about what was and was not important and how best to modify things to accomplish the desired result. It was a strange scenario they found themselves in, and one that seemed like it was more apt to be found in a Hollywood movie than in their real lives.

Observing Vangie's well stocked food cupboard with unmasked approval, Rob strongly suggested she not worry about expiration dates on the canned goods. He assured her that unless a can was bulging or showed other obvious signs of having its seal broken, the contents would not be harmful even if they were far past the "best used by" dates. At worst, he explained, the nutritional value, and/or the taste, might begin to slowly deteriorate after the food reached a certain age. Even so, it would be worth eating.

During the multiple trips in and out of the garage, Rob's attention had been drawn to a small off-road motorcycle that was stored along one of the walls. The machine was an old 1976 *Yamaha DT-175 Enduro* model. The motorcycle looked like it hadn't been operated since the Normandy invasion, but it nonetheless raised Rob's hopes. He was almost certain that the old dirt bike, designed primarily for off-road use, contained no electronics in its design.

He had two questions that would determine whether he might be able to use the motorcycle to get home. If the answer to either of the questions was no, then the plan wouldn't work.

Can we get the damn thing started? I know Don is a lot more capable than I am when it comes to vehicle mechanical ability. Maybe he could get the old bike running. Then again, I wonder if he would even be willing to let me take the bike from here. He might want it for himself. All I can do is ask I guess.

Rob finally decided the time was right to ask Don about the Yamaha parked in the garage after they had eaten a small lunch of crackers and peanut butter chased down with some re-heated coffee left over from the morning meal.

"Hey Don, I couldn't help but notice that old Yamaha dirt bike in the garage. I got two questions for you: how hard would it be to get that thing running, and would you let me take it to get home if we were able to get it running?"

Don smiled good-naturedly when he answered his buddy.

"I don't give a shit if you take it. I'm sure as hell not gonna be using it. And I don't think Vangie wants to use it, do you Vangie?"

Don's smile turned into happy laughter at his own joke. It wasn't really that funny, but Rob found that he was slightly envious of his friend's good attitude despite the stressful environment and all he had been through.

"Oh, you're so funny," Vangie said as she returned his smile pleasantly. The truth was that she was glad to see he was still in good spirits.

Don became serious again.

"I know that thing doesn't have any electronics in it, so the EMP wouldn't have hurt it, but it hasn't been run since the mid-eighties, so it might be useless anyway."

Rob dipped his head and studied his boots as he considered this information. Looking at the footwear he was reminded of the fact he needed to air out his feet and change his socks. So far he had avoided any foot problems, and he wanted to maintain this condition if possible.

"The question," Don said as he looked over at Rob, "is whether we can get the damn thing started or not. It's a two-stroke motor so we'll need to mix some oil with gas for fuel. That's no big deal; I can use my chainsaw fuel for that. But we'll have to take the carburetor apart and clean it up. Shit, that's assuming the carb parts are all still good."

"Well, do you think it's worth giving it a try or not? I'm no mechanic. I have to trust your judgment on this one, Don."

Although this comment was certainly truthful, he also wanted to give Don an easy out if deep down his friend wanted to keep the motorcycle for his own use. The two had been through much together—both having the right to claim they had helped the other get through life threatening situations. With this in mind, Rob didn't want to create the impression his inquiry about the motorcycle con-stituted calling in any kind of marker.

Rob laughed to himself as he considered this.

Yeah, I still have a damn conscience—it's just been seriously adjusted since this EMP thing happened is all.

Don answered with a jovial voice Rob could only attribute to the fact his friend was now reunited with his wife. It sure as hell couldn't be attributed to anything else going on.

"Yeah, what the hell; I guess we can give it a shot. Just don't get your hopes up is all," he said. "Let's go look at the old bike and see what we can do." With that, Don dismounted from his stool and began walking toward the garage. Rob followed his buddy, noticing with satisfaction that his limp had noticeably improved.

As the two friends were just about ready to enter the garage, they heard a commotion that sounded like it was coming from out on the street in front of the house. Several men's voices could be heard yell-ing frantically. The general tone of the voices was one of panic, and there also seemed to be a strong element of discord that was evident. The voices belonged to men who didn't agree on how to address whatever was happening. Though it was only identifiable in his sub-liminal brain, Rob sensed the nature of the problem was something other than an attack or similar threat, yet definitely some kind of emergency.

He ran to the front door with Don on his heels, the older man's knee pain all but forgotten with the sudden rush of adrenaline. What they saw was a sad enough event regardless, but it made Rob feel especially bad. The gruff man with whom he had exchanged words on the day of their arrival was lying on the ground, his *USMC* cap lying a few feet from his head like some tragic memento to the fallen sentry.

He was not moving other than being slightly bumped every few seconds by the man straddling his chest desperately performing CPR as he tried in vain to revive the dying man. Unfortunately his massive cardiac arrest gave him no quarter.

The man performing CPR jumped off of the supine man's chest, took a knee next to his head, and pinched his nose as he began breathing into his mouth. Rob ran over to assist the man administering CPR, taking over on the chest compressions while the other continued with his rescue breathing. After another minute or so of performing the CPR, Rob checked the man's pulse. There was none.

Shaking his head in the negative, Rob said, "Let's try it for another minute and then we have to call it man."

The man doing the rescue breathing looked at Rob without interrupting what he was desperately doing. He was confronted with a look he had seen all too many times as a patrol cop. It was the look of the desperate and pained individual suffering an inexplicable and unfair loss.

Rob was unable to tell if this man was in agreement with him or not, but he knew that he was right about calling it. Guys didn't come back after this long. Especially when there were no paramedics with professional equipment and well outfitted ambulances to transport them to a nearby trauma center with state of the art equipment.

Rob continued administering the chest compressions for another minute and a half before he stopped and climbed off of the dead man. "I'm sorry man, but he's gone."

The man who had been administering the CPR was the young guy that had been carrying the deer rifle as he performed his neighborhood guard duty with the other two men on the day of their arrival. Rob saw the young man's eyes well up and tear over as he let Rob's words soak in. The deputy sheriff figured the two men had probably become pretty close friends by mere virtue of having served together as watchmen for their cul-de-sac.

Rob had experienced and observed friendships that had developed between dissimilar guys working in a patrol car together for several shifts. Despite the vast differences that might exist between two persons when it came to age, ethnicity, their taste in entertainment, politics, food, sports, and other day-to-day activities, the bond established between them after serving together in that capacity was often a strong one.

"I'll be glad to move him or help you in any other way I can after you take a little time to mourn. I'm staying in this house right here," Rob added as he pointed to Don's house with his chin.

Rob got up and made one more comment before heading back to Don's house. "I'm sorry. I know how bad this hurts," he said.

"He was my uncle. Three tours in Viet Nam and raised six kids when he came back. Worked ten hour days till he was sixty two years old driving a cement mixer truck. Hell of a man."

Rob nodded, stood, and walked away. He walked past Don without making eye contact. He saw that Vangie was watching the event from the front porch, and he similarly avoided looking at her as he walked past, his shame eating at him something fierce. He let himself in through the front door, and sat down on a living room chair.

Rob felt bad about having challenged the cigar voice man after he had demanded to know why Rob was accompanying Don when they entered the cul-de-sac. While the man was probably overstepping his role a little bit, Rob now realized that he needn't have challenged him like he did. He should have kept his damn big mouth shut. The man was doing an honorable thing and Rob had just been acting like a cranky jerk that day. And now the man was dead. And Rob felt guilty. Actually that wasn't quite right. He felt absolutely like shit.

41

THOUSAND OAKS, CA

Rick had been forthright with Stephanie earlier when he stood in her living room with his wife and let her know about his intention to enter Roger's house to look for a gun. Unlike removing large quantities of food and water from the house, getting a gun out of the place was something that he could do by himself and in relatively short order. He was also convinced he could do this without any neighbors being the wiser--something that couldn't be said for carrying bags stuffed with food, and whatever else, out of the building.

All of the above notwithstanding, he couldn't quite get comfortable with what he was about to do. It wasn't a matter of his moral compass--or whatever else might constitute his rapidly changing conscience--Roger deserved whatever happened to him in Rick's opinion. What concerned Rick was the fact there was no guarantee Roger wouldn't return to his house before they had the opportunity to strip the place. Roger might be in police custody for the time being, but given the lack of predictability in the post-EMP situation, counting on his remaining in custody was a risky supposition. The entire public safety paradigm was in serious flux. No one could predict what would be in effect from day to day.

Shit, the situation seems to be changing from hour to hour, he thought.

Convincing himself to simply get on with the plan, Rick walked down the block to the house in question, noticing that the dual flags were still flying on the large flagpole. He was almost disappointed to observe the simple house with the covered front porch appearing so normal given what had happened inside with his wife recently.

He approached the property from the sidewalk, doing his best to surreptitiously watch for any neighbors that might be watching. Seeing none, he walked through the front yard and made his way to the rear of the house. He looked around again, for at least the tenth time since arriving. Nothing he noticed gave him any cause for concern. He considered trying to make a "clean" entry through one of the windows before discarding the notion and giving in to the idea of using a simple but faster method. He was going to force the back door.

Who gives a shit at this point anyway, he asked himself. *Just get into the house and get started looking for a gun.*

Rick's leg wound was still a long way from being healed, but he had faith in the power of his shoulders even though he was not as strong as he had been a few weeks ago. He stood about twenty feet from the door and charged it at a full run, limping but gathering considerable speed nonetheless. He dipped his shoulder just prior to contacting the wooden door, splintering the modest door jamb. The violence of the splintering door jamb surprised him with its sudden disintegration as his momentum carried him well past the doorway and into the laundry room just inside.

Overkill is under-rated, he told himself.

Wasting no time to admire his work, he visually took in the house interior. The kitchen was unremarkable, perhaps slightly better equipped than the typical bachelor's kitchen, but it offered nothing for him to focus on. For some reason—perhaps a subliminal need to see the scene of the crime—he went to the bedroom first.

He glanced around, noting a few art pictures mounted on the wall. Modern art that he had no appreciation for whatsoever. Several photos depicted the worldly man in various exotic locations around the world--none of which could be identified by the relatively untraveled construction worker. He suffered a short moment where he considered his own life and how it measured up against that of the man who had bedded his wife for the price of a couple days of food and water.

He felt a sense of regret that he had been deprived—or cheated--of his chance to avenge the forced pimping of his wife by carrying out his own plan of attack against this man.

Life was unfair...sometimes even downright cruel. He acknowledged the ugly fact that he would probably never be able to recapture the respect of his wife even if he lived to be a hundred. No monetary riches, spousal affection, or unconditional love he could provide from this point on would ever be able to rehabilitate their relationship. It might survive, or it might not, but it would never be the same.

Motivated by his increasingly consuming hate and resentment, he began searching the bedroom first, his manic removal of dresser drawers, opening of closet doors, and upending of the bed's mattress all nothing more than unsuccessful attempts at reducing his anguish. Other than a leather holster for an unknown type handgun located in a dresser drawer beneath a stack of t-shirts, he found nothing of any value or interest

Consistent with his actions since entering the residence, Rick purposely used far more force than necessary when he opened the medicine cabinet door in the bathroom. Yet, had he not done so, he might not have noticed the cabinet housing was unsecured. His background in construction told him that this was highly unusual. He pulled the entire housing out from the wall cavity, violently throwing it into the bathtub where the mirror shattered into pieces with a satisfying destructive crashing sound.

He looked into the cavity and discovered a cord had been tied to a large nail driven into the wall stud. Rick pulled up the cord, encouraged by the weight of whatever was attached to the other end. He was rewarded by a canvas bag that he quickly opened to peer into. The small amount of sunlight that found its way into the bathroom wasn't enough to see much. He yanked violently on the cord, separating it from the nail supporting it. He carried the canvas bag with its contents outside, this time not even bothering to check for neighbors that might be watching. He looked inside the bag.

A Glock 9mm pistol wrapped in an oily rag and two additional magazines, both loaded with hollow point ammunition, were contained in the sack. He also found the bag contained a box of 9mm hollow point ammunition, minus the rounds loaded in the two magazines. Rick briefly considered his find, knowing that the man had been arrested while wearing the same make of pistol.

I guess he kept a spare. If it makes sense to have one, then why not two?

He carried the bag holding the newfound items to the bedroom and retrieved the holster from the drawer that now lay on the floor, half of its original contents spilled out next to it. Sure enough, the Glock fit the holster. He threaded the leather device through his belt, checking to make sure it was secure. He spent a few minutes fumbling with the weapon before he was satisfied that he had loaded it properly. He recalled how Rob had mentioned one time that a defensive handgun should always be fully loaded—no empty chamber stuff if you wanted it to be useful for self- defense. He pointed the weapon, lowered it, then raised it again, using only one hand the way the non-trained often do, before finally securing it in the belt mounted holster.

Rick made his way through the entire house, leaving a path of destruction in his wake, and not feeling the least bit bad about his actions. He was actually surprised and slightly disappointed that he was unable to find any other firearms during his search. Given the man's demonstrated penchant for using creative hiding places, he questioned whether he had missed any additional items of value in the residence. Eventually he told himself to let it go.

When he discovered the treasure trove of food, water, and other staples Roger had stored in his garage, Rick allowed himself to smile for the first time in over a week. He was overcome with an uncontrollable urge to feed himself regardless of the promise he had made earlier about only searching the house for guns until he was joined by his wife and neighbor Stephanie. He went directly to the shelves housing the canned goods and retrieved a can of chili as he frantically looked around for a can opener. Grasping the chili can desperately, he ran to the kitchen in search of a means to get access to the ingredients it held.

Rick pulled out the drawers in the kitchen cabinets, dumping the contents unceremoniously onto the ground as he continued searching.

Before a full two minutes had gone by, he ran out of patience. He grabbed a sturdy butter knife and used a cooking pot to pound the blade through the can's lid over and over, working his way around the circumference. When he had removed enough to allow him to bend the tin cover out of the way, he scooped the chili out with a teaspoon located in the same drawer that had housed the butter knife.

When he had consumed all of the can's ingredients he went back and retrieved a second can of chili from the garage, taking an extra few seconds to grab one of several medium-sized bottles of water stored there. Repeating the same procedure to open the second can, he consumed the entire contents as fast he could get it down. Still not satiated, he returned to the garage a third time and found a can of peaches. He ate all of the sugary fruit, hardly pausing to breathe between mouthfuls.

Rick felt a little ashamed of what he was doing but was nonetheless unable to stop himself from gorging on the food. After having gone through two cans of chili, a can of peaches, and a dozen crackers, he felt his stomach protesting. His stomach was becoming used to only having only a small amount of food to digest, and he had just introduced way too much way too soon. He ran to the bathroom where he had ripped out the medicine cabinet either out of habit or instinct. He emptied his upset stomach into the toilet. The fact that there was no water available to flush the toilet didn't occur to him until he had already filed the toilet bowl.

He spent several minutes merely trying to get past the nausea and stomach cramps, sitting on the tile floor of the bathroom with his back against the wall. Finally regaining his ability to function somewhat normally, he got up and took another look around the garage. He located a box of heavy plastic trash liners on a shelf that housed cleaning chemicals and other sundry items.

That's what I was looking for. We'll use those to load this stuff up and carry it out of here.

He headed back to his own home. Despite the negative experience after gorging himself, he felt good about the 9mm pistol on his belt and the two loaded magazines in his pocket.

It took him a relatively long time to reach his house. The combination of his healing leg wound and general exhaustion was taking its toll on him. The added advantage of adrenaline had come and gone, and he collapsed onto the living room couch immediately after Rosalyn had opened the front door for him.

"I managed to find a pistol and some extra bullets while I was there," he said to Rosalyn, intentionally leaving out any mention of his food consumption while inside of the residence.

"He had some garbage bag liners in his garage too, so we can use those to get the stuff from there to here."

"Alright; that's good," she said.

Rick looked at her as if waiting for more in the way of a response. None came.

"Okay," he said, "I need to sleep for a little while before we head back down there to get that stuff."

He fell asleep on the couch while his wife was still asking him questions about what he had seen and how he wanted to go about removing the food and water stores inside the man's house. Rosalyn gently woke him several hours later by shaking his shoulder. He opened his eyes and sat up to seeing the living room lit only by candlelight. Stephanie stood several feet from Rosalyn holding a compact *Surefire LED* flashlight. She wore an intense expression on her face as she appeared to be looking out the living room window, even though it was completely dark outside. Charlie Wyatt was asleep on the other couch, his head resting on a pillow that Stephanie had brought with them.

Rosalyn began talking to her husband without delay, showing no concern for possible cognitive lag time accompanying his recent deep sleep. He used the palms of his hands to rub his eyes, now well aware he wasn't going to be given the luxury of gradually waking and acclimating himself to what was happening in his own living room.

She announced, "Stephanie and I have been talking about how to do this while you were sleeping."

Am I catching a little bit of resentment in her tone, he wondered.

She didn't bother pausing to get a response.

"Stephanie doesn't want to leave Charlie Wyatt here by himself, so we'll just trade off our tasks. First, I'll go there with you and we'll load up some bags while she stays here with him. Then we'll bring the bags here. I'll take a shift watching the little guy and then Steph and you can take a turn to get some things. We can keep trading off like that till we're too tired to carry any more stuff. Sound good?"

Rick agreed and rubbed the sleep from his eyes again. He felt a lot better being armed with the Glock as he and Rosalyn walked toward the house. Rosalyn didn't exactly feel good about what she was doing, but she felt a hell of a lot better than she had the last two times she had made her way to the man's house.

This time she had all of the control. Glancing quickly at the pistol on her husband's belt, she acknowledged that a small part of her actually welcomed the idea of Roger somehow finding his way back to his house while they were there. It was a sentiment that, unbeknownst to her at the time, was also harbored by her husband. The only difference was that there was nothing *small* about this desire in his case. He wanted it with every knowing part of his being.

The three of them labored over the next four hours filling the plastic oversized bags with miscellaneous food items, toilet paper, water, and whatever else they decided to remove from Roger's garage. Their first attempts resulted in the large plastic bags being loaded way too heavy, but this was remedied easily. They discovered doubling up the bags and filling them only a third to half was pushing the weight limit. It was well past midnight when they collectively decided to stop for the day--or night as it were. They repeated the same procedure, working only in the hours of darkness, over the next seventy two hours. Their efforts provided the three of them with a decent amount of food.

Transporting large quantities of water proved to be a far tougher endeavor than they had anticipated. Eventually they agreed to treat all of the fifty five gallon plastic water barrels in Roger's garage as a reservoir to be visited as needed. They would use one gallon jugs to make carrying the heavy liquid easier. There was no viable way to ration the water or monitor how much was being taken, so in the end it was simply agreed upon to use the supply at will.

Despite the inherent vulnerability of using the honor system, after all was said and done they each agreed it was better for any of them to have the water than a stranger--a scenario that wasn't exactly outside the realm of possibility.

The trio began referring to the task of carrying water from Roger's garage to their respective homes as "transfer runs". These were accomplished by bringing two single gallon sized empty water jugs in a backpack to Roger's garage where they were filled with water from the large barrels, placed inside of the pack concealed from view, and then carried back to one of their homes. It was a simple but effective system. With the exception of one occasion where a neighbor peered suspiciously out his window watching a backpack laden Stephanie as she hiked up the sidewalk toward her residence, no problems or challenges were encountered during any of the transfer runs.

Stephanie made it a point to carry her revolver with her during these runs as she couldn't dismiss the possibility of encountering the strange homeowner should he be released from police custody. And she knew Roger would be in a state of extreme rage--much of it directed at her--if this were to happen.

Five days after having removed the last of the food items from Roger's garage, Stephanie sat in her living room enjoying a hot cup of afternoon tea as she read to Charlie Wyatt from one of his favorite books. He had listened to the story dozens of times already, yet it continued to entertain him. She was grateful he had seemingly adjusted to the dramatic changes that had taken place over the past few weeks. Life was certainly a lot harder now than it had been before the EMP incident, but so far they had adjusted and were not suffering to the point where they couldn't cope.

She wasn't sure if the skewed concept of time contained within a four-year-old's mind was helping with the whole problem of a missing father who would be returning "soon", but Charlie Wyatt was dealing with this issue pretty well for the time being. For Stephanie, the hardest thing she had to contend with was worrying about Rob's well-being.

The sound of the ATV four wheeler was nothing more than a hum at first, but it gradually grew loud enough to where Stephanie recognized it for what it was. She put down the book she was reading, jumped up from her chair, and went to the window where she could see out to the sidewalk and street. She immediately recognized the same two policemen that had arrested Roger a week prior. Both were mounted on the ATV as it came down the street, its distinctive sound alerting the entire block of their arrival.

Was that a week ago? No, not that long ago.

She started to try to figure out how many days ago Roger had been hauled off, but gave up the effort after becoming frustrated. The days and weeks were becoming difficult to keep track of.

The off road vehicle came to a stop in front of her house and she felt her heart beat accelerate.

Oh no. Are they here to tell me they now know I lied about seeing Roger shoot those men? Do they have confirmed bad news about Rob? Why are they here? What do I do now?

The stocky patrol officer approached the front door first, his lanky partner coming up behind him a full twenty seconds later. He knocked loudly on the door, the force used being more than what was typically required to get the attention of occupants in most homes. Stephanie opened the door and hoped the panic she was feeling wasn't obvious to the policemen standing on her porch. The shorter cop, standing as though he were bracing for an imminent bum's rush or similar physical assault spoke first. He addressed her with the formality of a borderline officious patrolman who hadn't yet acquired the judgment to know when to come across as a hard-ass and when to show a softer demeanor.

In contrast, the tall officer stood behind his younger partner with a far more relaxed posture. He offered Stephanie a natural smile, his eyes containing a sparkle supporting its authenticity. She felt some of her panic begin to subside. Stephanie looked over her shoulder at her son and said, "Wait here honey; I'll read the rest of your book to you in a minute."

She thought about inviting the two police officers into the living room but suddenly remembered what one of them had said a week ago during their first meeting.

"We're looking for anyone who has large amounts of food or water stored, including swimming pools," he had said.

She didn't want to take the chance of one of them figuring out she had food stores in her house. She had promised herself that her food supply was not going to be shared with anyone outside her immediate family if there was any way she could avoid it. With this in mind she stepped out onto the porch and pulled the door almost completely closed behind her.

"I would invite you in, but my son gets his anxiety kicked up a little bit sometimes with uniformed police officers present. He even reacted a little bit like that when his father was in uniform and brought a partner by the house one time. He doesn't really get scared—more like he gets excited—as if I had given him a cup of coffee or something," she said with a shrug of her shoulders. She hoped her elaborate lie would get past the two cops.

The younger lawman didn't show much of a reaction to her comment at all, and the more seasoned officer only gave her another friendly smile.

"Kids can be funny about that stuff sometimes. I've raised three boys and a girl. She's getting ready to head off for college—or she was before all this happened anyway."

Stephanie only gave the man a pleasant smile by way of response. She was having trouble containing her anxiety and curiosity as she impatiently waited for one of them to explain the reason for their visit.

"Have you heard any news about what happened at the Nadeau Sheriff's Station in South L.A.?

The younger officer suddenly and quite visibly lost the confidence he had exuded in excess only moments earlier as he now found something interesting to look at on the porch floor's cement slab. His partner looked at Stephanie with an expression of genuine concern.

"Are you sure you don't want to go inside and sit down? I don't think there's any really terrible news, but some of it might be upsetting to you."

She felt her heart beat increase and the man's voice took on a more distant, or less clear, quality as she absorbed the meaning of what he had just said.

His voice sounded like a humming noise was surrounding it as she stood on the porch letting him speak. She tried to sort out the information in her head.

He said the news wasn't terrible, only that it might be upsetting to me.

"Okay, here's the best information we have at this time," he said by way of getting started. "There was an attack that took place against the Nadeau Sheriff's Station—that's where your husband is assigned, right?" he asked.

"Yes, yes," she said, obviously trying to hurry him along with his delivery. "What happened?"

"Well, like I said," he continued, "there was an attack, but the feds sent in a team afterward and they got a list of names of the deputies that were—uh, there weren't any deputies with the name of Flynn on that list," he added, hoping to provide even the slightest amount of comfort to the anxious and worried woman standing in front of him.

"Your husband was *not* one of the deceased deputies at the station."

Stephanie experienced a massive waive of relief flow through her body and mind. She realized she had been holding her breath as she waited for the information from the officer, and she now inhaled deeply before forcefully expelling it all. She leaned back against the house wall next to the front door to steady herself, not caring that she made a thudding sound as her body struck the exterior wall. She compelled herself to continue listening to the information coming at her.

"What happened to the deputies at the station during the attack? How many were killed? How many were hurt?" The questions were pouring forth before the patrolman could respond. She had met some of the wives of the deputies assigned to the Nadeau Station as well as many of the patrol deputies themselves, and she was now concerned about them.

"I'm going to tell you the truth Stephanie," the senior partner said, "and I'm really going outside the boundaries of what I'm supposed to be sharing with you."

He looked at her for some sort of acknowledgement on her part regarding the confidence he was entrusting her with. Her expression was closer to one of begging than acknowledgment of his trust, but he continued anyway.

"The attack was done by some sort of paramilitary terrorist types. Don't know much more than that. But they killed every one of the deputies that were in the station at the time. Apparently the deputies killed most of the terrorists attacking the station too. But like I said, none of the deputies killed was named Flynn. Not sure how they came up with all the names, but they did somehow."

Stephanie was overcome with a sense of grief as she considered the massive emotional pain the surviving family members of the slain deputies would be experiencing upon receiving this news. For some reason she looked at the junior policeman. He was now looking more like a young teenager who had found himself alone and in serious trouble than the cocksure cop pounding on her door a few minutes ago. Yeah. There was a steep adjustment curve in play now. And everyone was having it forced upon them after the grid crash.

Stephanie had wrangled control over her emotions somehow and was infused with the feeling that Rob was alright and on his way home to his family. She had no idea how he was going to get home, but she felt a strong sense of well-being as far as Rob was concerned. She also felt a genuine sorrow about the deaths of his fellow patrol deputies.

The tall policeman wasn't finished when it came to providing her with information.

"There's one more thing I want to tell you," he added.

"The man living down the block who we arrested last week was killed by one of our police officers a few days ago."

Christ, she thought, *does this stuff ever end, or does it just keep piling up like some sort of endless bad dream.*

He wasn't finished.

"This 'Roger' guy tried to escape from our station jail the day before yesterday. We have to walk any prisoners out of their cells once a day to use the latrine outside—due to there being no running water now. He hit one of our guys in the throat with his hand—not sure if the officer's gonna make it actually. He suffered a crushed larynx and he isn't doing well. Anyhow, another one of our officers saw it happen and shot the son of a bitch on the spot! Uh, sorry about the language, but the truth is that I wish I'd shot him myself the day you told us about him."

The man's jaw was clenched tightly as he spoke, indicating the anger he still felt about the way the situation had gone down. Picking up on the senior policeman's anger, his partner turned his head to look at him briefly and then glanced at Stephanie for a split second before returning his focus on the cement slab of the porch.

"Our orders are probably gonna change now anyway. No more arresting people and taking them back to the station. That system is broken at this point. Unless things get to improving, I wouldn't be surprised if we're looking at a situation where we either settle problems on scene or execute the bad guy after hearing all the facts—pretty much like they handled it in the old west. Probably won't get that bad, but it's bad." He shook his head for effect.

There was an overload of information she needed to try to sort through, and she experienced a sudden need to end the contact with the patrol officers. She asked them if they needed her for anything else. After receiving a negative response, she thanked them for making the effort to bring her the information and said she needed to check on her boy. As soon as she saw the partners begin to turn around she reentered her house and closed the door, throwing the deadbolt as a matter of habit more than anything else.

She found Charlie Wyatt playing with one of his toy dump trucks on the kitchen floor. It was getting close to their dinner time now, and she went to the garage where their newly bolstered food supply was located. She selected a can of stew, a can of green beans, and some saltine crackers for their dinner. She fired up the propane camp stove, combined the ingredients of both cans into a pot and warmed it up. She allowed Charlie Wyatt to break his crackers without supervision, ignoring the ensuing mess. She brushed the cracker crumbs into her hand and dumped them into the soup.

After finishing their dinner, she spent a half hour with him, finishing reading the story that had been interrupted by the arrival of the police officers earlier.

She lit an oil lamp resting on the kitchen table and then another identical lamp positioned on the living room coffee table. Carrying the latter to the bathroom, she set up a toothbrush with a small amount of toothpaste and a little bit of water poured from a plastic bottle. She then supervised her son as he brushed his teeth before tucking him into bed.

"Good night Charlie Wyatt," she said as she kissed him on the cheek and rubbed his hair. "I think Daddy's going to be coming home pretty soon," she added, feeling a confidence in her statement that hadn't been there for a long time.

42

CULVER CITY, CA

Rob and Don worked on the old off-road motorcycle for most of the next day following the heart attack related death of the neighborhood security volunteer. Don was definitely in his own element now as he removed the bike's old carburetor and then disassembled it, examining the parts as a surgeon would a patient on the operating table. He used gasoline from a gas can to clean the parts before reassembling them.

Rob did his best to help his friend, all the while being almost embarrassed about his own ineptitude when it came to engine mechanics. Nonetheless, he performed his role as a *gofer*--mostly retrieving tools and holding things when needed--without complaint or resentment of any kind. He even used an old manual bicycle tire pump to get enough air into the two tires to make the motorcycle usable.

The bottom line was that Rob was grateful for Don's generosity in lending him the motorcycle in the first place as well as for his willingness to spend the considerable effort on getting the machine up and running. By the end of the day, with the available natural light starting to diminish, Don had the old dirt bike ready to roll.

He admonished Rob, "These fuel lines are old and cracked, so keep an eye on them. If they start to leak you got a fire danger problem—obviously."

He looked at Rob, hoping for assurance that his friend was aware of this without Don having warned him. Rob nodded somewhat impatiently, urging his buddy to go on with his instruction.

"You *do* know how to use the clutch and shift gears on this thing right?"

Rob nodded again and said "Yeah, I had a dirt bike for a month or so when I was about fourteen. Took a bad spill and my parents made me sell it."

He chuckled at the memory.

"Gear pattern is one down and four up, right?" He looked at Don for confirmation and was rewarded with a nod.

Rob walked over to the handlebars and squeezed the clutch lever located on the left side. "If I have to I can actually shift the gears without the clutch if I remember right, but hopefully I won't have to." Don just shrugged his shoulders.

"Just remember this engine is a two stroke motor, so the power is up at the high end of the RPM's. This thing likes to be up there--so don't bog it down."

"Okay. That's coming back to me now."

"If you do get a leak in the fuel line, I'd use some of your duct tape to wrap it real good. That might carry you a few more miles at least. Of course you'll probably have a fuckin' fire to deal with before you even know you got a leak, so it might not even matter."

Don shook his head and looked at the old motorcycle as if considering whether he should even let his friend ride the thing—for his own safety.

He lifted his chin toward Rob and said, "Why don't you see if you can start this baby. I'm not gonna even try it with my knee the way it is."

Rob straddled the two wheeled machine and turned the throttle about a half turn, releasing it immediately after doing so. He folded the kick start lever out to allow purchase with his right foot. Keeping his foot on the lever he jumped up and then used his weight in conjunction with his leg muscles to thrust downward on the kick start lever. The bike failed to start until almost half a dozen attempts, but it started. He twisted the throttle to introduce more gas into the carburetor, revving the motor. He let the engine reach high RPM's for several seconds as dark colored smoke exited the tail pipe. The distinctive sound of the two-stroke motor instantly reminded him of his teenage years and the bike he owned at that time.

Don drew his bladed hand across the front of his neck signaling for Rob to shut down the engine. Rob complied immediately and looked at his friend for an explanation.

"I don't want any nosy neighbors coming around to ask questions if we can help it. They'll get to hear and see you leaving soon enough, and by then it won't matter. Plus you're gonna smoke us out of the garage with that thing--even if the door is open."

"Okay, I got it."

Rob excused himself and returned to what had become his temporary sleeping and resting area in the living room. His meager belongings were all packed tight and neat, either folded and placed directly next to his pack, or inside of the pack itself. He allowed himself to ponder over his present circumstances.

He was torn between starting back on his trek to get home as soon as possible and spending another day or two taking advantage of the decent food, shelter, and rest being provided at his friend's home.

On the one hand the emotional part of his mind was absolutely anxious to return to his family as soon as was physically possible, and he didn't want to waste another minute before doing so. On the other hand, the logical part of his brain was reminding him that his odds of successfully getting there would be far greater if he was well nourished and rested.

The unique nature of the friendship between he and Don—each having saved the other's life (if you counted the ambush against the robbers as having preemptively accomplished this)—was that no request from one could be denied by the other. But that didn't necessarily make it right in Rob's view.

He decided tomorrow would be his last day here.

Spending these days here at their home has been enough of a burden for the couple already. It's wrong to take advantage of their kindness. I need to go.

Rob spent the next day doing very little besides resting in preparation for what he hoped would be the last leg of his trek home. He tried to take naps on multiple occasions throughout the day, but found himself too anxious to actually sleep.

That night, while the three friends shared a dinner of canned soup, crackers, and weak coffee, Rob informed Don and Vangie that he planned on leaving the next morning after breakfast. Vangie insisted on letting him use some of their valuable water to wash his underclothes and socks. He heated water in a cooking pot over the camp stove and poured it into a plastic bucket. After adding a small portion of bleach to the hot water, he did his best to manually agitate the water and then hand wrung the items as dry as he was able. The clothes wouldn't have time to fully dry before his departure, but he would simply tie them to the outside of his pack and let them air dry while he headed toward home.

That night he spent the better part of a half hour going over the ingredients of his pack. He still had two energy bars and a small amount of peanut butter in a plastic zip-lock baggie. After asking Don for permission, he refilled his personal water containers as well. He checked the condition and operation of his firearms as best he could. The duct tape repair job he had performed on his pack after the crazy man had cut through the nylon canvas material with the machete appeared to be holding up.

God bless duct tape.

He slept well for the first five hours after letting his head hit the cushion on the living room couch, but he was visited by more nightmares after that. He woke up sweating and groaning. Despite his efforts he was unable to get back to sleep and spent over two hours lying on the couch dealing with his *brain traffic.*

The next morning Vangie fixed a big breakfast for them. She mixed water into some powdered eggs, fried a good quantity of small chunks of *Spam,* and scrambled them up together over the camp stove. Both men enjoyed the comfort food, savoring the tasty meal during every bite they took. As for herself, she only ate a small portion of the breakfast, but all three of them enjoyed their own large cup of coffee. The coffee was consumed in an uncharacteristically slow manner by all.

After thanking Vangie for her care and hospitality, he gave her a big hug and then shrugged into his backpack straps, once again feeling the familiar weight of the pack. He secured the shotgun to the cord hanging off the strap, just as before. This time he also used a small section of duct tape to pin the weapon against the pack's strap. Since he would be riding the dirt bike he was concerned that the little scattergun would bounce around too much unless it was secured with the tape. If he needed to get access to it quickly, he figured he could yank hard and free it of the tape.

He walked with Don to the garage, approached the motorcycle, and wheeled it out to the front of the house. Don had filled the tank with gasoline mixed with two stroke oil designed for use with this type of engine. Rob leaned the bike against the side of the house and approached his friend. Don extended his hand anticipating a goodbye handshake, but Rob stepped past his outstretched hand and said, "screw that," as he gave him a big bear hug and slapped his back a couple of times.

"You take care now, okay," Don said.

"You know it. And you take care of both yourself and Vangie. You better remember what I told you when it comes to protecting yourselves."

Not wanting to spend any more time on the farewell for fear of becoming emotional, Rob spun around and straddled the bike. He got it started on the second kick this time. He revved the engine, taking satisfaction in the whiny high pitched sound emitted by the engine. Then he pulled in the clutch lever, stomped on the gear shifter to get it into first gear, and released the clutch a little slower than he should have.

Rob kept the RPM's high and had the machine into fourth gear by the time he had ridden past the few men standing in the cul-de-sac, their looks of astonishment giving him a juvenile sense of satisfaction as he welcomed the adrenaline now rushing through his body.

He stayed in fourth gear after exiting the cul-de-sac until he had entered the main drag of Sepulveda Blvd again. Now he shifted into fifth gear as he rode in a northerly direction. He had the motorcycle moving at close to fifty miles an hour, traveling down the middle of the street and negotiating his way around the occasional stalled car in the roadway as he scanned for any obstacles or other threats.

He noticed several persons standing on their porches or front lawns staring at him, jaws agape, as he rode past them, pushing the two-wheeled machine to about ninety percent of its capacity. He was pleased to feel his old riding skills, unused for a quarter of a century, to be returning as he familiarized himself with the dirt bike. His only concern at this point was to eat up as many miles as possible before the motorcycle either ran out of gas or broke down.

At one point, after having covered approximately two miles, he entered a new residential block. Once again scanning as far ahead as he was able, he saw a group of young men running out toward the sidewalk on his right side about mid-block in front of him. Two of the men carried sticks that appeared to be cut-off shovel handles, and another had a long gun--either a rifle or shotgun.

It was clear to Rob they were planning on trying to stop him, probably by knocking him off of the motorcycle or shooting him. He had anticipated the possibility of others trying to separate him from his motorcycle along his route home; after all, the bike represented the ability to do a lot of things that most weren't capable of doing under the conditions. Yet he hadn't worked out a plan on how to avoid letting this happen. He had told himself he would figure it out on the fly, and now he had to do just that.

Just prior to reaching the middle of the block, he let off of the throttle to slow his speed, then stomped hard on the gear box lever twice, downshifting two gears as he veered left and yanked up on the handlebars just before the front tire hit the curb. He entered the left sidewalk without any problem and cranked the throttle back as far as it would go, enjoying yet another adrenaline rush as the engine let out its distinctive high-pitched sound attendant to reaching high RPM's. The bike accelerated past the threatening men and continued putting distance behind him and his would be ambushers.

Nice try shitheads.

For the first time in he didn't know how long, Rob was actually enjoying himself. It was nice to be able to experience the thrill of an adrenaline rush without having to hurt anyone for a change. He pushed the motorcycle along, trying to estimate--as best he could--where the engine was performing at about ninety percent of its maximum capability. He hoped this would reduce the chances of an engine failure, but he really had no idea if this was the case.

Rob came up to Venice Boulevard, turned westward, and travelled another mile or so before coming to Lincoln Boulevard. After covering a quarter mile he saw another group of young thuggish looking men that appeared to be planning some sort of ambush. It looked like he was the guest of honor for this one too. They were busy pushing inoperable cars into position to block the street, presumably for the purpose of preventing him from passing through.

These guys are obviously hearing the motorcycle's engine from a long way off, and they're mobilizing themselves before they even see me coming.

Uh-oh, he thought as he saw several young gangster types jogging into the street eighty yards or more ahead of his location, each carrying what looked like high capacity rifles, based on the long magazines protruding from below the weapons' receivers.

Fuck! Now what do I do? I can't get past them without the strong chance of getting shot as I try to blow by them!

Rob made an instant decision he hoped would prevent his ass from getting shot. He squeezed the front wheel's hand brake and stood on the foot brake for the rear wheel at the same time, all the while using his other foot to repeatedly mash down on the shifter. When the motorcycle had slowed enough for him to make a u-turn in the wide four lane street, he whipped the bike around in a full hundred eighty degree turn. Then, with the armed men now behind him, he opened the throttle as far as it would go. He began to zig-zag left to right and back again in case the gunmen behind him began shooting at him.

Might as well create as hard a target to hit as possible.

He heard three or four shots as he accelerated, pushing the bike for all it had. He had no way of knowing how close any of the rounds had come to striking him. Didn't matter anyway.

Just keep hauling ass, he told himself.

Rob thought about how he was seeing a substantial increase in the number of hostile groups and other problem types roaming outside their residences compared to what he and Don had encountered during their earlier travels. He wasn't sure whether to attribute this change to the locations he was now traveling through or the fact more time had passed. He considered the possibility it could be a combination of these factors.

It's been more than two weeks now since the shit hit the fan. I'll bet more people have gone through whatever food and water supplies they had by now, and they're probably starting to get pretty desperate.

Refocusing his attention on the road, he made a right turn at the first intersection, accelerated west-bound for two blocks, then made another right turn, once again heading north.   Pushing the motorcycle forward, he snapped his neck left and right in an attempt to release some of the tension that had built up over the past few minutes. He was pleased to hear the bike's engine still sounded like it was running strong and the torque similarly felt as though it were as strong as when he had begun the ride. He cut back over to Lincoln Blvd several blocks north of where he had originally detoured to get away from the ambush. He was now riding at full speed north-bound on the large boulevard again.

It was only then that he saw that the section of road fifty yards ahead had been completely blocked by several cars creating a blockade across the street. It appeared as though they had been pushed into the street from curb line to curb line.   There were also items—they looked like some kind of furniture--that had been positioned across the sidewalks on either side of the street where the barricade was set up.

He managed to un-sling his shotgun and grip it in his left hand as he slowed the motorcycle and scouted his surroundings for possible options. He would have preferred to have the scattergun in his strong hand, but he needed the use of that for the throttle control of the bike. As he came to within ten yards of the barricade, now in first gear with the wheels of his machine barely rolling, he saw the man—not much more than a boy really--running toward him, baseball bat grasped in his hands. Rob's peripheral vision had served him well. Had his head been positioned only slightly more to the left he would've missed him altogether and become a human *piñata*.

But his head had not been positioned too far to the left, and, unlike when he had been attacked by the machete wielding madman while sorting his pack, this time Rob had his shotgun in his hand—his left hand! He had no choice but to keep his right hand on the bike's throttle. He discharged the buckshot when the teenager was fifteen feet away from him. Only three of the pellets found their mark, but the guy went down, the wooden bat clattering as it hit the pavement. Rob had almost dropped the gun after firing it left-handed while manipulating the controls of the motorcycle with his other.

Seeing an opening for escape, Rob used his left foot to shift into a higher gear without benefit of the hand operated clutch. He went onto the sidewalk, trashed a dying flowerbed while gaining access to a front yard of sparse brown grass, and then entered the adjacent yard before returning to the sidewalk and finally the street. He had gotten around the barricade and was once again accelerating, getting all he could out of the old dirt bike. He brought the motorcycle to a stop a block farther north and reloaded the shotgun. Then he pressed hard on the used duct tape to once again anchor the weapon as best he could before taking off.

Rob allowed himself to enjoy the feeling of the wind on his face as he pushed the bike to its maximum speed, its distinctive high-pitched engine whine music to his ears. He had escaped yet another close call and was high on the feeling.

Yeaahhh!--None of you motherfuckers can stop me!

Spilling over with the exhilaration associated with all that was going on, he uttered a drawn out primitive battle cry--something between a yell and an extended guttural scream. It was so loud that it could be heard over the motorcycle's high pitched engine. He used the handle bars to dip and turn as he dodged abandoned cars, the vehicles and assorted items pushed into his path, and even the occasional object thrown at him. He had underestimated the level of effort that would be brought to bear against him by those wanting access to the dirt bike. But he didn't care at this point.

Fuck you all—come try to take it from me if you all want it so bad! Just try it!

He was now high as a kite on the adrenaline rush provided by the combination of the motorcycle's speed, the attacks, and the unending obstacle course he was forced to negotiate as he pressed on northward toward his home.

43

MALIBU, CA

Rob rode the Yamaha at a comfortable speed, traveling at about forty miles per hour north-bound on Pacific Coast Highway. He was now in the exclusive area of Malibu. After escaping the second ambush, he had taken Lincoln Boulevard north to the Ten Freeway entrance, and then continued on the freeway shoulder westward, working his way around an unending collection of abandoned cars--virtually all of which had been ransacked and/or cannibalized for parts. When he came to the end of the freeway in Santa Monica it turned into the Pacific Coast Highway. He continued in a northerly direction on PCH through the exclusive area of Pacific Palisades and finally into Malibu.

Prior to the EMP, Pacific Coast Highway had been a scenic drive for most, and an artery transporting commuters to and from work for others. While it still afforded Rob a beautiful view of the vast Pacific Ocean as he looked over his left shoulder, there was now an undeniable eeriness to his surroundings.

He attributed the strange and unsettling ambience to the fact there was an unusual lack of human activity in the formerly festive area. There was none of the typical vehicle traffic, virtually no pedestrian presence, and an unsettling quiet--although he shouldn't have been aware of the latter due to the sound of his motorcycle. Nonetheless, he could somehow *feel* the abnormal quiet.

He glanced at the small coffee shop located on the east side of Pacific Coast Highway, taking in its smashed windows and the fact there were no longer any tables or chairs visible within its confines.

The rustic wooden sign declaring the unpretentious name of the place--*The Coffee House*--remained intact above the shattered plate glass window that had afforded patrons a partial view of the Pacific Ocean prior to the grid crash. Rob recalled how he had stopped to have a cup of coffee at this place many a time over the past several years as a means of taking a small respite from the combined stress of the day's work and driving in heavy traffic on his way home.

He found himself succumbing to his penchant for letting his mind wander, wondering about the fate of the middle-aged couple who owned and operated his favorite coffee shop. He remembered when he had told the couple what he did for a living—something he almost never did during casual contacts—after an incident where he caught the woman's expression of startled recognition as her eyes focused on his front waistband area. Rob had accidentally allowed his shirt tail to ride up just enough to expose the edge of his handgun to the ultra-observant woman. The friendship between the two owners and himself was a casual one, but nonetheless one he enjoyed during his regular stops.

Where had they said they lived again? Was it in Agoura Hills? That was probably within walking distance for them if they had to walk home.

Rob returned his focus to his current situation as he strained to see what might be in the road up ahead. So far, so good. He had no way of knowing that a large number of Los Angeles County Jail inmates had recently been released due to the sheriff staff's inability to supervise or feed them following the EMP grid crash. No electricity, no working plumbing, and no resupplying of necessary items like food for the huge jail facility meant the system couldn't continue to operate. As if that wasn't bad enough, the sheriff's department staff was trickling out of the huge facility on almost an hourly basis. The ship was going down, and they all knew it--inmates and staff alike.

The release of most of the inmate population in the nation's largest institution of incarceration had produced some ugly results. Some might have referred to the phenomenon as an example of "unintended consequences" on the part of those making the decision, but truth be told, this was not an accurate description. The truth was that those rendering the decision knew full well they were dumping some seriously malevolent and dangerous individuals into a public venue currently devoid of any effective law enforcement presence. It wasn't that the sheriff's department personnel didn't care; it was simply that they felt they had no viable alternative. They had to choose between sentencing the incarcerated men to a slow and miserable death by starvation and/or violence while inside locked cells, or releasing them.

What this meant for Rob as he rode the off-road motorcycle through Malibu, was that the emptying of the huge jail system had prompted a lot of very dangerous men to migrate considerable distances from the massive facility. Some inmates went home, others sought out places in their neighborhoods or near their neighborhoods to hook up with old acquaintances. A smaller number--those with no family or others worth reconnecting with—opted to head for greener pastures. Simply put, they went to areas where they thought their opportunities were greater--exclusive places like Beverly Hills, Santa Monica, and Malibu in addition to dozens of other affluent locations thought to have valuables for the taking.

One hardened criminal in this category was enjoying his newfound freedom after having been locked up for ten months. A month ago he had been convinced he was heading for a fifteen year prison sentence that was sure to follow his trial. His recent post EMP release was nothing short of a windfall for him. Unlike virtually all of those around him on the downtown Los Angeles streets and sidewalks, he was so happy he could barely contain himself.

While walking along a sidewalk less than a mile from the jail facility, he encountered a bicycle riding young man out searching for food for his family of three. Based on what the inmates had been told by the jail staff just prior to being released en masse, the freed criminal was aware that the power grid had gone down and that it wasn't expected to be back up for a long time. He had also overheard a conversation between jail staff deputies indicating the cities in L.A. County were now without police presence or response.

He saw the bicycle and immediately knew he wanted it.

Still wearing the royal blue jail issue pants and a white t-shirt, he motioned for the man on the bicycle to stop. The thug had feigned a substantial limp in the hopes of reducing his threatening appearance. He knew full well his appearance--a lean muscular body of which over eighty percent was covered with dark colored prison tattoos--was likely to be met with caution, or even outright avoidance, by most. The religious family man decided to stop his bicycle and see what the limping guy with the tattoo covered neck wanted. Believing that the man was injured, he didn't view him as much of a threat. Perhaps he even had some information that could assist him in his search for food.

As the man on the bicycle came to a stop, his feet resting on the ground with his legs straddling the tubular steel frame, the jubilant criminal wasted no time on a greeting or other pretense. He closed the distance between them and lunged forward, swinging his right fist violently into the man's face. The blow landed hard on the bicyclist's cheek, knocking him off of his feet and sending the bike crashing on top of him. The jail-bird stepped around the bicycle and kicked the downed man several times as he lay on the sidewalk, knees pulled up into his chest while trying to use his hands to protect his face and head. There was very little if any anger in the predator as he viciously attacked the man; he simply wanted to ensure his victim wasn't going to offer any resistance as he took his bicycle from him. It was just business.

The thief rode his new bicycle off and on for the next twenty four hours. He wasn't familiar with riding a bicycle that had multiple gears and hand brakes, but he learned how to use these mechanisms within a couple miles of travel. He had made the decision to head for the coast where he knew there was a plethora of homes inhabited by people who had more wealth than they knew what to do with.

He arrived in Malibu on his bicycle as a tired man. But he soon found himself feeling invigorated by the large number of targets of opportunity here. There were so many targets he didn't know where, or how, to start. Although he had no way of knowing it, he was ahead of what would eventually be a wave of desperate mobs descending on this area like human locusts.

He found the second house he approached vacant. He observed what looked like an elaborate security system, including several security cameras mounted in different locations throughout the property and house, but none of that mattered after the grid had been down for so long. Besides, he knew there would be no police response.

After gaining entry through a window he drew the conclusion that it was a second home for a wealthy family. He helped himself to some packaged dry food and several warm beers that were in a refrigerator that had lost any of its cooling ability weeks ago. While ransacking the house he found a pair of jeans and a sweatshirt displaying a *Malibu* logo in front of a silk screened sailboat. He jettisoned his jail trousers and filthy t-shirt, glad to be replacing them even if the jeans were a few sizes too large. This was remedied with a thin leather belt located in the bedroom's closet.

The burglar located the real prize upon entering a den lined with expensive looking wood paneling and several mounted heads of big game animals. His attention was immediately drawn to a scoped .30-06 caliber hunting rifle displayed in an expensive glass and wood cabinet. He had no way of knowing the rifle was an expensive firearm that had been passed down for two generations, but he figured he would find a good use for it at some point. He pulled the rifle to his shoulder and looked out the large window toward the expansive sea through the rifle's telescopic sight. He figured out how to cycle the firearm's bolt action in order to prepare it for firing, and then fired the empty rifle several times to familiarize himself with its operation.

He found a box of cartridges for the rifle but it took him almost five minutes to figure out how to load it. He had difficulty in determining what he was looking at through the six power magnification provided by the rifle's scope, but after playing with it for the better part of ten minutes, he got to where he could clumsily use the telescopic sight for viewing.

He heard the sound of the motorcycle long before it was anywhere near him. Thinking that having a motorcycle would be far better than the bicycle he had used to get here, he set about seeing what he could do to acquire the motorized vehicle for himself. The impulsive sociopath had no experience in riding a motorcycle, let alone a dirt bike, but this fact didn't deter him in the least.

He ran toward the front of the house with the rifle, acknowledging the growing noise of the motorcycle's engine. He positioned himself so that he could see most of the street in front of the home he had burglarized. He positioned the rifle's fore-end across the stone wall that bordered the entrance to the property, creating a fairly stable shooting platform. It was hard enough to use the scope without having to deal with a bouncing or wobbling rifle.

He periodically looked through the scope at the street to the south of where he waited. He still had some difficulty using the scope, but was managing well enough. He noted Pacific Coast Highway looked a lot different now than it had when he was here two years ago working as a laborer.

He was, all told, a man of the streets, and as such had acquired a fundamental understanding of how to use certain weapons. But he was nowhere near any kind of a rifleman. He told himself he had watched enough movies to know he only had to hold the crosshairs of the telescopic sight on his intended target while pulling the trigger to hit it. As the sound of the motorcycle grew still louder, he didn't have to wait long before it appeared. He saw Rob riding the dirt bike through the scope. He placed the cross hairs on Rob's chest and *pulled* the trigger.

Had he understood even the basics of rifle shooting, he would have *squeezed* the trigger—some might use the term *press*--but he was simply a street predator with a new tool he had little knowledge of how to use. Still, his young eyes and good muscle control, coupled with the unfortunate coincidence of Rob's slowing, resulted in his shot doing some damage.

Rob had intentionally reduced the motorcycle's speed to less than twenty miles per hour well before he approached the intersection where the expansive Pepperdine University was located. He wasn't sure if he wanted to take Malibu Canyon Road over to the 101 Freeway or continue up the coast on the Pacific Coast Highway to get home. As he pondered the advantages and disadvantages of the two options, he felt a searing hot burning sensation in his right thigh. Due to the engine's noise, he never heard the report of the rifle shot that had sent the bullet through his gas tank and across his leg, but the resultant pain caused him to momentarily lose control of the motorcycle. This almost proved to be catastrophic for the former patrol cop.

The dirt bike's front wheel threatened to lose its equilibrium but Rob miraculously managed to right the machine and keep it traveling essentially in a straight line. Unfortunately that did nothing to help the gasoline now exiting the finger sized hole in the gas tank. Rob had glanced down at his leg to try to get some idea as to what was causing the sudden pain when he saw the hole in the tank and instantly connected the dots. Someone had shot at him.

He scanned his surroundings, looking ahead as well as to his left and right in a desperate effort to try to locate the source of the bullet. Failing to do so, Rob made the decision to ditch the bike before any number of bad things—or worse things—happened. He feared if he rode the machine until it quit he would either be shot again, this time possibly fatally, or that the motorcycle would catch on fire. In fact, he was wondering why the latter hadn't already happened given the amount of fuel that had leaked from the tank onto the hot engine, but he wasn't going to complain about getting some good luck for a change. Well, maybe it didn't actually qualify as *good* luck.

No longer getting the benefit of his naturally induced euphoria, Rob experienced good old fashioned fear as he applied both brakes as hard as he could and jumped off the bike just before it came to a complete stop. The rider-less motorcycle continued on for several yards before wobbling and crashing to the ground, the consequential sparks igniting the leaking gas and causing the bike to catch on fire. Rob lost his own balance as he dismounted the bike, falling on his good leg and sustaining some road rash to his left hand as he quickly got back on his feet and ran for all he was worth to the closest position of cover he could find.

Scrambling as though his life depended on it, Rob ran toward the fence line of the property immediately to his right. Running in an easterly direction away from PCH, he pumped his legs for all they were worth, taking a certain level of satisfaction in noting that his right leg still worked despite the pain. He came to a chain link fence and stopped just long enough to remove his pack and shotgun and then throw them over the six foot high barrier.

He considered the possibility that he was experiencing a déjà vu moment as he pulled himself over the fence. He hoped and prayed he wasn't going to hear any indication of vicious dogs on the property as he had several days prior in the Westchester neighborhood.

He was relieved to hear nothing at all. He remounted his pack and shotgun and headed out with a fast paced walk. He took in the huge house and large property he was currently trespassing on. He concluded whoever had been shooting at him was no longer likely to be interested in him now that his motorcycle was gone, but he none-theless preferred to stay away from the large street if at all possible. In fact, based on all that had happened to him during the last few hours, he wanted to avoid surface streets altogether. His plan now was to cover as much ground as possible by hiking through private land. Of course this posed its own risks, but he thought it was the lesser of the two evils.

Before he did anything else, Rob wanted to check out his injured leg. Discarding any concern for modesty, he dropped his trousers so he could get a good look at his injury. He observed a red line, perhaps a quarter inch deep, beginning an inch above his knee and continuing until only three inches below his hip. The shallow wound channel lightly oozed blood, but it was clearly not a serious injury. The bullet had merely created a shallow path across his leg--painful but super-ficial. A lucky break, unless you considered being shot at by some asshole with a rifle a significant piece of bad luck to begin with. The proverbial glass of water: half empty or half full?

Rob knew he couldn't risk having the wound becoming infected. Though he had no specific knowledge about the current status of hospitals and other medical clinics, he had no doubt that by now they were operating at a bare minimum level--if at all.

With no power, depleted medical supplies, and vanishing medical staff, could they even be functional, he wondered.

He broke out his small first aid kit and removed a small tube of *Neosporin* antibiotic ointment. He applied the ointment sparingly on the wound, pulled up his pants, and returned the first aid kit in his pack.

He mentally revisited the option of traveling on the road versus through private land as he made his way east. He laughed aloud as he thought about the possibility of a resident shooting him as he lumbered through their private land.

That would be just my luck. I manage to survive all this other stuff up to now only to have that Goddamn Murphy rearing his ugly little head as I hump through a back yard and get shot by some scared rich guy!

Rob had covered almost a full mile in this manner, confident he was maintaining essentially an easterly direction, when he observed an expanse of trees—he suspected they were Sycamores—a hundred fifty yards or more in the distance. As he stopped walking and squinted at the trees his hopes immediately soared; a collection of Sycamores generally indicated a water source.

Despite the encouragement gleaned from the Sycamore trees, his attention was drawn to a collection of waist high plants of unknown type thirty yards from where he now stood. Before traveling any farther he decided to take advantage of the privacy the plants provided to address his bodily waste functions. He had learned to use locations of opportunity when they presented themselves. One wanted to avoid having a need to go when the location wasn't a good one for the purpose.

He found a suitable place among the plant growth and prepared to take care of business. While squatting in a position that placed his hamstrings so close to his calves that they were almost touching, he suffered extreme leg cramps with no warning of their onset whatsoever.

Oh no...this has to be the result of dehydration! Not now God, please!

The cramps involved each of his hamstrings as well as the upper inside areas of both legs—and they were intensifying. He jumped up and tried to alleviate the excruciating pain by stretching out his legs, almost falling over into the dirt with his pants wrapped around his ankles in the process. He made sure to keep his legs straight so as not to aggravate the cramping as he reached down and yanked up his trousers. Not bothering to fasten his pants and grasping the holstered pistol to prevent its sliding off the belt, he began trudging in a circle in hopes of "walking off" the cramps.

The severe spasms would not let up—if anything they seemed to be intensifying. His leg muscles felt as though they were being pulled away from where they were attached to his bones so excruciating was the pain. Rob felt the beginnings of shock starting to present. Light headedness, nausea, a slight diminution of sound around him. All were symptoms portending a brief black-out if his prior experiences were any indication.

Rob fought off the shock by focusing on his anger. He recalled how more than once he had encountered seriously wounded gunshot victims who had kept the onset of shock at bay by drawing on their anger. None of these guys had done so intentionally, they had simply been extremely pissed off at the time and held onto that emotion. Rob had taken the lesson to heart.

After the better part of a minute, and having only noticed a marginal level of relief, Rob fished out three ibuprofen tablets from his first aid kit and chewed them up without water. He took a second or two to fasten his pants and resumed walking in a circle, knowing it would take at least fifteen minutes before he would feel any relief from the medication. He had no choice but to endure it until then. Walking over to his pack, he reached down and retrieved his water bottle. He drained its entire contents in large gulps, hoping this would help address the dehydration issue.

Finally, after fifteen or more minutes had gone by, Rob began to get some relief. The spasms were still present in both legs, but they were mild now. He had made it past the hard part for now.

He resumed his bowel movement, all the while taking care to avoid putting his legs into positions that might encourage more cramping. It was not an easy endeavor. He located some leaves suitable for the task and used them as toilet paper until almost finished, at which point he used a few squares of his dwindling supply of toilet tissue to complete the job. The method had helped him save the valuable commodity throughout his journey. A nickel sized application of hand gel rubbed into his hands, and he called it good. The physically beaten down deputy sheriff headed off toward the Sycamore trees.

Rob reached the Sycamores and found a small pond, no more than ten feet by twenty feet in overall size, at the center of the trees. It was full of murky water that didn't look suitable for drinking, but he was not dissuaded.

He took his empty steel water bottle and used his bandana to cover the opening. He filled the container by dunking the cloth covered opening beneath the surface of the pond, watching the air bubbles to know when it was full. He made a face as he observed the green substance trapped in the bandana after removing the container from the pond.

Now feeling fortunate just to be free of the excruciating leg cramps, he used another half hour to collect sticks and build a small fire. He utilized his water bottle, cable, and fire to purify the water and then allowed it to cool, just as he had done many times before. It was a slow process, but an almost foolproof one, and he didn't need to be sick along with everything else that seemed to be happening.

Rob could still feel his legs threatening to cramp up again—just the threat of the spasms really, not the actual condition. He decided to take advantage of the excellent little camp site to recuperate. He wanted to give his body time to rehydrate his muscles.

He finished off the peanut butter in his pack and downed as much of the purified water as he could keep down. He boiled more of the pond water and then allowed it to cool somewhere between warm and boiling. After pulling the empty *Platypus* flexible water bag from his pack, he put his gloves on and filled it with the hot water. He used it as a hot water bottle on his recovering leg muscles. For a while he cleared his mind as best he was able and simply allowed himself to bask in the warm comfort of the heat providing device. It was amazing what simple heat applied against the human body could do when it came to comfort and therapy.

Unlike when he had been hiking through the urban areas at the beginning of his trip home, Rob didn't want to travel in this semi-wilderness area at night. The topography here was prime rattlesnake territory, and he was well aware these snakes were active at night—especially at this time of year. Walking through this land without benefit of good vision would be a fool's errand. He decided he would try to travel during the day from this point on.

Rob spent what little remained of the day and the entire night in his makeshift camp, enjoying the partial protection afforded by the Sycamore trees as he propped himself against his pack to sleep. He utilized the setting to rest and eat a few meager food rations as well as to rehydrate his body until he felt he had completely saturated all of his tissues with the purified pond water. He topped off both of his water containers as well. Finally, he used hot water to rinse out his scum covered bandana.

Having somewhat reconstituted his energy level, and no longer feeling any cramping sensation in his legs, early the next morning Rob saddled up his pack and shotgun and started off in the direction of the sunrise.

Before he had covered even a quarter mile he encountered an eight foot high chain link fence topped with another eighteen inches of barbed wire. He looked left and right but could see no break in the fence that might allow him a way around the barrier.

The tired but optimistic family man took off his pack and shotgun, placing them on the ground in a manner that would allow him fast access to the weapon. He removed the small hacksaw blade he had stuck in his pack when he had first walked away from his disabled truck on the side of the freeway. He took a knee and used the blade to cut through the thick steel wiring that comprised the fence. It was a slow and tedious process, cutting one wire strand at a time, but he managed to get through enough of the wires to create a twenty inch square opening. He pushed his pack through, and then slithered through the opening.

Rob looked around for dogs, people, or any other obvious security features as he walked across the property. After continuing along on his original route for another hundred yards, he heard the unmistakable sounds of music. It was faint at first, but he realized he was drawing closer to the source as it grew louder. As part of his preference for classic rock music, Rob had listened to quite a bit of music from the 60's even though it was before his time. Now he was actually able to pick up the detail of the music he was hearing.

Growing ever closer to the source, a smile formed on his lips as he identified the song. He was hearing the 60's tune *Crystal Blue Persuasion* by a band called *Tommy James and the Shondells*. Rob had liked the song ever since he had first heard it years ago, and never failed to turn up the volume when it came on the radio despite the fact Stephanie considered the tune to be silly.

As he made his way through, and then exited, a thicket of unknown type plants and trees, Rob encountered a barbed wire fence that ran both directions for as far as he could see. There was no chain link fence on this side of the property—just an old-fashioned livestock type barbed wire fence that had three strands running horizontally, starting at about eighteen inches from the ground.

On the other side of the barbed wire fence he saw an old farm house and two large barns that looked like they could have been built in New England two hundred years earlier. The structures were located at the top of a grass covered rise no more than seventy five yards from where he now stood.

Adjacent to one of the barns were three smaller structures, each of which had its own chimney. He examined the chimneys for an additional second or two and concluded the buildings contained wood stoves--not fireplaces.

Interesting.

Rob was aware of the fact that wood burning stoves provided a great deal more utility than open wood burning fireplaces. One could use a good wood stove to heat water and cook certain meals, not to mention the stoves were far better at heating a home. All three structures were much newer than the other buildings, and Rob guessed they were used for additional residential housing--possibly for guests or perhaps the help.

Between the two old barns stood a large water tower built upon four six-by-six posts supported by X-shaped braces between the posts. A second water tank—this one at least four times the size of the elevated tank constituting the water tower--sat positioned on the ground below the water tower. An old fashioned hand water pump, presumably for drawing water from a well, was installed next to the ground tank.

A simple pulley system, including a rope and plastic open topped barrel with a rope harness around it, was attached to the top of the water tower. Rob quickly deduced the system was designed so that the barrel could be filled from the well or the ground tank and then hoisted with the pulley system to fill the water tower. It was labor intensive, but it would get the job done he figured.

At least three full cords of split firewood lay stacked against one of the barn walls under a corrugated tin roofed wood shed that looked like it had been built decades ago. He noted there was a long driveway on the opposite side of the property that ran in a north-south direction. He couldn't see the full length of the driveway, but he assumed it went all the way to Malibu Canyon Road, however far that might be. The property had plenty of seclusion, and it reminded him of a farm located some place far more rural than Los Angeles County.

Finally, Rob saw that there were two large propane tanks—he estimated five hundred gallons each—that were positioned on the side of the property's large barn. He roughly estimated that this was enough fuel to provide for a dozen people for two or three years, especially if it wasn't needed for heating a home.

The ex-cop drank the remaining water from his steel bottle and replaced the empty container in his pack, hoping he might get a chance to refill it while on this land. He removed his backpack and shotgun and then fished out his leather gloves. After putting on the gloves he slid the pack and shotgun under the bottom strand of barbed wire.

He rolled onto his back and slithered under the wire while using his gloved hands to push upward on the lower strand, ensuring that he wouldn't become snagged.

Having cleared the fence, he stood up, retrieved his pack, and put away his gloves. Again he repositioned the shotgun. He did his best to look around the property at the same time.

As soon as he slid into the pack straps he spent a brief moment lamenting the loss of the motorcycle, accepting that he would now have to make the remainder of the trek on foot. At least he had covered a good deal of ground with the motorcycle before losing it.

The music had changed, and he could now hear an old *Grateful Dead* song whose title escaped him. He had never cared much for their music, but he was certain this was the band he was hearing. As he came to the top of the rise the land leveled off, affording him a view of about a dozen people, all of them sitting in chairs positioned roughly into a circle adjacent to one of the barns. The group was a combination of men, women, and children. Rob saw the source of the music was a car stereo, complete with two modest sized car speakers, that rested on top of a rough-hewn wooden table placed in the middle of the chairs. Someone had wired the stereo to a car battery which rested on the ground below the table. He wasn't sure how the stereo had survived the EMP, but obviously it had somehow, and it was now being used to entertain this group.

Rob noticed the people all appeared to be what he considered hippie types based on their manner of dress in addition to something about the way they carried themselves. *Birkenstock* sandals, tie-dyed clothing worn by a few, as well as long hair and full beards on several of the men all contributed to his conclusion. He felt slightly ill-at-ease about his plainly visible shotgun. He tried to affect an overly jovial demeanor as he approached the group. He waived his arms and put on his best smile, all the while hoping they wouldn't see his phony performance for what it was.

One of the women, her young daughter sitting on her lap while she braided her hair, noticed Rob first. She said something to the others that he couldn't hear. Several more of the group looked in his direction. A few looked worried, or possibly even alarmed, at his presence. The others sported friendly smiles or similar expressions of welcome.

A man in his fifties with a long grey beard and hair almost to his shoulders stood up and began making his way toward Rob. He was carrying a large paperback book in his hand. Rob watched him stop briefly at the side of the main residence to lower a wooden door mounted at a forty five degree angle a few feet above ground level. He did so with the casual effort and nonchalance of one who had nothing to hide, yet Rob immediately suspected the significance of the man's actions. The door covered the opening to what appeared to be an old cellar under the house. A cellar that probably contained things a stranger shouldn't view.

As the man took his time approaching him Rob spent a moment taking in the surroundings. There was a large garden, including rows of tomatoes, squash, and miscellaneous other green vegetables located on the far side of the residential "guest" structures. Several avocado, orange, and even peach trees were growing on the property as well. Getting a closer look at the stacked firewood he couldn't help but notice the pieces were cut in short fourteen inch lengths. The short lengths of firewood were a strong indicator he had been right in guessing the "guest" structures had wood burning stoves as opposed to fireplaces in them. He knew most wood stoves required a notice-ably shorter length of firewood than fireplaces.

Rob caught a glimpse through an open barn door of a dozen pal-lets, most of which contained empty old-fashioned canning jars. Connecting the dots in his head, he assumed the residents were can-ning the vegetables and fruits grown on the farm so they could be preserved for extended periods. They were likely storing the canned items in the cellar the man had taken time to close a moment earlier. The cool subterranean location would be close to perfect for such storage, and it was a time proven method.

He entertained a brief thought. *This guy didn't want me to see whatever he has in that cellar--probably a whole bunch of canned food from their garden.*

Rob also took notice of an eighty by forty foot fenced pen located next to one of the barns that had been concealed from his view for the most part while he had first approached the buildings. Inside the larger section of the penned area were several goats, all of which were busy eating grass and weeds. A smaller section housed a collection of chicken coops.

As the man drew closer, Rob noticed the title of the paperback in his hand: *Natural Medicines and Cures for the Human Body.*

"How are you brother," the apparent group spokesman said as if he had known Rob for years and was glad to have him visiting. "Are you in need of anything for your travels?"

The average person who lacked the former street cop's experience with human subtlety in conversation might have merely accepted the offer at face value. However, Rob detected the slightest tell in the man's tone; or maybe it was something in his body language. Whatever the case, there was the unmistakable hint of a rushed request. He was convinced the man was asking if he could assist him so he could give him what he needed and then get him off the farm and on his way as soon as possible. And he didn't blame him. All of the "peace and love to everyone" stuff might be fine and well under normal circumstances, but Rob was pretty sure this guy knew things were different now.

"That's really nice of you," Rob replied, "but I'm just passing through is all. I really don't like walking on the main road out there if I don't have to--that's all."

He caught the hippie's eyes glancing at the shotgun hanging from his pack, but nothing was said.

"I understand. The roads can be dangerous," the hippie said. Rob thought the response was odd.

Was this guy aware of what was going on around here, or not?

"Would you like some water before you continue on your journey?"

He accepted the offer and the man called out for another in the group to retrieve it for him. Rob noted the fact he wasn't invited to sit down. He also noticed the group's spokesman hadn't asked him his name or inquired about where he was headed.

This guy is smart enough to know the less conversation that takes place between us the better the odds of having me be on my way. Definitely can't blame him for that. I think he knows what's going on. These folks have their own little commune--or whatever this is—going on here and they don't need any problems.

Rob said, "My plan is to get up to Malibu Canyon Road and then take it to the 101 Freeway, but I don't want to spend any more time walking along the freeway than I have to, so maybe I can find a different route."

The man looked toward the woman who was supposed to be getting his water before returning his focus on Rob, nodding his head to indicate he had heard him and approved of his plan. Or maybe only that he had heard him.

"Malibu Canyon Road is where this private road will take you," he said as he pointed at the long single lane road Rob had earlier observed. "I guess you can walk across these private lands for a while before you reach your destination, but I'm not sure that's really a good idea," he commented as he cracked a smile containing a trace of sarcasm. It wasn't lost on Rob that apparently this guy was enough of a capitalist to appreciate the sanctity of private property, especially when it was his land, or his neighbors' land, being trespassed upon.

A woman in her mid-forties with long greying hair arranged in a single braid and wearing a full length dress that could have been homemade, approached Rob with a mason jar of water and a genuine smile. He accepted the water and thanked her as he heard a new song coming from the car stereo. It was Neil Young's extended version of *Cortez the Killer*. The song reminded him of an earlier decade when he had spent nights hanging out with his younger brother in their family owned cabin in the mountains behind California's central coast.

Rob wondered what his younger brother and his family were doing to get through the post EMP conditions where they now lived in North Carolina.

Was North Carolina affected by the EMP? Well, my brother is a capable guy. He'll be able to take care of himself.

This train of thought prompted him to start thinking about his own family in Thousand Oaks again. The woman with the braid excused herself and left Rob and the group's head man alone as he slowly drank his water.

"I'm Rob by the way," he offered without extending his hand. The distance between them was sufficient to justify the lack of the somewhat formal gesture.

"I'm Edward."

"This is a nice little set-up you have here Edward. Looks like you're pretty close to being self-sufficient, huh?" He was answered with nothing more than a smile.

Rob was slightly irritated by the man's aloof personality. The logical part of his brain told him to be quiet and to simply get back on his route home, but there was something about the smugness of this guy that prompted him to broach the subject he was thinking about.

"Look, I get that you all seem to have a nice little situation here that's worked for you for however long. That's cool, and I can appreciate it being a nice way to live and all. I really can," Rob said with sincerity. "But here's the not so pretty reality part to all this," he said as he made eye contact with the middle-aged hippie.

"Not sure if you know this, but the grid is down and there aren't any first responders now--might not be for a long time either. Normally that might sound like a good thing to you, but believe me when I tell you it's not anything close to good right now."

He waited for a response from the man, but received nothing more than a noncommittal look. Not quite ready to let go of the point he wanted to make, Rob said, "Do you have a plan for defending all you have here? I'm guessing you have the responsibility for protecting these people here--am I right?"

The man called Edward responded with a slight smile and rolled his open hands outward in a placating motion. "We will help those who come here in need, just like we helped you."

Rob told himself he should let the issue drop, but he couldn't bring himself to let it go just yet.

"History is full of examples where good people believed they could triumph over bad people by merely responding to aggression and violence with kindness. It didn't usually end very well for those folks throughout history I might add."

"You mean examples like Gandhi," Edward replied with a not so subtle smirk.

Rob's rejoinder was not a new one, but it was new to Edward's ears.

"Actually," Rob said, "the only reason the pacifist thing worked for Gandhi was because the British were not a truly evil force. Yeah, sure, what they were doing at the time was arguably not right, but those holding political power in England at the time still possessed a collective conscience. At least enough of a conscience to listen to basic reason, and issues of right and wrong."

The worn out former cop shrugged his shoulders as if to suggest the new age hippie could either accept reality or ignore it; Rob wasn't interested in pressing the issue any further. He reminded himself that people had their own perspectives and he had to accept that. Not necessarily *respect* it, but *accept* it.

Rob noticed Edward was looking at him with thinly veiled surprise, presumably because until now he had thought his gun wielding guest to be the equivalent of a modern day Neandrathal.

Rob continued, even though it was against his better judgment.

"You know the more important lesson to be had from that whole Gandhi thing was that the same people who were so pleased with the success of the passive resistance against the Brits made their case to the Jewish people in Europe when the Nazis were doing their ugly shit." He had let himself slip into his second language--or maybe it was his first language now--street vernacular. But he was past the point of caring.

"Unlike the Brits", Rob said, "the Nazis were a truly evil force, and the pacifist approach didn't work very well for the Jews of Europe. Come to think of it, the pacifist thing didn't work very well for those who lived in Joseph Stalin's Soviet Union or Pol Pot's Cambodia either."

Fuck it. I'm tired of these dumb-ass people who refuse to acknowledge the way the world works, Rob said to himself.

Edward was absolutely quiet as he stared at Rob dumbfounded. As if on cue, Bob Dylan's classic song *Knockin' on Heaven's Door* came on over the battery powered music system. It was a song that fell like a heavy weight on his mood almost every time he heard it. Maybe it was because he had heard it being played too many times at funerals for those whom he had worked with--or at least known in his profession. Or maybe it was simply that he had actually listened carefully to the lyrics and was able to apply them to his own experience. Maybe it was a combination of the two things. Whatever the case, he had to force himself to ignore the song as best he could right now.

Rob told himself to lay off the hippie. He was storing more than a little anger and resentment currently, and he reminded himself it would be wrong to take it out on this guy. Finally he broke the silence between them.

"Okay, I won't push the issue any further. I appreciate your hospitality and I hope things work out well for you and your group here."

He lifted his empty mason jar as a half-assed gesture of gratitude while he uttered these last comments. As an afterthought, he removed his steel water bottle and took a few huge swallows despite the fact he was not thirsty in the least. Better to fill up with water while he had the opportunity, even though he felt water-logged. He asked Edward if he could have a piece of fruit and a refill for his water bottle before he went on his way. The man consented and held out his hand for Rob's water container. Promising to return shortly, he turned and walked away.

While the man used the old pitcher pump to fill Rob's water bottle before heading off to locate a piece of fruit for him, the former cop thought about the little farm and the group of people living here.

This isn't all that bad of a way to live I suppose. A simple life with everyone's responsibilities clear cut. Only minimal, if any, outside bullshit to deal with. Maybe the rest of us don't have things figured out as well as we tell ourselves we do. But I wonder what the deal is with this Edward guy, he asked himself.

Edward returned two minutes later with a large orange, half of an avocado, and his water container full of water. Rob thanked him and devoured the food in just over a minute. It had to have been pretty evident that Rob was still hungry, yet the man standing next to him offered him nothing more. It was now becoming uncomfortably obvious Edward wanted the visit to be over.

Rob wiped his hands on the front of his jeans, taking care to avoid touching his leg wound as he did so. He wished Edward luck with his farm, tightened his pack straps, and began hiking toward the driveway connecting the property to Malibu Canyon Road. As he approached the road he turned around one last time to take in the idyllic small farm. Turning back toward the road, he considered the place and the people he had just visited. They had a good self-sufficient situation, but he feared they were going to be visited by serious trouble before long.

I guess this Edward guy thinks he has it all figured out. Either he has some means and plan for protecting the place that he wasn't making known, or he's going to be in for one serious life changing surprise at some point.

He forced himself not to think about how the children on the little farm would be affected by the trouble that would sooner or later visit the group.

Dismissing the little commune and the potential problems the future might hold for its residents from his thoughts, he began to think again about his own family. He wondered what Stephanie and Charlie Wyatt had been doing to deal with all that had happened since the EMP. He comforted himself with the knowledge that he and Stephanie had set aside some disaster supplies a while ago and that Stephanie had a basic means of protecting herself and their son. He further consoled his worried heart by reminding himself that Stephanie had a strong dose of common sense and had proven herself a solid problem solver in the past.

A sudden spurt of energy caused him to quicken his pace as he realized he would probably be home within forty eight hours-- maybe even sooner. This injected him with a sense of well-being he hadn't felt since the EMP incident had occurred, and he welcomed the feeling. He allowed himself to imagine the nearing reunion with Stephanie and Charlie Wyatt, the sweet emotions washing over him like a rejuvenating warm shower. He assured himself they would establish a system to get through the post EMP disaster until things returned to normal, or whatever the "new normal" was going to be. They would work it out; of this he had no doubt.

Fortunately--or maybe not--Rob couldn't see the growing volume of smoke that had begun to fill the sky several miles to the south. Virtually the entire city of Santa Monica would soon be engulfed in flames, and those lucky enough to survive the ensuing destruction and mayhem would be migrating in search of any place offering a chance at survival.

44

SANTA MONICA MOUNTAINS, LOS ANGELES COUNTY

Rob walked for another two hundred yards before he realized there was now a massive amount of smoke a dozen miles to the south. He had no way of knowing that almost a quarter of the city of Santa Monica, and now portions of the adjacent Pacific Palisades, were on fire. But he could tell that it had to be one big fire to be causing all that smoke. With structures built close to each other, and no fire fighters to battle the burning buildings, it didn't take long to have an out-of-control conflagration moving through a residential area.

He similarly had no way of knowing the huge fire had been started by angry and petulant sociopaths. Sociopaths who, having been unable to get past a well defended home to pillage food and water stores inside, had decided to set fire to the place. As sieges went, fire was an ancient and historically successful tactic. Moreover, it was a tactic that the well-stocked and well-armed residents had not prepared for. The gasoline aided blaze had engulfed the house rapidly and then jumped to the neighbor's home, whereupon the process continued until dozens of homes were ablaze. Soon after that, entire neighborhoods were burning.

Rob reached the canyon road he had been aiming for and was now walking north toward the 101 Freeway. He felt the weight of the pack pulling on the straps against his shoulders. It was a sensation he should have been used to by now, but the opposite was true. It was wearing him down more and more each passing day. Yet his spirits were high. He anticipated he would be home and reunited with Stephanie and Charlie Wyatt soon. He was determined to press hard so that he would arrive tomorrow. His thoughts returned to the fire.

That fire is really bad. I wonder how many more people will die as a result? I'm just glad I got out of there when I did. One day's difference and I would've been in serious trouble.

Then the realization hit him hard.

That fire is going to displace one hell of a lot of people. People without food or water. People who were already desperate before the fire. How will this impact the Thousand Oaks area? Many of the people fleeing the burning areas will be able to reach our neighborhood in a few days.

For what had to be close to the thousandth time since the EMP, he forced himself to shift his thoughts. There was nothing he could do about the future problem of hordes heading into Ventura County where his family lived. He would address that later—after he was home.

He was glad that his leg wound--not much more than a deep scratch but still technically an open wound-- wasn't bothering him much. Even more than that, he was glad there was no infection as of yet. His pace had reached the point where he would've had to jog to be moving any faster. He felt the moisture on his body and welcomed it. Not a heavy sweat, just a light one. Had he been in a colder climate he would've slowed his pace a little, realizing that moisture of any kind was an invitation to hypothermia. But he wasn't worried about that here.

He removed his *boonie* hat and ran his palm across his forehead, wiped it on his jeans, and then ran it over the back of his neck. Replacing his hat, he wiped his wet palm across the crown. He was once again using his hand to pin his shotgun against his chest in order to avoid the weapon's irritating *bump, bump, bump* bouncing against his body as he walked. Two hours after he had left the hippie farm he had reached the frontage road that ran west, or south-west, of the 101 freeway. Pleased with his progress for a change, he busied himself looking around at his surroundings. Rob had decided to avoid the freeway itself because, unlike the frontage road, it would be difficult to get off that travel route and disappear in a hurry if trouble presented itself. Trying to get over the chain link fence bordering the freeway would slow him down.

The frontage road in this area was comprised mostly of sparsely arranged commercial buildings with a few small stores mixed in. Everywhere he looked he saw buildings in a similar state. Broken windows, ripped apart interiors, and assorted items—apparently of no value—strewn about in front of the buildings. It was obvious to Rob that there was not likely to be any areas--in Southern California anyway—that had been spared the destructive aftermath of the EMP.

He saw cars of every type abandoned on the freeway. Virtually all of them looked as though they had been gone through and stripped of anything of value. He wondered if the gasoline had been siphoned from the vehicles yet. There were cars that had been abandoned on the frontage road as well, but nowhere near as many as the freeway.

As he ran his hand over his face feeling the couple weeks' worth of beard he had been growing, he entertained the possibility of using one of the car mirrors to shave with.

I'll have to use either my folder or the big Kabar. Doubt either one would be fun to shave with. And I'll have to heat water.

He was starting to think about how his homecoming would take place. Absorbed in his happy mental sidebar, he realized he was smiling inanely. Embarrassed by his lapse, he looked around to see if anyone was watching him. He preferred to look unapproachable. The less inviting he appeared, the better, as far as he was concerned. He put his poker face back on and continued walking.

He heard the dogs before he knew where they were. A few were snarling and snapping at each other, but not in the way associated with a dogfight. It was the snapping and snarling that occurs when individual dogs become overly excited about the pack's objective. Thanks to cable networks that showcased dogsled teams in Alaska, Rob knew that at times this excitement caused dogs to engage in brief displays of aggression toward the dog beside them. The short-lived but ferocious snarling was a good indication this was what he was hearing.

Yeah... That sounds like a pack alright, and something has them excited. I can't see anything else around here that they could be focused on besides me. Where are they coming from?

Rob knew he had very little time to get ready for what he feared was an imminent attack. Once the dogs got hold of him it would be too late to defend himself. He would be bitten, pulled to the ground, and dragged around, unable to effectively use any of his weapons. He raised the lightweight shotgun and cocked the hammer, his head on a virtual swivel in an attempt to locate the approaching pack.

The lead dog rounded the corner of an abandoned locksmith shop with both of its front windows smashed out. It was a large short-haired tan colored unknown breed, with a huge head. It wasn't snarling or barking, but rather simply breathing heavy as it came directly for him from a distance of fifty feet. He could see three more dogs tight on his heels. Two were long haired dogs easily weighing eighty pounds apiece, while the third was a mongrel that almost looked like it was part coyote.

He pointed the shotgun at the lead dog and squeezed the trigger. As the concussion of the powerful round filled his ears, he saw the dog go down, his feet folding under him instantly. The rest of the pack was closing on him quickly. He saw the attack as though it were happening in slow motion. He saw one of the canines had a lot of white foam-like froth at its mouth. He thought it strange that he noticed this detail at such a moment.

Realizing he had no time to reload the shotgun, he let it drop on the makeshift *Paracord* sling and yanked his pistol free. He tried to get a front sight on the closest animal running at him, but it was moving too fast. He fired twice and missed twice. Three more shots and still no effect. Two of the dogs were almost on him by the time he was able to get two rounds into one and a single round into the other. One went down snorting and stopped breathing a few seconds later. The other, hit between its chest and hips, began yelping and biting at the wound. But it was no longer intent on attacking Rob.

The last dog—the one that looked like it was part coyote--stopped running at him. It began moving side to side, forward slightly and then back again, baring its teeth at Rob in a menacing snarl that gave him pause even though it wasn't advancing on him. As the coyote-mix closed to ten feet, he took careful aim and shot it through the head, dropping it like the proverbial "sack of potatoes". Then he finished off the dog that had been gut shot, ending the animal's suffering.

Rob looked all around him, now concerned about the possibility he had attracted unwanted attention with all the shooting. He opened the shotgun and replaced the empty chamber with a double aught shell from his shirt pocket. Then he removed his partially depleted pistol magazine and replaced it with a fresh one. He would top off the half empty magazine later when he came to a suitable spot. Right now he wanted to get the hell out of here. He started walking at a fast clip as he scanned his surroundings, hoping he hadn't brought himself a whole new episode of trouble.

A man in his early thirties-- who had the appearance of someone used to being transient and living out of the full-sized dirty backpack he wore-- passed Rob walking the other direction on the frontage road. They stopped to talk for a moment, each ostensibly sharing any news about where he had just come from. In Rob's case his comments were meaningless. In fact, they were complete bullshit. There was no way he was going to let this guy know about his having to shoot the pack of dogs. As for the transient, he mentioned only that all of the stores had been looted and that people were doing the best they could to eat and find water.

"Oh yeah," the man said, "there is one place that's open—well sort of open I guess. The Costco in Westlake."

Rob looked at the guy to try to get a read on what he was saying.

Is this guy joking or what's he getting at? He can't be serious, can he?

"Okay, I guess I have to plead stupid. What are you talking about? I'm at a loss here."

The man replied, "Let's just say the local cops decided to take the place over and do their own business."

Rob just looked at him.

"Are you talking about the Sheriff's Department or what?"

A head nod.

"The boys in tan and green have set up shop there from what it looks like. If you go past there, you can judge for yourself I guess."

"Okay. Wow. That's kinda interesting. Wonder what's going on there?"

The transient shrugged his shoulders.

Rob's mind was working fast. He wondered if what this guy said was even close to being accurate. Then he wondered, if true, whether he could expect to get any preferential treatment. He could show his identification and tell them he was a LASD deputy. He was slightly ashamed of his thinking, but the shame was quickly replaced by a desire to help his family—and himself.

With nothing more to say, the two wished each other luck and continued on their respective routes.

About an hour before nightfall, a worn out and hungry Rob Flynn stopped in an industrial area in Westlake Village. The buildings were made of concrete and cinder block. Broken windows were now the norm, and this place was no different. He found a small alcove between two buildings, no more than three feet wide, with twenty foot high exterior building walls on all three sides. It would do just fine for what he hoped would be his last night away from his family.

Rob found a large cardboard box that had been discarded in the parking lot, its original contents no doubt stolen days—or weeks—ago. A little cutting with his folding knife and he had six pieces no bigger than two feet square. He brought them to his sleeping spot and placed them on the ground where the rear wall formed the end of the alcove. In keeping with his practice, he would sleep sitting on the ground leaning against his pack supported by the wall. The multiple sheets of cardboard would provide a little bit of insulation. It wasn't going to be comfortable, but it would be better than sleeping on bare concrete.

He didn't even bother to try to make a fire. He drained what remained in his steel water bottle, refilled it with the plastic bladder in his pack, and finished off the remaining little bit of food he had left.

I wonder if I should've thought about taking some meat from one of the dogs I killed? Probably won't matter. I should be home by tomorrow sometime anyway.

While there was still some natural light, and before going to sleep, he loaded the pistol magazine he had used earlier, and then put it back in his belt pouch. He slept fitfully through the night, his back and neck keeping him awake for at least half of the eight hours he spent on the cardboard bed. He was relieved when the first sign of dawn revealed itself.

Okay, here it is...the last day on the road before I get to see my family.

He had his gear ready to go in less than five minutes from the time he got up. No hot water, no food, and no morning constitutional to deal with today. Just a hunger induced rumbling in the stomach. Since it was on his route anyway, he decided to go by the Costco store to see what the situation there was all about. With any luck he might even get something to eat.

He arrived in the parking lot of the huge warehouse store well before noon. He saw that there were four uniformed male LASD deputies standing at the large entrance of the place. Each of the men carried a shotgun. None looked older than thirty, and they all appeared to be bored.

While he had never considered it before, it now seemed obvious to him that the Costco building was close to the perfect place for a capable force to commandeer following a major disaster. Not only was the building full of almost everything a person might need to wait out a catastrophic storm, its windowless concrete reinforced cinder block wall construction was conducive to defending against attack.

Rob appreciated that someone had seen to it that multiple cars were positioned tightly against the outward opening double emergency doors. It was an obvious measure to prevent access at these points.

As he approached the main entrance to the building, Rob displayed his LASD badge and identification card. He walked slowly as he did so, making every effort not to convey an attitude of special privilege or expectation. All eyes were on the sawed-off twelve gauge hanging off his pack strap. One of them immediately stepped away from the group and began to flank him. Rob heard the metallic *"click"* of the safety being removed from the man's weapon.

"Hi guys. I work Nadeau Station, and I've been trying to get home since the grid crash happened. I live in Thousand Oaks."

He came to a halt to wait for a response. He thought he caught a slight indication of unease coming from the four patrolmen, but that was to be expected. Things were different now. That made sense.

A very fit Asian deputy in his late twenties stepped forward and pushed his Oakley sunglasses onto the top of his head. He gripped his shotgun with his right hand, holding it tight against his body, muzzle up, while he extended his left toward Rob.

"Mind if I take a look at yer ID?"

Rob allowed him to take his identification and badge wallet from his hand. The deputy looked it over briefly and handed it back. He motioned the flanking deputy back.

"What station did you say you worked at?"

"Nadeau Station."

Because of the reputation of his station, Rob was used to getting varied reactions by LASD cops assigned to lower activity stations. Sometimes there was resentment and sometimes admiration. On some occasions suburban patrol deputies viewed him as being soft in the head for choosing to work at Nadeau Station. So when all four looked at him with expressions he couldn't quite put his finger on, he dismissed it as insignificant. The fact was that his fellow patrol cops had heard rumors about a horrendous attack on the legendary sheriff's station. Yet none broached the topic directly.

As he adjusted his Oakley sunglasses, the deputy asked, "When did you leave Nadeau Station and start heading home?"

"Actually, I never made it to the station. I started for home the day of the grid crash, but a ton of shit happened along the way, and it's taken me till now to get here, believe it or not."

There was another furtive glance at the others. Then he changed the subject. He couldn't bring himself to share the rumors about the Nadeau Station with Rob. He saw no point in it, and apparently none of the other deputies present did either.

The deputy gestured toward the huge cinder block building.

"Our captain ordered us to commandeer this place and not to let anyone in till further notice."

Rob asked, "So what did you do about all the perishable food in there? I mean, I'm assuming you guys didn't let it go bad, did you? I know there's no refrigeration in there, right?"

"We have one of our patrol cars that still runs. Runs like shit, but it runs good enough to get back and forth between here and the Agoura Station. So we took all the food needing refrigeration outta here. We used that one piece-a-shit car twenty four-seven to empty it out. But lots of the non-perishable food is still here."

Rob was surprised one of their patrol cars had survived, but he didn't want to open up a new subject right now.

"So the deputies at your station ate all of the non-perishable stuff then?"

"Well, one of our guys had his motorhome stored at the station lot. It wouldn't start, but the refrigerator and freezer was propane powered, and it still works. So we're using that. Plus, we gave a lot of the food away to people coming up to the station looking for help. No sense in wasting all the food we couldn't store or eat ourselves."

Rob stopped to consider what he had just heard.

"Hey, I was wondering if you guys could spot me a little somethin' to eat. My stomach is shakin' hands with my backbone right now."

The Asian cop looked at the others, seeking their approval. One shrugged his shoulders and the other two nodded.

"My name's Derek. This is Mark, John, and Todd," he announced as he pointed out his team mates. No hands were extended, just slight nods of the heads.

With a wave of his hand, Derek summoned Rob to follow him through the store entrance. As he crossed the store's threshold he saw two additional sheriff's deputies wearing tactical gear. They both looked to be about Rob's age. Each stood next to a stack of canned goods that Rob suspected was arranged to provide cover in a gunfight as well as easy access to the food. Unlike the four uniformed patrolmen outside, these guys held AR-15 rifles along with several extra magazines in their tactical vest pouches.

"He's a deputy," Derek proclaimed to the two tactical cops.

Neither responded other than to look at Rob. They stared at his shotgun, just like the others.

One of the tactically outfitted deputies, a wiry man about Rob's age of average height with a boyishly handsome face, had a cloth name tag sewn to his vest. The name displayed was *BABBITT*. It caught Rob's attention due to his associating the name with a well known incident that had occurred close to two years earlier. If this was the same guy, and he was sure it had to be, this SWAT deputy had gained department wide respect among the rank and file for his display of honor.

It didn't involve a heroic gun battle, pulling someone from a burning house, or any other act of physical courage, but rather a more rare form of valor. John Babbitt had taken a month's suspension without pay rather than allow a fellow SWAT officer to be forced out of the highly sought after LASD tactical unit. The details of the matter were never made available to Rob, but the gist of the incident was known to virtually all on the department.

He decided to mention the incident to the deputy now serving sentry duty.

"Are you the same Babbitt that took the thirty day suspension so that what's his name wouldn't get kicked out of SWAT?"

The boyish looking tactical cop, clearly embarrassed by the subject, smiled at Rob.

"Yeah; that was me. I did it for a good cause, or at least I thought so then."

Rob replied, "Well, a lot of us respected you for doing that."

Babbitt nodded slightly but offered no more comment on the matter.

Feeling a little uncomfortable now, Rob changed the subject.

"Do you live near here? Just wondering how you ended up here."

"Yeah, I live about a mile away. Got kinda bored sittin' at home." Another flash of a smile.

Rob said, "Well, I can't wait to get back home myself. Been away since all this shit happened. Been drivin' me crazy, but I had to hunker down a bunch of times if I wanted a good chance to make it home at all. Bein' reckless coulda got my ass killed I figure."

Babbitt nodded again without saying anything. Rob was definitely getting the point that this guy wasn't one for unnecessary conversation.

Derek retrieved two hard plastic packages of tuna and crackers from a stack piled not far from the entrance. He tossed them to Rob, who had to use two hands to catch them.

"Grab a bottle of water if you want. Shit, grab two," Derek offered as he pointed to a large stack of heat-wrap packaged sixteen ounce bottles.

"Cool. Okay if I chow down inside here? It won't take long. Just rather not have anyone outside watching me...might cause you guys trouble you don't need."

"Go ahead," Derek replied as he pulled up one of several nearby lawn chairs and sat down.

Rob ate standing with his pack on his back. Using the small spoon provided, he finished every bit of the tuna, crackers, and even the small packets of relish provided. He cleaned the spoon with his mouth and dropped it into his shirt pocket. Then he chugged down the water, stopping only once between pulls. He stashed the second bottle in his pack.

"Thanks, Derek. I was fuckin' starving, man."

He was actually still hungry, but he would be alright for now.

"So I take it you guys know all about EMP and why the power grid went down and everything?"

Derek looked over at one of the cops holding an AR-15, and asked, "Think it's okay to tell him about the EMP info we got yesterday?"

"Why not...he's a deputy."

"Our lieutenant got some info from a fed of some sort--DHS maybe--who said they think the Iranians might be behind this shit. The DHS guy—or whatever--was really tired and more than a little pissed off I guess. He said they think the Iranians got nuclear capability after some deal to kick ass on the Islamic State assholes a few months ago. So then the fuckin' Iranians use that shit against us by hittin' the U.S. with an EMP!"

Rob was silent as he sorted the info out in his mind. Although he had no way of confirming the information, It all made sense. He wondered how badly things had been screwed up for America now.

Now that he had put something in his belly, he was once again in a hurry to get home. His house was within five miles of the Costco building. He figured it should only take him two hours travel time--plus any further delays—to reach home. Excited and upbeat despite the terrible news about the possible source of the EMP, he adjusted his pack straps and prepared to leave.

Rob pointed to the large volume of smoke in the sky to the south of them.

"Hey, not sure if you guys know this, but the reason for that smoke is that there's a major fire burning down near Santa Monica or thereabouts. I'm talkin' huge. All those displaced people are gonna be lookin' for a place to go. You might be getting' a major problem heading your way here pretty soon. Just a 'heads up' is all."

The other tactical deputy, Babbitt's partner, spoke for the first time since Rob's arrival.

"That's fuckin' great," he said. "Just what we need."

***

There were still a few hours of sunlight left when Rob entered his Thousand Oaks neighborhood. Other than observing quite a few depressing scenes along the way, the trek from Costco to this point had taken place without incident. Throughout this last part of his journey, it surprised him to see how many resident run security operations were in place. He estimated one out of every five or six residential blocks in the suburban town had some sort of citizen security operations being employed.

The variations and degrees of security measures ran the gamut. Virtually all of them had sealed off the entrances to their residential blocks by some means or another. Cars were the most common method used, but a couple streets had heavy chains pulled across their entrances. Their ends were secured with padlocks to telephone poles or similarly immovable objects. Some blocks had unarmed men—and even a few women—performing foot patrols. Others had armed men performing patrols and/or sentry functions. He even saw one house with a rifleman positioned on the roof.

This doesn't even seem like my town anymore. I wonder if things will ever be the way they were before this damn EMP thing happened.

As he came to the street adjacent to his own, Rob ran his hand over his beard. He had abandoned the idea of trying to shave before going home. Heating water and using a knife seemed like it would involve too much effort. Stephanie would just have to accept him with a beard for the time being. But he could at least freshen up a bit.

He stopped and dropped his pack on the sidewalk, and then peeled off his outer shirt and t-shirt, draping them over the pack. He noticed how thin he was compared to the day his world had changed. He used the remaining water in his *Platypus* container to wash up as best he could. He was counting on Stephanie having enough water at their house to make his use of it at the moment unimportant. The truth was that he was only able to focus on one thing right now—the forthcoming reunion with Stephanie and Charlie Wyatt.

After shoving the *Platypus* bag back in his pack and putting his shirts back on, he was so excited he could hardly contain it. He rounded their street corner and took note that unlike many of the other streets in the area, there was no security operation--at least nothing visible.

We will definitely have to address that later.

He recalled how he and Don had tried to come up with the best way to approach his house in Westchester without alarming his wife any more than necessary. After failing to come up with a good way to approach his own house other than simply knocking on the front door, he let go of the idea. Besides, he didn't want to prolong the moment a second longer.

Rob reached the edge of his brown lawn and dropped his pack and hat on the ground without concern for the shotgun or machete. He was within fifteen feet of the front door when something caught his eye. There was a guy standing by the side of the house. And he was looking in through the window.

Rob could have no way of knowing he was looking at the sole survivor of a trio of vicious hoodlums who had been intent upon robbing Stephanie--and possibly worse—ten days earlier. He had no way of knowing this cretin had returned to see if he could finish the business that had left his two cohorts dead. He was planning to watch Stephanie and confront her when she was unarmed. And he could be patient. Rob might not have known any of this, but he could tell the guy was a criminal...just by the look of him.

The returning father didn't want to create a violent scene where his wife and son would have to view the incident, or the aftermath, so he planned on running him off. He would scare the shit out of the guy and convince him to look elsewhere for his victims. He had had more than enough of the violence. He decided not to draw his handgun. It would be his first mistake of the confrontation.

The revenge seeking sociopath peeking through the window saw Rob as he walked toward him and reacted instinctively. He rushed the newly arriving husband and father without a second thought, or a second's delay. Experience had taught him that hesitation only lessened the odds of winning a fight. In an instant he was fully engaged!

Rob only had time to get his hands in front of his face and crouch in the hopes of lowering his body mass before the imminent collision of their bodies. As the lean but muscular *Peeping Tom*--twenty years his junior--reached him, Rob attempted to step aside and sweep him with his foot. It didn't work out the way he hoped.

He avoided getting tackled, but as the punk was partially thrown aside, he caught Rob with a glancing right hook on the side of his head. The young hoodlum sprung forward and came in swinging. Rob got his hands up, half clenched, in front of his head. He kept his forearms in tight, almost vertical, to protect his face and neck. He felt several punches landing on his arms.

This asshole knows how to throw a decent punch, Rob told himself.

The thug, not getting the instant results he was planning on, backed up and began slowly circling his older opponent.

I'm not going to give this guy a fair fight. Screw that, Rob thought.

He pulled his pistol and pointed it at the criminal ten feet across from him, making certain to keep the gun in close to his body to reduce the chances of it being grabbed. Rob thought about shooting the guy right then and there. It would be easy and the son-of-a-bitch deserved it. And it wasn't as if he hadn't recently killed other men under similar circumstances. But he hesitated as he thought about his wife and young son being so close by. He reverted back to cop thinking.

"Get on the ground! Now!"

Rob could see the man's brain trying to process what was happening, and what he should do. The guy had a disturbingly creepy expression suggesting a penchant for savagery and cruelty that came through even when being held at gunpoint.

He heard the front door open and then a woman's voice. It was Stephanie.

"Rob? Rob? Oh my God!"

He heard Charlie Wyatt call out, "Daddy! Daddy!"

Then Rob did something stupid. Something he knew better than to do because it was a rookie mistake. He took his eyes off the creep for just a second—if that long--to look at Stephanie.

With all that was going on, the *Peeping Tom* recognized his chance, and took full advantage without a split second's pause. He turned and sprinted away until he had made it to the end of the block and then rounded the corner.

Rob, aware that he was now in full view of his wife and boy, never considered shooting the fleeing malefactor, despite that he now had to worry about a future visit.

Switching gears, he holstered his gun and ran to Stephanie and Charlie Wyatt. He wrapped one arm around each of them and lifted both off the ground. He lowering them back down but kept his arms around them both.

"I missed you so much," she said as she began to cry.

"Daddy, we did all kinds of stuff while you were gone, and we have a camping stove, and we have to use flashlights now, and Mommy has a gun too. When can I show you?"

Rob just squeezed them both for another full minute. When he finally released them, he wiped his cheeks so that Charlie Wyatt wouldn't see his tears.

Stephanie looked at Rob. She used her index fingers to brush away her tears.

"Who was that guy? I saw you were pointing your gun at him. Tell me what's going on."

"He was just some guy I saw walking in the front yard is all. Some loser lookin' for somethin' to steal or scavenge probably. I just ran him off. No big deal."

"Were you gonna shoot that man, Daddy," Charlie Wyatt asked with the typical naivete of his age.

"No, Charlie Wyatt. I wasn't going to shoot him. I just thought he might be a bad guy. But he got scared and ran away really fast."

The boy looked at his father as if trying to digest the information.

"Okay, let's all go inside," Stephanie announced.

Charlie Wyatt led the way through the front door, running into the house, filled with a child's eagerness to show his father all he had missed while away.

No sooner had they entered the house than Rob grabbed Stephanie and pushed his body against hers. She backed up and pulled him toward her until her back was against the entranceway wall. They shared a long passionate kiss until Charlie Wyatt returned.

"C'mon Daddy, I have stuff to show you." The four-year-old took Rob's hand and pulled him to where the camping stove was set up. And then the boy's tutorial began. Rob listened to every last bit of it, grateful for the chance to do so.

That night, after Rob had taken a four gallon hot water camp shower and put on clean clothes, Stephanie made a dinner of canned chicken chunks mixed into vegetables soup with crackers. Then she brought out *Snickers* bars for desert.

They both put Charlie Wyatt to bed. Rob read a book to him until he fell asleep. He spent a long moment just looking at his son as he slept peacefully, secure for the time being.

Before Rob turned in for bed, he poured himself a double shot of *Jameson's* Irish whiskey. He was enjoying the warmth it left in its wake on the way down when he thought about the creep he had encountered at the side of the house earlier. There was something about the guy that emanated evil. Something that set off the alarm bells in the deepest part of his being. And he was on the loose somewhere not far from here. Loose in a neighborhood with no police service to speak of. He stole a quick glance at his pistol on the nightstand.

Stephanie saw the look on Rob's face and knew that he was worried. Of course, she had her own worries—like the fact she still had to break the terrible news to her husband about the fate of his friends at the Nadeau Sheriff's Station. But she had decided it could wait until tomorrow. She didn't want to lose the value of tonight.

"C'mon now honey. Right now you need to get some sleep...well maybe not for a few more minutes," she said in a sexy voice as she stepped out of her nightgown and came over and rubbed his leg.

She was almost purring now. "Tomorrow we have a lot to talk about, and some of it isn't good. But at least our family is together now. I love you so much." She kissed him slowly and passionately on the lips.

"I love you too Stephanie. And I can't tell you how proud I am of you. We've got a lot to do... you know that. We need to set up security protocols and..."

"Shhh. Yes, I know. Now you stop talking and let's just enjoy tonight."

THE END

ACKNOWLEDGMENTS

Like most authors, I feel it is imperative that I thank those who have made this first attempt at a novel possible. First and foremost, after my wife, I want to thank those family members and friends who read my book in its stages of development and provided feedback.

Of course I would be remiss if I didn't thank those whom I have had the absolute honor and privilege to work with throughout my career in law enforcement. While literally speaking I wrote this book without benefit of technical advisors, the truth is that I received excellent technical advice on a regular basis from the outstanding men and women I served with for over two decades.

I am grateful to every one of you.

ABOUT THE AUTHOR

Frank LaFlamme spent almost a quarter century in a law enforcement capacity in Los Angeles County serving for three local agencies as well as an assignment with the DEA Los Angeles Office. His varied assignments included uniformed patrol, narcotics investigation, gang enforcement, robbery and homicide investigation, tactical warrant service, and a terrorism liasion officer position. He holds a Bachelor of Arts in political science from the University of Southern California and a Master of Arts in Criminal Justice from Chapman University.